The Mystery at Sag Bridge

The
Mystery
at Sag
Bridge

Pat Camalliere

First Edition   ISBN 13: 978-1-937484-30-9

AMIKA PRESS   53 W Jackson BLVD 660 Chicago IL 60604   847 920 8084
info@amikapress.com   Available for purchase on amikapress.com

Edited by John Manos. Front cover and author photography by Richard Hoyt Lee. Back cover photography by Herman Brinkman. Designed and typeset by Sarah Koz. Body in Janson Text, designed by Miklós Tótfalusi Kis in the 1690s, revived for Mergenthaler Linotype by Chauncey H. Griffith in 1937, digitized by Adrian Frutiger in 1985. Titles in Dwiggins Uncial, designed by William Addison Dwiggins in 1935, digitized by Richard Kegler in 2001. Thanks to Nathan Matteson.

~ ~ ~

To the women who inspired my lifelong love of books:

Mom, who from my earliest memory took me to the library, read to me every night, saw that there were books in the home, and set an example of daily reading.

Aunt Isabel, who bought Little Golden Books for me when I was a child, every payday from the time I was born.

Whenever Cora Tozzi drove through these woods, as she did daily, she wondered what was behind the trees she saw from the road. The woods had invited her exploration for years. Today she would find out. She never expected the parking lot to be empty, though.

She wasn't about to allow the absence of people to scare her off. She closed the car door carefully in reverence of the silence, but the metallic click was as jarring as if she'd slammed it. She glanced nervously around the desolate lot and picnic area to the edges of the forest. The place both fascinated and frightened her. Nothing appeared alarming, but...maybe it *wasn't* safe for a woman to be here alone.

Well, I wanted to come here...here I am. Unpaid bills, food shopping, a hundred other tasks...can wait. I will walk in my forest...don't waste this perfect day! But...it's not what I expected....

Foolish or not, she had decided to come alone, to experience the woods at her own pace, free to savor thoughts, impressions, and observations. Another presence, even Cisco's, would interfere.

But was this a good idea? Was it safe? A small woman, not young, nor as fit as she'd like, she was pretty vulnerable. Maybe she should think about it again...no, surely nothing would happen to her. Good fortune had followed her all her life, as if an unseen presence guarded her, and she had come to count on that. She would be vigilant, though, and she was prepared: she carried a trekking pole with a sharp carbide tip.

Could I actually use it, if I needed to?

A faint trail led into the trees from the picnic area. She tossed off apprehensions and, heeding her dermatologist's warning to take precautions against more skin cancers, she tugged a floppy hat out of a pocket, pulled it over her graying hair, and stepped onto the path, carefully listening for unusual sounds.

But every sound was unfamiliar, so what would seem unusual? Unseen, a small creature rustled across the forest floor, and she jumped, and then laughed at herself. *Silly old woman.* She heard a car pass on the road nearby, reassuring. She trudged deeper into the trees, and road noise faded.

She mulled over her fears: what was threatening in the woods? As the road noise had just reminded her, she was near civilization, just follow the noise and she wouldn't be lost. But people had been lost, in these very woods or other woods nearby, sometimes their bodies not found until years later, likely due to the density of the underbrush, and the infrequency with which anyone ventured off a path. In fact, she read in the paper just last week about a man who was last seen walking into woods a mile from here two weeks ago, and he had not yet been found.

Foreboding of evil might occur to a woman alone out here. Perhaps some sadistic man lurked in the underbrush, planning to have his way with her, to leave her battered or worse. Women are warned to fear men in lonely places. Maybe some unknown creature lay in wait, like in the movies. The forest primeval—or just evil? Cora didn't believe in alien or supernatural beings…but in the woods alone, anything seemed possible.

She shook it off, laughed again. She'd walked for ten minutes, and nothing she saw, heard, or sensed was ominous. Her confidence returned as the woods deepened, and she became captivated by their beauty.

~~~

Every day on her way to and from her job, Cora passed through these woods. Her commute, and her days, were long, beginning at daybreak, or earlier, and ending in twilight, or later. Her daily trip turned out to be a respite of quiet thought in her hectic world. She cherished the drive, especially through the peaceful forest, and the opportunity to reflect on beauty around her she otherwise took no time to see.

She watched the trees, shrubs and groundcovers change with the seasons; the light never illuminated them in quite the same way. The sights delighted her: the fresh greens of spring, the golden arches the trees made over the road in fall, the crisp new-fallen snow, a brilliant cardinal flashing boldly across the road. She caught glimpses of wildlife: deer, coyotes, raccoons, turkeys—even wolves on the rare occasion, but she had seen them, at least she thought so—possible evidence of wildlife repopulation. She had read that wolves were hunted out of the area over a hundred years ago, but in recent years a rare lone wolf was sighted in Northern Illinois, ranging out of its territory, probably in search of food or a mate. There was plenty of food here, with the overabundance of deer.

The forest's mood could be gloomy, but the woods have many moods, and on other days, sunlight streamed through the treetops—Cora heard it called *God's light*. The sight sometimes brought a lump to her throat and a tear to her eye. Easily moved, which she attributed to her emotional Irish heritage, she was glad she could feel joy this deeply.

A number of roads passed through the forest, but Cora's favorite took her past an old Catholic Church, Saint James at Sag Bridge. The small building sat on a hilltop, surrounded by a cemetery, the cemetery surrounded by dense woods. When Cora attended Mass there, ushers rang the church bells by pulling ropes—one to ring, another to toll, calling parishioners. Cora felt that she stepped into another time and place. Inside, above the altar, a remarkable stained glass window depicted the eye of God.

Stories of ghosts and other mysterious happenings around the churchyard were plentiful, which was not surprising as the encroaching deep and impenetrable woods created an eerie atmosphere.

Cora referred to this rare place as her forest, and considered it a gift. But that was just what she saw along the road.

She had to know what was in the woods behind the old church.

~ ~ ~

Now she was here, completely shut off from the outside world. She looked around, and her senses took over.

Shrubs occupied the forest floor. She recognized maples, seedlings and old monsters; some had fallen, some laid broken in tangled masses. There was a magnificent old oak, with majestic branches and massive trunk. A glorious thing, and words from Joyce Kilmer's poem, "Only God can make a tree" came to her mind.

Her skin warmed by a gentle breeze rustling the leaves, she walked easily along the dry level trail, overgrown here and there by thorny brush that caught her clothes. Today the woods emitted a damp, earthy odor, not the wonderfully pungent dry leaf smell of fall. Whispering sounds and birdcalls descended from the canopy, and sharp crackles announced the travels of woodland creatures, squirrels and chipmunks on the ground. Cheerful sounds, the music of the forest.

How different from her yard, with its roar of air conditioners, banging of construction projects, drone of lawnmowers. A small plane hummed overhead, reminding her of childhood, lying on the lawn in summer, dreams and images suggested by clouds.

Suddenly Cora was surrounded by a cloud of gnats and, yes! Mosquitoes! They swarmed around her face, neck and hands, searching, penetrating any open skin, ears, eyes, hair. *No you don't. You're not gonna feast on me!* She broke into a trot, flailing her arms—not easy to do while carrying a trekking pole. Glad no one was there to witness her foolish flight, she left the nuisance behind as the trail came to an end at…*what?—a road?*

Panting, she wished she could shed a few pounds as easily as she was able to when she was younger. She found herself standing on an old asphalt road, neglected and cracked with countless weedy fissures. *A road? In the woods? Paved? Service roads would be gravel…odd. It must have gone somewhere…but where? Saint James? But it has its own roads….*

Curious, no, compelled, Cora followed the road uphill, to find out where it used to go. She labored up and up, curve after curve, pausing now and then to catch her breath and let the burn in her legs ease. She saw only trees. The road seemed endless, a road to *nowhere.* Maybe a scenic overlook was up ahead. But if so, why was the road abandoned? At each bend she expected to see something ahead but saw only another bend.

At last, almost ready to give up, a post, a weathered 4 × 4 next to the road, barely noticed. *Something* was ahead, must be—if there was a post there must be a reason to put it there. As she approached, she felt lightheaded…from exertion—or a surreal daze? To the side of the post, which on closer inspection may have been part of an old gate, was a faint trail leading back into the woods, and down that trail she saw butterflies, more butterflies than she had ever seen, an astounding, incredible show!

From an inch to more than six inches, brilliant and varied, some iridescent, others royal blue, black, white, yellow, swallowtails. They fluttered over and around the path, so thick Cora couldn't see beyond them as they streamed from the woods. *Do butterflies live in the woods? Don't they like sun, live in gardens?*

Awed, then entranced, Cora walked into the cloud of butterflies. They danced around and ahead of her down the trail, but all was oddly still. There were no birdcalls, no other insects. All was silent except her footsteps, muted on the soft grassy path as she followed the butterflies, as if in a dream.

The path penetrated dense brush, and ended at a clearing; intuitively she knew the clearing was where she was supposed to go. It held the explanation to what just happened and was the reason for the road.

In the center of the clearing was a large stone slab, a cube of about four feet. *Like* 2001: A Space Odyssey, *in miniature.* The rock appeared to be a monument, and the clearing man-made. Fascinated, she approached the granite monolith and read the words carved on it: Caution—Do Not Dig. Buried in this area is radioactive material from nuclear research conducted here in 1943–1949.

A memory of something she read, somewhere, sometime: Cora put it together. The old road led to Argonne Laboratory, a large national research facility that was hidden in the woods in these Forest Preserves during the Manhattan Project. It was an ideal location, for then, as now, one could walk for miles in these woods and remain unseen. She pictured Enrico Fermi and Albert Einstein walking this very ground, although she was only guessing.

This, then, was the secret hidden behind the trees that Cora had come looking for. She had no idea anything was left of the Manhattan Project and was surprised the waste was buried near the old site, as the present location of Argonne was across the valley two miles away—in fact, she would have been able to see it, were it not for the trees. She felt the same sense of history and being in another time and place as she had when she visited Saint James, just a short distance from here.

She looked around and realized the butterflies were gone. *What just happened? Were they really here? Did I imagine them?* Wandering in a dreamlike state, she explored the clearing. The longer she stayed, the more she imagined she felt something leaching from the ground and detected a slight sharp odor. *Maybe this stuff isn't harmless…causing some sort of cellular damage!* Her hands tingled, and it was difficult to concentrate, as if in a daze. *Real? My imagination? Shit! I'd better just leave!*

~ ~ ~

Eating fast food in front of the television that evening, she talked to Cisco about it.

"Don't you think the butterflies were bizarre? Why would they be there? Why do you think I'm so fascinated by that place? Is it what I found or something else I didn't find?" she asked.

"Why do you need a reason? Can't you accept that sometimes it just is?" he replied.

Cora sighed and let it go. That was reason enough for Cisco, but not for her.

Cora returned to the woods a number of times that summer. She never saw butterflies there again. She wondered if it had something to do with the time of year or the time of day, but in her heart she knew there was no logical, natural reason. She knew the real explanation: the mystical butterflies did not return because she no longer needed them to lead her—now she knew the way.

In Cora's life, the inexplicable was common, just another day.

Angel of God, my guardian dear
To whom God's love commits me here.
Ever this day be at my side
To light, to guard, to rule and guide.
Amen.

—Traditional Children's Prayer

~~~

When at night I go to sleep
Fourteen angels watch do keep…

Angels hover round me,
Whisp'ring they have found me…

—Engelbert Humperdinck,
"Evening Prayer" from *Hänsel and Gretel*

Cora

2012

Chapter 1

"You know what I think retired means?" Cora said, lugging china and serving pieces up the basement stairs—her fourth trip. She sighed. "I think it means tired all over again. I thought life was supposed to get easier after I quit work, but it seems nothing is changed."

"Why are you bringing that stuff upstairs?" Cisco was reading the paper at the kitchen table. "Don't we have stuff up here you can use?"

"Yeah, well, all our good stuff is stored in the basement, and we never use it. We're going to go to our graves without using it."

"You'll have to wash it."

"Of course I'm going to wash it. Do you think I'm an idiot?"

She filled the sink with hot water and piled in dishes, shaking her head.

"You want some help?" he offered, looking up.

"No, I got it. I'd rather do this myself."

"You're your own worst enemy, you know. You don't need to get involved in so many things." Cisco turned his eyes back to the paper.

Yet again— how often does he have to remind me?

"I was afraid I'd be bored. I joined things so I *wouldn't* get bored." She glanced in his direction. "You think I went too far, huh?"

"You could say that. It'd be an understatement," he said, without looking up.

"I'm going to get it under control…after I finish a few things…" Cora started stacking washed dishes on a towel on the countertop.

"I've heard *that* before. You know it never happens," he said, eying her over the top of his glasses, closing the paper and adding it to one of several piles on the table.

"Well, I'm going to *make* it happen this time."

"Why should this time be different?"

"Because there are other things I want to do, that's why." They both laughed at the contradiction.

"No, I'm serious. I want to travel, spend more time with the kids, see if I have any writing talent. The things I retired to find time for," she said.

"So why are you volunteering at the library, the chorus, the historical society, and the book club? Why all the board commitments? Why aren't we traveling, spending time with the kids, or fixing up the house?"

"I like doing those things. Besides, the library and the historical society will help me write." Cora rearranged the accumulating stacks of clean dinnerware to prevent disaster.

"You just made my point. I reiterate, how are you going to find time to do other things if you won't give anything up?" He looked up and watched her face.

Cora shifted her eyes away evasively. "Well, I don't know. By finding a better way to do things, I suppose, so it doesn't take so long. And I'll give some tasks away to other people."

"Yeah…right." He rolled his eyes toward the ceiling.

"We've been over this before, and the girls will be here soon. I'm sorry I brought it up," Cora said. She closed her eyes for a moment. How did a simple comment about retirement almost turn into a disagreement? She picked up a kitchen towel and began to dry china.

Cisco got up from the table, and leaving piles of newspapers scattered across the tabletop, pulled the vacuum out and began to clean the kitchen floor.

Cora bit her tongue. She had just cleared the table and couldn't understand why he couldn't make a single pile instead of strewing piles all over. And why didn't he wait until she finished cooking and washing to vacuum? He'd have to work around her and have to do it all over again when she finished messing up the kitchen. She set tableware on the island counter.

"Lasagna is a lot of work. Why did you have to make that?" Cisco shouted over the vacuum.

"We make things suggested by the book we're discussing. Today's book is about Italian–Americans, and I make good Italian. There will be leftovers...." She caught his eye and grinned.

He smiled, then asked, "And the salad? Couldn't someone else make that?"

"I make good salad dressing," she said meekly, avoiding his eyes, having no good answer to his objection.

"I give up." He shook his head and pulled the vacuum into the family room.

Cora felt guilty. Cisco was helping her prepare to entertain a group he was no part of, and here she was, impatient because he was underfoot and not doing things in the order she preferred. Her eyes grew hot and moist. He was the best, and she didn't show him that enough.

She looked through the kitchen window into the yard. Bare, weedy lawn when they moved to Lemont, Illinois, she and Cisco had filled the large lot with flowering trees, shrubs and perennials, an activity they enjoyed. Not that disagreements hadn't taken place along the way, until ultimately they figured out they made more progress if Cora did the planning and Cisco did the physical work, and they kept their grumbling under their breath. There was always something to do, though, and Cisco did the better part of it. *It looks lovely—thanks to Cisco.*

Cora peeked in the oven, hung up a dishtowel, and walked into the family room. Coming up behind Cisco, she wrapped her arms around him, nuzzling her face against his back. "I really do appreciate you, you know," she said. He leaned against her for a moment. "Too," he responded, the intimate way they said, "I love you too."

~~~

It was almost eleven o'clock, her guests would arrive soon, and Cora wasn't yet dressed for company. She left salad ingredients on the counter and ran toward their bedroom to change. When she was halfway up the stairs, a crash came from the second floor office she shared with Cisco.

Cora found a large wall clock lying face up on the floor. She grumbled as she bent to retrieve it. *I don't have time for this!* She placed it on its back toward the rear of her desk, surrounded by piles of unfinished work, and then rushed to her closet and grabbed a pair of pants and a top.

As she stood at the bathroom sink brushing her teeth, nagging doubts assailed her. She was sure she had attached the clock firmly to the wall the last time. It shouldn't have fallen. This was the third time it fell this week—what was going on?

Whatever it was, she'd have to worry about it later.

~~~

Lu, Cora's best friend since school days, arrived while Cora was finishing the salad. Cora was glad Lu was a few minutes early, so they could chat a bit before the others arrived. Cora exclaimed, "Oooh, I like your hair! You look good!" She took a platter of garlic bread from Lu and set it on the kitchen island.

Lu ran her hand through her thick auburn hair and grinned. "Fired my old hair stylist and got a new one."

"Good move! How are the boys?" Lu was on her second family, mama–grandma to a divorced son and two grandsons. Their children had grown up together, and now Lu and Cora each had two grandsons of similar ages.

"More of the same," she said. "Nothing serious. Always some scrape or another." She launched into a detailed rendition of a series of misfortunes, and Cora listened distractedly as she cut tomatoes and cucumbers and scraped them into a bowl of salad greens.

The doorbell sounded, and Frannie stomped in before Cora could answer it. She carried a large chocolate cake, which she set down in the center of the island, pushing items aside without regard to others working there. Outrageous, outspoken and energetic, Frannie made a startling, albeit endearing, impression when Cora invited her to join the club. Although only moderately overweight, her most obvious physical characteristics were huge breasts that gave her a top-heavy appearance, and today's outfit did nothing to minimize the effect. She wore brown leggings that tapered from her waist to her feet, a clingy pink top that highlighted above-the-waist bulges, and a bright red cloche hat.

Cora exchanged glances with Lu, thinking Frannie resembled a large sugar cone with strawberry ice cream and a cherry on top. Cora grinned at the image.

Frannie had worked for Cora years earlier, but Cora had been forced to fire her due to Frannie's inability to work harmoniously with staff. She was always coming up with "a better way." She drove her coworkers mad. Despite the awkward situation, Cora and Frannie remained close friends.

"She fired my black ass," Frannie had said, shocking the club members, "but I wasn't about to let her fire me from being her girlfriend!" She had subsequently gone through a series of jobs, always landing on her feet, but never for long.

She and Cora had similar tastes in reading, music, and crafts. Frannie's boisterous and upbeat manner, easy laughter, and refusal to accept defeat in the midst of challenges, was refreshing. Both Frannie and Cora had cared for and then lost aging mothers in the past couple of years, and their grief had drawn them closer.

The doorbell chimed nonstop, and a voice demanded, "Stop that!" The commotion heralded the entry of Cora's daughter-in-law, Marty, and Cora's two grandsons, Sean, ten years old, and Ryan, six. The door burst open, and they charged in, talking loudly at the same time. Marty was married to Cora's older son, Patrick.

It wasn't that long since she had seen the boys; how did Sean get so tall? Ryan, though, was still a little ball of boyish energy. She pulled him squirming into a tight hug and then tousled his thick curly hair.

"Patrick got called into work, and I couldn't get a sitter," Marty explained. "I hope you don't mind I brought the boys."

"No problem," Cora said. "They love to spend time with Grandpa. They can play Nintendos and if they get out of control, he can take them outside to run it off. See they have something to eat, though, if you would. No sugar!"

"Cisco won't mind?" Marty asked.

"He misses having kids around. It'll be fun for him." This was an exaggeration. She knew what Cisco really liked was a quiet house; he would certainly keep an eye on the active boys and even enjoy it but would probably prefer to watch golf on TV.

"Sean! Frannie's here!" Ryan yelled excitedly, ran into the large family room adjoining the kitchen, and launched himself at Frannie. Improbable as it seemed, Ryan and Frannie were fast friends.

Raised in a black community, Frannie had met and married a white man shortly after high school and lived in a white neighborhood. Her vernacular slipped back and forth, from professional to ethnic. Although she spent many years in the fashion industry, an occupation she and Marty shared, Frannie's personal style was bizarre, not only ill-fitting and unusual clothing combinations, but also odd hair styles. Her dark round face rarely smiled, but her eyes gave her away, sparkling with intelligence and good humor. She wasn't like anyone Ryan knew, and he found her fascinating. Now a widow, Frannie's only son had joined the Marines last year, leaving a void in her life, a void she was happy to fill with Ryan.

Cora disappeared to retrieve a hidden stash of Goldfish crackers. The boys would devour the entire supply if she didn't hide it. Her face took on a concerned expression when she left the room. The demands of Patrick's job were too great. She was concerned about his health and how the family was dealing with his frequent absences. It wasn't her place to interfere, but once a mother, always a mother—the worrying would never end.

When she reentered the room, Sean grabbed the bag. "Goldfish! Wow! Thanks, Grandma. You always have the best snacks!"

"Share with your brother!" she called after him, shaking her head as he ran to plop onto the family room sofa with his Nintendo.

Jean, who lived next door, arrived, followed almost immediately by Sissy and Betty.

"You know, we should call ourselves the Two Sons Book Club," Cora said with a laugh. "I have two sons, and two grandsons, and Lu does too. Marty has two sons, and so do Jean, Sissy and Betty. Ever think of that?"

"Sounds like something out of a Charlie Chan movie, don't it?" Frannie commented, and, after the laughter died down, put in, "I only have one son, so I'd be the odd woman out."

Lu said, "Of course, there's also Valerie…."

"Ah, yes. There is Valerie…Valerie with one daughter," said Jean, with a frown, as the women moved toward the kitchen. "Heaven forbid we should forget Valerie."

The last person to arrive, as usual, was Valerie. Valerie and Jean, both nurses, worked at the same hospital, and Jean had invited her to join the book group. Valerie, a too-thin divorcee with an eight-year-old daughter, was an avid reader, but the women didn't like her. For her part, Valerie didn't appear to enjoy the meetings either. Cora supposed she came because it was hard for her to make friends. She doubted she would make any in this group either, but the women couldn't figure out how to ask her to leave.

~~~

The women sat crowded around the kitchen table, littered with desserts in various stages of demolition and half-full cups of coffee.

"It's hard to believe," Sissy commented. They were discussing a tell-all book about the Chicago Mob. "Doesn't this stuff just happen in novels, movies and TV shows? It's exaggerated, right? Did anyone here ever run across a member of the Mafia?"

"Yes, actually," said Cora, leaning back in her chair, arms crossed over her chest.

"Really?" This from Marty, eyebrows raised in surprise at her mother-in-law's comment. "You never told us that."

"I guess I never thought to tell you. It's pretty much part of growing up around Chicago, if you're close to an Italian family." She chuckled and looked in Lu's direction. "Right, Lu?"

"Oh, yes!" Lu said wryly, nodding her head vehemently. "We had quite interesting experiences with our Italian families and friends."

"You, too?" asked Sissy. "Tell us more, Lu."

"I dated a boy from an Italian family, and his cousin was in the Mob." She gazed out the window and paused, remembering, and then looked back at the women. "They didn't all live in the city, you know. Some connected people, important guys, live in my suburb. It's a small community; you get to know everybody. Eventually it no longer seems unusual." She shrugged.

"So who did *you* know?" Betty asked, turning to Cora.

"We just read about one," Cora replied.

"The guy who wrote the book? The Mob lawyer?" Valerie challenged. "Excuse me, but I find that hard to believe. Why would you know him?"

"It's not very interesting, actually. A local politician was forcing our suburb into a project we didn't want. Some of us got together to fight him, and John was an attorney who helped," Cora said.

"*Did* he help?" Valerie asked with a smirk.

"Not much," Cora admitted. "He acted important." She picked up a fork and pushed some crumbs around on her plate and then shook her head. "He warned us that he was involved in something big, that he might have to disappear, and eventually he did. As you know from the book, he was an informer and went into witness protection. I don't remember exactly, it was years ago. He was a strange guy."

"I don't believe you," said Valerie, looking at the tabletop as she rubbed at a spot with her thumb. "I don't believe you knew him. He wasn't even Italian, anyway—he was Irish."

"Believe what you like, Valerie. I suppose I have a reason to make it up?" Cora's face reddened. Valerie had hit a hot button: Cora hated being accused of lying.

Sissy jumped in. "Back East we used to think Chicago was a terrible place, with mobsters, street gangs and police brutality. 'You're from Chicago! Really?' We thought everyone from Chicago was bad. When I moved here, people would ask me what nationality I was. I didn't understand; I was American. I finally caught on they wanted to know what *country* my family came from. I couldn't understand why they'd want to know that."

"Yeah," Lu said with sarcasm. "All these ethnic groups, we have to keep ourselves straight."

"So what are *we?*" Betty asked. "I'll start—I'm German." She stood up and carried her cup over to the counter to refill it.

"German, French, and American Indian," said Lu.

"One hundred percent Irish," said Marty with a smile.

"I'm from Pennsylvania—I'm American!" Sissy said. The women laughed, and she shrugged and said, "Seriously, I'm not really sure."

"Uh, huh. I think it's written all over me!" said Frannie. The women burst into laughter, and when it stopped Frannie added, "Could be appearances are deceiving though. I sure have a lot of fun with my name."

Cora, who had just taken a sip of coffee, choked and reached for a napkin. The others, realizing they never knew Frannie's last name, looked at each other, confused.

"Berkowitz," Frannie said, with a huge grin. "My husband's family were Jews from Poland. Don't you all just expect to see a big black woman with unruly hair when you hear Frannie Berkowitz is coming?"

"I don't know about the rest of you, but my mind turns to serial killers," said Lu.

"But really, could be all mixed up—who knows what slave owners did way back in the day, up to a lot of no good I suspect. I could be related to royalty, for all I know." Frannie struck a pose and mimicked placing a crown on her head.

As the women chuckled, Valerie said, rolling her eyes, "I'm not playing. Who cares? This is silly."

"And I'm half Irish and half Polish," Cora said, ignoring Valerie. "I fit right into this town. Lemont started with Irish immigrants, and then many Polish people came."

"So where are all these Italians we been talking about?" Frannie demanded. "Not one in the bunch. Kind of odd, looking at all this here home-cooked Italian food! Must be married into it, right Mrs. Tozzi?" She waved an arm at the buffet, largely empty now.

"And Cisco is....?" asked Sissy.

"Sicilian."

"What's Cisco short for? Francisco?" Jean guessed.

"No, his full name is Arturo Valentino Tozzi."

"Why is he called Cisco then?" she persisted.

"When he was a kid he was obsessed with the Cisco Kid on TV. He would dress like him, galloped around yelling 'eeeehhh Panchooo' all the time. You remember the Cisco Kid?" Cora glanced around the table.

Lu, Frannie, and Betty nodded. The younger women looked blank.

"Well, Cisco was about five when the series started, and it ran for about five or six years. By then the nickname stuck."

"What about the 'Arturo Valentino' part?" Sissy asked.

"Uncle Arturo and Uncle Valentino, of course," Cora said with a chuckle. "Sicilian boys were always named after uncles until they ran out of uncles."

"Was Cisco born in Italy?" asked Marty.

"It's Sicily, not Italy. Some people are sensitive about that. No, his grandparents came first, but his grandfather died soon after they got here. Cisco's grandmother was left with five kids to raise, and she tried to keep going by taking in laundry. In those days they boiled clothes to get them clean, and she would heat huge pots over gas burners in the basement. She was exhausted one night, fell asleep, and a pot boiled over and put out the flame. The gas filled the basement, and they found her dead the next morning."

Cora paused, rested her elbows on the table and her chin on her hands. "The kids, they were young, too young to take care of themselves. They went to a Catholic orphanage in Chicago. As each child got old enough to leave, they stayed in touch with the others…they stayed close. Cisco's mother was the baby of the family."

The women were quiet. Cora stood up and began collecting empty plates from the table.

"What about the women, what were they like?" Sissy asked.

"You know the old joke," Cora replied from the sink, where she was running water over dirty plates. "What's the difference between an elephant and an Italian grandmother? Give up? Twenty-five pounds and a black dress." The women laughed.

"Really, some of the older women *were* pretty big," Cora went on, returning to the table and wiping her eyes. "They talked a lot, they cooked a lot, they were very generous and very social. You would like them. We always had a good time, a lot of laughter. And there *were* a lot of black dresses!"

The group was startled by loud crashes from upstairs. "Is anyone up there?" Betty asked. "I thought Cisco and the boys went out."

"They did." Cora frowned and got up to investigate.

When she returned to the room, she looked at Lu and smiled wryly. "It was just Angel, throwing things around," she said. Her tone was light and casual, but her forehead was furrowed and suggested concern.

Lu laughed. "Is Angel still around? I haven't thought about her in years!"

"Who's Angel?" Marty looked around the table. Lu and Cora exchanged glances and laughed, but the others appeared puzzled.

"You want to get into it?" Lu asked.

"I don't know why I said that." Cora sat back in her chair, put her elbows on the table, rested her chin on her hands, and looked around the table, where the women all waited expectantly. "I guess I have to explain now. The short story is, Angel is a name we use when something weird happens, sort of like naming a poltergeist. Sometimes strange things happen to me, and we say Angel is acting up."

"So what did Angel do just now?" asked Betty, looking back and forth.

"She threw a clock on the floor," said Cora.

"You mean, a clock fell, and you called it Angel's work?" Valerie insisted, leaning back in her chair with her arms crossed over her chest.

"Not exactly…the clock fell off the wall this morning, so I put it flat on my desk with stuff piled around it to be sure it couldn't fall again, to keep it from 'getting away'. Somehow it made its way to the floor again, in an empty room." Her face reddening, Cora met Valerie's eyes, provoked by her insulting tone. She hadn't meant to explain this much.

"Why did you pile stuff around it? Wasn't that overkill?" Valerie challenged, rolling her eyes.

"Because the clock kept moving when no one was there," Cora said defiantly.

The women looked at each other skeptically.

"Did *all* the stuff fall on the floor?" asked Sissy.

"No, just the clock. The stacks of books and papers were right where I left them," Cora said.

"Booga, booga!" Jean said, fluttering the fingers of both hands.

Valerie stood up. "You guys are taking this crap seriously? You're all nuts," she said. "I got to go." She grabbed a bottle of water and a handful of cookies and walked out, without pushing her chair back under the table.

Frannie rolled her eyes. "Miss Congeniality," she quipped.

"Yeah. Well, I got to get going too," Sissy said. "Just tell me before we break up though, how long has this 'Angel' been around, and why do you call her that?"

"I don't know exactly. A long time—maybe when I was first married," Cora answered. "She comes and goes, around for a few days, then she disappears for years. Lu came up with the name Angel because it felt like a benign, reassuring presence. She said it was like having a Guardian Angel."

"Aren't you afraid when this stuff happens?" Sissy persisted.

"Not really. I think it's unusual, but it's happened so many times, and nothing ever comes of it. I just go, 'Oh well, one more thing that doesn't make sense'."

"What does Cisco say? Does he know about it?" Marty asked.

"Oh, yeah, he knows. He's a guy. He looks for a rational explanation, then shrugs, just another strange thing, nothing we can do, just forget it. I don't forget it, but I don't make a big deal out of it either."

"This ain't no big *nothin'!*" Frannie said. "You need to be careful, look into this business! You do that, girl."

"Yeah, Cora," Betty said. "You never know. You should be careful."

Cora shrugged. This sort of thing was normal for her, but she understood her friends' reactions, which was why she didn't talk about Angel much. Unexplainable things had gone on most of her adult life, and nothing bad ever happened, in fact, quite the opposite, she thought she'd had an unusually fortunate life. The incidents did seem more annoying lately, though. She wondered if she *should* take them more seriously.

~ ~ ~

After the women left, all but Marty, Cisco returned with Sean and Ryan.

"Want some help?" Marty asked, as she carried dirty cups to the sink.

"No, that's okay," Cora said, taking the cups from her. Perhaps mindless work in the kitchen would help her sort out her thoughts about Angel.

"Grandpa took us to the farm down the street!" Ryan exclaimed, pulling on Cora's shirt. "We saw a rusty old tractor and the woods where Grandpa says deer and coyotes hang out!"

Cora looked at Cisco with disapproval. "Anything could be living in that thicket!" she objected.

She noticed Sean staring at a cactus blooming near the front door.

"Wow, that's cool!" he exclaimed.

"I have a story about that cactus," Cora told the boys, putting an arm around each of them. "It's called a Christmas cactus, because Christmas is when it's supposed to bloom. My father, your *great*-grandfather, had one for many years and it never bloomed. He got disgusted because he wanted flowers, and so he gave it to Grandpa Cisco and me, and said we should try to get it to bloom. Well, we had it for years too, and it never bloomed for us either, not once. Then Great-Grandpa got sick, and one day he died, and after we got home from his funeral, what do you think happened? It wasn't Christmas, or anywhere near, but that cactus, for the first time ever, was *blooming!*"

Sean thought it over. "Wow!" he said. "It must have *hated* him!"

Chapter 2

Cora forced the crumpled, near-empty toothpaste tube into its holder on the bathroom counter, took off her nightshirt, and with trepidation began her monthly full-body exam. Plagued by skin cancers, the less-dangerous kind fortunately, she had procrastinated. She didn't trust her observations, was fearful of finding something new, running to the dermatologist with a false alarm, or worse, ignoring something important.

The need to do this made her feel old. She hadn't gained weight since retirement, but she could stand to lose twenty pounds. Okay, twenty-five. Thirty? More disturbing were the sags, the wrinkles and dimples on her arms and thighs, these especially because exercise would have little effect—she was stuck with them for life.

She finished the exam with her face: no new lesions, but pouches under her eyes and drooping cheeks. She wished she could stay between fifty-five and sixty—the perfect age: plenty of experience and confidence, a comfortable lifestyle, and nothing hurts or droops yet. She sighed—she'd never see sixty again.

Something else she saw in the mirror—her mother's face looking back at her. Well, not her mother's face, but the familiar expressions her mother had worn now appeared on Cora's own face, showing worry, or irritation. Heredity? Or being together for a lifetime? Images of the adjacent rooms, the bedroom, bath and sitting room her mother had occupied, now guest rooms, filled her head and reawakened grief. Eyes shiny, she turned from the mirror.

Like Grandma used to say, it's hell to get old. She stepped into the steaming shower.

When Cora left the shower she almost stepped on the crumpled tube of toothpaste. Startled, she looked at the ceramic holder still in place near the vanity mirror, behind her hair dryer and a folded towel. A chill went down the nape of her neck, and her stomach clenched, a moment of terror, thinking of Janet Leigh in *Psycho. Who's here?*

It was an ordinary thing, only a used tube of toothpaste for God's sake, but eerily frightening, more menacing because she was standing there nude and vulnerable. Okay. How did it get there? Her mind sought logical causes. She was alone in the house—she thought…Cisco went golfing…did someone break into the house?

Why would an intruder throw my toothpaste on the floor and leave?

Not taking time to dry herself, she threw on a robe and searched the house. As expected, no one was there, and Cisco's car was gone.

I know the tube was in the holder—I'm positive. It couldn't roll…how did it get over the towel and hair dryer?

Angel again? Whoever, whatever, if there was an Angel. But this morning it wasn't the same warm, comforting Angel; no, it was more alarming. Maybe her friends were right and she had to take this more seriously.

But Angel's never been threatening—why?

Cora said aloud, "Angel, I'm getting tired of your nonsense! Cut it out already!"

Of course, nothing happened. It never did.

~~~

After dressing, Cora wandered around tidying the house, mulling over past incidents she jokingly referred to as Angel dust.

She supposed other people had odd things happen they couldn't explain. Cora thought she probably had more than most, but she had gotten accustomed to them over time. It had been years since she'd had such weird experiences, but in the past few months little odd phenomena had resumed, such as finding things where she hadn't put them. One day she reached for a book she left on the bedside table, but it wasn't there. She searched the house, then there it was, on the same table, where it had just *not* been. She watched drawers slide open untouched and paper clips jump across her desk. Rational explanations, like being out of balance, didn't seem adequate.

Last week she found two batteries on the edge of her desk in front of her laptop. A small clock Cora kept behind her laptop lay face down in its normal place with its battery compartment open. At first she thought Cisco opened the clock and forgot to put the batteries back—for whatever reason she couldn't imagine—so she asked him about it.

He gave her a blank look. "What are you talking about?"

"Didn't you take the batteries out of my desk clock?"

He shook his head and gave her and irritated look. "No. I haven't left the room. Why would I do that?"

"Well, it's sitting there on my desk, open, and the batteries are sitting somewhere else. Come and look." Cora dragged Cisco into her room.

"See? How did it get like that if you didn't do it?" she asked, pointing.

"I guess you must have done it. There's no one else here, and I sure didn't."

"Well, I *didn't* do it—I'd remember." She crossed her arms over her chest. "The battery compartment didn't open itself, the batteries jump out and leap over the laptop, and stop at the edge of my desk. So what happened?"

"Old-timers' disease?" he guessed, shrugged his shoulders, and went back to his office.

Cora's first encounter with Angel happened when she was pregnant with her son, Patrick. After fixing dinner, she would lie down in the bedroom to wait for Cisco to come home from work. She knew the sounds of his arrival: a key clicked in the lock, the downstairs door creaked open, footsteps ascended the stairs, a key turned in the apartment door, the door brushed over the carpet. One day she heard the familiar sounds, but Cisco didn't come to her room. When he came in a short time later, Cora asked, "What happened? Did you forget something?"

"No. Why do you ask?" he said with a puzzled look.

"Didn't you just come home, then leave and come back?"

"No. I just got home now."

She told him about the sounds, and he thought it was strange, but perhaps she was half asleep, dreaming, didn't that make sense? Well...maybe. But the same thing kept happening.

One afternoon Cora and Cisco were sitting together at the dining table, facing the apartment door. Cora looked at the door, then at Cisco, who nodded that he heard too. Key in lock, door open, footsteps, doorknob squealing, and they *saw* the doorknob turn! Cisco jumped up and sprang for the door, as Cora yelled, "No—don't!" Ignoring her, he threw the door open, but no one was there—no one in the hallway, no running footsteps, no sounds at all...only silence. The strange events then stopped—for a time.

Six years later, in their first house in the suburbs, Cora knelt at the head of her bed watching through a window as her two young sons played in the yard. With her back to the bedroom door, she heard Cisco enter the room and felt the bed sink as he sat behind her. When Cora turned to him, there was only a depression in the bed, as if someone *was* sitting there. She put her hand into it; it felt real, but it slowly disappeared. Was she going crazy? Could it be Cisco sat down, snuck out again, but the depression stayed? Silly, but if not, then what?

She had to ask Cisco. She found him in the basement, and he insisted he had not been in the room.

Afterwards, from time to time, Cora would occasionally sense a presence on the bed beside her, and she would find a depression there.

She talked to Lu about it, filling her in about the other experiences. Lu, as expected, didn't question Cora's story. "What should I do?" Cora asked her friend.

"Are you scared when it happens?" Lu asked.

"Surprisingly, no, I'm not," Cora said. "In fact it's calming, sort of... like someone cares and is *watching over* me and wants me to know. When I put my hand in the depression I feel calm, not so tense. Like I have a buddy, a protector or something."

"Like a Guardian Angel," Lu said, and Angel she became from then on.

Angel had a playful side. At Cora's job, she would act up in front of visitors. She'd play her drawer prank, the person watching wide-eyed while a drawer opened itself. A staple might fly off the desk and strike the visitor on the arm. A paper clip would bounce with a *tink* from one desktop to another, or something would jump off a shelf. "What happened?" the person would exclaim, startled, and Cora would smile, look puzzled, then laugh and say it must have been a poltergeist. It could be embarrassing, but Cora thought it was funny.

Some twelve years ago, in their fifties with their sons grown, Cora and Cisco finally bought their dream house in Lemont, a suburb far southwest of Chicago. Semi-isolated by forests and situated on a rocky bluff overlooking the Des Plaines River Valley, the town's remoteness gave them the comfort and peace they wanted.

Angel's antics stopped, until their recent return.

Did she really think a supernatural presence watched over her? She was iffy about belief in the spiritual world. Her Catholic upbringing supported belief in an afterlife, and that presupposed the possible existence of spiritual beings, didn't it? Communication between the two worlds was harder to accept though.

Nonetheless, she seemed to have more than her share of spiritually suspicious events. She couldn't explain them, but she wasn't going to waste a lot of time worrying. The incidents were curious, that's all. Worth puzzling over for a bit, fun to talk about with the *right* friends, then put out of mind where they belonged. She had things to do—her life was busy. Odd things didn't happen often and no harm was done. They could be ignored. Couldn't they?

If there was a spiritual presence, though, why did it follow Cora? Luck of the draw?

Perhaps she was, as Cisco thought, embellishing when she couldn't find rational explanations. These things happened to everyone, didn't they?

Well, whatever Angel is or isn't, seems she's back. I wonder why?

~ ~ ~

Cora did *not* like the summer heat. This afternoon was pleasant though, and she decided to fix a drink, sit on the shaded deck, and relax with a crochet project before making dinner.

Cora went to her liquor cabinet, which was in a buffet that had once belonged to her grandmother. She and Cisco lived in a brick two-story Colonial home, furnished predominately in traditional style, but a smattering of contemporary and antique pieces snuck in.

Studying the contents of the cabinet, she selected a bottle of Scotch whiskey, a bottle of cheap amaretto, and something called watermelon schnapps, all with about two inches remaining. Taking them into the kitchen, she found margarita mix and an assortment of soft drinks in the refrigerator. The margarita mix was out. She wrinkled her nose at the watermelon schnapps and settled on amaretto and Diet Coke.

She filled a tall glass to the top with ice, added a single shot of amaretto, and topped it with Diet Coke. This single drink would last the rest of the afternoon and evening, although it would probably make her fall asleep in front of the television. She took a sip; surprisingly, it wasn't bad. Sometimes she hit a home run, other times it was awful, but she drank it anyway.

At this rate, at her usual two or three drinks a week, she should empty these bottles in about three months. The idea of throwing away an unfinished bottle was not an option. That would be wasteful.

The liquor cabinet was on Cora's list of objectives to stop accumulating and start using things up. Brought up in families that lived through the Great Depression, both Cora and Cisco were raised to save anything usable and stock up when prices were low. Having done that for a lifetime, their home was now filled with more *stuff* than they could ever use.

Adding to the clutter, Cisco's mother had been a hoarder, and her belongings ended up with Cora and Cisco after her death. To amuse herself, Cora counted items. "There are a hundred and five coats. How could one woman use a hundred and five coats? Some still have price tags on them. And there are forty-seven cans of spray starch. Why would a woman who never left the house need forty-seven cans of spray starch?"

"You're trying to make her sound logical. That's impossible. Don't even try," Cisco said.

He didn't admit they had a clutter problem too; there was stuff, so what? They had space, what's the problem?

"We can't *find* anything!" Cora would say, exasperated. "We must have forty pairs of scissors in the house, but where are they? Somewhere in the stuff. So what do we do when we need a pair of scissors? We go out and buy another pair because we can't find any. In fact, we probably find them on sale and buy *five* of them. Two weeks later we can't find them anymore. And screwdrivers—we must have over a hundred, but our table knives all have little crooks on the ends because when we need a screwdriver we can't find one." She exaggerated intentionally, hoping Cisco would see humor in the situation, but he didn't get the joke.

To be fair, the living areas of the house were neat and clean—so long as no one looked in the basement, drawers, or closets. And Cora couldn't deny she was a collector. Every room was full of overflowing bookcases. She had good intentions about giving books away, but she would find only a few to part with. Most seemed like friends.

Photos were also out of control. She had hers, many printed in duplicates, some on slides, some in albums and some in boxes, with negatives. And she had her parent's photos. And her grandparents albums, interesting, but full of people she couldn't identify. Her hard drive was cluttered with digital photos, duplicated on CDs and DVDs, so she couldn't lose any. She spent months organizing until she burned out on the task. She managed to sort them into smaller boxes and store them neatly, but she didn't throw any away.

And there was music: on CD, tape, LP, even old 78s and 45s.

And the cut glass, crystal, bone china. Oh, yes, she had to admit she was a collector. But her stuff was *good*.

Maybe Cisco was right about her cluttering up her life with too many activities. It seemed to go with too much stuff. Of course, he needed to heed his own advice.

Having made a minute step in the right direction, Cora picked up her drink and her yarn, went out on the deck and settled into an Adirondack chair, resting her feet on a footstool. It was peaceful, alone here among the birds and the rustling leaves. Maybe she could procrastinate about Angel after all.

~ ~ ~

"Hi, Hon. I'm back" Cisco said, joining her on the deck, dropping a kiss on her forehead, and sitting down in a chair next to her.

"Hey. Can I make you a drink?" she asked, holding up her glass in demonstration.

"What are you drinking?"

"Amaretto and Diet Coke, and we have Scotch and watermelon schnapps. I can put together anything you like."

He made a face, wrinkling his nose. "No, thanks. I'll get myself a beer."

Returning with beer in hand, he sat down again and gazed around the yard. "The maple needs pruning," he observed. "What do you think?"

"Yeah. I'll help you if you want. How was golf?"

"Great! I shot an eighty-six. Had a good back nine. My short game could use a little work, but I was really hitting my drives today." He chatted on, demonstrating with enthusiastic waving of arms and hands, and Cora lost some of what he was saying. She wasn't into the technical aspects of the game that so absorbed Cisco, but she was lulled by the familiar sound of his voice. Eventually he had nothing more to say, so they sat companionably, Cora crocheting and Cisco assessing the yard.

Thinking about how to begin, Cora finally just said, "I'm afraid Angel is back, Hon."

"What makes you say that?" he asked warily. Cora knew Cisco didn't take Angel seriously, but she wanted his input and common sense.

She told him about the toothpaste tube that morning and reminded him about the clock batteries. "And when the girls were here for book club the wall clock crashed on the floor, and drawers are opening again, stuff like that. I didn't make a big deal about the clock with the girls, but that was actually the fourth time it happened this week."

"You told the girls? Why did you do that? You shouldn't have told them." Cisco frowned, a little angry. He would rather keep Angel between them.

"I shouldn't have," Cora said, nodding in agreement, "but it happened while they were here, what was I supposed to tell them? They were looking for an explanation, and it just came out. Of course, Lu already knows. It's different this time, Hon. It seems like Angel is pushing to go public. It's almost like she's a kid, saying, 'You don't pay enough attention to me, so now I'm going to act up in front of your friends'."

"Don't let your imagination run away with you now."

Cora glanced at him, and recognized the look, the one that said he was humoring her.

"I'll try not to. But you've got to admit there's strange stuff going on. Some of the girls think we should take this seriously—maybe something dangerous is happening. What do you think?"

"I don't know what to think. Crazy stuff happens, then—nothing. That's the pattern, right?" Cisco said, trying to be patient, but with irritation in his voice and concern on his face.

Chapter 3

"Hello, it's me— Cora!" she called from the bottom of the stairway, so as not to spook the women upstairs in the creepy old building.

"We're here, come on up!" a cheerful female voice replied.

The Lemont Area Historical Society, or LAHS, was located in an old stone church, appropriately named "The Old Stone Church." Cora climbed the dim, narrow, groaning stairway to the choir loft where the archives were housed. A large library table dominated the area, and seven-foot tall shelves lined the walls, along with an assortment of mismatched file cabinets and desks. A computer, scanner, copier, and bulky microfilm reader stood ready for use. Extension cords created obstacles across the floor and added to the cramped appearance, connected to table lamps that augmented whatever light penetrated the stained glass windows.

Cora and a few other dedicated women met one morning a week to keep order and answer research and genealogy requests from the public. Cora's mind was focused on Angel this morning, but keeping to her schedule provided an opportunity to leave the house and distract her from that problem.

She greeted Ania, a compact seventyish woman with twinkling blue eyes and a pleasant smile, who was already busy at the microfilm reader. Cora set down her belongings and started sorting through new acquisitions on her desk.

"You've made an early start, I see," she said, untying the string that held together a large atlas from 1875 so she could prepare a description of the item.

"True. Requests stacked up all of a sudden. A number of people want to come in to do research too. I'll have to make appointments," Ania said with a frown. Despite her complaint, Cora knew Ania enjoyed meeting with researchers. She worked with death records and genealogy requests and had been a volunteer for over twenty years. Knowledgeable and undemanding, she was a pleasure to work with.

Since joining the LAHS, Cora learned the interesting history of Lemont's churches. "The Old Stone Church," built in 1861 with stone from a local quarry, was believed to be the oldest church in the "Village of Churches." It was located across from notorious Smokey Row, a collection of shady establishments that sprang up as early as the 1860s. Reverend Tully, then the pastor of the Methodist congregation, waged war against Smokey Row. He took credit for clearing the town of corruption and sin, when in fact the businesses simply closed on their own, having little business after the canal was finished and the transient workers moved out.

However, another nearby church also claimed the oldest-church distinction. Perhaps both were right, since Saint James, located in the forest about four miles east, was in an unincorporated area of Lemont, an area once called Sag Bridge. The cornerstone for Saint James was laid in 1853, and the church sat on a hill between the Des Plaines River Valley and Sag Valley. It took six years for the Irish parishioners to lug enough stone to the hilltop to complete the building.

Cora was fascinated by Lemont's past and found the reading, recording, and preservation of documents entertaining. She grew fond of the other volunteers, who chatted while they worked, sharing interesting facts as they came across them. She felt fortunate, at this stage of life, to have found a new and meaningful passion to ignite her imagination.

"How about you, Emily?" Cora asked, turning to a spry woman in her early nineties. "Are you enjoying the summer?"

Emily and Ania had worked together for many years and were close friends. Emily's family traced back to the earliest Lemont settlers, and she was able to recall people, names and events going back to the 1920s and 1930s. It amazed Cora when Emily identified people in photos that were eighty years old. She was so reliable that the other workers said if Emily didn't remember it, it never happened.

Emily looked up from the table, where she was cataloguing the contents of one of the map drawers, magnifying glass in hand. "I went to visit my daughter, but it's nice to be back. There's no place like your own home. My daughter's place is so loud, people coming and going at all hours. I rest much better at home, and you know at my age you need your rest," Emily replied.

The society received donations to the archives regularly—valuable to preserve, but where to put them? Space was limited, as was the budget. With Cora's management experience, she was asked to take a fresh look at organizing the collections. It was her goal to bring the collections into the digital age and compile an improved searchable inventory, as an archive wasn't much good if no one knew what they had or where to find it. It all boiled down to cost and available labor; each project was an enormous task.

"Anything new going on?" Cora asked. As they chatted, she examined newly-donated items and entered the acquisitions into a logbook, numbered, described, labeled and filed them. The society also maintained a museum in the basement of the church, with displays recreating vintage settings. Some acquisitions ended up there.

"Not really," said Ania. "Just that pile in front of you."

"Say, I've got a question," Cora said. "Cisco and I were walking by the quarries, and I was wondering why they filled up with water. Is that what ended the quarrying industry?"

Numerous abandoned quarries were scattered through the floor of the Des Plaines River and Sag valleys. Previously a major industry in Lemont, walking and bike trails now went past the quarry pits, which were also popular fishing spots.

"I can answer that," Emily said. "It was the other way around. Sometimes the workers struck underground springs while cutting stone, and then too, rainwater collected. When the quarries were operating, they pumped the water out. When other stone became more fashionable and cheaper than ours, one by one the quarries went out of business. No more business, no more pumps, nature took over, and the quarries filled up."

She set down her pen and began arranging the loose documents in their drawer. "I always thought it was interesting that when the quarries were abandoned, much of the machinery was just left. It's still down there."

Ania, noticing that Emily had completed the drawer she was listing, rewound her microfilm reel, removed it from the viewer, and returned it to its metal box. She turned to help Emily put back the contents of the map drawer and carried the heavy drawer back to its cabinet.

"The quarries were popular for swimming then," Ania said. "People came from other suburbs and from Chicago to swim until the 1950s. The water was up to eighty feet deep, and it was extremely cold where the springs ran, and there were too many drownings, so they closed them for swimming. But our parents used to swim there, and people came for years. Sometimes vendors even set up stands and sold food."

"My parents and Cisco's parents used to talk about swimming there too, and they lived in Chicago. My mother told me a story about coming here with a bunch of friends when she was young. Her shoes got stolen, and shoes cost a lot of money back then, so her mother wouldn't talk to her for days. I think she remembered losing her shoes more than swimming in the quarry, but nonetheless..." Cora dropped off. Although it was two years since her mother died, she still found it hard to talk about her.

"There's more than just machinery down there," Emily went on, as she opened a folder and began flipping through photographs. "People used to dump anything they wanted to get rid of, especially old cars, in the quarries. Sometimes it was to cover up crimes or auto thefts, or even mobster-style murders, with bodies in the trunk. Scuba divers used to train in the quarries, and they found a lot of cars down there."

"Some of it's more recent. About thirty years ago or so, a woman was found in the trunk of her car in the canal just north of Sag Bridge," Ania added. "It was in the papers for months, and it's still talked about. Her lawyer husband was convicted of arranging her death, and it was always suspected the Mob was involved, but no one ever proved it."

"I remember that! How odd! We were just talking about the Mob at our book club last week. Submerged evidence of dirty Mafia deeds, right in our back yard. Quite a coincidence," Cora remarked, turning back to her work.

Chapter 4

Cisco got out of the car, but Cora remained in her seat, consulting a trail map. Resembling tangled skeins of yarn Cora wrestled with when knitting, the trails looped and crossed each other as they wound through thickets, up and down hills and ravines, over streams, and detoured around lakes and swamps. Although never more than a mile or two from homes or roads, the woods were desolate, and people who did not know them well could easily become disoriented, wandering in circles until too dark to see their way. Cora knew bodies had been found in these forests, people who wandered off the trails, became lost, and not discovered until years later. Taking time to review what lay ahead made good sense, but Cisco left that to Cora. He was impatient to get moving.

"Aren't you done yet?" he called.

Like a kid. Are we there yet? Cora sighed. It was part of his charm.

Cora scrambled out of the car and reached into the back seat for her trekking poles. Cisco thought the poles were useless. A man of average height, he was lean, fit, and energetic. He had developed an effortless marching stride many years ago during Army basic training, and he could walk miles over any terrain with ease. The poles helped Cora keep up a pace that didn't frustrate him, and he would slow his natural pace to match hers. The compromise worked pretty well, allowing them to walk companionably.

"Okay, Chingachgook, where are you taking us today?" he asked, settling a baseball cap over his balding head, and adjusting thick glass frames on his rather large Roman nose.

"That trail—" Cora pointed at a wide gravel path behind a picnic grove, "leads up the back side of Swallow Cliff. It's a more gradual climb than the steps up the cliff face. There's a good view up there, and then we can walk along the top edge of the cliff, work back down, and return on the lower trail. That'll be about three miles."

"We'll need to climb the steps to get back to the car. Are you okay with that?"

"I'll make it. Just let me set the pace."

"I don't remember any trails along the top of the cliff," Cisco said, looking ahead along the trail where it began a gradual climb.

"There aren't any, but there are paths. We'll follow the edge—how hard can it be? Then we'll catch the trail on the other side."

"Okay. Let's get going then."

They struck out up the trail, chatting as they walked, Cora swinging her poles with each step. "I used to ride my bike out here with a friend when I was a kid. We'd pack a lunch, rent horses and picnic, then bike back. Boy, did our butts get sore! I never knew what was on the other side of all those trees, and now we live there."

"I remember toboggan slides here at Swallow Cliff," Cisco said. "Now people use the old steps for exercise."

The grade got steeper. Cora paused to catch her breath and let the burn fade from her calf muscles while Cisco waited patiently. After a short break, they started up again.

"There was a picnic grove near here with a hill of sand, like dunes, and a spring bubbled in front of it. We'd climb it—you know how hard it is climbing through sand—then run down and try to stop before landing in the water. We didn't always make it," Cora said, laughing.

"I thought this whole area was clay. That's all I run across in our yard. I never knew there was sand around here," Cisco commented over his shoulder, finding it difficult not to outpace Cora.

"Yes, it was a surprise—a hill of sand in the middle of the forest. Farther down the spring, away from the picnic grove, was a little hidden clearing. We'd picnic there, cool our pop bottles in the spring, just sit around and laugh and talk until dark."

"Sounds like fun. Why don't I know about that place, and why don't *we* go there?" Cisco asked.

"It's not like that today. Well, it's still there, of course, but the hill is covered with shrubs and trees, and you don't see sand anymore. The clearing is just a wide spot next to the trail, nothing private or special about it. When I went there a few years ago, I thought I was in the wrong place. Few people remember it anymore."

"That's a shame," he replied.

Cora's breathing was a little labored, despite her poles. Looking ahead, she saw no end to the incline. She suggested Cisco go on at his own pace and wait for her at the top.

"Thanks for the history lesson!" he called, as he strode out ahead.

"Are you thanking me or complaining?" she called cheerfully after him.

It was a lovely, balmy day. Leaves still clung to trees and underbrush, brilliant with color. Fallen leaves rustled when stepped on, releasing a burst of musty odor into the fresh fall air, which Cora found reminiscent of her childhood. She loved their walks together, but she also relished solitary moments in nature. She slowed her pace, now that she needn't try to keep up with Cisco, and let her thoughts wander.

A few years ago, Cora would have defined herself by her work, telling others what she did rather than who she was. She decided to retire when she admitted to missing things that were important to her. Once she shed the job, she threw herself into things she wanted to do with abandon, too much abandon it now seemed. Instead of a single focus, work, her life now consisted of periods of frenetic energy followed by periods of exhaustion. She found herself avoiding friends because she was too busy, tired, or irritable. She felt she wasn't pulling her weight with household obligations. Up until two years ago she had to fit in the care of her elderly parents. Now she no longer had that burden, but physical limitations were beginning to take their effect.

She knew Cisco was trying to help, to divert her. He urged her to take this walk today, to get away from problems and obligations. He also wanted her to stop worrying about Angel, and perhaps he was right. Then again, maybe her friends were right. Her conflicted thoughts weren't getting her anywhere, so it could be a good idea to just not think about Angel for a while.

Cisco was out of sight now, somewhere on the trail up ahead. He would stay within calling distance and double back if she didn't show up in a reasonable time.

More than halfway up the incline, she noticed rustling in the woods along the trail. It sounded like pacing, heavy and regular, something bigger than a squirrel or chipmunk scrambling in the underbrush. Perhaps a deer? An image of someone lurking in the trees popped into her head. She stopped, and so did the sound. She looked around, unsure where the noise had come from, and saw nothing to account for it. Reassured, she resumed her walk.

As she approached the hilltop and saw Cisco waiting for her, a sudden commotion, a *thrashing*, shook the woods. It came from near the same place as before. She looked anxiously in that direction, saw motion between two large trees forty feet away, and caught a faint foul odor. She stood still, trying to identify what she saw and heard. Something big was in there, the size of a large dog, but its shape and density were indistinct. It moved slowly between the trees, and looked like dirty grey smoke or a small patch of fog. As she watched, the ominous crashing stopped and the shape faded away. She peered into the trees intently, but all was silent, the forest completely still, even the breeze halted.

Was something following her? What?

She hurried up the remainder of the path to where Cisco waited.

Cisco started walking as soon as Cora caught up to him. "You always forget!" she panted. "*You're* rested now, but I just got here, and I *haven't* rested yet. *Stop*, will you!"

She took a few heaving breaths, leaning on her poles. "Something weird is down there," she said between breaths, pointing off into the trees. "Were you watching me come up? Did you see anything?"

"I was watching, but not constantly. I didn't see anything. What do you think it was?"

"Did you hear anything?"

"No, nothing. In fact, it was very quiet."

"Yes! I mean, that's part of it—the quiet. First there was this crashing, thrashing in the trees, then complete silence, no sound at all, like something shushed everything in the woods. Even the breeze stopped. And it stank!" she said.

"So? I'm sure it happens. Maybe it was a deer?"

"I don't think so. The second time it happened I saw something, and it was nothing like a deer."

"What *was* it like, then?" he asked.

She pointed a pole toward the place. "It was about the size of a large dog, kind of gray or dirty white, hazy-looking, and it just sort of went away...."

"It ran away?" Cisco raised his eyebrows.

"No...I didn't see it run off—it just wasn't there anymore. It happened fast—I heard it, turned around, got a glimpse of it, then it was gone...," Cora swiped her pole through the air in emphasis. "Just gone—like that."

"Well, there doesn't seem to be anything there now. Probably a deer plus your imagination. Are you rested enough yet?" Cisco turned toward the trail, ready to move on, dismissing the incident.

"Uh...yeah...sure. Let's go. Maybe that's all it was." Cora drew her eyebrows together doubtfully, but started walking, taking the lead this time.

When they reached the top of the hill they came to the overlook on the cliff top, and they stood watching turkey vultures making wobbly circles through the sky. "Look how they hover over the road." Cora pointed at three of the large black birds. "I read that their sense of smell is so sharp they can find road-kill by sniffing the air."

They wondered if the swallows that gave the cliff its name would appear to dart around and catch insects. Although they stood on one ridge of the valley, lush foliage prevented them from seeing the waterways they knew occupied the valley floor, nor could they find the steeple of Saint James on the opposite ridge. A scattering of cars were parked at the foot of the cliff, and a solitary man in sweat pants climbed the stairs cut into the cliff face.

They moved on, following the edge of the cliff. As expected, thin, partially overgrown paths kept petering out, forcing them to backtrack and push through areas of undergrowth to hike along the cliff edge, making for slow progress, and a feeling they didn't quite know where they were.

"Listen," Cora whispered. A soft but steady crunching of leaves came from behind them.

"Did you hear that?" Cisco asked, holding out a hand to stop Cora.

"Yes! It's like what happened before," she nodded, looking around, her eyes wide. "See? I told you!"

They went on, and the steady pacing returned. They stopped. The sounds stopped. They walked. The cushioned noises resumed—stealthy, matching their steps. Stop—look around again—nothing there. Quiet but for their breathing, their footsteps, and the pursuing crunches, in an utterly calm forest—not a breeze, not a bird, not even an insect marred the silence.

"It's not our imagination, is it?" Cora asked, heart pounding, eyes darting, face white.

"No. Something's there, only I can't *see* it!" Cisco said in a whisper, looking about nervously. "I think it's following us."

"What should we do? Should we turn around…go back?" Cora stopped in confusion.

"We're probably halfway. It'll be as far to go back as it is to go on. Jesus! I don't know! Let's just keep walking." He grabbed her elbow and began to pull her through the brush.

"Following us? Or pursuing us?" Cora said, puffing a little, fighting to keep up with Cisco and prevent her poles from getting tangled in the undergrowth. As she finished saying this, they broke through the dense brush and arrived back at a main trail.

Cora experienced a momentary illusion of safety, having arrived at a marked trail. She slowed her pace, took a deep breath, and wiped sweat from her brow with her arm. She hoped they'd encounter other people now, but no, it was desolate, and her relief was short-lived. The sounds didn't disappear, but got closer, louder, came from the left, then from the *right*.

"How many things are out there? Are there two?" she asked, turning her head, trying to see through the trees on her right now.

"I wish I knew! Maybe…" Cisco said, stopping, turning in a circle, searching the forest again. Cora stopped and moved to his side.

Suddenly, there was turbulence behind them, loud crashing, and they spun in the direction of the racket, then stood frozen in shock. Huge branches and tree trunks moved violently about forty feet away. Trunks six inches in diameter bent and swayed as if a giant were shaking them, but they could see nothing to cause the frenzy. Then the commotion raced through the forest, as if a tornado was sweeping through it, but oddly there was no wind. It rapidly passed, and moved on, until they could no longer see or hear it.

"Oh my God! What was *that?*" Cora cried when it was over. "Did you see the size of those trees bending? That's no *deer!*"

"Whatever it is, it's *ahead* of us now," Cisco said in a strained voice, spinning around, eyes darting, jaw set. "Let's go back!"

"If we do that…what if it comes *behind* us again?" She grabbed Cisco's arm. "The trail is easier here…what if there's more than one of those things?" Like Cisco, her eyes searched continuously all around.

"Maybe we can find a way off the cliff right here," Cisco suggested.

Before they could move, another rustle caught their attention. They turned toward the sound, and a large gray animal, over a hundred pounds, walked slowly and purposefully, head held low, onto the path about thirty yards away. It stopped and stared fixedly at them.

"What *is* that?" Cora exclaimed in a hushed voice. She grabbed Cisco's arm and cowered behind him, heart racing, terrified.

Stunned, Cisco had no reply, and stood frozen.

"It looks like a huge dog…or a wolf," Cora went on, peeking out at the animal.

"It *can't* be a wolf. It must be a dog." Cisco, transfixed, recovered his voice but still didn't move.

"I don't know…is it going to attack? It's just standing there…what should we do?"

"If we run it might attack. Does it look like it's going to attack?" Cisco whispered, while he, Cora, and the animal maintained uninterrupted eye contact.

"Attack? How can *I* tell? Should we wave our arms, try to scare it off? Wild animals are supposed to be more afraid of us than we are of them," Cora suggested.

"It may not *be* a wild animal. It could even be rabid. That could make things worse. Okay, then…we should make ourselves look bigger, more threatening," Cisco moved beside her, touching heads and shoulders. "Now we look like one big thing instead of two small things. Give me one of your poles, and hold yours up."

If she hadn't been so terrified, Cora would have laughed at the ridiculous solution. However, before they could lift their poles, the animal put its head down, took a few steps toward them, and stopped, its keen eyes never wavering.

"It's like it knows we're talking about it, trying to plan a defense," Cisco whispered, his mouth touching her ear.

The animal sat down on the trail, continued to stare at them, its eyes gleaming with a yellowish light. It did nothing aggressive, only watched them intently.

"Okay," Cisco whispered. "That's not threatening. Hold out your pole, show it you can defend yourself."

They did that, and the animal stood up, put its head down again, silently took a few more steps toward them as if in warning, then stopped and stared again.

"All right, no good," Cisco admitted. "We can't outrun it...."

"I'm afraid to turn our backs on it. Maybe we can start *backing* away," Cora suggested.

They tried that. The animal moved toward them again, stopped when they stopped, stared.

"It's like it wants to keep us here," Cora whispered. "Are we imagining this? Is it a dream?"

"No, it's no dream—I wish it was," Cisco whispered back.

"Is it going to attack us?" she said again. "We have the poles, but...."

"We can't just stand here—we have to do *something*," said Cisco, frustrated and bewildered, as he waved an arm in the air.

The animal took a few more steps, still eyeing them intently. Then it began to pant, its long tongue lolling out of its mouth.

"It looks like it's laughing—playing with us," Cisco said.

"Playing, hell! This is no fun!" Cora declared. She straightened her back, planted both feet, and set her jaw.

As if it understood them, the animal lowered its head, walked closer, only fifteen feet away now, and without breaking eye contact, squatted and urinated on the trail. Then it stood up, turned its back to them, flicked its tail, and trotted off jauntily, down the path and out of sight.

Chapter 5

Cora and Cisco wasted no time but took the shortest route off the cliff, even though the animal was gone.

As they went down the cliff steps, the man they had seen training earlier passed them on his way up. Cora called after him, "You should avoid the woods above the cliff. We just saw a big menacing animal there."

"Really?" the man stopped, turned around, and inquired, looking interested. "What was it? A deer?"

"Oh, no—not a *deer*. It looked like a wild dog or wolf."

"There's no wolves around here." The man's eyes shifted away from Cora, apparently deciding she was odd.

"No, that's what I thought too. Nonetheless...."

"Did it attack you?" he asked, edging away.

"Uh...no. But I'd be careful anyway," Cora said in a weak voice, face red.

The man gave Cisco what seemed to be a pitying look and went on up the steps.

"You told that guy the animal was menacing. Did you think it was? Did we blow this out of proportion?" Cisco asked.

"Well, I felt terrified up there. Now, I don't know. Sometimes it seemed like, whatever it was, it was playing with us. But there was that following part and the shaking in the trees. I couldn't tell the guy about that. He'd think we were nuts," Cora said.

"I suspect he thinks that already," Cisco said, smiling in her direction.

They trudged toward a two-lane road to avoid the woods. It was a roundabout route to where their car was parked, with late afternoon traffic, but *safe*. Gradually they calmed down and discussed their impressions of the incident, as they walked at the side of the road at a moderate pace.

"I feel dazed, even now. Like I'm going to wake up soon." Cora's eyes were focused on the road ahead.

They walked in silence, deep in thought. "I don't think that was a dog," Cora said after a while.

"Why not?"

"It didn't *look* like a dog. It looked and acted more like a *wolf.*"

"Wolves and dogs look a lot alike, don't they? Besides, there aren't any wolves around here, remember?"

"Well, you do at least agree it wasn't a coyote, don't you?" Cora stopped, turned to Cisco and searched his eyes.

"Yes, you're right there." He reached for her arm and pulled her along. "I've seen enough coyotes around the house, and that was definitely not a coyote. It outweighed a coyote by more than fifty pounds, and the color was all wrong. This thing was gray, not tan."

"I told you *before* I saw wolves near here, from the car. You never believed me, so I did some research, checked out behavior and physical differences."

"And?" Cisco asked.

Cora's voice became more confident and less shaky as she backed up her reasoning with facts. "For one thing, people most often tend to confuse German Shepherds or huskies with wolves. German Shepherds have more black and brown in their coloring, and a longer nose, and their ears are taller. They can have some grey, but it's usually mixed with black and tan."

She was walking briskly now, poles clicking as they struck stones along the shoulder of the road. "Huskies do look more like wolves, but Siberians have a white mask and blue eyes, which distinguishes them. The Alaskan huskies are smaller and their tail curls over their back. Wolf eyes are brown or yellow, and their tails don't curl. The animal we saw was all gray, with yellow eyes, a short nose, short pointy ears and a low tail."

She glanced at Cisco to see if he agreed with her. "They don't look that much alike when you really pay attention. We got a good look today, staring at it for so long."

"Could be a mixture," he argued.

"True. But habits are different too. A dog wouldn't be living in the forest and catching its own food. It would hang around close to homes and raid garbage. And dogs growl, but wolves stalk silently, and the one we saw was silent—they're hunters, right? Now that I'm thinking about it, it's a good thing we didn't turn our backs on it," Cora said, waving a finger in the air, pole swinging from its strap around her wrist.

"Why's that?" Cisco asked, turning toward her.

"Because wolves hunt by chasing down fleeing prey from behind."

"Uh—yeah—good thing we didn't do that," he agreed, reaching over to pull her off the road as he spotted a car that was traveling too fast. "I'm not sure I agree with all your points. Garbage isn't far away—a dog could live in the forest but raid home garbage cans after dark, for instance. And, if it's a wolf, how did it get here?"

"I read wolves can travel up to five hundred miles to search for food or a mate. There are gray wolves in northern Wisconsin and in the UP. That's less than five hundred miles, so it could happen, right? They follow high tension electric wires, because it's faster."

"Well, we know it's a female, that was obvious," Cisco said with a chuckle. "But how do you explain the shaking trees in the forest? A wolf wouldn't be powerful enough to do that. Maybe something *else* shook the trees?"

"Two things, you mean? The wolf *and* something else? Or something *more* than a wolf? Maybe...." They came to the entrance to the parking area and turned into it.

Cora stopped and put her hands on the roof of the car, looking over it at Cisco. "Did you get the impression it was intelligent? The way it followed and stared, and it looked like it was playing with us, don't you think? Don't you wonder about that? I get the sense this was personal, not an accidental encounter. Like it wanted something from us."

"Well, *that* could be your imagination," Cisco suggested, reaching into his pocket for the car keys.

"Could be. Or I could be right. Whatever. But it's messed up my appetite for walking in the woods. I hope I can get over it. I *like* our walks in the woods."

Chapter 6

Halloween was two days away, and the Lemont Area Historical Society's *Fright Night* program was about to begin in the Old Stone Church. People gathered to tell, and listen to, scary stories about local ghosts. Candlelit, the atmosphere was gloomy and mysterious. Volunteers, dressed in frightful costumes, greeted and seated the audience. A creepy-looking manikin, a butler in a tuxedo with red, black-rimmed eyes, stood at the door glaring at those who dared to enter. Historical society staff had named him Bill Mum.

A casket, made of rough boards, sat on a pedestal beyond the altar railing. It was sized to fit a child, and it added a sobering, poignant note.

Cora was the last speaker. Her talk was about Saint James at Sag Bridge, a popular location for ghost tales. It was known that Indian villages had once existed on the site, so legends included phantom Indians, but also disappearing carriages, monks and brides, glowing infant caskets, and other eerie sights were reported, many tales allegedly told by reliable witnesses.

Cora was dressed in black and wore no jewelry or makeup. Her pale face and demeanor suggested a macabre appearance as she glided to the lectern, standing stiffly erect behind it, hands resting on its reading surface. She stood silently, somberly eyeing the audience for a full minute before beginning to speak, slowly and dramatically, in a hushed voice that forced the audience to strain to hear her.

"My story is a true and remarkable tale.

"In the sixties, during my college days, one of my friends was a priest who was fascinated by the supernatural, and he sometimes visited cemeteries at night. He told us stories about his experiences in graveyards, stories that frightened and amazed us. So when he invited us to go with him to the old cemetery at Saint James at Sag Bridge, we were delighted. He knew the pastor there, and arranged for the gates to be left open for us. But at the last minute, he had to visit a sick parishioner. Not wanting to disappoint us, he told us to go anyway. There were five in our little ghost-hunting group.

"Tall gates guard the entrance to Saint James, but they were open, as we were told they would be. We parked in the deserted lot. Fierce dogs protected the place at night, we were told, but the dogs wouldn't be out if the gates were open…would they? We were very cautious anyway.

"With our headlights off it was seriously dark, forest all around, and what about those vicious dogs…who knew what other creatures could be out there, unseen? We looked around anxiously and contemplated the next step—to venture out into the cemetery. Our every sense was heightened, every movement, every sound, even odors, everything seemed ominous. We imagined creatures lurking in the woods, and listened apprehensively, startled at little noises from the forest, each creak or snap or rustle suggested sinister intent.

"Heh, heh, heh—," Cora barked out a malevolent laugh, and the audience jumped and then laughed in embarrassment.

"Do you know what it's like there? Have *you* been there? The old church is on top of a hill, ringed by an old cemetery, and surrounded by dense forest, impenetrable with underbrush. There are abundant places for *things* to hide at night! Heh, heh, heh."

Cora paused. When she spoke again her voice was bright, lively, and amused.

"Initially the girls in our little group were fearless—once we were sure the dogs weren't out, that is—because we didn't really believe we would see anything. So we three girls led our party up the hill, with the two boys lagging behind, and we entered the cemetery.

"The boys, though, were clearly having second thoughts, groaning and whimpering and acting as if they didn't want to be there. We laughed at them. How silly they were, what wusses! Girls are more logical, not to mention brave."

Cora's words became slow and distinct.

"You know that fear breeds fear—and that was what happened. The boys made such a fuss going, 'Ooooh,' and 'What's that?' and 'Aaahhh-hh!' and jumping at imagined things, and by the time we passed around and behind the old church...."

Cora's voice lost its playfulness, and became low and portentous.

"Now—the cemetery was even *spookier*...our car, our means of escape, was out of sight, and we thought maybe this wasn't such a good idea after all...and so we turned back, and as we crept nervously through the cemetery, the boys leading now, we went faster and faster, and then we were all..."

Cora's speech got fast and excited:

"...*running* down the hill, with me at the rear. And..."

Cora paused dramatically, then, in a slow, distinct low voice, went on.

"...as we approached the parking area—beyond our car—in the forest right behind it...

"There!" She exclaimed loudly, throwing up an arm, and pointing to the back of the church.

The audience reflexively jerked around to look, then laughed at themselves and turned their attention back to Cora. She resumed, this time in a stage whisper.

"There...," she pointed again, "...just there, at the edge of the forest, among the trees—an apparition! Do *you* see it?"

Cora paused, looking from one set of eyes to another, giving the audience time to envision a ghostly presence in the forest. They squirmed in their seats, looking around the dim sanctuary, avoiding Cora's stare. Then she continued to describe it for them in a calm hushed voice.

"It was white, but transparent, like mist, but *glowing* inside, softly lit among the trees on that dark and gloomy night, and *hovering* above the ground. I could see objects indistinctly right through it. It was shaped like a person, but I couldn't tell if it was a man or a woman. It seemed suspended two feet above the ground, and it didn't move, but I thought it was watching me. I stared at it, stunned and unable to move.

"My friends had reached the car by then, and were impatient to leave, to get out of there. I pointed at the shape, speechless, but it was already fading. By the time the others looked where I pointed...look!—there, see what I see...! It was gone, disappearing in front of my eyes."

" 'Why did you stop? What were you pointing at?' my friends asked.

" 'Something was there, in the forest, right there,' I said, and pointed to the spot again. 'Now it's gone, but...I think I saw a ghost!' "

Cora paused again and then continued in a normal speaking voice, perplexed:

"What did I see in the forest at Saint James that night so long ago? What could it have been? I can't guess. Was it mist or fog, drifting in the trees? It could be, I suppose, but then why did it glow? I saw it clearly for...I don't know...thirty seconds? Maybe longer. Longer than a fleeting glimpse, that's for sure. I had a good look. Was it watching *me*? I sensed it was.

"But this I *know*—"

Another pause:

"It hovered...it glowed...it never moved...and it just faded away...."

~ ~ ~

"You should have been an actress!" Maureen said afterwards. "What a great way to end our program!" She bustled off to help serve refreshments.

"Good job, Cora!" Diane, the president of the LAHS board, approached Cora and shook her hand. "Can you tell the same story again next year?"

Cora was evasive. "Maybe once is enough. I'm not sure I want everyone thinking I *believe* in ghosts!" she said, joking but half in earnest.

"Was it really a true story then?" Diane asked.

Cora's reply was evasive. "Basically. But of course time has a way of exaggerating the facts. I'd rather have people wonder."

"Well, true or not, the audience enjoyed your story. Thank you for telling it."

Chapter 7

"How's your daughter, Valerie?" Sissy asked, looking up while tossing salad. "She's what, nine now?" Valerie, as usual, didn't bring food, leaving that for someone else. There was always plenty of food, but the others found it annoying.

"I know it's a cliché," she said, running a hand through her pixie-cut dark hair, "but Molly is nine going on twenty-nine. She's quite the little person, elegant and dignified. When we shop she turns her nose up at everything *I* pick. I always thought I had good taste, but let me tell you, that little girl of mine is quite the fashion guru. She's very particular what she wears to school every day, and smart! She amazes her teachers, they tell me." Valerie was animated, clearly delighted by Sissy's interest in Molly.

"You're not proud of her, are you?" Marty's tone said she was commenting, not asking.

"She's the center of my life. I don't know what I'd do without her." Cora was surprised to see Valerie's eyes shining with emotion, which seemed uncharacteristic.

"Does she see her father?" Sissy asked, as the women filled their plates and took seats around the kitchen table.

"He's in California. She visits him every summer, by court order. I'm a wreck while she's gone, afraid he's trying to take her from me. Now that Thanksgiving is coming up, I'm getting nervous he'll try to pull something. I've had a visit from a social worker, thanks to him, and I just found out he's got a detective trying to prove I'm unfit. I'm furious!"

"I'm sure you have nothing to worry about," said Jean.

Valerie went on and on about Molly as the women ate. In an effort to open up the conversation to other topics, Jean turned to Cora. "How is the library election campaign going?"

Cora laughed. "It's not much of a campaign—I just get signatures and write a bio for the paper."

"Do you think you'll be re-elected?" Sissy asked.

"I hope so. I've been on the board for ten years, and I think I've done a good job. Voters don't pay much attention to the Library Board, but with only three people seeking two positions, I think I have a good chance." Cora's words were positive, but her eyes shifted uneasily and she focused them on her plate.

"How would you feel if you didn't win?" Betty asked, picking up Cora's concern.

"Pretty bummed, I guess," she admitted. "I suppose it could happen. Many voters just pick a name that sounds good to them and don't know anything about the candidates." She hesitated and set down her fork, blinking rapidly. "I really enjoy serving the library. I'd feel like a failure, like my work was no good, if I didn't win."

"Well, I'm going to tell everyone in town to vote for you!" Betty said.

"Me too," Jean echoed, wiping her lips with a napkin.

"Thanks. Would you mind spreading the word and sending some emails? I guess it's more important than I let on." Cora looked around the table with a sheepish grin.

"Say, Cora," Lu said, "I hope I'm not insulting your Irish heritage when I tell you Italian food is a whole bunch better than Irish food."

"You wouldn't say that if we were having her corned beef," said Marty.

Valerie remained silent, looking alternately at her nails or the empty plate in front of her. The moment of enthusiasm she had shown earlier seemed to have spent itself. Cora guessed she was sulking since she was no longer the center of attention, or because no one had picked up her empty plate. The plate would probably still be sitting there when she left.

"Have you heard from Joe and Rosie," Marty asked, helping Betty carry empty dishes to the sink. Joe was Cora's other son, Rosie his wife. They lived two hundred miles away, which meant Cora saw little of her grand-daughter Maria, soon to be a year old. Both professionals, Joe and Rosie needed to be where the jobs were, and that was not, unfortunately, Lemont.

"I did," she replied. "I hope the weather is decent in December, so we can drive out for Maria's first birthday."

"Juggling new jobs, *and* a new house, *and* a new baby. I have to give them credit," Lu said.

Cora wore a worried expression. "Yes, I'm sure it's hard. But that's the life they chose."

"Say!" Betty threw in, sitting back down at the table. "What's going on with your angel? Any more funny stuff?"

"Well, yeah, some," Cora admitted. "Nothing earth-shattering. Let's not waste time talking about Angel though. Maybe if there's time later...."

Marty led the discussion of Frank McCourt's autobiography, *Angela's Ashes*, as the women nibbled dessert. "Cora," she prompted, "you told us all about Italians at our last discussion, and you're not even Italian. You are Irish, though—I bet you have some Irish stories."

"Uh...yeah...okay." Cora grinned, meeting the women's eyes, hinting she was ready to hold court. She forked a last bite of cake into her mouth and washed it down with a swallow of coffee.

"I spent a lot of time as a kid with my Irish grandmother. She was born in Chicago, but you'd never know it to talk to her. She was always talking about the 'auld sod' and being 'full of the blarney' and stuff like that. She didn't have a brogue, but pretended to, and talked about living in Ireland, although she'd never been there." She set her hands on the table, interlocked the fingers, and leaned forward.

"She'd take me to visit her stepfather, who lived to be a hundred and three, cared for by his three spinster stepdaughters. They lived on the south side of Chicago on a double corner lot, and had chickens, goats, puppies and cats, like a farm right in the city. I heard them call people 'shanty Irish', but their own life wasn't any different." She laughed, shaking her head. "They put on airs, as they described it!"

"Did the men drink, like McCourt's father?" Marty asked. Not only was Marty Irish too, but her children were descendants of the people Cora was talking about.

Cora shrugged. "At weddings and wakes. Irish wakes were big social occasions, more like parties, and they went on for days. Irish women *scrutinized* the obituaries, and showed up at the funeral parlor if the obit mentioned anyone they knew, even if they never met the deceased."

Betty laughed. "I heard that!"

Cora was on a roll. She settled herself more comfortably in the straight-back chair, leaning back and crossing her legs at the ankles. "The women cried when they arrived, wailed for a while, but then they'd sit talking and laughing in loud squeaky voices. The men paid their respects, then went next door to the tavern—there was always a tavern next to an Irish funeral parlor, which I suspect was a requirement for an Irish wake. They hung around on the sidewalk in front, no matter what the weather was, red in the face, talking and laughing, some not too steady on their feet—who cared?—most of them lived within walking distance."

"Did Grandpa join them?" Marty asked, leaning over the table. "Did he drink?"

"I only saw him drunk at parties, weddings, or funerals, and then he was a happy drunk, not a mean one. Everyone thought he was the life of the party, but it embarrassed me, and I didn't think he was very funny." Cora rolled her eyes and shook her head.

"There are a lot of Irish in Lemont." Betty said. "You must know that from your work at the historical society."

Cora nodded. "True. The Irish came to build the first canal, in the 1840s and 1850s, and many of them stayed. They used to say all you needed to build a canal was a pickaxe, a wheelbarrow, and an Irishman." Cora put her hands together and made a chopping motion, and the women laughed. "And—"she went on, "they spent a lot of time in Smokey Row."

"Smokey Row…really?" asked Sissy, raising her eyebrows in question.

"That's what it was called. Hard to imagine, looking at this sleepy town now, but there were over a hundred brothels, taverns and gambling joints in the center of town, quite the den of iniquity. Most closed down toward the end of the twentieth century, after the workers finished the canals and moved away."

Frannie was uncharacteristically quiet. She stared at her plate and pushed cake around without eating it, and didn't seem to be paying attention. Betty asked, "Is something wrong, Frannie? You haven't said much today."

Frannie put her elbows on the edge of the table, rested her chin in her hands, and let out a slow breath. "I'm not sure I want to talk about it. It's very personal," she said. The women looked at each other, wondering if Frannie would say more. Cora experienced a moment of chagrin that she hadn't noticed her friend was uncharacteristically quiet.

Watching their expressions, Frannie went on. "I don't say much to you all about living in the black community. It's a part of me I'm not sure you'd understand."

The women squirmed and looked at the tabletop, uncomfortable. Frannie was leading up to something, but she might be right—they might not understand. She was welcome in their circle, but they weren't so sure about being invited into hers.

Frannie turned her gaze away, and looked out the window at the leaf-less trees in Cora's yard. She appeared to be thinking over what to say. "You all know I moved back into Mama's house, right? Well, now I'm not so sure that was the right thing to do."

"Why not?" Betty asked.

Frannie turned to Betty, who all the women knew was a sympathetic listener. "The folks there are still pissed at me for leaving the neighborhood so long ago. They can't forgive me for hooking up with a white man. That wasn't accepted so much back when I did it. They call me uppity."

"Maybe they have a point," mumbled Valerie. The others ignored her.

"So, are they giving you a cold shoulder?" Lu said.

"They're mad at me, too, because my brother, he told them Mama's house should belong to him, not me, since I left and he stayed, and I got no right living in it. They think I stole it from him."

"That's not fair," said Betty, banging a fist on the table, and looking at the other women for approval. "You're the one who quit your job to take care of your mama when she got sick. He never showed his face except to hold out his hand. That's why she left that house to you."

"I was surprised when you moved back there too. You never said why you decided to do that," Marty said. She selected a cookie from a plate remaining on the table and broke off a small piece.

Frannie clasped her hands under her chin and rubbed them together, then she looked at Marty. "I gave up a lot to live with Mama and take care of her, but by the time she died I knew I really didn't want to be a working woman anymore. I'm not good at pretending to be someone I ain't, and you got to do that on a job, to get along—act like everybody else. That's not me. But it won't be too long, only a couple of years, before

I can collect Social Security, and with my savings, and living rent-free, and a little money coming in if I rent out the downstairs apartment, I can make it till then. So I thought I'd give it a try."

"So I don't understand," said Sissy, picking up a fork and pushing it around, squeaking a little on the empty plate. "Are the neighbors making it that bad for you? Just forget about them."

"It's my brother making trouble." Frannie said, closing her eyes and shaking her head. "He didn't live with Mama or help her, but he thinks since he stayed in the neighborhood when I left, her house should be his. He's so angry, and he's riling up everything and everybody."

"Riling them up? How?" asked Betty.

"Well, he thinks the court screwed up big time when the judge told him the house was rightfully mine."

"Your brother took you to court?" Sissy asked, jerking upright and staring open-mouthed. "That son of a...."

"Your own brother, how awful," Betty said, placing a hand sympathetically on Frannie's arm.

"Yeah, well, the neighbors, they side with him, he's got them all riled up about it."

"They'll come around, Frannie," Cora said. "Just give them time. But why didn't you say something? We had no idea you were going through this."

"I don't like passing my troubles on to nobody," Frannie said.

"So why are you doing it now then?" Valerie, her mouth partly obscured as she rested it on her open hand, grumbled under her breath.

"That wasn't called for, Valerie," Lu, sitting next to her, leaned over and whispered.

"So he's angry, so what? What's he going to do? You won in court," said Jean.

"Well, I thought, okay, so he is my brother, and he's in a bad way, doesn't have a job, maybe hanging with the wrong people. I'm not gonna give him the house, he'd just lose it, but maybe I can let him live downstairs, just for a while, 'til he can get on his feet, maybe I can help him better himself. Maybe get rid of some of that anger, too, if I'm nice to him. So I try that."

"Uh oh, I got a feeling this isn't going to turn out good," said Lu.

"You got that right," Frannie said, shaking her head again. "That man's dang worthless, and no way he's ever gonna let me help him. Well, he's gone now though."

"What do you mean? What happened?" asked Marty.

"He come home one Friday night, just over a week ago, real late, and he been drinking, and he come in my apartment—he still got a key, I made a big mistake there not changing the locks when I moved in, but who knew? He drug me out a bed, started yelling, ranting, how I robbed him of his home, how I'm asking him for rent all the time—like he ever paid me rent, fat chance that ever happen. He act like I'm the cause of every bad thing ever happened to him, and he done nothing to help *himself*." She wrinkled her nose and curled her upper lip in disgust.

"That must have been pretty unpleasant," said Jean.

"Don't I wish that was all that happen! You know it's not my style to talk nice when I get upset." Cora noted that the more distressed Frannie got the more she slipped into vernacular. "He picked up a big heavy mug and threw it through the window, glass falling all over the place. He came over to me, and he pushed me with both hands, and I fell into the counter—almost went down on the floor. I had enough and I started giving back to him, and we're standing there and we're yelling as loud as we can yell, and then he hauled off and he punched at me with his fist, but I turned and he missed my face, but he hit my shoulder and this time I *do* go down, and I let out a scream, loud as can be, and the next thing I know there's banging on the door, and it's the police, and I guess a neighbor called them."

"Oh wow! So what did they do?" asked Jean, her eyes open wide.

"Well, these two policemen came in—Michael left the door open, of course—and we're both still screaming at each other, and the police are trying to shout over us, yelling 'Just calm down now'," but we're too much into yelling and we don't stop. Then Michael he moves real sudden toward me, and then the police went crazy."

"They didn't know what you guys were going to do," said Lu.

"That's right, they didn't know, and so they both grabbed Michael, and not too gentle either, and they put handcuffs on him, and when he stopped struggling they asked me, 'You alright ma'am?' and I say I'm okay, only madder than hell, and they say to Michael, 'You live here?'

and he says no, that he lives downstairs, and they take him down there to talk it out."

"I hope they did more than that," Cora said, trying to catch Frannie's gaze.

"Well, two more policemen come then, a man and a woman, and they were real nice to me. We sat down to talk about it, and they said when they get a call like this they're expected to arrest someone, and they wanted to know if I want to bring charges."

"What did you do?" asked Betty.

"Well, he's my brother, my only kin, but I told them I tried to help him but now I know I can't, and I don't want him living in my house no more, I'm scared he might hurt me if he gets mad again, and it seems he's mad all the time. I never had no dealings with the police before and I don't know about rights or anything, I only know I don't want Michael near me no more, whatever that takes, and that's what I told them."

"So did they arrest him?" asked Marty, wide gaze riveted on Frannie.

"I guess so. They didn't exactly tell me, but they called someone on their phone, and said the judge gave what they called an emergency protective order. They said because I was a 'complainant asking the person to leave the premises,' that's the words they used. They took him away, and gave me the name of someone to change my locks, and said he can't come here no more." She paused for a moment, took a deep breath, and sipped some coffee before continuing.

"I don't know where they took him and I don't want to know, but he must of got religion or something because he ain't been around. He came only one time, with another policeman, and I let him get his stuff from downstairs, and he took everything, even stuff that belongs to me, but he's gone now, and it's worth it to have him gone. Girl next door, she says she heard he went to Vegas where he knows a guy, gonna give him a place to stay."

"Are you sure?" asked Cora, her eyebrows raised in doubt.

"Well, he's gone for now anyways, and maybe he'll learn how to behave before he comes back. I got those locks changed though, and I sleep with a big old butcher knife under my pillow, just to be safe."

"So if this is all over, why do you say you're not sure you should be living there?" asked Jean.

"No one talks to me. Everyone looks away when they see me coming. I have no friends there and I feel uncomfortable and alone. I thought I was going home—it's not what I expected. It's not a good place to be, but I'm determined to stick it out."

Cora noticed a small quiver in Frannie's frown. She realized Frannie's story explained a lot about her friend's personality. Her bravado and stubbornness were defense mechanisms that compensated for the realities of her life. Having rejected her only living relative, and rejected by the people she grew up with, she now sat in a room of white women trying to explain her misery.

"I understand why you would do that," said Lu, nodding her head as she looked around the table at mostly doubtful faces. "Sometimes you just have to prove you have the guts to be where you are. I've had to fight my way through life too. Maybe not so hard as you, but still I've had my battles. If you can't prove it to *yourself*, you just don't have what it takes to keep on going, you lose your confidence. If you don't have your self-image, you have nothing, your life goes in the toilet."

Valerie, who had been rubbing her ear with her thumb and forefinger, said, "Well, I *don't* understand!" Cora thought she acted like a selfish little girl. "Why are you forcing yourself on those people, staying where you're not welcome?" She laughed, but no one joined her.

"Can't you see she's upset? You're not helping with comments like that," said Lu.

"Well, is that the end of the story *finally?*" Valerie said. She wasn't about to back down.

Frannie, provoked, sat up straight and glared defiantly at Valerie. "These are not *bad* people, they just need time to get to know me again. They think *I'm* the one who did something wrong."

Valerie let out a breath dramatically. "Why am I even trying to argue with you? These 'good' neighbors—you're only getting what you asked for!"

Frannie said. "I'm just trying to make my life best as I can, and now you're blaming me too. It's hard enough to be talking about this. I'm sorry I ever told you!" She brushed tears off her cheeks, her emotions obviously at a volatile point.

"Are you happy now, Valerie?" asked Lu, glaring at her across the table.

"You think *I* made her cry? Well, guess what—"

"That's enough!" Cora interrupted. She stood up abruptly and loomed over Valerie.

Valerie looked up at Cora, momentarily taken aback, her jaw dropped. "I—," she started.

"Just—stop—talking!" Cora enunciated between clenched teeth. There was shocked silence in the room as the women looked at each other, then at Frannie, Cora and Valerie in turn.

Cora continued calmly. "We've all had enough of your rude and mean comments, Valerie. You're not welcome here anymore."

"What...are you asking me to leave?" Valerie snorted and gave a one-sided smile. "We haven't decided what book to read next time—"

"No, you don't get it, Valerie. No next time. I think I speak for everyone here when I say we don't want you to return to book club, not next time, not ever. Just leave, please, before this gets uglier than it already is?"

Lu's eyes sparkled with approval and she nodded slowly.

Valerie looked around at the others and saw no support. With a flushed face, she narrowed her eyes, stared at Cora and said, "You'll regret this!" Then she grabbed her purse and stomped out.

"Oh dear!" said Betty.

After Valerie left, the women looked at each other uncomfortably.

"I'm sorry to be the cause of all this," said Frannie, chin in her hands and staring at the tabletop.

"Don't be! We're all glad it's over, and it wasn't you to begin with. Valerie was just using you as her target of the day, ticked off because you took the spotlight off her. I think I speak for everyone when I say we're very ashamed at how she talked to you," said Lu, with a warm smile.

"I'm *so* glad to be rid of her. I was starting to dread coming, knowing she'd be here. I had to bite my tongue not to be as rude as she was," said Sissy, nodding.

"But I'm still worried about your safety, Frannie," said Cora, with a wrinkled forehead. "Let's assume this son of a bitch is gone, are there any other threats? Is it safe where you live?"

"It's not a bad place to live. You all could walk down the street and be fine, but you probably wouldn't *feel* comfortable about it. People hang out on their front stoops and socialize in good weather. Most have jobs and pay their bills. There's some homes with no father living there, but no drive-bys or that kind of thing." Frannie's eyes remained downcast, not looking at her friends.

"Is there anything we can we do to *help* you?" Betty asked, resting a hand gently on Frannie's arm.

"Not much you *can* do. You're sure not going to follow me home and confront my demons, and even if you did it'd only add fuel to the fire." She looked up now, and glanced around the table. Everyone's eyes were on her. "No, I have to figure out how to fight my own battles. Just knowing I have friends here who think kind about me, that's the best help you can give me."

The women resettled themselves in their chairs, fidgeted, and reached for cookies. Cora thought they seemed somewhat at a loss. She knew them well enough to know they sincerely felt empathy for Frannie and wanted to help her, but also that they didn't understand the life she led and probably felt their own lives were better. They didn't consider themselves to be bigots, but Cora couldn't begin to define where bigotry began or ended.

"Maybe if there was just one person in the neighborhood you could get through to, it could make a difference? Is there anyone you think you might be able to turn into a friend? Someone others might listen to?" Betty finally suggested.

"It's awful to think about, but maybe you can use this experience to your advantage," Lu said. "Surely someone is shocked at what happened, and isn't speaking out. Watch people, see if anyone looks guilty, ashamed, something like that. Look for someone who will meet your eyes. Then try to find an opportunity to gain that person's favor."

"You all know I'm not so good at schmoosing and pretending stuff. Blunt and outspoken, that's more like me." Frannie said. She barked a laugh, but it was a poor imitation of her usual infectious good humor.

"We know you have a soft side, Frannie—maybe now's the time to show it. There's a saying—people respect you for your strengths, but they love you for your weaknesses. Think about that while you're trying to get a little love from the neighborhood." Sissy said.

Chapter 8

Cora was making de-cluttering progress, sorting old magazines for the trash, when she was interrupted by the phone. Irritated, she hurried to her office to pick it up, tripping over a pile on the floor and narrowly avoiding a fall. Why was she killing herself to get to the phone? It was probably only Rachel from Cardholder Services for the umpteenth time this week, wanting to alert her to some bogus problem with her un-named credit card. Telemarketers should realize how inconsiderate, not to say dangerous, they are, she thought.

"Hello?" she said as she grabbed the handset, her irritation clear.

"Is this Cora Tizzy?" the caller asked.

"Tozzi...who's calling?" Cora said, reluctant to give information to an unknown caller.

"This is Megan Flynn from the *News Local*. Is this Cora?"

"Yes...," she admitted cautiously. She subscribed to the *News Local*, a weekly newspaper.

"I'm calling to verify a story. You're running for re-election to the Lemont Library Board?"

"Yes, I am." Cora allowed a smile. The election was the following week, and she was pleased the paper was covering it at last. She began to move randomly about the room.

"Do you confirm or deny that you believe in ghosts, and are regularly visited by a spirit?" Megan asked.

"I'm sorry...what?" The smile abruptly disappeared.

"We've been informed you believe in ghosts. Did you speak about a visitation at the historical society's *Fright Night?*"

"Oh that!" She gave a short chuckle. "Yes, I told a story that night. It was all in fun. We tell scary stories once a year before Halloween."

"Then it wasn't a true story? Didn't you tell it as if it was true?" the reporter persisted.

"Well, yes...I did say it was true—but again, it was all in fun."

"So it *wasn't* true then?"

"You know, just about everyone has had an experience they can't explain," Cora evaded, her brow furrowed.

"Okay, then it's true—I'll go with that. What about a ghost, named Angel, I believe, who you claim has been visiting you for years?"

"Who told you that?" Cora demanded. She froze in place and felt her face growing hot.

"I'm sorry, I don't reveal sources. Is that ghost true too?"

"Not like you describe it, no. Again, sometimes things happen I can't explain. I joked about it with friends, and we gave it a name, Angel. I wouldn't call it a ghost."

"So I'll confirm that too. What about your dealings with the Chicago Mob?"

"I don't have dealings with the Mob!" she exploded. "What's going on here? Who's telling stories about me?"

"Sorry. So we'll print we have information you have dealings with the Mob, but you deny it. Thank you."

"Wait a minute!" Cora said, gripping the phone tightly and raising her voice. She exhaled slowly to calm herself. She realized she was still standing, and dropped into her office chair. "Can we start over? I don't know who you've been talking to, but I'm starting to guess. I had a group of women to my home last week, and one of them got out of line. I asked her to leave, and she threatened me. You can't *believe* these stories she told you. In fact, the word 'libel' comes to mind."

"But you're not *denying* the stories," Megan said.

"Well, I certainly deny being involved with the *Mob!*"

"Where did she get the idea then?"

"My husband is Sicilian. I mentioned to friends that there were people in the family who hinted they knew people in the Mafia, and I told a few family stories. Rumor or truth, I have no way of knowing; it's just interesting conversation, blown out of proportion. I've certainly never had any 'dealings,' as you say, with the Mob!"

"And the ghost stuff? Do you believe in ghosts?"

"I sure don't *think* I do. Haven't you ever had anything happen you couldn't explain? You think you see someone out of the corner of your eye and then look directly and there's no one there? Or something moves without a rational reason?"

"I can't say I have. Do you think that's common?"

"Of course, it's common! When we talk about things like this, most people have similar stories." Cora waved an arm as she talked.

"Then there's a *group* of believers?"

Cora widened her eyes, incredulous at the reporter's conclusion. Then she laughed. "This is getting crazy. There is *no* group. There is *no* belief. There was only an odd incident and a mean woman trying to get back at me because she's angry."

After a pause, the reporter laughed too. "I *do* get your point, but put yourself in my shoes. Someone tells me something voters should be informed about if true and I have to check it out, right? I wouldn't be doing my job if I didn't give you a bit of a hard time, would I?"

"I understand, but certainly you can't believe these insinuations. I've been on the board for ten years and served the community well. Why don't we talk about that, not this unfounded nonsense?"

"Okay, let's talk about your record then, and why you feel you should be re-elected."

When the call ended, Cora thought she had the reporter's respect. She felt sure nothing would be printed about Valerie's accusations.

~ ~ ~

A few days later, Cora came into the kitchen to find Cisco reading the paper at the table. He waited for her to pour a cup of coffee and seat herself.

"Morning, Hon." He folded the paper to a page, and then rubbed the back of his neck, shifting his eyes away from her. "I hate to start the day with bad news, but you're going to find out anyway. You're not going to like this," he said.

Color drained from her face. "That interview? I was sure she was going to write a nice piece. What happened? What did she say?"

"No, it's not the article, which was quite complimentary. It's the *Sound Off* letters. The letter is signed with a different name, but it must be fake; it's obviously from Valerie. You really pissed her off!"

"Let me see."

Cisco handed the paper to Cora. The letter got right to the point:

Most people don't pay much attention to candidates for the Library Board, but for the upcoming election they would be wrong. The incumbent candidate, Cora Tozzi, admitted to me in private conversation that she is regularly visited by a ghost that guides her decisions. She also disclosed ties with organized crime. These issues will certainly affect decisions made regarding programs, books, and spending at your library.

Is this the sort of influence you want your children exposed to? The candidate has even gone so far as to speak at community events about her visitations! The organized crime connection should raise a question regarding how your tax dollars are spent. Is money being siphoned off and diverted to the Chicago Mob? Mrs. Tozzi has been on the Library Board for a number of years, and who knows how much damage has already been done. What else is she doing you should know about?

Call the library and demand an immediate investigation of its financial dealings, and join me in telling everyone you know this person should not be elected again.

Lilly White, Lemont, Illinois

Cora sat stunned, eyes brimming with tears. When she was able to speak, she said, "Lilly White. She signs herself Lilly White. She thinks this is a joke...."

Cisco's face was flushed, a muscle in his jaw jumped, and his hands clenched into fists. "Cora? Hon?" He got up from the table, pulled her up and held her. "I wish I *was* connected to the Mob! I'd put a hit on her! That bitch!"

Cora's shoulders shook and tears flowed freely as she buried her face against Cisco's chest, but she couldn't speak past the burning lump in her throat.

The phone rang. "I don't want to talk to anyone," she choked out. "Let it go to voicemail."

She controlled her emotions eventually, took a deep breath and stood back. "I'll be okay," she said. She went into the bathroom, splashed water on her tear-stained face and rubbed it with a towel. She put on a light jacket and her floppy-brim hat. "I need to take a walk. I'll be back soon."

"Do you want me to come with you?"

"No, please...I'll be fine. Just let me get it out of my system, okay?" She went out the kitchen door.

When she returned, she was composed. She started taking food out of the freezer and cabinets, lining up ingredients on the counter, making busy work to distract herself. Cisco was gathering up papers to put in the trash.

"Wait, let me see what the reporter wrote," she said, retrieving the paper from Cisco. She read the article and was pleased the reporter had focused on Cora's accomplishments.

"Well, that's good, at least," she said to Cisco, closing the paper. "Hopefully people will read this and skip the opinion letters. We'll see."

"How could both things run in the same paper?" he wondered. "Do you think people can distinguish between a journalist's opinion and a crank? Must have been some mix-up. People should be more willing to believe the reporter, though."

"Will they? Would you? I wouldn't. If I didn't know me, I'd say 'Who knows what's true?' and I'd vote for someone else, someone there was no question about. Much as I hate to say it."

"Well, a lot of people know you. Word will get out."

"You think so?" She went to check voicemail. The earlier call was from the reporter, saying she just read the letter. Cora called her back.

"I can't tell you how sorry I am," Megan began. "After you and I talked she called me and I told her I couldn't print her information. She was angry, called me a bitch, and hung up on me. I thought that was the end of it. I had no idea that letter was going to run until I saw it. It makes me look bad too, like I don't know what I'm talking about, like I didn't investigate you before writing my story. I see what you mean about her. She got both of us, didn't she?"

"I appreciate your call, but I don't understand how it happened. Aren't letters screened? Doesn't someone at the paper have to decide to print it?" Too restless to sit or stand still, Cora wandered between the kitchen and family room, aimlessly picking up items from tables or counters and setting them back again.

"It shouldn't have happened, and believe me I'm going to talk to the editor. It must have slipped past him somehow—I don't know. Or maybe she put pressure on someone here." Her loud sigh came over the line.

"And what about that name, Lilly White? Surely that was a tip-off?"

"People have to identify themselves, and we check. Maybe the editor was in a hurry," she theorized. "It's a challenging job—there are deadlines. Sometimes things that shouldn't happen just get overlooked."

"Yes, but there must be a way to fix this," she insisted, standing still now.

There was a thoughtful silence on the other end. "We can't print a retraction, since we didn't write the letter," Megan said finally. "We could print an apology, but it might appear as if we were trying to excuse the paper for printing contradictory information."

"If you *did* print an apology, it would be in next Friday's paper, right?" asked Cora.

"That's our next edition, yes."

"The election is Tuesday. How would it help me after the fact?"

"Oh. True. Do *you* have a suggestion?"

"How about if you write a letter of explanation, say someone called with allegations, and you found out they weren't true? Say the editor was unaware of your investigation, printed the opinion letter in error, there is no truth to it, and the paper is sorry." She dropped down into a chair at the kitchen table.

"Well, something *like* that is what we would print, of course, but you said it would be too late."

"Yes. But you could take copies of the letter around town, to places like the library and the village and township offices for people to pick up. And call the library to explain so they can hand them out. And put it in your web version of the paper."

"Uh…we don't usually do all that…," Megan began.

"Sorry, but your paper needs to correct the mistake. How about if you convince your editor the paper would make a favorable impression on its readers by acting responsibly to correct the error?"

"I'll try to sell the idea to him," Megan agreed hesitantly. "No promises, but he might go along."

After the call, Cora went to the garage, where Cisco was putting away gardening tools for the season. Like Cora, he was staying busy to control his anger.

Cora repeated the phone conversation, and the proposed solution.

"Let me start a phone campaign and ask the neighbors to spread the word. I bet we can reach a lot of people," he suggested, trying to wedge a rake into an overcrowded corner.

"Would you? That's a great idea! If I did it myself it would be awkward and involve a lot of explanation. It'd be such a help if it came from you!"

"Now's when we find out who our friends are, right? Trust me, Cora—you have a lot of friends!"

Cora wandered upstairs to her desk. Only ten in the morning, a whole day still ahead of her; she knew she wouldn't accomplish much, anything requiring any real *thought*, for sure. But she could plod away at routine tasks, to keep from focusing on her resentment.

Few things hurt as much as betrayal.

She would check her emails first, expecting a slew of messages as a result of Valerie's letter. She might as well get it over with. Some would be pro, some con; she hoped most would be pro.

She turned her computer on, waited for it to boot up, and logged on. She opened her browser, clicked on her mailbox. Before the emails loaded, a pop-up appeared in the center of her screen:

**I'll fix this, Darlin'.
I LOVE YOU!**

Chapter 9

Valerie grinned as she drove alone down the dark, deserted road. She was confident her letter to the *News Local* had served its purpose and wrecked Cora's election chances. Pleased with her efforts, she chuckled and shot a fist into the air. "Yes!"

She drove into a fierce wind, trees bending violently and debris swirling across the pavement. She was only ten minutes from home, though, and could probably make it before the storm hit.

The polls closed three hours ago. Valerie pictured Cora checking the results on the County Board of Elections website and discovering she had lost the election. She would shed tears of disappointment, and surely guess who was responsible. Valerie hoped she made some trouble for that snotty reporter, too. She smiled widely, waved her arms and wiggled happily in her seat, doing a little celebratory dance, singing, "We will, we will, rock you, *boom*, da-da *boom*."

Suddenly a powerful gust of wind hit her car, knocking it into the oncoming lane. Not a problem—no other traffic on this road. Then a downpour struck, and Valerie could barely see the pavement.

That's okay, she'd be home in minutes. Molly was safe with a sitter, but she was terrified of storms, and Valerie was anxious to be with her.

Wiper blades on high speed swept back and forth, thumping with each pass. Sharp claps of thunder, the deluge pounding on the car roof, the wind—the din was deafening. Continuous flashes of lightning created a strobe-like, disorienting effect. She felt isolated, as if nothing in the world existed but her car and the storm.

She slowed the car, visibility improved, and she relaxed as she drove carefully down the narrow and now slippery road, feeling in control of the car and allowing her thoughts to return.

Valerie traveled this road frequently and knew she was moving into an area of open fields with nothing to shelter the car from the wind and rain. Instead of the increased battering she expected, the rain abruptly slackened and revealed unbelievably on the road ahead...

"No! It can't be!" She screamed and rammed her foot frantically on the brake pedal.

It was over in an instant—the car went into a spin, there was a loud thud, and incredibly the driver's side window just exploded, glass flying, the car struck nose down, dizziness....

Then excruciating pain, loss of consciousness, and she saw no more.

~ ~ ~

"Jean, you know Valerie Jablonski pretty well, don't you?" the aide asked, entering the ER unit, where Jean was dressing a face wound.

"I suppose so, although there's been a recent change in that. Why?" Jean asked.

"Well, get ready for another change. An ambulance just brought her into Unit Three, and she doesn't look so good," the aide said.

"What do you mean? What happened?" Jean turned her head to face the aide.

"An auto accident. She's pretty banged up, and she's not coherent, ranting nonsense."

"Maybe I should go in there. A face she knows might calm her," Jean said. She put the last strip of tape over the dressing on the elderly woman's cheek. "Stay here just a minute," she instructed. "I'll send someone in with home instructions, then you can go. Is your son waiting to take you home?"

At the woman's nod, Jean pulled the aide into the hallway. "Get a copy of wound care instructions from the desk, call this lady's son, and arrange transport. I'll complete the discharge, but I want to check on Valerie first," she said. She headed toward the exam room.

Jean heard wailing before she entered the cubicle. When she walked in another nurse and a paramedic were holding a struggling Valerie while they placed restraints on her. "I know her. Maybe I can help," Jean said as she approached, snapping on a pair of exam gloves.

"Valerie," she said. "Valerie? Can you hear me? It's Jean, Valerie." She reached out and took Valerie's blood-streaked hand. A large bandage covered Valerie's eyes, under which were wads of gauze, placed to keep pressure on the eye sockets. So much for Valerie recognizing her face.

"Jean?" Valerie said, and stopped struggling. "I can't see you. I can't see anything. Why can't I see?"

"You have bandages covering your eyes, Valerie. You won't be able to see until they take the bandages off. You're in the ER, Valerie. Are you in pain? Did you get anything to make you comfortable?"

Jean glanced at the paramedic, who nodded as he removed his exam gloves and scrub cap.

"I'll talk to the doctor, and then I'll stay with you, Valerie. I'll be sure they take good care of you. Let me step away for a minute and get someone to cover me so I can sit with you. Is that okay Valerie? I promise. I'll be right back."

Valerie nodded. She seemed sleepy, as if the medication was taking effect.

"Jean?" she said. "Jean, you tell them. It was the wolf, Jean. They don't believe me."

Jean turned with a puzzled glance at the paramedic, who shrugged and then motioned her to follow him out to the hallway.

"Has the doctor been in yet?" Jean asked.

"No, we just got here. You know her, huh?"

"We're not close but we work together. I think having someone she knows in the room will help reassure her, and she doesn't have family nearby. I'll stay with her as much as I can. What happened, do you know?" She glanced anxiously through the doorway.

"Someone called 911 for a car in a ditch. When we got there she was out behind the wheel, and her face—well, I've been doing this for years but I never saw anything like that before," he said, shaking his head. "Glass shards all over, bloody as hell, lots of deep lacerations, gouges really, like she was clawed or something, especially around both orbits. At first I thought that her eyes were punctured and decompressed, but on further examination they weren't in the sockets at all…it was…nightmarish." He rubbed his head, letting out a long slow breath.

Jean looked away for a moment, blinked rapidly, then hugged her arms to her chest, directed her gaze back to the EMT and asked, "What did you do for her?"

"Put pressure over the orbits and a big bleeder in the temple, stopped the bleeding, and got her out of the car. That was tough, but we managed, and she woke up while we were pulling her out. There was no apparent trauma except to the face—the airbag helped there—and her vitals were good except for tachycardia, which is to be expected, and the usual soreness, swelling and bruises, of course." He looked away down the hall for a moment, perhaps picturing the scene, then back at Jean.

"From the looks of things the car went nose down into the ditch. She must have struck the side window with her head and concussed—there was no side airbag. Maybe some glass punctured her eyes and she tore at them—that would account for the gouges and the blood on her hands too. She keeps screaming and she's not responding to questions, at least not rationally. We sedated her, and it's taking effect." He shuffled his feet and edged toward the exam room door.

"Wait," said Jean, reaching out to grab his arm. "You say she's not rational. What has she been saying?"

He shifted his eyes away toward a wall, frowning. "She keeps repeating the same thing—the wolf, she says. From what I could put together, she says a wolf was standing on its hind legs in the middle of the road and after the car crashed it attacked her. She must have hallucinated that while she was out, I'm thinking."

CHAPTER 10

Most mornings Cora lingered in bed reading. Today she got up as soon as she woke, dressed quickly, and made Cisco a full Sunday-style breakfast—eggs, sausage, potatoes, scones— loaded with the fats and carbs they usually tried to avoid. Then she washed and dried the dishes instead of piling them in the dishwasher, humming happily. She felt energized, despite the excitement that had kept her awake much of election night, after she convinced herself she had won.

When the phone rang Cora was busily sorting through account statements, her third cup of coffee close at hand. Cisco was in the basement, doing whatever it was he did down there.

"Did you hear the news?" Jean asked after Cora picked up.

"About the election?" She grinned and leaned back in her chair. "I don't know if it's because of all our calls, or if Valerie's letter didn't mean much after all, but thank God, and you, and *all* my friends, I won—not by a narrow margin, but substantial. I am *so* thrilled! But aren't you at work? You didn't have to call from work. Why didn't you wait until you got home?" She hugged the phone to one ear and shifted a pile on her desk to make room to start another one.

"I'm home now. I worked midnights last night." Jean hesitated. "That's great about the election Cora. I know you're happy, and I'm happy for you. But I meant about Valerie. About the accident."

Cora turned away from her desk and gazed at the window, giving Jean her full attention. "Accident? No—I *haven't* heard about an accident. Valerie was in an accident? What happened?"

"It was bad, Cora." Cora heard Jean's long breath over the line. "She was driving home, along that empty place through the golf course, when last night's storm hit. Her car ran into a ditch."

"Is she okay?"

"I was on shift when the ambulance brought her in. She was unconscious when they found her, and she hadn't been wearing her seat belt, so she got thrown around some. She had a lot of injuries, but she'll recover. The tragic part is that she'll be blind."

Cora jerked upright in her chair. *"Blind?* Why? From head trauma?"

"It's ugly, Cora. It appears the driver's side window blew out and glass particles flew into both eyes."

"I thought car windows had safety glass."

"Maybe that's just windshields—or she has an older car."

"I don't understand why she's blind," Cora said, wrinkling her brow. "Can't they remove the particles and re-pressurize the eyes, like when I had my retinal surgery?"

"It gets worse. Both eyes were ripped out. The doctors think she was having so much pain before she lost consciousness, she tore at her eyes to stop the pain and clawed them out. There was blood on her fingers and nails. The ER doctor said it almost looked like some animal got at her."

"Oh my God...how awful!" Cora stood up and paced, holding the cordless phone tightly, recreating the scene in her mind.

"I stayed with her all night, and when she woke up, of course she couldn't see, and that was pretty awful. She didn't know yet that her eyes were gone, just that they were covered. When she was calm enough to answer questions, it became clear she doesn't have complete recall."

"Shock, unconsciousness, all that, it's no wonder," Cora said. She stopped wandering around the room and gazed unseeing out the window. "Does she remember *anything?*"

"She just says the storm hit, and she couldn't see through the downpour, but then there was an animal in the road, she tried to avoid hitting it and spun out of control."

"An animal? She probably would have been better off to hit it—what kind of animal?"

Jean hesitated and then went on in a rush. "What she says is bizarre. She's probably still delusional about that part, it couldn't be...."

"What?" Cora prompted, motionless, feeling a sudden chill.

"She says it was a wolf, Cora. That's what she was babbling about when she was incoherent, and she *still* says it was a wolf, standing upright on its hind legs, and glaring straight at her."

Cora blanched, remembering the wolf she and Cisco encountered in the woods—when was that? Over a month ago?

"That's...crazy," Cora said, and put a hand to her mouth.

"Yes, it is, but...."

"But what?"

"You're going to think I'm crazy too, but while I was waiting with her, I washed her up a little, cleaned the blood from her hands, and when I looked at the gauze...I swear, Cora, there were a few short hairs on it, like dog hair, you know? Does Valerie have a dog?"

"I don't know. She never mentioned one, but maybe she does." Cora said, with a rapidly beating heart and intensely dry mouth.

"I got to go, Cora," Jean said. "It was a rough night. I couldn't sleep thinking about it. But I thought you should know."

"Thanks Jean. I don't know what to say," She put the receiver down and rested her mouth on a closed fist, struggling to sort out her thoughts.

She had been so happy a few minutes ago, on top of the world, her self-worth restored after the election, a real vote of confidence, she couldn't stop the pun that jumped into her head. Despite the shocking events, Cora gave a wry smile, realizing she was acting like her father again, who habitually injected bits of humor during stressful situations.

Blind! God...how awful!

How would she take care of Molly? Would Molly go to live with her father, the very thing Valerie was so afraid of?

What was all that craziness about a wolf? Does Valerie have a dog?

Surely she'd change her story when she could think clearly again. But Cora had been seeing wolves—she thought so anyway. Was it just a coincidence that now Valerie claimed to have been attacked by a wolf?

Cora headed downstairs where Cisco was puttering with his tools. He guessed from the look on her face something was wrong. "Who was on the phone?" he asked. "What happened? A problem with the election?"

After she told him the story, Cisco said, "It's awful...of course, it's awful...but sometimes bad things happen to *bad* people too, not only good ones." He hung a screwdriver on a pegboard.

She folded her arms over her chest and slowly tapped her right foot on the floor. "I don't want to think about bad people or good people. Her whole life is changed! Some people might say she had it coming, but no one had this coming!"

She wandered over to his workbench, picked up an empty plastic bag and threw it in a garbage bin. "What about the wolf thing? What do you think about that?" she asked.

"Who knows? Probably her imagination, as Jean said."

"But we saw a wolf too. Remember the wolf we saw a few weeks ago? You weren't convinced, so I put it out of my head too, but now?" She raised her eyebrows, inviting him to agree with her.

"We saw something that *maybe looked* like a wolf. And it wasn't standing on two legs."

"True," Cora admitted. She pressed her lips together and bit on them. She looked around the basement, then back at Cisco. "I think you should take this wolf stuff more seriously. Something odd is going on. First there was the Angel stuff, then the wolf in the forest, and that note on my computer. You said you didn't do that, so how did it get there? And now this business with Valerie, and a wolf again. How can all of this be a coincidence? It's too much."

"Oh Cora...don't go blowing things out of proportion. Valerie's not herself yet—I'm sure there's an explanation," Cisco said, waving his hands and shaking his head.

"Sure. An explanation for a wolf running Valerie off the road and tearing her eyes out, right after she did something nasty to me!" She was tapping her foot on the floor again, more quickly now.

"Calm down, Cora," Cisco said, and turned away to continue puttering at his workbench.

After lunch Cisco went out to work in the yard and Cora returned to her desk and powered up her computer. Immediately a new pop-up appeared in the center of its screen.

> I told you I'd fix it
> Darlin'.
> Máime did it again!

Chapter 11

As Cora stared unblinking at the message, scalp tingling, heart pounding, the phone rang. She reached for it without taking her eyes from the laptop. The pop-up disappeared as she picked up the phone.

Am I going crazy?

It was Frannie. After her disclosure at the last book club meeting, she and Cora's friendship had deepened, and they spoke almost daily on the phone.

"I told you there was nothing to worry about, girl," Frannie began. "There was no way that trash was gonna get the best of you. You won by an f-ing landslide! She can just stick that nasty old letter of hers where the sun don't shine."

Not listening, Cora stared at the now-empty computer screen, her face white and hands shaking.

What did it mean?

"Frannie...a whole lot has happened since then," she said. "You've... got to hear this." Cora told her about Valerie's accident. "We had good reason to be angry at her, but this...this just shouldn't happen to anyone. It's awful."

Frannie said, "Well, I'm not callous or anything, I *do* feel bad, but I'm ashamed to say, that girl didn't make herself no friends. A wolf, huh? You believe that nutty stuff?"

Frannie didn't know about the messages on Cora's computer or the encounter she and Cisco had in the forest—and Cisco wasn't open to further discussion about the matter. Upset and confused, stunned by the new message, Cora didn't know what to do or where to turn. Now here was Frannie, and she knew intuitively Frannie was the person to confide in.

Any two people, Cora believed, form relationship patterns through the years that affect the way they communicate with each other, not only the way they talk but the things they talk about—or don't talk about, and this was especially true of married people. Admitting one feels inadequate to face a problem, even to a spouse, is not easy, she thought. The fears and emotions she had been suppressing were about to spill out. She didn't want Cisco to witness that. He was supportive, but women understand each other in a different way. And *that* way was the way Cora needed now.

She would tell Cisco about the latest message, but later, when she was less emotional and he wasn't so reluctant.

Frannie's voice came through the receiver again, heedless of what was going on in Cora's mind. "I think Valerie did say she had a dog. I bet it was a Corgi—seems like a Corgi's the kind of dog Valerie would have, don't you think?"

"Frannie," Cora said in a shaky voice, "I'm having a bad day. Can we get together?"

~ ~ ~

Cora strode into the library, and after a brief search she found Frannie in an out-of-the-way corner of the adult section, seated on a comfortable sofa. Frannie's hot-pink sweater was too tight and clashed with her pants. Her hair was pulled unevenly to one side, and an errant wisp of gray hair stuck out at an odd angle.

Despite her worry, Cora smiled at her friend's appearance. It jogged a memory of book club, when Frannie told the women, "I was in the fashion business, but never had the body myself for them clothes…." Frannie then stood up and shook her more-than-ample chest, which flowed in waves from side to side, bringing the women at the table to screams of laughter.

Cora wondered why Frannie didn't apply her fashion sense to her own wardrobe, but that was Frannie, full of contradictions and surprises. Like her unpredictable and sometimes inappropriate vocabulary. You never knew what would come out of her mouth, but as a friend she was absolutely loyal, and willing to throw herself wholeheartedly into any request.

Warmth washed over Cora at the sight of her friend and took an edge off her anxiety. Things couldn't be all that bad with such a friend willing to drop everything to meet her, no questions asked. She dropped onto a sofa across from Frannie.

"Where's your pad and pen?" Frannie asked. She ran her eyes over Cora as if looking for something she had missed. "You never go anywhere without a pad and pen, girl. Something's missing. Look sort of naked without them, you ask me."

Cora gave a short mirthless laugh. "And I'm probably going to regret not bringing them. We'll be more relaxed, uninhibited, don't you think? Pad and pen make it seem like *work*."

"What if you forget something, now?"

"Good! Lately I *want* to forget!" She laughed again nervously, and her gaze roamed around the library. Partially blocked by rows of shelves, she could see about half of the small, single-floor building. A few patrons browsed through the shelves, more sat at work tables concentrating on the laptops in front of them, and two staff members were busy at the reference desk.

"Must be something important going on, you dragging me here. I got a question before we start. Why are you telling *me*? Why aren't you talking to Lu, she being your best friend? Or Cisco?"

Cora shifted her gaze from Frannie, then back. She put her hands on her knees and rubbed them absently. "I guess it started with a gut reaction. You were *there* Frannie. I was upset, and the phone rang, and it was you, and the words just came out of my mouth. But I've had time to think about it now, and I know you're the person I want to talk to."

Cora paused and let out a long, slow breath. She glanced around the library again, and then continued. "I thought about Cisco, but he's too close to this, and he's tired of hearing about it. Men all the time want to just *fix* things, and I don't even know *what* to fix. He'd start making suggestions, and I'd go 'I don't know' and he'd go 'Why not?' until we're yelling at each other. I want to get things straight in my head before I bring him back into it. As for Lu, she and I already worked out what Angel was and wasn't, but that was long ago—not what's happening now. I need *fresh* thoughts, not old ones."

"So this is about Angel then? Not Valerie?" Frannie leaned back in her chair with a wrinkled forehead, found a comfortable position, and crossed her legs at the ankles.

Cora shifted her eyes and picked at a loose thread on the arm of the chair. "Well, it's all related. That's what I need to sort out."

"You're a take-control gal yourself, that's the Cora I know. How am I going to help you with that?"

Cora gave Frannie a half smile. "What's been happening is off the wall weird, and it's got me doubting myself. I need someone to tell me if my thinking's on the right track or if I'm getting carried away. You understand me, and you have guts, imagination, an open mind..."

Frannie's boisterous laugh rang out, interrupting Cora, and some library patrons looked curiously their way. "Uh, huh, I got it. You need somebody *crazy* enough to buy into *crazy* thoughts. Well, I suppose you got the right person for that. I'm a loose cannon, all right, and you can depend on me to swallow *harebrained* ideas and even carry through with *harebrained* schemes! Just what you need, girl. Stick with me, I'll straighten you out."

"I'm glad you said that so I don't have to." They looked at each other and laughed. "Of course I have no idea what we're getting into. After what happened to Valerie—are you sure you want to get involved?"

"You ever know me to shy off from anything, girl?" Frannie raised her eyebrows and grinned.

Cora turned serious, fidgeted, put a thumbnail between her front teeth and sighed. "I don't know what's going on, Frannie, and I'm starting to get scared."

"So I was driving here, and thinking about what you told me on the phone, of course I was *thinking*...but before I start running off at the mouth, what's this about Angel? What else is going on and getting you all upset? You sure it's not just your mind being too busy with all these events, the whole mishmash of thoughts, so your feelings are out of whack?" Frannie lowered her chin and directed an unblinking gaze at Cora.

"Maybe...." She shifted her eyes again, refusing to meet Frannie's gaze.

"So what are you upset about?" Frannie asked again.

Cora rubbed her mouth, then put both hands behind her head, closed her eyes, then opened them and looked back at Frannie. "I can't talk about this slumped in a sofa. I'm too edgy. Can we move to a table?"

"Sure thing. Next thing you be wanting that pen and paper you didn't bring."

"You could be right. I do think better when I keep my hands busy. Can't read my notes when I get home half the time, though." They got up, gathered their belongings, and moved to an empty table, settling into straight-back chairs. Cora put her elbows on the table and rested her chin on her hands. "That's better!"

At first they just looked at each other. Then Cora burst out, "I don't know what this *wolf* business is all about! Did what happened to Valerie have anything to do with *me?* I didn't tell you on the phone Frannie, but Cisco and I saw a wolf last month. We were walking in the woods, and it came toward us, and acted really strange." Cora told Frannie in detail about the experience. "And that wasn't the first time. I saw what I sure *thought* was a wolf a few times before."

"Maybe there *are* wolves out here, and Valerie *did* see one." Frannie rubbed at her upper lip with her forefinger as she considered Cora's story.

"Well, maybe...but the way that animal behaved when we saw it in the woods? It was like *more* than a wolf, so powerful. It was like it *knew* us, and wanted to tell us something. Like it had real intelligence, *human* intelligence. It even seemed to be *playing* with us."

Frannie leaned forward, inviting confidence. "Did you think you were being threatened? Scared? Awed? What? Explain."

"Amazed, confused, I don't know...it was scary, but at the same time I didn't think we were going to be attacked. I *can't* explain. Oh! This makes no sense! It all makes no *sense!*" Cora leaned back in her chair, and crossed her arms over her chest, hugging herself and searching Frannie's face.

"Maybe it was this same wolf Valerie saw when she had her accident? A real wolf, maybe, or like you said a spooky thing, some big old animal that didn't belong there? And you saw that same thing in the woods?" Frannie suggested, copying Cora's posture.

"Well, sure...anything is *possible*. But if it was just some old lone misplaced wolf, why did she say it was standing on two legs in the middle of the road in a rainstorm and staring at her?"

"Well...okay...yeah...that's strange. Maybe she got all drama...from the trauma." Frannie didn't notice the inadvertent witticism, put a forefinger over her lips, and then pointed it at Cora. "Tell me what's bothering you here, Cora. I think I know where you're going with this, but say it out loud."

"I don't want to admit this Frannie! It's just unbelievable; you'll think I'm crazy, *anyone* will think I'm crazy." Her eyes were shining with tears, and she shut them for a moment to clear both her vision and her thoughts. Then she leaned forward, put an elbow on table, and rested her chin in her hand again, not saying anything.

"Okay then…I'll say it for you," Frannie went on. "You think it's tied up with something *supernatural*, and has something to do with Angel. Am I right?"

"Yes, that's it…thank you." Cora expelled a slow breath, relieved to hear her worry put into words. "Maybe there *is* a real Angel, not just a series of odd coincidences. And maybe she *has* been protecting me. And maybe for some reason she wants me to know she's for real now. And *maybe* she knew what Valerie did to me, to us, and wanted to punish her. And *maybe* somehow she made this stuff happen with the wolf, I don't know how." Cora reached into her purse, pulled out a tissue and blotted her eyes.

"Whoa, hold on there, girl. You're moving too fast now. How do you jump from wolves and throw Angel in there, and now Angel's protecting you and punishing people? Did I miss something here?"

Cora had forgotten Frannie never heard the whole story of Angel's antics and knew nothing about the pop-ups on her computer. She took a deep breath and filled her in, in detail, back to the very beginning, and answered all her questions.

"Oh, God, this is just so far-fetched! I can't believe I'm actually considering these thoughts, but I can't stop them. I feel like it's not real—this can't really be happening to me! Then I force myself to think clearly, and it *is* all real, but no less *crazy!* I feel warm, then clammy, and my palms are sweating *now*…." She rubbed her hands together, then crossed her arms and tucked her hands under them.

A look of concern on her face, Frannie said in a calm tone, "I can see that. Your face is red too, and your eyes are jumping like you're on something. Take it easy. Let's just sit a minute, take a little break."

Cora sat back and looked around the library. She noticed a young girl, about three years old, stop to stare at Frannie. The girl slid behind her mother, eyes wide, and pulled on her skirt for attention, then pointed at Frannie. "Mama, why is that lady dressed so…" she began, but her mother shushed her, glanced at Frannie, lowered her head and whispered to the girl, then took her hand and pulled her away. Frannie took no notice.

"Let's analyze this now," Frannie said, calm and practical, rubbing one finger after another as she put things together. "So you think Angel is putting these messages on your computer, and the messages hint she's taking vengeance for you or some such thing, attacking Valerie. You keep saying 'she'—you sure Angel is a 'she'?"

"I don't know it's a 'she', just always thought of her that way." Cora shrugged her shoulders. "So these strange things are happening again, even stranger and more often than before, and we see a wolf—maybe—and Valerie gets attacked by a wolf—maybe—and then these messages on my computer, no explanation for any of it. It's too much weird stuff going on—got to be related somehow. How could it all be coincidence?"

"Let's think, then. Are there any clues in those pop-ups? Tell me again, what did they say, word for word?" Frannie leaned forward and rested her chin in her hand.

"The first one said, 'I'll fix this, Darlin'. I love you.' That's Darlin', with no 'g' at the end."

Frannie sat back, looked toward the ceiling and closed her eyes. "Uh huh…when did you get that one?"

"After I read Valerie's letter in the paper."

"Right after? Did anyone besides Cisco know you read Valerie's letter?"

"Yes to right after, and no to Cisco. There's only Cisco and me in the house, remember?"

Frannie opened her eyes and met Cora's. "Could it be Cisco put it on your computer?"

"Not the Cisco I know! First of all, he wouldn't know *how* to make a pop-up. Second, he said he didn't do it, and I believe him. Third, he calls me 'Cora' or 'Hon.' He's never called me 'Darlin''—why would he do it anyway?" Cora was calmer now that she was working on her problem, her tears gone and her facial color back to normal.

"Maybe that's a clue—Darlin'. Who *does* call you 'Darlin'?"

"Nobody."

"Well that's no help." Frannie made an exaggerated frown.

"No."

"Darlin'—not *Darling*. Why, do you think?"

"One might assume Darlin' was a term she was accustomed to using?"

"Could be *that's* a clue, using a little different word. Maybe it's Southern. You know anyone from the South?"

"Yes, but I haven't seen them for years."

"And the second pop-up? You got it this morning, and it said...what?"

"It said: 'I told you I'd fix it, Darlin'. Máime did it again!'." Cora spelled the name.

"What do you *think* that means?"

"I'm afraid she's taking responsibility for what happened to Valerie. All this weird stuff lately...."

"Let's say that *is* what it means. Worst case. Who's Máime then?"

"I have no idea. I never called anyone Máime, or knew anyone who referred to herself as Máime."

Frannie looked at the ceiling, worked her lips, and then closed her eyes to think. "So...so far all we have is questions. Who is 'Máime' and why does she call you, if indeed she is referring to *you*, 'Darlin''? And what's she mean fix it?" She opened her eyes and looked directly at Cora. "Now here's a more disturbing thought, occurs to me. Why does the message say 'did it again'? What's this *again* part? Did anything like this ever happen to you before?"

"No, of course not. Nothing I can think of. I never had a strange pop-up, that's for sure. But...oh!" Cora stopped abruptly and jerked upright, her open hand over her mouth.

"What?"

"Well, this is a stretch, I'm warning you." She leaned close to Frannie confidentially. "Years ago, I had this worker in the office that was totally unmanageable. She thought office procedures didn't apply to her, worked when she felt like it, did what she felt like, and the rest of the staff wanted to know why I put up with her. She tried to get me in trouble, told lies, caused me a lot of stress."

Cora ran her hand through her hair. "She wasn't married, but she got pregnant. Then one day, a couple of plainclothes policemen came to the office and asked for her. They took her away in handcuffs."

"What for?"

"I called the station for information, asked if I could expect her to return to work. They told me they had been looking for her for embezzling from a previous job, she had moved and changed her name. They would be holding her, at least for a while."

"So what happened?"

"I didn't want her back, of course, but had to complete paperwork, and I called her home, got her roommate. He told me she had gone into labor while being held, but it turned out to be a false pregnancy. I can't explain, I just know it happened. I never saw or heard from her again."

"That's wild. How could Angel make that happen?" Frannie raised her eyebrows and peered into Cora's eyes.

"I never thought about Angel at the time, but it's such a weird story...I thought she might have faked the labor so they'd release her, but the false pregnancy part...I just wanted her out of my office, out of my life, and then this strange stuff happened—Oh! Wait! There's something else." Cora stiffened.

"Tell, girl," Frannie prompted, waving an arm to go ahead.

"At a different job, long time ago, maybe twenty years, I caught one of the receptionists padding her hours, and when new owners bought the company she complained about me. They were looking for a reason to put in their own managers, and I lost my job. Six months later this employee was diagnosed with mental illness and hospitalized. She's still not out, and her husband divorced her and married someone else."

"So you think Angel caused..."

"Oh, no!" Cora interrupted, eyes wide with excitement as thoughts kept occurring, "Then, one of those owners, the one who made the decision to fire me, stole from the company, and got caught, and went to jail. When he got out his wife left him, took his kids, and he couldn't find another job. He got depressed and committed suicide...and the person who took my place, she was killed in an auto accident a month after she replaced me...and then the company filed bankruptcy less than two years after I left. The owners lost everything they had."

She stopped, eyes wide, face pale, arms crossed over her chest to keep her hands from shaking.

Frannie looked at Cora intently. "Remind me not to get on your bad side. And you thought all this was *coincidence*, girl?"

Cora sat thinking with her fist over her mouth. Finally, she lowered it and said, "Yeah, I did. I mean…it didn't all happen at once, but over a lot of years…I never put things together. It looks different now, in hindsight. Doesn't it?"

"So people who got in your way got 'fixed' somehow. By Angel?"

"I'm not ready to say that."

"Are you ready to *suspect* that? Or do I need to fetch you up alongside your thick head?"

"I'll think about it," Cora said, shifting her eyes from Frannie's piercing look and shaking her head. "That can't…be true."

"Well, you just do that. And while you're thinking about it, when you go home, you take out that pad and pen you didn't bring with you today, and you do some more remembering, and you write down every time someone was mean to you and then something bad happened to them. You write it all down, and then we'll talk again…and then we'll see if this is coincidence or something unnatural going on here." Frannie leaned forward to catch Cora's eye again, punctuating each point by poking a finger on the table.

Cora opened her hands, exasperated. "So what good is that going to do? If this has been going on all my life, and I never did anything about it before? I've always been practical and that worked for me. Why should I think different now?"

"What's different is now you *know* something is happening." Frannie leaned back and folded her arms over her chest. "When you didn't have any idea, you just went on with your life, Angel protected you, and you didn't even know it. Maybe she let you know she was around some little way, heaving a paperclip at your boss or something, like she's joking with you. But now you *know*. Now you're *obliged* to bring this to a stop, or you become an *accomplice*. Can you live with being an *accomplice*?"

"Uh…I guess not."

"And you can't do *nothin'* until you find out what's going on. Who is this *Máime*? Why's she attached to you? That's what I want to know." She poked the table again.

Shrugging her shoulders, Cora held both open hands out.

"You got to take this serious. You got to find out. Take action."

"What kind of action do I take against an Angel?"

"You know *research* girl! You know how to research, from that historical place you go to. You got research *tools*. You get information, you put down notes, you piece it together—you got to start doing all that, look for some reason this business is going on and what to do. And you got to go and see an *expert*." Frannie pointed a finger at Cora every time she said "you".

Cora burst out laughing. "God, Frannie, that's why I love you!" she said, wiping her eyes with the back of her hand. "That's the first good laugh I had since this started. What *expert* did you have in mind? An expert in *angels?* An expert in *spooks?* An expert in *wolves?* Or how about a good *psychiatrist?*"

"Maybe you start with a priest. Yeah, that's a good idea. We're both Catholic. Priests know about angels and devils and that kind of stuff. They even do exorcisms. You start with a priest, you ask him about angels, and you ask him about spirits, and you see if he's got any ideas to put you on track."

Cora was thoughtful. She gazed away at nothing, chin in her hand, a finger over her mouth. "Silly as it sounds, that's not a bad idea. Our friend, Father McGrath, is just the guy, actually. I don't know why I didn't think of him. He's a psychologist and a counselor living at the church. He's easy to talk to, and interested in 'other-world' stuff. He might take this serious, at least more than any other professional I might approach."

With a place to start, with a friend like Father McGrath who would surely give advice and comfort, and Frannie's ideas and moral support, Cora felt her confidence returning.

"I'll call him when I get home. I still can't believe there's really some sort of *being* out there monitoring my life though."

"You know, girl. You may not *know* you know, not yet. But you wouldn't be here today talking with me if you didn't *know* deep down this is real peculiar and you got to stop it. You talk like you're not coming to that conclusion, but deep down you *know*. *You* may be living a charmed life, but my life has been *far* from charmed. I've seen lots of bad things, and lots of bad people, so maybe I recognize a serious problem better than you. You got to get right on this."

Frannie leaned forward and jabbed a finger at Cora. "Because here's something else I can see after we just talked this out now. Whatever *is* going on, like you said, maybe it's not new and things chug along with nothing going on for years, but there's more happening now and it's pretty ugly. I mean, Valerie's a piece of work, no question there, but what'd she do bad enough to get her eyes tore out her head? Man, did she suffer for that!"

No answer came to Cora.

Waving a finger in the air, Frannie said, "You listen to Frannie now. I got a feeling it's gonna get even bigger and go even faster, now you have real contact, real words from this Angel. Seems to me, something's happened to get your Angel moving and she's wanting something from you, and she's not *getting* it, so she's determined to get you *directly* involved. If you believe only one thing, believe *this* one: this here Angel is es-ca-*late*-in'!"

Chapter 12

I bet *Mom will love my haircut.*

Hot tears formed suddenly in Cora's eyes. She dashed them away, hoping the young hairstylist wouldn't notice, but too late.

"Is something wrong?" the girl asked, taking a step back and removing the comb and scissors from Cora's hair in alarm. "Did I hurt you?"

Her eyes shiny, Cora shook her head. "No," she said. "I just was looking forward to showing my haircut to my mother." Her voice shook and she cleared her throat and swallowed a few times. "We liked to show new things to each other. My mother died two years ago," she went on. "I forget it sometimes, like she's still here. Just give me a minute." Cora reached to the shelf below the mirror, took a tissue, and blotted her eyes as the girl watched, unsure what to do or say.

"It's okay," Cora said. "I'm okay. You can finish."

Cora paid for the haircut, and back in the car her tears started again. This time she let them flow as she drove toward Saint Brennan's Church. She'd better pull over to compose herself, or Father would think he was dealing with an emotional cripple.

Two years, and I miss her like it happened yesterday.

She pulled into the public library parking lot and walked into the rest room, thankful she didn't run across anyone she knew. She entered a stall and sat.

Most of the time she was able to put her feelings about her mother out of her mind by promising herself she would think about it later, a later she consciously put off again and again. She buried it and went on with her life, not allowing herself to think of how much she missed her, and she was even able to forget. Times, like this morning, she would just break down for no apparent reason.

She knew, like all daughters know, she would lose her mother one day; but knowing that, knowing all women expect to have that experience, knowing it wasn't the only time she would cope with grief, didn't help her when it occurred. A brutal realization, she thought, that we don't value sufficiently what we have until we don't have it, let alone how painful it will be when it's no longer there. Mothers, grandmothers, great-grand-mothers, daughters, granddaughters, great-granddaughters—those are bonds we experience firsthand, going forward as well as back through the years, threads into the past and the future, loss and longing linked across the generations.

If only I can stop remembering!

She finally controlled her tears and left the stall. Looking in the mirror, she saw what she expected—signs she had been crying. She took a paper towel, wet it with cold water and held it against her eyes until the burning stopped.

Why did she take time for that haircut? When life got intense, Cora functioned best if she arranged distractions, forcing problems out of her mind until she felt better able to confront them. Such respites prepared her to reason more effectively. She thought getting a haircut before her visit with Father McGrath would provide just such a break. Well, that sure backfired.

She took a few deep breaths, walked back to her car, and got behind the wheel. She didn't want to be late. She just hoped she didn't look like a basket case when she got there.

~ ~ ~

She didn't get her wish. Father Dennis McGrath, pronounced "McGraw", was watching for her when she arrived. "From the look on your face I'm glad I decided to see you right away," he said in greeting, with his gentle smile.

Father McGrath was a short, slight, balding priest with a round reddish face that suggested kindness, intelligence, and good humor, and wire-rimmed glasses that often slid down his nose. He dressed casually in black jeans, a black polo shirt, and black sneakers. He led her to a large parlor with four comfortable-looking overstuffed chairs facing in a circle in the middle of the room, and closed the door. Bookcases lined the room, full but neat. Cora recognized a classical work playing softly.

"It seems strange to be seeing you here instead of at our dinner table," Cora said, as her gaze roamed the room, wondering where he wanted her to sit. "This is nice. I love Mozart's *Requiem*. Remember when we went to the Chicago Symphony performance, and Cisco fell asleep?"

His eyes twinkled and he nodded, then gestured to one of the chairs, inviting her to sit. He turned the music off and took a chair across from her.

"I'm sorry, Father," Cora said. "This is going to sound pretty immature for an old lady like me, but I've just been crying because I miss my mommy!" she admitted, with a wry smile and a chuckle.

"Sometimes the pain comes back, even a year or two later; that's quite normal, as long as it doesn't dominate your life. How bad is it?" He focused his eyes on her face, but she avoided eye contact, sitting rigidly with her purse on her lap.

"It's okay. I bury it, and don't let myself think or talk about her. Avoidance, isn't that what it's called?"

He nodded. "It works sometimes."

"I miss having someone to go to who will care about little things. Who can I tell when I'm miserable with a cold? It's no big deal to anyone else, but it would be to Mom," Cora said.

"Yes, moms are good about that. But you said when you called that it wasn't grief that's troubling you. You wanted to talk about something else that's going on?" Father leaned back and crossed his legs, slumped comfortably in his chair, and watched her closely.

Cora and Cisco met Father McGrath shortly after moving to Lemont, when they worked together on a community project. She represented the library, and Father the local churches, in a project to enhance communication and share resources. It was a great idea that failed despite the enthusiasm of the committee, primarily because each organization refused to give up independent control. Cora, Cisco and Father hit it off and stayed friends. Cora took pleasure in their intelligent and lively discussions, and Father appreciated Cisco's open and unpretentious views on life. When Cora's mother moved in, they saw less of each other, although they emailed frequently.

The room was pleasant, with a huge mahogany desk that would dwarf the diminutive priest. Sheer curtains covered a long row of windows along one wall, looking onto a porch at the front of the rectory, which had been converted from an old home. Late afternoon sun pierced the curtains, warming and brightening the room, flickering with moving shadows of nearby bare tree branches. Cora watched the shadows for a moment before answering the priest's question.

"Yes, uh…some really *strange* things. I hoped you could help me put them in perspective, figure out what's going on and what I should do." She held one hand tightly with the other.

He raised an eyebrow. "Things…like?"

Cora was uneasy. It was hard to admit she entertained the possibility of a supernatural visitor. She felt silly, uncertain how to approach the subject. "Like angels, like spirits, like what is real and what is not. Like how to relate to an angel?" she said in a small, embarrassed voice, trying to ignore the lump in her throat.

He appeared unfazed. "*Lions, and tigers, and bears, oh my!* And things that go bump in the night? Your fears?" he teased kindly, tapping a forefinger on his gently smiling lips, lightening her tension and making it easier for her to go on.

"Yeah," she smiled, "especially the bump in the night part. But no. More than that, I think."

Never having consulted her friend professionally, Cora wondered if she was supposed to imitate his relaxed posture. She realized she was hugging her purse unconsciously, so she put it on the floor and settled back into her chair. She crossed her ankles and laid her arms on the armrests. She still felt awkward.

"You aren't comfortable here today, are you? That's not like you," Father said.

She shook her head. "No, I'm not. I feel—sort of like I would if I were seeing my neighbor for my annual physical instead of my doctor."

Father burst into a hearty laugh and Cora joined him, breaking the tension.

"Father, you know the Church's teachings about angels and spirits, and I thought you'd take me seriously," she said, leaning forward slightly. "I don't want to think I have a supernatural visitor, but I don't know what else to think."

He raised an eyebrow again, but smiled gently. "Okay. What's going on, my dear?"

The story tumbled out, slowly at first, and then she talked nonstop for twenty minutes. She told him everything—held nothing back, even her deductions and fears. Now and then he interrupted with a question. Nothing in his face or body language indicated surprise or disapproval and he seemed interested and concerned. She was relieved. She had been worried he would question her sanity. At last, she felt she had covered it all and stopped.

Father rested his chin on his interwoven fingers and closed his eyes in concentration. Cora waited nervously. Did he think she was blowing this out of proportion? Or imagining it?

At length he dropped his hands and looked directly at Cora. "Awful as it is, much of what you say could be coincidental." He held up a finger. "It could be real, with no apparent explanation." He held up a second finger. "It could be imagination, or exaggeration." He added a third finger. "Or we can consider a supernatural cause. What is concerning to me is the appearance of the pop-ups. Are you absolutely positive about those?"

Cora nodded emphatically. "As much as I can be. I know I didn't dream them. How could I be mistaken about something like that?"

"That's right, of course. Can you think of any natural explanation for the messages?"

"No, I can't. They don't even make sense from a paranormal perspective. What kind of angel communicates by computer?"

"That would seem to be a first," he admitted, with a lopsided grin.

"Most of what I know about angels is from movies, TV, and Bible stories. What does the Church say about the appearance of angels on earth? Do we believe that happens today? And why would it happen to me? I mean, what's happening doesn't seem to be a religious matter."

Father uncrossed his legs, switched his weight to one hip, placed an elbow on an armrest, and rested his chin in his hand, watching her. "What makes you think these happenings are the actions of an angel?"

"Well…because it's protecting me—it *seems* like it's protecting me," she repeated. "It's been there a long time, maybe all my life. *If* this is really happening, then what is it, if not an angel? Isn't that what angels do, protect people? What else could it be?" Cora squirmed in her chair, found a more comfortable position, then crossed her arms over her chest.

"Well, in my opinion, I hardly think an angel would tear out someone's eyes. I'm not going to try to give you an opinion about those people you say may have been punished, whether that's coincidence or due to some other behavior. You seem to be suggesting something like an avenging angel, and that doesn't fit either." He tapped one foot rhythmically.

Cora's eyebrows went up in surprise. "It doesn't? Why not?"

"An avenging angel, or fallen angel, or devil, or your 'Angel,' call it what you will, would be seeking retaliation or punishment. Did Valerie do something so awful it deserved that brutal retaliation? What did any of those people you mentioned do to single them out for such extreme punishment? People do a lot worse things, and an angel doesn't come down to earth to deal with them. Do you see?" He dropped his chin and looked over the top of his glasses, inviting her response.

She went on stubbornly, "My friend Frannie said that too, that it was out of proportion. But, well, couldn't an angel be angry because of something that was done to me?"

"Unlikely, but let's think about something besides angels. Perhaps we should consider a spirit." He folded his arms across his chest.

Cora drew her eyebrows together. "What's the difference?"

"An angel is a being that never lived on earth as a human. An angel can visit earth in various ways, usually to deliver a message. A spirit, on the other hand, once lived on earth, then died, and for some reason is unable to cut ties to its earthly existence and accept its spiritual existence. It's not usually concerned with giving a message or otherwise assisting someone on earth. Instead, it's seeking whatever resolution it needs to accept its own death. In a word, it's selfish. It wants something." His glasses slipped down his nose as he spoke, and he pushed them back into place.

Cora's gaze moved around the room as she considered what he said. "Neither of those descriptions seems like what's going on. So what then? Is this a bizarre coincidence? Or am I jumping to conclusions, taking something ordinary and making it something it's not, like Cisco thinks?"

He searched her eyes. "You say Cisco thinks you're making it something it's not? Could he be right? He knows you pretty well, wouldn't you say?"

"He's tired of hearing me talk about this, I think." She shifted her eyes away from his. "I suppose I sometimes put things together that don't go together, and nothing comes of it, and okay, I have a tendency to exaggerate."

"Does that make your description of these events unreliable?"

"I don't think so—I've asked myself a lot of questions and I've tried to consider other possibilities." She cleared her throat. "So do you have an opinion? Is something paranormal going on? Am I nuts? Do you think I'm in any…danger? Do I need an exorcism or something?" She forced a little laugh, not joking, but seeking reassurance.

He let out a long slow breath. "I don't think the pop-ups on your laptop could be mistaken for something else, do you?" Thoughtfully, he took off his glasses, rubbed the sides of his nose, put them back on, and leaned on the armrest, bracing his body with an elbow. "But you asked if this is really happening, so let's explore that. It appears at least some part of what is going on is factual. Your conclusions may or may not be correct. Let me ask—do you feel frightened?"

She looked at him, blinking rapidly. "I didn't…now—especially when I think my friends could be attacked…it puts a new light on things."

"When exactly did Angel start appearing?"

"Well, as I said, I've been noticing bizarre things most of my adult life. It started after I got married and moved out of the house, when I was expecting my first baby. But there have been long periods when Angel, can I just call her Angel—for conversation purposes?"

Father nodded.

"There were long periods Angel wasn't around. Lately her actions are more obvious and more frequent."

"Why didn't you take her seriously before now? Seems some extraordinary things have been happening, and yet you didn't make a big deal out of them. Why not?"

"Like, one morning, I couldn't get my shampoo to lather from a near-empty bottle. Strange, that never happened before. Did water get in it? No, it was still thick. Did Cisco alter it some way? No, he didn't. Well, a fluke. Next bottle of shampoo, different brand, same thing happened. Why? Who knows? It takes a long time to go through a bottle of shampoo—see, it's a little thing, but it's weird. Did I remember right? Just when does it get so strange I want to do something about it? And if I did, what exactly would I do? Things like this happen to everyone, we just can't explain them, right?" She watched Father hopefully.

With a long direct look over the top of his glasses, Father slowly shook his head.

"Oh." Cora's face fell, then she went on in a rush of words. "Well they seemed commonplace, at least to me. I'd talk about them now and then, but it was for shock value, more like a joke.

"Cisco, well, they happened to me, not to him, and mostly when he wasn't around. He couldn't explain them either and I'm sure he just wanted them to go away, so it's no wonder he tuned out."

She tucked her hands under her thighs and leaned forward in the chair. "I felt a sort of bond, like a friendly presence was communicating with me, getting my attention, when these things happened. But it's different now, more often and more weird, and I'm not feeling comforted anymore either."

"Do you fear physical harm? Do you think Angel will hurt you?" he asked, watching her closely through narrowed eyes.

"No! I'm afraid something bad will happen *because* of me, to people I love."

Father considered Cora's reply. "When did the...uh...*visits* start to recur?"

"I guess it was after I moved to Lemont, about ten years ago, maybe six years before I retired. At first doors drifted shut, things showed up in places I know I didn't put them, stuff like that. Similar to what used to happen years earlier." Her eyes drifted away to watch the flickering shadows again.

"Was the move to Lemont a major change in your life?"

"It was, really. We found what our family and friends call our dream house. It was the culmination of what we worked for all our lives." Cora smiled, returning her gaze to Father. "It's not all that great, but it's more than we thought we'd have."

"Why did you pick this house, this place to live?"

"It's a nice house, on a large lot, in a quiet neighborhood. We could afford it," she said, still smiling. "We just drove out there one day on a whim, and as soon as we saw it something clicked. It was like it was meant to be, right off the bat, and we didn't even look anywhere else. The town is quaint, with lots of places to walk—we like to walk. Our home is next to a farm and some small forested areas, and we see deer and other wildlife."

"Like wolves?" He looked over the top of his glasses.

"No! Not wolves. I saw them in other places, not by my house. And the house had two extra rooms for my mother."

"Why didn't she move in with you right away?"

"She wanted to stay independent as long as she could." Cora felt her mouth getting dry. She picked up her purse, rummaged in it, took out a mint and put it in her mouth.

"I remember your mother as a quiet lady who was always smiling."

"She was a good mom." Cora turned her head away and stared at a wall trying to keep the tears from forming. "I can't remember if I told her that," she said in a shaky voice.

"She knew Cora. You were there when she needed you. How did you feel about taking care of her? Was it difficult?" He poked at his glasses again.

"I actually took care of *both* my parents for many years. They lived in their own home, but they needed supervision. When my father died, my mother was frail by then. His final illness took a lot out of her. She didn't want to be a burden, but she needed us. It got hard running back and forth and taking care of two homes and it made more sense for her to move in with us. We weren't getting any younger either!" Cora crossed her arms over her chest and pushed her chin forward.

"I thought if she lived with us it would make all our lives easier. It didn't turn out that way. I thought we'd enjoy doing things together, but by the time she moved in, she had little interest in anything. I felt bad—it was hard to watch her struggle." The tears had returned and Cora wiped them away with her hand.

"But she was easy to live with?" He watched her closely.

"For the most part, I liked having her around. We had to prepare special meals, help her get around, give her a bath, be sure she didn't fall, shop for her. It was work, but not a lot of work. But sometimes she got crabby, and one of us, either Cisco or I, had to be home most of every day. We couldn't take trips or vacations together, had to refuse social events, and I admit I resented it. It wasn't that it was hard, but there was no let-up. I was tired and I felt guilty when I spent time on myself, like I should be doing more for her." She clenched her hands tightly in her lap.

"No siblings, no other family?"

"No. My sons don't live close and have their own families and jobs. They would have helped if they were closer, but they weren't. There's no one else, really. Cisco, of course—you know how he is—was wonderful to her, more patient than I was most of the time. But sometimes she just wanted me."

"How long did you care for them?"

Cora thought for a moment, adding it up in her head. "I'd say around twenty years, I guess."

"Twenty years. You and Cisco were tied down for twenty years, with no significant break. Trapped." Father noticed Cora opening her mouth to object and held up his hand, then directed a meaningful look at her. "And then she died," he said softly. "And you thought your burdens would be gone, but instead you miss her, and that's why you were upset when you arrived today. You're experiencing sorrow."

He paused, watching it sink in. "We keep waiting for life to get easier, but it doesn't, does it?"

"Exactly. I wanted to make it better for her, and I couldn't," Cora agreed, nodding.

"So then Angel started, shall we say, watching more closely over you, after your mother got sick and died?"

Cora considered. "I guess that's true. I hadn't put those things together. I must have more stuff in my head than I realized." She bit on her lower lip.

"Do you think the two circumstances are related?"

"How do you mean?" Cora tilted her head and rubbed behind one ear.

"Ten years ago you moved to your dream home. Six years later, you retired from a job you were at for a long time, then your mother moved in with you, and then she died. Sounds like a lot of big changes. Then Angel started getting more...uh...obvious, shall we say—when?"

"About two years ago, but the incidents have really stepped up the past couple of months."

"In what way? Explain."

She shrugged her shoulders and waved an arm aimlessly. "More frequent, I guess, more obvious. Instead of catching movements out of the corner of my eye, I see them directly, like drawers opening, things jumping off furniture. I'd be looking right at something and it would move all on its own. Bigger things moving."

"What about sounds? Voices? Did anything accompany the acts?"

"No...no voices. When things moved they made thuds, screeches, crashes, like what you would expect." She smiled. "And of course, those same 'things that go bump in the night' we mentioned. I didn't check them out, only waited for them to repeat, and they never did. Maybe it was house-settling sounds, but there was a regular beating, very soft, like a machine pumping away in the corner of my bedroom, most nights. Never did find out what it was, and Cisco said he couldn't hear it. Stuff like that."

Father pressed his upper lip with a forefinger and gazed at the ceiling, thinking. "Two years since your mother died—Angel steps things up. Looking for patterns here...."

"It may have been about then. I suppose it was."

Father took off his glasses, and tapped his upper teeth with an earpiece. "You said life was clicking along pretty well, you felt sad about your mother, but that was normal and you were dealing with it. Then all of a sudden a previously non-threatening but unidentified presence comes into your life in a *new* way and something awful happens. You think that presence may have caused the awful thing. Then it occurs to you that some bad things happened earlier in your life, people met with tragic events after making trouble for you, and that could be related too. You think a priest's opinion may help, because you think an angel is causing your problems—in fact, you even *name* your problem Angel. Are you asking me if God or His angel is trying to tell you something, or if you should look for some other cause for your experiences?"

"Yes! And I want to figure out if something is actually going on, or am I delusional? That's the word, *delusional*. Wish I'd thought of it earlier. It fits better than imaginary." Cora searched his eyes, babbling nervously.

He uncrossed his legs and put both feet on the floor, sat a little forward in his chair, and pointed the stem of his glasses as he talked. "All right, let's sum up. You first noticed a protective presence many years ago after you married and moved from your home, away from your mother. This presence became more apparent when *you* became a mother. I bet the presence, or Angel, came back when your children moved away from you, *their* mother. Then Angel came back when your responsibilities for your mother increased, and really started to kick into gear after your mother died. Does that seem about right?"

As Cora considered his words, her face relaxed and she nodded. "I don't know if I'm more relieved you believe me or more concerned you think a spirit is possible."

Father McGrath asked gently, "You wanted to protect your mother. Is it possible you need protection in turn? Are you looking for that subconsciously, or is a supernatural presence picking it up? You said Angel called herself Máime in her message to you. Do you know that that means?"

"No, I was puzzled by that." She shook her head.

"It's Gaelic, Cora. Máime is Gaelic, pronounced like Mammy, or Mommy, what Irish children call their mothers. Mother is máthair, but when children address their máthair they call her Máime. If we assume this Angel is real, for whatever reason and by whatever means, might one conclude she is Irish, and might be calling herself your mother?"

Cora clapped a hand to her mouth and looked at the ceiling, then said, "My God, Father, you're a genius! Of course! That's the reason she visits and protects me. But why does she think she's my mother? I had a mother! And my mother wasn't Irish, she was Polish."

"Whoa!" he said, waving a hand in the air. "We haven't proved anything. I didn't say she's real, just postulated a theory if that were true."

Cora stood up, moved behind her chair, clenching the back of it tightly, gazing over Father's head and saying nothing.

"I'm putting this back in your court before we talk further, my dear," Father McGrath concluded, standing up and moving toward his bookshelves. "You have more thinking to do, but I have some books here somewhere that might help. They talk about angels and spirits—not in the same book of course!" He laughed, scanned the shelves for a few moments, and then shrugged his shoulders, giving her a sheepish smile.

"I'll dig them out for you and drop them off at your house. Meanwhile, you sort out your feelings and see if what we proposed throws any light on the situation."

Cora bounced her fists softly on the back of the chair, trying to concentrate on his words.

How can Angel think she's my mother? She should know I had a mother.

Chapter 13

Cora turned off the highway onto a street marked with a DEAD END sign and slowed the car to avoid occasional broken pavement and potholes. What looked like an old farmhouse sat beside a huge new luxury home with an elaborate playhouse in its yard. Cora shook her head as she drove by, wondering how people with young children could pay for such homes, and why they thought they needed that much space. She and Cisco never could have afforded such grand housing when they were raising their children, and wouldn't have needed it after the boys moved out.

At the end of the road was an overgrown area of shrubs and grass which dropped sharply beyond the foliage to a two-lane road. Cora pulled into the driveway of a modest frame ranch home, noting fresh paint on the window frames and a burnt-orange door that accented pale blue clapboards. A shiny brass knocker and kick plate adorned the door, and an assortment of pots on both sides of the entry welcomed visitors. Yellow mums brightened flower borders, and the lawn was well tended. This was a surprise. Bridey must have a lot of energy for an eighty-plus-year-old widow.

Cora almost called off her meeting with Bridey to spend the morning researching spirits; however, Father McGrath hadn't brought the books he promised yet, and she had already changed a number of appointments and didn't want to reschedule Bridey again.

Procrastination was not always a bad thing, Cora believed, but could be a tool. By removing her focus from problems she could see them more objectively when she returned to them. Sometimes they solved themselves in the meantime, saving her any effort at all. Incubation, she called it. Cisco called it rationalizing.

Bridey Boyle, a tiny, energetic woman with surprising bright red hair in a wedge cut, answered the door.

No way that's natural—it's got to be dyed.

After exchanging greetings, Bridey led Cora to her living room and invited her to sit on the sofa. "Would you like a cup of tea?" she asked. "I'd like one myself, and I hate to drink alone," she said, with a chuckle at her little joke.

"I'd love a cup of tea," Cora said, with an answering smile.

Cora glanced around the room while Bridey was in the kitchen. Like everything else she had noticed about Bridey's home, it was neat. The furniture was old but well cared for, the typical heavy blond wood and simple lines of the 1950s. The plush carpet was new, and showed tracks of recent vacuuming. The upholstery was clean but somewhat faded. Fussy knickknacks made the room seem personal and comfortable. On a small round table, centered in front of a picture window, was a professional portrait in a simple wood frame, showing a smiling Bridey and a handsome man of a similar age. It appeared to be fairly recent. The large man had warm blue eyes, a round ruddy face, and a full head of white hair. The picture reminded Cora of her own Irish relatives.

"You have a lovely home," Cora said when Bridey returned. She accepted a cup of tea in a deep red and gold bone china cup and saucer. "Can I set this on the table? What pretty china!"

"Of course you can." Bridey settled herself into a straight-backed chair in front of the window, set her own beverage down on the table, and swept the room with an arm. "This old furniture is hard as nails. It's gotten by all these years, the only real furniture we ever owned, after the hand-me-downs we started off with, that is. Jack was real particular about everything we bought. He wasn't much for shopping, and only wanted to do it once. Everything we bought was intended to last a lifetime."

Cora sipped her tea, then set the cup and saucer down. "Jack sounds like a great husband. Is that the two of you in the picture?" She pointed to the photo. "He's very handsome."

"Yes, he was. We took that picture back in 2000, to celebrate the new century." Bridey's face beamed. "Jack was healthy then," she said. "He didn't get sick with the cancer until almost ten years later. He's been gone two years now."

"I'm so sorry. Two years. That's the same time I lost my mother."

"You still miss her, I bet, just like I miss Jack. Not a day goes by...," Bridey said sadly.

"Yes. I keep thinking she's still here. I want to show her something or talk to her, and then I remember and tear up." Cora could feel her cheeks warming and moisture in her eyes, and changed the subject.

"Thank you for agreeing to talk to me," she began, fussing with her fingers on her leg. "There are few people any more who lived in Sag Bridge before it became part of Lemont. I've been talking to people who remember it when it was a town of its own."

"Oh, I'm happy to talk to you. No one wants to listen to us old folks anymore. Young people these days aren't much interested in the past."

Lemont and Sag Bridge were once important and separate canal towns during the construction of all three waterways that were responsible for Chicago's prosperity. Similar towns only three miles apart, Cora wondered why Sag Bridge disappeared and why little written or photographic evidence of the town existed. Even the history of the name, Sag Bridge, remained a debated issue. When Cora brought it up, the historical society's president suggested she develop an archive on Sag Bridge.

Leaning forward a little, Cora asked, "Do you know why Sag Bridge isn't a town anymore?"

"Some time in the 1950s, I don't remember the exact year, the town thought it was too much trouble and expense to keep running itself, and voted to un-incorporate—there weren't enough people here anymore. But the school stayed open until 1961, you know. It was the last one-room schoolhouse in Cook County. I went there all eight years, I did. Same teacher that whole time, and she taught good. No assistant either, like they have today," Bridey laughed, waving a finger in the air.

Cora smiled. "I read about the school. The historical society has photos of the building and some class pictures. What I wanted to know was what it was like to live here, you know, before the industry, trucking companies, and junk yards took over. When Sag Bridge was something other than a corner of Lemont." She leaned back and crossed her legs as she waited for Bridey to think it over.

Bridey considered, rubbing both chair arms while she thought. "Well, I'm not sure I can be of much help if that's what you're looking for. Most of the early folks pretty much moved on after the last canal, the Cal Sag, was done, and that was before my memory. They started building that one in 1912, the third canal, and I think it took 'em ten years. I was just a baby when they finished."

"I realize that. I thought maybe you might remember stories you heard, from your family, or from your husband's family. I'm more interested in the town than in the canals," Cora explained.

"Well, why don't you ask me some questions? Something might come to me. My memory isn't what it used to be. In fact, before you got here, there was something I was thinking I needed to show you, something you'd be especially interested in, but I'll be darned if I can remember now what it was." She scratched her head and gazed toward some bookshelves against the far wall.

Cora smiled. "I do that too, all too often. Okay. Why don't you tell me about your mother and father? Where did they live, and what did they do?" Cora reached into her purse and took out a note pad and pen.

"Máime was a simple housewife, like me." The word jumped out at Cora: *Máime*. "And Dadaí worked on the railroad, various jobs."

Apparently, Cora assumed, she called her father Dadaí, which she pronounced DAH-dee. Cora looked up. "Your mother and father? You said that a little different. Can you spell it for me?"

"Sure. It's m-a-i-m-e with one of those little marks over the 'a', and d-a-d-a-i, with a mark over the 'i'. Most Irish people don't call their mothers and fathers that much, but people in Sag Bridge used the old names for their parents."

That explains that!

"He was a brakeman when he retired, I think. We lived on the family farm in the old farmhouse, but didn't work the land. We rented out the land to a farmer down the road." Bridey turned slightly, and turned an unfocused gaze toward a corner of the window.

"So your parents didn't live 'in town' so to speak?" Cora looked up from her note pad and Bridey turned to meet her eye.

Before replying, Bridey sipped her tea, set the cup down again. She ran her hand through her hair. "Well, *in town* wouldn't have been like you think of a town nowadays. There weren't a lot of what you would call nice houses, just for the business owners. People from the farms nearby came here to the post office or general store, the meat market, the blacksmith, like that. I heard tell of a couple of hotels, but they were more like boarding houses. And of course, Sag Railroad Station and the Electric Railway stopped here. People still used horses back then, but it was easy to get around, to Chicago or to Joliet, on the train or the electric streetcar. It was cheaper and faster than now, in fact." Again, she was looking off toward some distant point, not engaging Cora's eyes, as she talked.

Once she got started, Bridey rambled freely. Cora smiled as she made notes.

My God, she's great! Doesn't know if she can help—baloney!

Encouraged by Cora's interest, Bridey rambled on, looking at Cora now, and smiling more confidently. "Behind that cluster of buildings, a block or two, there were a few blocks of shanties around the businesses, where the transient canal workers used to live. Most were deserted after the canal got finished. Then there were nearby farms. And the church up on the hill."

"How many people do you think lived here then?" Cora prompted.

"Oh, maybe a thousand. No more than that." Bridey pointed a finger. "Oh! I forgot to mention the saloons—all the old canal towns had saloons. Working men wanted their drink after the day was done, and there wasn't much else to do at night. We had a reputation for brothels too, but most of those closed after the second canal, long before I was born." She laughed after making this clarification.

"A thousand people—that was a lot in those days," Cora said. "Let's work backwards. You said the school closed in 1961. Why did it close?"

"After the town shut down, we still had a school district, but there weren't enough people that lived right here and wanted to go to a one-room school. The schools in Lemont were better, so the kids went there."

"So the population was declining then?"

"It had *already* declined, right after the canal was done." Bridey fidgeted with the cover over the arm of her chair. "It was easy for people to get around, to Lemont and other places, and the businesses at Sag, they were small anyway. Nobody came to Sag just to shop, and Sag people started going to Lemont and Joliet and Chicago too, so the Sag businesses closed. There was no business here even when I was a girl, just a scattering of homes and farms."

"Would you say the population of Sag was a thousand when you were a child?"

Bridey shook her head vehemently. "Oh, no, not then. Maybe three hundred were left, including the farms. When they built the last canal, much of the town was in the way and was torn down, and the forest preserve district had bought up a lot of remaining farms and turned them back to forests, even before that. Kind of silly after all that work to clear the land, don't you think?"

"How far back does your family go at Sag Bridge?"

"Oh, back to the very beginning," Bridey said, with a few quick little nods of her head. "The first canal, the I & M? My great-grand-dah worked on it. The canal contractors made a lot of promises but then they were always running out of money. Worked the poor *Micks*, they called them, real hard—backbreaking work. Then there was no money when it came time to pay the men. The contractors *said* they had no money, but they always seemed to make out okay themselves. They paid the workers with something they called land scrip instead, and the workers used the scrip to buy cheap farm land." She shook her head and frowned.

Cora scribbled for a while, and then asked, "So that's why there were so many Irish at Sag Bridge?"

"That's right," Bridey agreed, nodding. "They used to say, 'You want to build a canal? Well, all you need is a shovel, a wheelbarrow, and an Irishman.'" She laughed heartily, and Cora joined in, although she had used a version of the saying herself.

"So Great-Grand-dah came here to farm before the canal, back in the 1830s and 1840s," Bridey continued. She told about his struggles establishing his farm, encounters with the Indians along the river, and that when he died the farm was left to Bridey's Grandfather Nolan.

"The farm was just south of Sag apiece, in the valley where it wasn't so swampy, and Grand-dah and Grand-mah had sheep and pigs—the pigs liked to forage in the trees. They grew corn and of course potatoes. The Irish always had to have potatoes, didn't they?" She laughed again, enjoying her joke, and looked at Cora for encouragement.

Bridey talked at length about her grandparents and her life growing up on the family farm. "The farm was left to Dadaí, but he had no interest in farming—oh, I said that."

Cora looked up from her notes, chewed on the end of her pen, thinking, then asked, "You say your father worked on the railroad?"

"When Dadaí was young, he wanted to leave the Sag, like a lot of folks, 'cause there was nothing for people here, and he tried to find work in Chicago or just about anyplace else. He wound up back here though, on the railroad, and worked for it most of his life."

"What did he tell you about his life as a child in Sag?"

"Oh, Dadaí was quite the story-teller, he was!" Bridey chuckled in anticipation.

"Tell me some stories, if you don't mind." Cora knew Bridey wouldn't mind—she was having a great time.

"When he was a boy, about eight years old, he was already expected to work. He had to cut wood, weed the garden, go out to the fields and knock off potato bugs. But he hated it, and whenever he could run off, he would sneak to the river to fish."

"Go on."

She leaned forward. "When he got a little older he dreamed up schemes to make money to buy candy. He'd meet trains at the station and carry bags for a nickel. And he'd go to the quarries to find fossils, *trilobites* he called them, and sell them. He had a secret spot." Bridey reached for her tea, drained the cup, looked at it and frowned.

Cora didn't want Bridey to break the flow to run to the kitchen for tea. She asked quickly, "Did he go to school?"

"Yes, but in those days boys were expected to get a job and bring in some money for the family. Dadaí got a job at the aluminum factory in Lemont, made fifty cents a day." Enjoying her story, she lowered her voice as if telling a secret. "He hung around with a gang of boys after work, and got in trouble. They let boys in the saloons in those days, and Dadaí and his friends hung out to watch the goings-on."

She described the men sitting around pot-bellied stoves, drinking and chewing tobacco, spitting into spittoons or on the sawdust-covered floors. There were no bar stools—men stood around the rail. "Dadaí and his buddies waited until men got drunk, then played tricks on them for laughs until the owner chased them away.

"Dadaí met and married Máime, got a job on the railroad, and moved from job to job, water boy, brakeman, maintenance crew. They lived in the farmhouse."

"What happened to the farm? Is it still there?" Cora asked.

"No, there's subdivisions there now. Other farms sold, and Dadaí was never fond of it, as I said, so he sold our farm too."

"When was that?"

"Probably in the sixties, or thereabouts. It was after Jack and I married."

Cora caught up on her note taking. "You mentioned Saint James. Was that your church?"

"Surely was. Great-Grand-dah helped to build it, lugging stone up from the quarry. It was built with stone from Sag quarries, did you know?" Bridey said proudly. "The family always went there, four generations of us. The parish was mostly Irish, and even before it was a church it was a cemetery. And the church anniversary book says, before that it was a French fort, and before that an Indian village."

Bridey ran her hand through her hair again, and gazed out the window, picturing something in her mind. She began talking in a dreamy manner. "I remember what I wanted to show you now. Dadaí told us a story about the cemetery, something that happened when he was a boy, in the late 1890s. A man and woman were murdered there, along with a little just-born baby, a baby girl. Dadaí knew the dead man, who was a foreman in one of the quarries. The man had always been nice to him, gave him fossils to sell. Both the man and woman had their heads bashed in, and the little baby girl was in the woman's arms and dead too."

Cora stopped taking notes, caught up in the story.

"The priest at Saint James found the bodies when he was hunting early in the morning. There was a church meeting the night before, so the killings must have happened during the night. Strange thing, the priest said when he discovered them a wolf was lying there too, sleeping curled against the woman with its head on the little dead baby. When the wolf saw him at first it just laid there and glared at him, but when he tried to get closer the wolf started to snarl and come at him, and he had to shoot and kill it. There were wolves here back then, you know."

Bridey was lost in the tale, but she turned to look at Cora for her reaction. "The murders really happened, but the part about the wolf is a legend, of course, and not too many people believe it. I don't know how you feel about priests and all, but I think the fact a priest told that part of the story means it's probably true. What reason would he have to add to what was already an incredible story?"

Cora was stunned. A wolf again! Despite the tingle at her hairline, she managed to say calmly, "How strange! How did it happen?"

"No one knows. They never found out who killed them. It was in the papers, of course, as it caused quite a commotion for months." Bridey looked at Cora hopefully. "Would you like some more tea? I know I would. I can make more."

"Wait a minute," Cora pleaded, setting down her writing materials and placing both hands on the sofa cushion. "Can you tell me more about the woman first? Did your father know her too?"

Bridey looked pleased. "I can do better than that," she said with a small laugh. "That's my little surprise. I have her diary."

Cora could hardly contain her excitement. *A diary!*

"Oh! Do you know where it is? Could I see it?" she exclaimed, her eyes sparking with delight.

"Sure, Honey. It's right in this cabinet, with some old pictures too." Bridey walked across the room to a bookcase and reached for a box on a bottom shelf, drawing it out. "I haven't looked at this in years, but I'd enjoy doing it with you. Do you have time now?"

"Do I have time?" Cora beamed enthusiastically. *"Absolutely* I have time!" She jumped up. "Here," she said, reaching for the box, "let me help you carry that, it looks heavy. Can we sit at a table?" she asked, leading the way to Bridey's kitchen.

Chapter 14

Feeling that she was wasting too much time this morning, pressured by urgent matters, Cora struggled to put her thoughts in order. Bridey had allowed her to borrow the diary, and what she wanted to do more than anything else this morning was read it from cover to cover, but she had to make some decisions about Angel, and that was more urgent, much as she wanted to put it off.

For forty years, Cora had started her day at five in the morning, but since retiring she treated herself to relaxed mornings, waking at seven o'clock, eating a leisurely breakfast, chatting with Cisco, reading for a half hour to engage her brain. This morning she had abbreviated her routine, but she needed at least a little down time. Without it, she would jump aimlessly from one task to another, making little progress.

She entered her office and sorted her u-shaped desk to clear ample workspace. She gathered documents from the printer l on the left, pausing for a moment to look out the window to see if anything was happening on the street. She sat down and put incomplete items in holding bins labeled *urgent* and *whenever* on the l on the right, and filed completed paperwork on the shelf above her main workspace, leaving her desktop clear except for her laptop, note-making materials, and the tasks for the morning. This was her *preparation* phase.

Then came *organization*. She labeled two manila file folders: *Sag Bridge*, and *Angel*. She sorted scraps of paper, notes, and other materials in her task piles and placed them in the folders. Now she was ready, at last, for *work*.

Before retirement, Cora's life was divided into two categories: work, and everything else. Now there was historical society, library, chorus, book club, writer's club, and yes, still, everything else. There still weren't enough hours to squeeze in family, home, garden, travel, and other interests. Angel now threatened to take over everything.

Staring over her laptop at the cluttered tack board facing her, she let out a long slow breath and squared her shoulders. She had to quit procrastinating and start getting something done.

If she dealt with yesterday's interview quickly, she could devote the rest of the day to Angel. She opened the *Sag Bridge* folder, intending to get that out of the way.

Along with the diary, Bridey had loaned Cora some old photos of Sag Bridge. The pictures were of family members standing in front of farmhouses; none showed what the streets and buildings looked like in the town's heyday. She was looking for written and photographic evidence to help her visualize the town at its peak. She reviewed documents, starred items for further action, decided nothing needed immediate attention, and closed the file.

Smiling as she picked up the diary, Cora turned it over in her hands. It had been a delightful surprise. She would make a number of copies at LAHS, work from a copy so she could mark it as she read, and probably scan it to a flash drive as well. She was anxious to get a feel for the life of the young woman who was killed at Saint James. She wondered if the authorities at the time had known of the diary. If they had examined it, it must not have contained any clues or they would know who killed her and why. If not ...well, who knows, maybe Cora would find something overlooked, or that would be seen differently from today's perspective. Or it may just be an interesting bit of history. But there was no hurry— the mystery had been unsolved for over a hundred years, a few more days wouldn't make any difference. But she had to at least take a peek at it before she began concentrating on Angel.

The diary was ten inches tall and seven and a half inches wide. The binding and corners were red leather embossed with gold, over a multicolored marbled cloth cover, and the lined pages had no headings or columns. At the end were charts and tables, calendars for the years 1890 through 1900, train and electric line time tables, and random generic information such as interest tables, foreign coin values, dates for full moons and eclipses, wind direction and velocity signals, and other such statistics of interest back then. The pages were yellow, brittle, and fragile, and some were separated from the binding. The entries were closely written, in a tiny fancy script, surprisingly easy to read.

The first entry was dated December 25, 1889. The date embossed on the cover was 1890, so Cora deduced the book had been a Christmas present. The last entry was July 10, 1898. She made some calculations. If the writer was in her early twenties when she was killed, which would have been an approximate age for a young married woman, she would have been maybe twenty-two when she made her last entry, and subtract eight, that would make her about fourteen when she began the diary—give or take. Turning to the inside back cover of the book, Cora noted an inscription she missed, as she would expect an inscription at the beginning, not the end. "To my favorite niece, the one who will be a famous writer someday, I give you a *journal* to begin the *journey*." It was signed "Uncle Denny, Christmas, 1889".

Cora read the first entry:

December 25, 1889–Christmas Day, in the evening, but Christmas Day Eve, not Christmas Eve. Uncle Denny says I am his favorite niece, and that is good because he is my favorite uncle. Maybe that doesn't say a lot because no one knows where my only other uncle ran off to. I wonder what Sally would think about him saying that? I think Sally thinks she is his favorite. Well, I won't tell her, that will be between me and Uncle Denny.

Only Uncle Denny would know how much I would love this beutifull book. I will write in it faithfully but I will save it for important things and thoughts so it does not get used up to fast. Where will I hide it though? I must have a secret place, because I can't be totally honest about what I set down here unless I know for sure that no one else will ever, ever see it. I will have to think about that very carefully, because it is also important that it be easy to get at, or I will be defeated in not being able to use it if it is not conveenint.

How charming. Cora smiled, delighted at the childish misspellings. Reluctantly, she put the book aside, after making a note to call Bridey to see if she knew where the diary was found. She was tempted to read the last entry before putting it away.

No! If I do that, I'll be lost.

If she spent any more time reading, she would want to keep digging away at the mystery, and she had procrastinated too much already—she had to start dealing with Angel. If she didn't get into that problem right now, she'd want lunch before she began, then she'd be groggy after lunch and not in the mood, and next convince herself it was okay to put it off until the next day. No, she had to get started. Father hadn't dropped off the books he promised yet, but she could write down what she knew and brainstorm some ideas.

She slipped the diary into a desk drawer and closed it, her hand lingering on the closed drawer front. She rolled her shoulders, stretched her arms over her head, rummaged through a cup of pens for a favorite, pulled a note pad in front of her, bent over it and stared at the blank page for a short time. She then began jotting handwritten notes in no particular order, as they occurred to her:

– *List bizarre incidents that may have involved Angel—including "punishments". Relate them to what was going on in my life when they happened.*
– *Is Angel real, spirit, or delusion? Column list: things that point to real versus delusion.*
– *Why might Angel think she's my mother and what does my mother have to do with it?*
– *If Angel has been around for a long time, why is she escalating now?*
– *Why "Máime"? Why "Darlin'"? And where did this wolf come from?*
– *Prioritize. Which thing on this f-ing list do I do first?*

Cora felt a sense of accomplishment, but struggled to decide what to do next. She decided to type the list into her computer and fill in ideas under each item. Thoughts might come to her as she did the mindless task of transferring the information from paper, and she would follow where they took her. If not, she'd start on an easy question, in hopes of jump-starting her thought process.

She opened her laptop, booted it up, and checked her emails first. Nothing important, just ads, spam, funnies from friends. She played a game of computer solitaire.

Just one, I promise. I deserve a break.

She lost the game.

She opened a new word document. As she placed her fingers on the keyboard, words started to appear in the blank document on her screen in a large bold font, although she was not pushing any keys:

Where did that come from Darlin'?

"Cisco!" Cora yelled. "Can you come up here? Right away?"

Chapter 15

"Look!" Cora demanded. Seated at her desk, she pointed a shaking finger at her laptop screen, then turned to watch anxiously for Cisco's reaction.

Cisco leaned over her shoulder and read:

Where did that come from Darlin'?

He straightened up, drew his eyebrows together, and dropped one side of his mouth. "Yeah? So? Why are you so excited? What does that mean?"

"That's what I want to know! What do *you* think it means?" Cora waved her hand at the screen, and then searched his eyes again.

Cisco shook his head and folded his arms over his chest. "Cora, what are you asking me here? You show me something you typed and then ask me what you mean. In reference to what? I haven't got a clue what you're driving at!"

"I *didn't* type that! That's the *problem!*" Cora said, rapidly tapping one heel on the floor, frustrated that she had to explain what seemed obvious to her, that he wasn't as blown away by the message as she was.

Cisco rolled his eyes and glanced at the ceiling, clearly struggling to remain patient. "What do you mean, you didn't type that? Who typed it then?"

"That's just it! That's the question!" Cora opened both eyes wide and jabbed her finger at the screen.

He threw his arms up in the air and rolled his eyes again. "Cora, back up. Give me a break. *Talk* to me here!"

Cora took a breath, stretched her neck, rolled her shoulders, and leaned back in her chair. Cisco plopped into his chair, swiveled it around to face her, and waited, hands tucked into his armpits.

"Cisco, I was working, sorting things out, whatever—working. The laptop was off. I turned it on, checked emails, played a game of solitaire. Then I opened a Word document. These words just started to flow onto the screen. Like an f-ing Ouija board or something! And I called you right away. That's it. I don't *know* how it happened." Her eyes kept moving back and forth between the screen and Cisco, and she put a thumbnail between her teeth.

Cisco, leaning back in his chair, exhaled loudly. "So someone hacked your computer. Or you stored a series of keystrokes to your clipboard unconsciously, and they appeared in the document when you opened it. Computers do crazy things. Nothing to get so excited about."

"Come on! That's pretty far-fetched. Why would I type those words?" She shook her head and turned down a corner of her mouth.

"I don't know. What were you doing last time the computer was on?"

Cora crossed her arms over her chest, imitating his position, and glared at him. "Cisco...no. Don't go there. That didn't happen."

He shook his head slowly from side to side and let out a low groan. "Fine. Why do you ask me if you don't want to hear what I have to say? How do *you* think the words got there?"

"I think Angel did it."

He exhaled loudly and shook his head again. "Come on! That business again? Can't you give that a rest?"

"When stuff keeps happening? I should give it a rest? Don't you think I should try to figure it out?" Cora's voice rose as she glared at him.

"Well, if you're figuring it out, can't you consider something besides this Angel crap?" Cisco stared fixedly at the screen as he flung an arm toward it.

Cora turned from him, put her chin in her hands, then rubbed her nose and cheeks, and took a deep breath. "No—I can't think of anything else. If I had a logical reason for what's going on, don't you think I'd be talking about it? Can *you* explain it? Do you have any ideas? I mean, that stuff with Valerie, that was pretty weird, not to say scary. What do *you* think happened there?"

Cisco shifted his eyes and set his jaw. Cora knew he hated to back down once he'd stated an opinion. "I *haven't* been thinking about it. Valerie had an accident, that's all. And this other stuff, well, I don't know. Maybe your mind is running away with you."

"You've seen strange stuff too," Cora reminded him.

"The wolf, you mean, and a long time ago? Yeah, but...I can't explain any of it, but I don't buy *supernatural* stuff, and this mythical Angel you keep trying to make into a person." He scratched the back of his head.

"Father McGrath isn't so sure Angel is mythical. He thinks...."

"Father McGrath? You brought Father McGrath into this? Why would you do *that?*" He threw both arms in the air.

"Because I thought it was serious and you didn't. I needed another opinion." She raised her chin defiantly.

"Because mine's no good, right?" His eyes flashed and a muscle in his jaw jumped.

Cora suddenly realized why she and Cisco were on different pages. She had been so preoccupied by the excitement of the past few days that she had never filled him in on the events. After he indicated he didn't want to think the first message on her computer and Valerie's attack had anything to do with Angel, she had put off telling him about the second message and her conversations with Frannie and Father McGrath, intending to do it when things were less hectic and she had a better handle on it herself. That time had not come.

"Oh, Cisco, let's not fight about this!" She dropped her eyes and then rubbed her face before looking up at him again.

"There's some things you don't know, but you've been so dead set against my ideas about Angel, I didn't want to argue with you about it. It only made me more upset and I needed someone who wasn't so involved—who would approach it with an open mind. So I talked to Father, and I talked to Frannie, too."

He stared at her, blinking rapidly, but didn't say anything.

She took a deep breath, and let it out slowly. "This isn't the second strange message on my computer. It's the third," she said. She glanced nervously at the laptop screen and around the room, but nothing had changed. Her anxiety was ebbing, and she launched into a short version of recent events, interrupted by multiple questions and explanations, but in the process they both calmed considerably.

She reached out and placed a hand on his arm. "I'm sorry, Hon. I should have told you right away, but I was so mixed up. But now, can you just humor me for a minute? Let's just *pretend* this is Angel on the computer then. What could this message mean?"

Scratching the back of his head, he gazed for a moment out the window, and then turned back to her. "Okay...you think there's some all-seeing entity out there, watching over you, and it's handing out sanctions to people who offend you. Somehow there's a wolf involved. And now this 'being' is communicating with you through your computer. Is that about it?"

"Yeah, pretty much," Cora said in a weak voice, avoiding his eyes.

"So who is it then, this entity?" He turned both palms up. "Or what is it? And why is it protecting you? If we *suppose* it exists, that is?"

"I can't answer that. But let's talk about what's happening *now*. Let's suppose an angel or spirit *is* communicating with me right now, on my laptop. What do I do?" She pointed at the message on the screen again, then turned to watch his face.

"I suppose you should try answering it." Cisco raised his arm and made circles in the air with one finger.

"That's what I thought too. But I don't understand the question, so how can I answer? I don't know what it *wants*. And I wanted you to be here, Hon, to see, in case I got an answer." She reached over and touched his arm again.

"Yeah. Right. An answer from a supernatural being," Cisco said, taking a slow deep breath and staring at the ceiling.

She removed her hand and shot him a look. "Stop!"

"All right...but if it's an all-seeing being, why does it have to ask you *anything*? Why doesn't it *know*?" He lowered his chin and looked at her over the top of his glasses.

Cora rolled her head from side to side. "Can't you try to be helpful here?"

"I *am* trying. I'm trying to figure out what it's looking for. What doesn't it know? And why doesn't it know it?"

"Ah, I see. You mean, if it's been following me and seeing what I see, then it knows what I know. Unless it's something new? Or something I don't know myself yet?"

Cisco pointed a finger at Cora. "Right! So what's new?"

Cora spent a moment in thought. "Let's suppose she would want to know as soon as something happens—she's impatient."

"She?"

Cora ran a hand through her hair, then put her elbow on the desk and rested her chin on it. "Don't ask—bear with me. I just know it's a she. Intuition...whatever. We're assuming here."

"Fine," Cisco said, playing along. "So what's new, what just happened, that the two of you don't understand, since the last time *she* had a chance to contact you?"

"Well...I interviewed Bridey."

Cisco held out both hands, palms up, inviting. "And....?"

"We talked about Sag Bridge, and I borrowed photos and a diary from her. I looked at them at my desk this morning."

"Could Angel be interested in old photos or a diary? Why?"

Cora considered the question. "The photos are nothing special. The diary is interesting though. It talks about when Sag Bridge was a thriving community, and it was written by a young woman who wound up getting killed along with her husband and baby."

"Did you do anything else?"

"I made a list of things to work on, to try to figure out more about Angel."

"Maybe she doesn't like the idea of being figured out. That could make her angry." Cisco pushed his chair closer and leaned over Cora's shoulder, looking at her screen with more interest.

"Yes, it could. But why would she ask where I got that? Wouldn't she ask why I'm doing that?" Cora said, shaking her head.

"So you think Angel wants to know about the diary? Why would she? Do you think she recognizes it?"

Cora shrugged. "Well, it's a place to start. I could ask her, respond to her message with a question, but how do I do that?"

Cisco threw his arms up in the air, but he was smiling. "How should I know? I never tried to send a message to an Angel before!"

"Well, if she's listening to us, then she's hearing us now, and she already has her answer. Only *we* don't know she knows, so we'd like some kind of confirmation from her."

"Assuming here, she's communicating through your computer. So type it, I guess. Below her message," Cisco moved his chair closer and leaned toward the laptop.

Cora placed her hands on the keyboard and tried to type into the document. The computer was locked.

"Reboot it," Cisco said. Cora powered the laptop down and turned it back on. When it came up the message was gone.

"That's not surprising, as we never saved it," said Cisco. "See if it was auto-saved."

They checked all possible locations, but found no trace of the document. Cora opened a new Word document and typed in bold letters and large font:

Are you asking about the diary?

Nothing happened. They waited five minutes, staring at the screen. After ten minutes more, they moved around the office, making busy work and checking the screen frequently. After half an hour, in the event Angel didn't want to communicate while they were in the room, they went down to the kitchen, reheated coffee from breakfast, came back and checked again. Still nothing.

Cora moved the cursor down the page and added:

Are you there?

No response.

"What now?" Cora asked, feeling foolish.

"Leave it open. Go about your day and check your screen now and then. If nothing happens by tonight, forget it, and ask yourself if this whole business is nonsense." Cisco turned away to leave the room.

"Cisco," she said, ignoring his last suggestion, "something bothers me here. You brought it up before. If Angel has the power to know about what happens to us, why doesn't she know about the diary? Why does she have to ask?"

"Maybe she knew about it, or it was hers. Maybe it got lost. I don't know." He shrugged.

"I'm glad you said that— that's what I was thinking, too. If there *is* a ghost around here, how many could there be? And this diary falls into my hands, a diary of a woman who was murdered? Just when things are getting hot around here? If it isn't Angel's, at least she recognized it." She searched his face with wide, unblinking eyes.

"Don't get carried away, Cora. You didn't get an answer. This is probably just a pile of coincidences, not some ghost." Despite his words, his furrowed brow suggested uncertainty.

They went downstairs. Cora put her arms around Cisco and hugged him. "Thank you," she said.

"For what?" he asked, hugging her and rubbing her back.

"For humoring me. And for not saying I told you so."

Chapter 16

After lunch, everything remained as they left it, Cora's question still unanswered.

"Nothing is going to happen, Cora," Cisco said, shaking his head. "Admit it and move on. You can wait until tonight if you want, but nothing's going to change."

"I suppose you're right. It just seems…every time I turn around, something odd happens. How do I get it to stop?"

"Try ignoring it," he said, with a meaningful look.

"I'll try," she sighed. She would. But she knew she would fail.

~~~

Cisco left for some practice time at the bowling alley. Cora, wanting to take a step away from the events of the morning, made an attempt to read and thought about taking a nap, but she couldn't relax or concentrate on her book. She vacillated between her gut instincts and Cisco's logic, but couldn't shake the feeling of pending danger. Restless, she decided to work some more on the list she made earlier that morning, hoping that activity would settle her mind and put things in perspective.

She went upstairs and found the office door closed. She never closed that door, and wondered why Cisco would have. Then she remembered that he ran upstairs before he left the house, and thought he might have left a little surprise for her. He did that now and then.

That sweetie! He knew I was upset. Just like him to try to cheer me up.

She opened the door, a smile on her face—a smile that quickly faded as she looked around the room. The Sag Bridge diary was lying open in front of her laptop! She knew for certain, she *remembered*, placing the diary in a drawer when she finished with it. It had been in the drawer when she and Cisco were talking earlier. The drawer was now fully open. Cora was obsessive about closing drawers.

Cora moved slowly to the desk. The diary was open to an entry dated May 30, 1898, the page titled *Decoration Day*.

The phone rang and she startled, pulling her eyes away from the diary. As she turned toward the phone, her gaze swept across her laptop screen and then stopped there, the ringing phone forgotten, a chill at the back of her neck.

There, in the center of the screen, below her earlier messages, was another cryptic text box:

> **Yes. Start here Darlin'.**

The phone rang again and, as if in a trance, she picked it up. "Hey there girl, how's it going? You got it all figured out yet? Well, now, just you wait until I tell you what I found online…"

"Wait!" Cora exclaimed. She set the phone down and covered her mouth with both hands, concentrating, sudden thoughts clicking into place.

Angel was real and communicating with her…she recognized the diary and wanted to tell Cora something about it…the diary wasn't in Cora's house until yesterday…the argument with Valerie, Cora's distress about the letter in the newspaper, that happened in her house too…other incidents, Angel found out what was going on in Cora's life because she talked about it at home or at work…those long periods Angel had no contact with her, that was after Cora moved or changed jobs….

Angel only knows what she can see in this house, as if she were a visitor. She doesn't know what happens other places, just here, here where I am, in this house.

She wrapped her arms around her shoulders, looked at the floor, swayed, then turned in place and looked at the ceiling. Does that make sense? She wasn't sure, but…were Angel's powers limited to places she expected Cora to be? The vengeful acts didn't take place there, or their encounter with the wolf, but...she'd figure that out later. Maybe she could read Cora's mind only in her house, or witness things there, but could go elsewhere to do things, once she knew...and Cora and Frannie were plotting against her—what would she do about *that?* She couldn't let Frannie talk about Angel on the phone! She'd have to meet her somewhere else.

"What's going on there? You okay?" Frannie's voice came through the receiver.

Cora grabbed the phone. "No, I can't talk now, Frannie, or I'll be late. I have to do something right away before I meet you," Cora said, the words tumbling out. *Please, please, Frannie, don't mention Angel!*

Frannie caught on that Cora couldn't talk. "Uh...meet me...uh... where was that we're meeting again?"

"Oh—that's right—we never confirmed the place, just the day and time," Cora babbled, pacing the office as she spoke. "I thought we said Starbucks, but maybe not. It's a good thing you called to confirm."

"Uh huh...confirm...right," replied Frannie. "And...uh...what time did we say?"

"Right now. I'm running out of the house right now, and we have to hurry so I can get back before Cisco gets home for dinner." She walked over to her desk, picked up a pen for no reason, pushed papers around the desk aimlessly.

"So why don't I just come to your house then, wouldn't that be better?"

"No! Uh...no. I have to pick something up at Starbucks anyway, so it'll save time. See you there." Cora hung up before Frannie could say anything else.

She grabbed the list she had written that morning, a pad of paper, her purse, and raced out to her car.

~~~

Cora spotted a car backing out of the only remaining parking spot and rushed over to grab it. She waited as the driver slowly backed up...and *backed* up...and backed up some more, senselessly. *Where is he going?* She put her car in reverse, but another car pulled behind her and she couldn't move. She blew her horn to no avail. The driver struck her car.

She jumped out, marched angrily to the driver and demanded, "Where did you think you were going? I was sitting right there! You backed right into me!"

The man looked annoyed, as if she, not he, were the offender. He mouthed the word, "Deaf," and pointed at his ear, his eyes hard with anger.

She stared at him, pointed at her eye, and mouthed explicitly, "Can you see?"

She stomped back to her car, mumbling beneath her breath. "No excuse to back into me, idiot! If you're gonna drive a car, you got to watch what you're doing!" She assessed the damage while the man stood near his car door, apparently unwilling to be involved. He got back into his car and drove away.

On examination, there were scratches, but no dents. Cora should chase after him and notify her insurance company, but really, what was the point?

The driver of the car behind Cora spied the vacant spot, pulled around her and took the space. By the time Cora managed to park elsewhere and walk back to Starbucks she was livid.

Frannie waved to her from across the parking lot and met her at the restaurant door.

"Arrrggghhh!" Cora said in greeting.

As they entered Starbucks together, Frannie blinked and asked, "What you all hot and bothered about?"

She told Frannie about the incident as they got coffee, a small black coffee of the day for Cora, a large mocha with extra sugar for Frannie. "You think he was really deaf?" Frannie asked, taking off her jacket and plopping down heavily into a chair at a small table.

"Who knows," Cora answered, seating herself across from Frannie. "I know he was *ignorant.*"

"Those are fighting words," Frannie said, raising an eyebrow.

"They are." Cora agreed. "I'm in a fighting *mood.*"

"Fed up?"

"And fired up!"

"Ready to tame the tiger!"

"Tackle demons!"

"How about angels?"

"That's a bit harder."

They burst into laughter.

Cora grew serious, "I didn't need more tension in my life, but maybe I ought to be thanking the guy. The distraction took me away from my self-imposed pity party. How are you doing, Frannie?"

"Better, better. I've been talking to one of my neighbors this week. 'Jennie,' I said, 'I'm having trouble getting accepted back here. Maybe you can tell me what I'm doing wrong.' She came over, we opened a bottle of wine, and we talked 'til all hours, and she's gonna put a word in for me here and there, pave the way for me with the others." She grinned and wiggled in her chair.

"I'm so glad to hear that." Cora smiled.

"I'm trying not to be so high-handed. Sometimes I even succeed. Sometimes I just can't stop being Frannie, though." She laughed boisterously, knocking her purse on the floor and bending to pick it up. "Bottom line, I think I'm putting that particular devil to rest. But enough about me, that's not why we're here."

"Okay then," Cora said, turning to be sure her own purse was securely hanging on the arm of her chair. "To angels."

"Uh, huh. Angel business. I take it something important has developed. We have to hurry, right?"

"Well, we should try to finish up in an hour." She pulled out her cell phone and checked the time. "I should fill you in before you tell me why you called. I talked to Father McGrath and had more communications from Angel."

"We gonna do all that in an hour?" Frannie lowered her chin and raised her eyebrows.

"Maybe not. Then we'll just have to make another date."

"But not on the phone?"

"Absolutely not." Cora shook her head. "You'll understand why."

So much had happened it was hard for Cora to believe it was only four days since the election. She told Frannie in detail about Father McGrath and his suggestion that she look at key events in her life. "He's bringing me some books so I can learn more about angels and spirits. His ideas about my mother's death and Angel thinking she's my mother are worth considering."

"Yeah, that's a thought." Frannie sipped coffee, then pinched her lower lip. "Máime…mother…your Mom…that makes some kind of sense. We can put that down, think about if it fits. You bring your pad and pen this time?"

Cora smiled, reaching into her purse for writing materials. "Sure did, all prepared." She jotted a note, more to keep her hands busy than to record the point.

Cora told Frannie about her visit with Bridey and the diary, and about Angel's latest messages.

"And then you called while I was reading her message. You always seem to call when I hear from her. It's getting spooky. You sure you're not working *with* Angel?" she asked with a grin and a chuckle.

"Anyway, Cisco doesn't know she answered me yet, but I'll tell him when he gets home. The reason I stopped you on the phone, I think her powers are limited to my house. She's like a visitor, who sees and hears what goes on, but doesn't travel with me and doesn't know what's in my mind. That's why she's questioning the diary, because she didn't know I had it until I brought it into the house, or where it's been or how I got it." As she talked, she pulled out the list she had made earlier.

"Why do you think that?"

"It was a sudden thought, but I was going over it again while driving here. I was thinking about past incidents, like we talked about, and it seems anything she might have reacted to she would have known about when we talked about problems at home or stuff that happened at work, things that she would have either seen or heard if she were there, like she hung around where I spent most of my time. I didn't want her to know we were talking about stopping her, figuring she wouldn't like it."

"Uh huh. I see what the hush-hush was all about, and yeah, you're right about that! But if she's taking vengeance for people who do nasty stuff to you, like we talked about, she didn't do that in your house. In fact, you're not even there when it happens. How'd you explain that?"

"I *can't* explain that." She shifted her eyes, looked at the floor, exhaled slowly, then looked at Frannie again. "Maybe I'm all wrong Frannie. But something is sure to hell going on!"

Frannie said, pointing her finger at Cora. "Did you bring that diary with you?"

"No. I figured Angel wouldn't like it. She doesn't know I'm telling any-one about her messages, except for Cisco. We know she's unpredictable and can be violent, but we don't know what sets her off. I'd rather not give her ammunition."

"You got my vote on that, girl! So what was it about, that part she told you to read?"

"You called right then Frannie, and all I could think about was stopping you from saying anything revealing and getting out of the house. I haven't read it yet."

Frannie nodded. "Uh huh, you did that right. But she didn't actually admit that was her diary, right?"

"No, but I think Cisco hit the nail on the head when he said Angel recognized it, even though he was being facetious at the time." Cora leaned back in her chair, and looked away. "I feel so out of my element here, Frannie. How do I deal with something I can't even identify, with powers I can't guess, something we think is attacking people I know? I feel helpless."

"The Cora I know is no way helpless. You're the most persistent wom-an I ever met—you never give up on anything. Here's what you got to do—you fight your way with what you got, your brain, your determi-nation, your skills, like research and planning stuff. You look at what we dig up and something will come to you—it always does. All you need is a nudge, that's all, and that's what Frannie's here for, to keep listen-ing and keep nudging. And some busy work." Frannie took a large gulp of coffee and winced. "Wow, that's still way too hot! I never learn to sip first. Let me see that list you made."

Frannie took the list and studied it while Cora leaned back in her chair, doodling on her note pad. Finally, Frannie placed the list on the corner of the table, where they could both see it.

"Okay, so…did you do this first thing on the list, make a list of punish-ments and all that?" Frannie asked, pointing to the first item on the list.

"No…I didn't start working on the list yet."

"Maybe we don't need *all* this anymore. Let's see…is there anything we can cross off? Is there any benefit in looking at what Angel did in the past?" Frannie asked.

Cora thought for a moment, pulling on a lock of hair behind her ear. "Only if an incident gives a clue as to who Angel is, and what makes her act."

"The idea is—" Frannie poked her finger at the item on the page, "you didn't think a *person* was behind the events when they happened. So if you think about why a *person* would react that way, it could tell us more about her."

"Okay," Cora nodded, jotting a note. "What about the wolf business? Bridey's story about the murders at Saint James involved a wolf. A wolf keeps coming up. I don't think that could be coincidence, do you?"

Frannie flashed a grin. "Here's where your girlfriend gets to show off. I'm real good on the internet, and I got time on my hands." She reached into her purse and pulled out a bulky printout.

Cora thumbed through the pages: pictures of wolves, comparisons to dogs, characteristics, habits, lore, and more. "There's too much here for me to absorb. Why don't you tell me the high points?"

"What you said, about you saw a wolf, not a dog…you still think that?"

"I do, based on what I saw and researched before all this began."

"Okay then, here's what I think are the *salient* points. I've been reading that wolves are being seen in Wisconsin and in Illinois too. So you're not off base there. What I think, we have three choices here: one, there can be a real *live* wolf hiding out there, no relation to anything happening to you, just living out there somewhere; two, Angel can be *manifesting* as a wolf, to accomplish whatever she wants to do; three, it can be a wolf *spirit*, a separate spiritual entity, not Angel at all." Frannie grinned proudly.

"Let's assume it's *not* a real wolf—that leaves two choices. Do you have an opinion?" Cora asked.

"Uh huh. Not an opinion, but comments. There's this story, by Algernon Blackwood, called 'Running Wolf,' about a wolf spirit. You should check that out, see how it fits."

Frannie leaned toward Cora. "What I'm talking about, especially now after you told me what Father McGrath said, is I read stories of wolves as substitute mothers. You know, Rudyard Kipling and Mowgli? Mowgli was lost in the jungle and brought up by a pack of wolves, you remember that? And the story of Romulus and Remus, the twin brothers that founded Rome and were suckled by a she wolf? You ever see that sculpture? You heard the expression, raised by wolves? It's all myth, but what was it made people buy into it if they didn't think it could happen?"

Cora raised an eyebrow. "I never related wolves to mothers. That is curious." She scribbled on her pad, murmuring, "Read 'Running Wolf', Blackwood, and visit wolf farm."

"Wolf farm?" Frannie dropped her chin and looked at Cora.

"Yes, there's a private wolf farm about six miles south of here. I want to see living wolves up close, and talk to the owner about wolf habits, if one could be living out here, how they live in the wild, stuff like that." Cora smiled. "I love what you've found. I assume I can take this with me?" She held up Frannie's printout.

"Absolutely. Don't take it in the house though!" Frannie cautioned in alarm.

"Certainly not!" Cora promised and flashed a grin.

"Next…." said Frannie, pointing to the list again.

Cora read, "Is Angel real, spirit or delusion?"

Frannie leaned back in her chair with a little wiggle of excitement and fluttered the fingers of both hands in the air. "Doesn't seem to be much doubt after her latest tricks, does it? But I didn't know that before I came here, so what I did is, I looked online about how angels and spirits communicate with the living. There's a ton of stuff out there—all different theories, but I go along with what Father McGrath told you. If Angel is real, she's likely a spirit. I was gonna tell you all that on the phone, but now you already went there when you told me about Father McGrath. But that's good…we got to the same place."

"So you agree I don't have a guardian angel, but a spirit—a ghost," Cora summed up.

Frannie nodded vigorously. "Uh huh. Or a spirit guide—they're the ones that *protect* people. But here's the thing: ghosts and spirits and guides, they all do things different, and they got different motives. Then there's poltergeists, the guys that move things and throw clocks on the floor. Your Angel, she seems to be a little bit of every kind of thing. This stuff is a whole field of knowledge here, but it's all theory, nothing proved. It would take years to try to figure out what we're doing on our own… we got that kind of time?"

"So I should get another expert, you mean? If experts think so differently, how do I know who to pick?"

Frannie waved her arm dismissively. "I'm just letting you know. Let's wait until you get those books from your priest, see what they say, then decide."

"That makes sense." Cora nodded.

"One thing turned up good to know, about poltergeists. In more than one place, it says that poltergeists link to an *earthly energy source* that lets them do what they do. So when there's a poltergeist around, things like electric lights, telephones, TVs, like that, go all goofy."

"Yes?" said Cora, frowning, missing the point.

"And Wi-Fi, and wireless, and…you fill in the blank girl."

"And computers."

Frannie beamed. "You got it!"

"Ah—" said Cora, "I see—and computers."

"Uh huh." Frannie grinned. "Looks like we got us a Cyber Angel!"

Cora burst out laughing. "That's a first, isn't it?"

"Say, I'm hungry," Frannie said, glancing toward the counter. "Are you hungry? If we're gonna still be here a while, I need sustenance."

"Sounds like a plan," Cora agreed. They got up and purchased bakery, a sweet roll for Frannie, and a bagel for Cora. They also refilled their coffee cups.

After returning to the table and taking a few bites, Frannie set her roll down and asked, "Did you ever try to contact Angel before, you know, with a séance or Ouija board or something like that?"

"No, I don't believe in that stuff. I did try reading tarot cards for a while but I gave it up pretty quickly," Cora said, after swallowing, taking a sip of hot coffee, and wiping her mouth.

"Why'd you do that?"

"I got too good. I kept seeing things I didn't want to see, nasty stuff, sometimes about people close to me."

Frannie thought about that, rolling her eyes, then said, "Well, this here Angel found her own way to communicate—via your computer. Next," Frannie fired, pointing a finger at Cora, "what about the mother business?"

"Well, I guess my mother's death hit me harder than I thought, but I've always been good at coping, like with avoidance and tincture of time. I make myself think about something else, or make myself busy, and eventually things get better."

"What about closure?"

"That's a buzzword, and in my opinion a lot of crap," said Cora, shaking her head. "The important thing is accepting the situation and moving on. You don't need the involvement of others to do that. And you don't let the past wreck your life, waiting to fill in the blanks."

"Do you have any guilt feelings? Might be throwing you off subconsciously?"

Cora set her bagel down, let out a slow breath and shifted her eyes. "Doesn't everyone have guilt feelings? When I took care of Mom, I was good to her, but I was bossy, and underneath I resented the responsibility. I wanted her last years to be happy, but the time I spent taking care of her didn't leave time to enjoy *being* with her. I'm sure she picked up on some of that." Tears began to gather.

"What're you talking about here? Think you're Superwoman? You know you did all you could do," Frannie said, as she fished a tissue out of her oversized handbag and handed it to Cora.

Cora took the tissue and held it, finishing her thought. "No one but me. I had to pick between hard things, and I'm not sure I made the right choices. But what's done is done." She wiped the tears.

"But Cisco and Father McGrath think this might be bothering you enough that it comes out you imagining Angel. You doing that?" Frannie searched Cora's eyes for a reaction.

"After today I can hardly think that anymore. She's got to be real. But what does Angel have to do with my mother?" Cora shook her head.

Frannie watched without comment. "Okay, let's leave that, move on. Why is Angel acting up *now?*"

Eyes on her plate and playing with the remaining bagel, Cora said, "Father McGrath told me spirits would be selfish, would want something. What could she want? If she's been protecting me all these years, what did she get from that? And what made her re-energize lately? The only thing I can think of is my mother's death. But if Angel thinks *she's* my mother, what would Mom's death have to do with anything?"

Neither of them had an answer.

"Well, let's go on…why 'Máime' and 'Darlin'?"

Cora shrugged her shoulders. "Like we said, referring to herself as my mother. That's very confusing. I have no idea."

Frannie pushed her empty plate away and tapped her pen on the table, consulting the list and mumbling. "The wolf...we talked about that. The diary...we talked about that...you think it's Angel's?"

"I think she recognizes it at least. How many murdered dead girls do you think are out there that could be Angel?" She shrugged her shoulders.

"Well, when are you going to read it then?"

"As soon as I get home." Cora crumpled her napkin and put it on her empty plate. Glancing around the room, she noticed tables filling and a line forming at the checkout counter. It seemed the rush hour crowd was arriving.

"Lastly, prioritize, what to f-ing do first—getting a little colorful there, aren't we Darlin'? We're doing that now...." Frannie looked up. "So, what've we got left?"

"Down to three items. One, analyze prior incidents and look for clues. Two, learn more about spirits. Three, brainstorm ideas about why she might call herself my mother." She held up fingers as she counted off the new list.

"You're going to read that diary, and don't forget those books from Father McGrath. So what do you want me to do?" Frannie leaned back in her chair, placed her hands on both knees, and rubbed them while watching Cora.

"Let's see. I'll make a spreadsheet, with, what, four columns: describe incident; ask why Angel would do this; what was going on in my personal life when it happened; clues."

"Good plan," said Frannie, nodding approval.

"Some of that information about wolves was pretty interesting. Do you think there's more, now we're considering a spirit wolf?" Cora suggested.

"I can dig further. Do you want me to go to that wolf farm you mentioned?"

"I'd like to go too, but let's let it go for a few days. We have enough to do."

"Okay then. So you concentrate on analyzing incidents, Father McGrath's books whenever he gets them to you, and the diary. Meanwhile, I'll try to find out more about spirits on the internet. I want to read about spirits manifesting as animals, in case we change our minds and decide Angel turns herself into a wolf. Maybe we want to check demons while we're at it?"

"God, I hope not! Let's not go there unless we're forced to, right?"

"Right." Frannie looked up, her face beaming. "We're done!" She opened her cell phone to check the time. "We got two minutes left."

"Oh Frannie, it's so much easier with your help. I don't know how to thank you." Cora's emotion showed on her face.

"You don't need to give me no thanks," Frannie said. "We're a *team.*"

Oblivious to nearby coffee shop patrons, the incongruous pair high-fived, grinning.

Chapter 17

An unfamiliar car was parked in front of Cora's house when she got home. The meeting with Frannie had encouraged her to some extent, but the stress of the last few days left her exhausted.

Shit! The last thing I want right now is company. This has been…I just want to curl up on the couch…throw a blanket over me…forget everything….

Entering the house, she recognized Father McGrath's voice. He probably brought the books he promised. She panicked.

What are they talking about? Angel!

She hurried into the kitchen. "Good afternoon, Father," she said, unsmiling, setting her purse in a corner and hanging up her keys. Today he was dressed in full clerical garb, she noted, and the stop at their house was likely one of many calls. Good—perhaps he would be in a hurry to leave.

"I just offered Father a cup of coffee and put on a fresh pot. It's almost done. You want some?" asked Cisco.

Cora groaned inwardly. Father had to leave before he said something dangerous. How was that going to happen if he was waiting for coffee and chatting? Certainly he would bring up their talk, if he hadn't already.

Maybe she could distract him. Desperately trying to figure out what to do, she bustled around the kitchen, pulled things out, put a frying pan on the stove, and began to slice vegetables and meat.

Cisco looked at Cora and narrowed his eyes. "Can't you let that go and sit with us?"

"I'll be done in a minute. Let me get dinner started," she said, and kept chopping.

"Maybe I should get going," Father said, glancing back and forth as if sensing tension.

"I'm sure we're keeping you from something important," Cora agreed. "It was good of you to bring the books, but if you're busy, you don't need to stay to be polite."

"Cora," Cisco said succinctly, with another puzzled glance at Cora. "Father was just saying it was a relief to get *away* from the church for a while, and he'd love to have coffee and some of your cookies."

"Oh...sorry...I didn't mean to be rude. I thought I'd taken enough of his time the other day, and now here he is doing another favor." She didn't look up from her work at the counter.

"Not at all," Father said. "I haven't had the occasion to delve into parapsychology for years. It's been an interesting diversion. I could point out some particularly informative sections of the books...," he began.

"No!" Cora interrupted, and then tried to cover her involuntary outburst. "I'm sure you marked the pages. To tell you the truth Father, it's been a difficult day and I'm not sure I'm up to discussing this now. Do you think you could leave the books and I'll call you after I read them?"

Cisco set a cup of coffee in front of Father, ignoring her words. If he had any idea she was trying to get Father to leave, he wasn't going along with it.

"We were talking before you got home..." Cisco began.

"Do you want salad with the casserole?" Cora interrupted again, before Cisco could say more, turning away to open a cabinet and retrieve a casserole dish.

"Sure. Say, would you like to have dinner with us?" Cisco invited, holding out an open hand toward Father. "Cora always cooks too much. If there's leftovers she doesn't have to cook the next night. I suspect she does it on purpose." He laughed and Father joined him.

"I'll take a pass, but can I have a rain check?" Father said. Cora let out a slow breath in relief.

"You're sure now? It's no trouble," Cisco said, waving an arm again in invitation. Cora said nothing. Cisco gave her another irritated glance, probably wondering why she was acting so unwelcoming.

"Coffee and cookies will be just fine," Father said.

"Oh, yeah...the cookies. Sorry...I forgot." Cisco went to the cookie jar and piled a mound of cookies on a plate. "You don't mind my hands, I hope."

"No, that's fine." Father tried to catch Cora's eye. "I was telling Cisco I thought these books might help figure out how to put an end to your troubles with this spirit."

Damn it!

He couldn't have said anything worse! There was no point in avoiding the subject and no telling how Angel would react now he had mentioned putting an end to her—unless Cora could salvage the situation by trying to make it look like the books would be helpful instead of threatening.

Cora put down her knife. She turned off the stove and took a seat across from the priest, looking him in the eye fondly. He was happily crunching a cookie, his cheeks full.

"Maybe we don't want to put an *end* to Angel, Father," she said. "Maybe we just want to understand her so I can work *with* her instead of against her."

Father and Cisco exchanged a look. Father swallowed and reached for another cookie. "That wasn't what I thought we were trying to do. I thought you sensed threats."

She shifted her eyes away, then resolutely back to his. "Well, that's changed. I just want to understand her better. Will these books help me do that?"

"Perhaps. But in my opinion you should decide if your problems are exaggerated reality or figure out what it is this entity wants from you and find a way to stop it. These are great, by the way," he said, holding up a cookie.

Cora turned away without reply, at a loss for what else to do. Her efforts to save the situation were making it worse.

Jumping back in, Cisco frowned and shook his head. "As we were saying before Cora got home, maybe this is all blown out of proportion. You seem to be encouraging her idea there could be some *entity*, as you say, visiting her. I find it hard to believe you would do that."

"Why should you find that hard to believe? I'm a priest. Who else should know about the afterlife?" Father gave Cisco a gentle smile. "Right now I'm speaking as your friend, not as a priest. Cora told me you thought she exaggerated the situation. I'm not convinced either way, but I do think she *believes* it's real. We should be helping her assess her problem and deal with it."

Cisco's distorted smile indicated he was dubious. "What would make you think it was real?"

"Some facts point to real experiences. Didn't you witness one this morning, the message on the computer you told me about earlier?" Father asked.

Cisco glanced at Cora before answering. "We thought that could have been a hacker. We never got an answer, but Cora was sure it was a *message*."

Cora was silent. Would it make things better or worse if she told them about Angel's latest message and what she now thought about the diary?

"I bet Cora thinks a hacker is improbable, and I'm of a mind to agree with her."

"You can't seriously think there is an evil spirit in the house!" Cisco exclaimed, waving his arms.

"No, but neither can I say I've excluded it. I hope when Cora reads the chapters I marked a thought or memory will prompt what we should do."

Cisco and Father glanced at Cora, who wasn't taking part in the conversation. She had to convince Angel she was on her side. If she didn't tell the others what happened that morning, would Angel suspect she was harboring secrets and become angry—and dangerous?

Cora lifted her head and looked at Father, then held Cisco's eye. "She did answer the message. She answered it after you left, Cisco."

"Right," Cisco said, shaking his head. "How did she do that?"

"When I went upstairs after you left, the office door was closed. You didn't close it, did you?"

"I don't think so. It drifts shut sometimes, though."

"It drifts over, not shut. Not clicked shut so I have to turn the handle to open it, right?"

"Uh...yeah," he admitted.

"Well, I had to turn the handle. And when I opened the door, the diary was lying open on my desk. I didn't put it there—I put it in a drawer. But when I entered the room it was open by my laptop." She crossed her arms over her chest.

"Maybe you forgot..." Cisco began.

"I didn't forget, Cisco! Please believe me and listen. I *know* this!" She held his eye. "And on my computer screen was a new message. It said 'Yes. Start here Darlin'."

The color drained from Cisco's face, and he appeared to be struggling for a logical explanation. "If it turns out you're telling stories for some strange reason, I'm not going to take it very well."

Cora narrowed her eyes and looked directly into Cisco's. "I'm not telling stories Cisco. That's what happened."

"Maybe someone snuck in…" Cisco began. He was interrupted by Cora's snort and obdurate expression.

Father cleared his throat, reminding them he was still in the room. "What do you think Angel's message meant?"

"This time I'm sure I *know* what she wants. She wants me to read the diary, starting at the page she opened it to. There must be something she wants me to find in the diary."

"What's that?" asked Cisco.

"I haven't had time to read it yet." She threw her hands up and shook her head. "Frannie called and I had to run right out. With everything going on, I almost forgot I was meeting her today." She hoped Angel wouldn't catch the fib, and wondered if Father would figure out that the diary might belong to Angel. She looked at him to check his reaction.

Father McGrath pinched his lips between thumb and forefinger, deep in thought. Finally he said, "In view of the new message, I think we should assume there's a spiritual presence and deal with it. But I don't think it's wise to continue investigating on our own. We should get help."

"Do we really have to get someone else involved?" Cora asked, frowning. "Shouldn't we wait until something really threatening happens? All she's asked me to do is read a diary. How threatening is that?"

He placed both hands on the table and looked directly into her eyes. "The first issue here is establishing her existence. Once we accept she exists, we have to act, because we suspect she caused harm to others. We don't know how much was done already, or if or when another awful thing will happen. We should prevent that, but we have no idea how."

"I'm reluctant to call anyone in too. I agree with Cora," Cisco said, waving his arms to emphasize his opinion. "We've done all right so far. Why take that step? Even if we do, who do you go to for this sort of thing? These people who investigate the supernatural don't seem very credible to me."

"*You* haven't been hurt so far, and Cora thinks this entity is protecting, not threatening her. But I doubt Valerie would agree the situation is harmless." Father looked over the top of his glasses. "No—we have to act. There are reliable people in the church. Let me make some calls to see if I can find someone, and we'll stop this Angel. I'll start as soon as I get home."

Cora tried one more time. "Can't we wait until after I read the diary? I can read it tomorrow. Surely we can wait that long?"

"Why don't you bring it down and we'll read it now," Cisco suggested.

Cora dropped her chin into her hand, her elbow resting on the table. "Cisco, I'm just so exhausted. It's been the craziest day, maybe the craziest day of my *life*. I just don't think I can do another thing. If I'm going to tackle the diary I need a clear head, but I have to have a break. I just can't...not today."

Cisco looked at Father. "You heard her, Father. I think we wait a day, okay?"

Father nodded reluctantly. "I'll wait for your call, then, but no later than two tomorrow, all right? That should give you enough time, and I'll have the afternoon to reach people."

Father stood up, and began to put on his jacket. "Read the diary first, but check the books I brought too, at least the pages I marked with sticky notes." He zipped his jacket, patted his pockets, and pulled out a set of keys. "I loved the cookies."

Cora followed Father to the door, relieved he was finally leaving. "Thanks so much, Father. I hope you're not disturbed by our differences of opinion."

The priest smiled. "How can I be of help to anyone if I can't take a little disagreement in stride? Talk to you tomorrow."

As Cora opened the door, she heard a rustle and noticed movement in the shrubbery beside the front entrance. "What was that?" She startled and jerked back into the doorway, tense and wired after her emotion-packed day.

Cisco, who had been beside her, stepped out onto the front stoop and looked around. "I don't see anything, Cora," he said. "You're really jumpy."

"She's got reason to be jumpy, don't you think?" Father McGrath said, joining Cisco outside.

Cora glanced toward the shrubbery again nervously, but, not seeing anything out of the ordinary, stood next to Cisco as they watched Father walk toward his car. As he reached for the door handle, a large animal darted silently from the shrubbery. Catching the motion out of the corner of his eye, Father turned and jumped away in alarm, too late to prevent the animal from clamping its jaws around his ankle. He screamed in fright and pain as the creature pulled him off balance and he fell down on the driveway.

Horrified, Cora recognized the wolf, who released the hold on Father's ankle and now stood over the priest; mouth open wide, teeth bared in an aggressive grimace, it snarled and arched its neck. Father attempted to scramble away, screaming and throwing his arms protectively in front of him. The wolf slashed at his arms and Father pulled them away reflexively, leaving him momentarily exposed, and the wolf forced its body over him, ripping at Father's jacket, shirt, and clerical collar, trying to reach his throat, as Father writhed, uttering guttural screams, struggling frantically to protect his head and neck and to push the animal away.

Cora screamed, "No! Stop! Leave him alone!"

She ran to the wolf and began pounding her fists on its back, thinking of nothing but stopping the attack. Behind her she heard Cisco yell, "Cora! No! Get away from that wolf! It'll kill you!" He rushed to her, grabbed her around the waist with both arms, and pulled her away.

"Let me go!" She twisted wildly, broke away from Cisco and with both hands grabbed handfuls of fur on the back of the wolf's neck, trying to pull it off the priest. "Get away, Cisco! I mean it! I'll be okay. Call 911!" she shrieked.

Cisco cried, "We need a weapon!" and ran into the house.

Cora forced her hands around the animal's neck, interwove her fingers to lock her arms around it, and buried her face in its musty fur, straining to lift it off the priest with all her strength, heedless of personal danger.

The three struggled, Cora wrapping herself around the beast, fighting to maintain her footing and not be pulled over. Hugging it, she could sense its immense power, feel its muscles pull powerfully with each reach, each snap of its jaws, feel the chest expand with every raspy breath, smell the foul odor of its mouth. Beneath the fur, its rib cage felt thin and bony, the fur soft but dull-looking, like a starving dog.

All the while Father screamed, thrashed, batted at the wolf's face, jerked away from slashes to his hands and arms, while the wolf continued its attempts to rip at his throat.

Cisco rushed back, brandishing a golf club, watching for a way to hit the wolf without hitting Cora.

The wolf lifted its head and snarled, snapping its jaws wildly from side to side, avoiding Cora behind its back, and squirming powerfully to break her hold. Having succeeded in dislodging the wolf from the priest, Cora released it, took a step back, and stood facing it with heaving breaths, arms out and ready to grab it again if it resumed its attack.

The wolf took a stance between Cora and Father, and snarled again, staring at her, ears erect. Cora reached out an arm to stop Cisco, preventing him from swinging the club, sensing the animal was done. It backed away a step, lowered its tail, and looked from Cora to Father bleeding on the ground, then back to Cora. It looked toward the house, up at the second floor, as if watching something in the window of Cora's office.

Father clutched his neck and moaned, struggled to draw a wheezing breath, blood flowing between his fingers and dripping off his arms.

Now the wolf noticed Cisco with the golf club, lifted its tail, turned its attention to him, and moved toward him menacingly. Cisco raised the club and waited.

Cora watched the action unfold as if she were a spectator, her heart pounding.

The wolf slowly turned its attention back to the office window. It tilted its massive head to the side, hesitated, took a slow step back, turned, then raced for the farm at the end of their block, and disappeared from view.

Cora dropped to the ground beside the now unconscious priest and put pressure against his neck with her bare hand. "He's bleeding—bad! Damn it! Got to stop it! Oh, my God! Get me a towel! Call 911! Jesus, please!"

Cora looked up and saw a few neighbors, drawn by the commotion, assembling in the street, saw Jean from next door running out of her house—thank God, a nurse!— and she heard a distant siren. Help was already on its way.

Come back to Erin, Mavourneen, Mavourneen,
Come back, Aroon, to the land of thy birth
Come with the shamrocks and spring-time Mavourneen,
And its Killarney shall ring with our mirth…
Oh, may the Angels O wakin' and sleepin',
Watch o'er my bird in the land far away
And it's my prayers will consign to their keepin'
Care o' my jewel by night and by day…

    —Charlotte Alington Barnard (Claribel),
     "Come Back to Erin," 1868

Mavourneen

1898

Chapter 18

My mam named me Mavourneen, one fine thing she did for me, at least. Mavourneen...what a grand name 'tis! It translates to *My Darling*, from an old Gaelic word meaning *delight*. It's pronounced Mah-VAH-neen, with the accent on the *vah* part, and when you say it, it sounds a wee bit like *my darling*, and it suits me, it does. Yes, it truly is a grand name, but also 'tis hard for people these modern days to get their mouths around, and so I am called Meg...and that suits me too.

Packey, now, he calls me Mavourneen, especially in tender moments. The Irish are big on nicknames, they are, so although his given name is Patrick, 'tis Packey he is called. I have my own nicknames for him, but only in private. The boys would have a bit of a gay old time if ever they heard the names *I* call him. But a sweet darling man he is, for all of that, at least to me. At the quarries, he's giving the orders, and 'tis another thing, for sure.

My mam is always complaining. "Meg, there ya go lass, with your nose in a book agin!" she'll say. "Don't ya know there's plenty of work that needs takin' care of, an' ya surely won't be expectin' *me* to do it all now. With child or not, ya need to be pullin' yer weight an' helpin' yer pore ole' Máime, who raised you from a babe an' all. Sure and those jelly jars wouldn't be being too heavy for ya to lift; cain't ya put them on the shelves where they're belongin'?"

That would be just like Mam, ungrateful and bossy. She never can stand to be seeing anyone taking her own sweet time. It's not as if I don't pull my weight as she says. Reason I'm here is to help her do her work and listen to her guff when no one else will be bothered. I may move slow these days, but I know what I'm doing and I'm smart about it. She just can't stand when I stop moving. It makes her bonkers, it does, even when the work's all done. She's fluttering around all the time, looking busy, but she's not getting anything done, just *wasting* time. Her mouth, though, she makes real good use of *that*.

Mam changed her mind of a sudden, and turned to me with her hands on her hips like she does, and ordered, "Go on down on Archey Road an' take the 'lectric train to Lemont an' fetch me some tea from the general store. Mr. Bell here at the Sag store don't have that extra choice morning tea I like, but they have it in Lemont." She went into her bedroom and returned with her purse and handed me a dollar in coins.

"While you're at it, pick up some cookies an' cocoa powder. I'll be baby-sittin' Josie's boys, an' there's no bakin' oven in these rooms. I'm sure I'll niver know why these Bells can't provide a cook stove for their boarders."

"Now Máime," I told her. "We've been through this. They can't be pipin' gas lines into every room an' the parlor heater is more practical. If you had a cook stove, you'd be complainin' how cold the winters were without a parlor heater. You should be thankful you have a toilet with a pull chain an' a bathin' tub with a water heater. You're better off than us, as we don't have indoor plumbing on the farm, ya know. An' you don't *need* to be cookin'. You can eat in the hotel dining room, as it comes with your board."

Truth be told I was happy to be getting away from her whining and welcomed the errand. So I grabbed my bag, put on my bonnet, and went out.

The dollar Mam gave me didn't cover what she wanted me to buy. When I figured it in my head, the tea was fifty-five cents, forty-five cents for the cocoa, the cookies twenty cents, and the fare for the electric line five cents each way, which meant I'd have to dig into my own purse. It surely was expensive to keep Mam in her own rooms, but Mick had put his foot down about her staying on the farm, and Mam had given Sally no peace when she lived with them, making their lives full o' the misery. Now that Packey and I are living on the farm too, it's worth the cost to put Mam up at the hotel. It would just about kill her to admit it, but

I'm sure she's just as happy to be back in town, as she never liked it on the farm from the beginning. It was too much work for the likes of her.

I walked out the door and up to the end of the block to catch the electric streetcar. It came every half hour, only a short wait. Mam had put me in a mood to spend the waiting time dwelling on troubles.

Mam surely had a great many irritating ways about her, like talking as if she just come over from Ireland, which she does all the time. She was born right here in Sag Bridge and never stepped foot in the Auld Country in her life. Still, she talks like Ireland is the whole world. I don't understand it. The Irish are so looked down on; why ever would she want to be always reminding everyone she's Irish? Most Irish hide where they're from so they can get on in the world and not be stuck to swinging a shovel in the quarry, like my Packey.

My Packey's a fine man and I love him like nobody's business, but he's been known to protest that being Irish, 'tis assumed shoveling or swinging a pickaxe are the *only* things he can do. He must take the same jobs other Micks do and would never be thought suited for a more skilled position. Well, the Irish are *politicians* of course…but then that's another thing entirely, and not for the likes of my Packey. He's a natural leader, but he doesn't have a political bone in his body. Nor do I for that matter.

I wished we had our own place, but we're happy enough living with Sally and Mick on Pa's farm, at least until after this little one is born. The newspapers say the hard times are supposed to be over, but that's not true for us yet. Since Pa died we can't hardly get all the work done. With Uncle Denny working on the railroad, and my babe due soon, and Packey's no farmer—it's more than Mick and Sally can do. The money I made working at Field's would have helped, but with the babe and all I just can't be traveling to Chicago every day.

When I lived downtown I got away from this dreary place. I wished I was still working in Marshall Field's grand store. Although his partner thought him a fool, Mr. Field knew there was no future in Sag Bridge and he was smart to leave this town behind. I couldn't help but wish it had worked out as well for me. I miss buying grand clothes and hearing grand music at the Chicago Symphony and all the exciting things they don't have here.

And oh, how glorious the Fair was! I know I'll never see the likes of it again all my born days, the crowds and the exhibits and all. Sparkling White City, white buildings and white lights shimmering; over 100,000 bulbs it is told! It cost dear to go, it did, but as soon as the dates were set I started to put a bit away for the day and sure didn't I save enough for Packey and me, and I'll never regret that, I won't, although some thought it a foolish waste.

An age of technology, they called it. I can hardly wait for the future, when things like a kinetoscope will be in every town, and make pictures move on a screen, *pictures* that can go over and over again, all the day long, not only when the actors or singers are ready.

One of the new inventions will make jobs for *women* to get into business. A Remington typewriter it was called, the same company that makes guns. A man let me try it, pushing buttons he called keys, to make words on paper, and I know I can learn to work it and someday I will sit at a desk and make words flow like magic without ever touching the paper.

There was even an Irish village, a reconstructed village made to look just like a real one in Ireland, with a huge Irish castle, and you could see the whole fair if you climbed to the top. Every visitor got a piece of genuine sod from Ireland. I gave mine to Mam.

Mam refused to touch it. She backed away from me a step and put her hands on her hips. "What is that dirty lump?" she asked me, her face all wrinkled like an apple left too long in the sun.

"That is sod, Máime—genuine sod from the Auld Country, like you're always talking about."

"Oh, you're just full of the Blarney," she told me. I don't know if she ever believed me or not.

So I came back here when I married Packey, to spend all my days and nights in this shabby little town, where the biggest excitement is the Saturday prizefights, and the only other place to go is Smokey Row in Lemont, that dirty old place near the canal with all the bars and brothels. That's not for decent folk the likes of me, but 'tis for the men in town and those that come from all over. To be fair, I guess Smokey Row brings people to spend their money. But not people I care to associate with, at all. 'Tis not much here for fun for the ladies, and it's missing Chicago I am for that, but 'tis worth it to be with my Packey.

The streetcar approached, and I picked up my bag and stepped into the car. I saw my friend Maggie waving to catch my eye. I squeezed in beside her, carefully lowering myself and holding the back of the seat. Getting seated was an accomplishment with my bulging belly.

"Here come Meggie an' Maggie," our friends used to say when we were in school together. I was happy to see Maggie. Truth be told I would be happy to see any friend who wouldn't be putting an added burden on me. Now that I was out on the farm and Maggie moved to Forest Springs three miles down the line, it was only seldom we got to talk. I missed having a friend to share things with, a woman friend. I had Sally, of course, and she's a good sister, but not someone you pick, someone who sees things same like you do and makes no difference if you have faults.

"How are you feeling, Meg?" she greeted me, scooting toward the window to make room for me. "It must be taxin' bein' so heavy now that it's getting so warm an' all."

"It surely is," I said, arranging my skirts. "Right now 'tis just a relief to get away from Mam an' sit myself down."

"She still bellyachin' all the time, even now she has her own rooms an' all?"

"Even worse, it is. Sally don't visit Mam but once a month, an' I go every Monday. So 'tis like she saves up all her moanin' for Monday an' that's all I hear from the moment I arrive an' she doesn't leave off 'til I go home again."

I noticed myself talking like people in Sag again. When I lived in the city I tried to hide my brogue, but sure I'm right back to the sing-songy Irish way of speaking. It seems natural, it does, hearing the sounds from my own lips and the mouths of everyone else around.

"The divil's in that woman, for sure," said Maggie, shaking her head from side to side.

"I guess Máime wanted more out of life. Her family was shanty Irish, just about, although she always made them out to be somethin' better. When she married Pa an' moved to the farm, why, he was part English, an' she was ashamed of that. She forever put on her high horse, an' no wonder she turned into an old biddy," I told Maggie, and let out a long breath.

"An' are ya happy to be back in the Sag? Do you miss the exciting life of the city at all?" she asked me.

"Truth is, I do miss it, Maggie. Not just the excitement, but the comfort of it. The fine big buildings an' modern conveniences made life easier. Life is so much harder out here on the farm. But tell me, are ya goin' to the picnic on the Fourth?" I asked.

"I wouldn't miss it for the world an' all! Is your whole family goin'?" Maggie asked.

"Oh sure an' they are," I said. "Sally an' Mick will bring us in the wagon."

"What about your máthair?" she asked me.

"Oh, we couldn't leave Mam out, much as we might like to. She'll walk about an' keep herself busy talkin' an' tryin' to avoid Aunt Catherine. She'll wear the same navy dress with the dots—it's the only one looks half decent on her short dumpy body. It's a great opportunity for her, to complain to people who may actually listen, since they don't hear her every time, like me. Sure an' she'll enjoy it to no end."

We chatted on merrily, wondering if the Quarrymen would win the base ball game at the picnic, and Maggie asking if the men would set up a ring for fights. If they do, I know Packey will be there, as he is one of the best amateur prizefighters hereabouts.

The car arrived in Lemont and Maggie and I went our separate ways. I was sad to see her go. Before heading to the general store, I took a wee break and wandered toward the canal. Fortunately, the spring rains were done, and instead of a mire of mud and horse droppings I only had the dust to deal with. I climbed onto the wooden sidewalk and followed it as far as it went, to save my skirts and make walking easier. The alley by the drug store had a terrible stench on this warm day. At its far end I noticed Mrs. McCauley was still allowing her pigs and chickens to run free in the garbage. We needed a law to stop that sort of thing, we did.

I had to pass through Smokey Row, but this time of day was safe enough. There were no drunks loitering in front of the establishments, and 'twas quiet as I walked by, but it would be quite another matter come evening.

The sidewalk ended and I made my slow and waddling way down the street, struggling with my skirts dragging. I grumbled once again about how inconvenient women's styles were. The big puffy sleeves were hot as all get-out in the summer and the long skirts picked up dirt. And bustles, well those made no sense at all. If I had anything to do with setting fashion, there'd be a lot of changes, there would.

Three barges were tied up at the canal dock, and about a dozen mules resting over by the towpath. Dockworkers carried boxes into the tunnels that ran under the streets direct to the businesses that ordered the goods. Other barges waited their turn, and in the distance I saw grain being loaded. This early in the summer, of course, there would be little farm produce to transport.

I knew the tunnels saved carting heavy boxes and barrels to street level and back down to basements, but I wondered about how far they went. I peeked into a tunnel once and it seemed to open to a vast dank maze that disappeared into darkness.

I had little time for thinking about tunnels, though, and soon dragged myself to the general store to make my purchases and catch the car back to the Sag, where Mam would be waiting, of course, with some other complaint she dreamed up while I was away.

Chapter 19

Back at Mam's place, I tried to make everything to her liking, and listened to more crabbing while I was at it. Didn't the store charge too much for the tea—regardless of the fact I paid the difference myself—and was that the only kind of cocoa powder the store had? And the cookies, didn't they have those ones with the white in the middle, the ones the boys liked best, and whatever possessed me to buy the ones I did?

After I left Mam at the hotel, I took my sweet time walking home to our farm with my duck-like gait. I'd spent enough time hurrying today, so I welcomed the opportunity.

Strolling down the dirt road, I thought about what sort of mother *I* would make. Máime was a fine example of the kind of mother I would *not* be, a burden on her own family, who could barely tolerate her. Her sister now, Aunt Catherine, she and Mam had not talked for years.

Truth be told, I had to admit children doted on Mam. Adults had no patience for her irritating ways and incessant jibber-jabbering, so she spent more time with children. The little ones loved being minded by Mam, because their families were too busy getting on in the world to spend time on things that interest children. Mam did what children liked. She took them on long walks where they wanted to go, and let them pick what to talk about, and paid attention to their every word. She played as many games as they wanted, and made their favorite foods when they visited.

Mam prattled to them about the Auld Country, as they had not heard tell of the Auld Country before. She would take down her thin gray hair and show how she braided it, wound it at the base of her neck, and pinned it in place with thick tortoiseshell hairpins. I'll never know why but even young boys watched this with interest.

She told stories about things like the cat-o-nine-tails her Pa used when she was a bad little girl. I never believed that story about the cat-o-nine-tails, but I did wonder how Mam came by it. She would go to her closet, take down a box and there the awful thing was, rolled up in newspaper. The children would listen, eyes wide and mouths open, as she showed it to them and told them that if the boys were really bad Pa would put a pin in the end of each tail. Oh, the little ones loved Mam and her tall tales, they did.

But *I* will be the *best* máthair. My Darlin' will feel *real* love—not like Mam, only because no one else will have her—and she will grow up loving life like her Pa, and have lots of friends. We will enjoy being together, and when I'm Mam's age, my Darlin' will *want* to be with me, not like a chore to be done with.

I smiled and rested my hands on my belly over my Darlin' and talked to her quietly. "I know you already, my little girl, I just feel it, an' I have an uncanny way of knowin' such things. I will pick the perfect name, one you will thank me for callin' you. I can barely wait to meet you, my Darlin'."

I dragged along even slower when I reached the lane to our farmhouse, the same house I grew up in, savoring the last few quiet minutes alone—but not alone, with my little girl. In truth, I may have been stalling too because I was dreading more work that would surely greet me when I got home.

It was near to suppertime when I entered our kitchen. Sally was bustling about, like she always does. You'd think she'd be thin as a stick, and I'll never know where that broad butt comes from—no one else in our family has that. She doesn't need a bustle to stay in fashion. But her clear lovely face makes up for it. "How's Máime?" she asked without looking up.

"Same as always. Nothing pleases her," I told her, taking off my bonnet and hanging it on a hook near the door. "Where's Mick?" Mick is Sally's husband, and he is nice enough, but always thinking about farm work and no real fun at all.

"He took the wagon up to Lemont for some part he needed. I 'spec he should be back soon."

"I had to take the 'lectric car to Lemont to get some things for Mam. I could have come home with Mick and avoided all that walkin' if I knew he was goin'." I didn't tell her the walking was the best part of my day, as I set down my bag and took a chair at the table.

"He left just an hour ago." She wiped sweat from her face and glowered at me. I thought she looked exhausted. "I could have used your help here," she said.

Likely she was unhappy with me because she worked hard all the day without me, but I couldn't have relieved her of the heavy things even if I had been home. Dealing with Mam was not such a grand task either, and she wasn't giving me credit for that.

"Maybe you'd like to take my place puttin' up with Mam on Mondays?"

"Niver! If I had to be with her all day like before, I don't know as how I could stand it. If I heard one more time about owin' her for raisin' me from a babe, or gripin' how could I say such a thing to my poor máthair, I think I would have taken the back of my hand to her. She used to hide things, you know, just to make my life harder."

"I know," I told her. I wanted to say she had told me that at least *twenty* times already, but I bit my tongue. I was tetchy too, from spending the day with Mam.

"I don't s'pose Packey's home yet," I said.

"It's a bit early, isn't it?"

"Yeah, 'tis." Truth was I just wanted to see him. I needed his cheery good humor to lift me out of my melancholy mood. Although we were married for two years and I'd known Packey for four, I still smiled every time he walked into the room. A big strong rough-looking man he may be, but there's not a mean bone in his body, and he loves life like no one I've ever known. A joy my Packey is, and I thank the good Lord for bringing him to me.

I sighed. "Let me wash up an' get the dust off. I'll make the supper tonight. Leave the fixings an' go rest a bit," I told Sally, although I was tired myself.

I climbed the narrow stairs to my room, poured water into the washbasin, and washed my face and hands with sweet-smelling soap. It felt good, and the scent cleared the cobwebs from my head.

Sally was fine as far as sisters went, but sure we didn't think much alike. The both of us were short with fair skin, bright blue eyes and thick auburn hair, but there our resemblance ended. She was a year younger than me, but didn't she act more like the older sister. She was forever and a day serious-minded, not concerned with much of anything beyond getting the work done. She accused me of having my head in the clouds and studying and dreaming all the time, and I s'pose she's right about that. We got along well enough, but it was Maggie I needed to really understand me, to be myself and talk silly. But Maggie moved away. Friends do that, but sisters are always there.

I returned to our kitchen to tackle supper. It wouldn't be too much of a chore. Sally had fetched meat from the icebox and vegetables from the root cellar, and they were sitting out on the big trestle table in the middle of the large room, waiting for me. I rummaged in the pantry for herbs and spices. Sally's cooking was plain and bland but I liked to make it more interesting.

I put wood in the cook stove firebox, lit it, and adjusted the exhaust and air vents. I wiped sweat from my brow with the back of my hand, and rubbed the damp hair at the base of my neck. Using the oven in the heat of the day was near to torture. When the firebox was good and hot, I scraped the cut-up meat and vegetables into the cook pot, added my herbs and spices, and put the pot on the cooktop. I found biscuits in the breadbox, left from breakfast, and put them in the warming oven.

Almost done, I dipped water into another pot and put it on to boil, to make ready for clean-up after supper. We didn't have piped-in water or a kitchen pump like most of the homes in town, but it was not so easy to do out here on the farm, nor did we have the money for such luxuries.

Our Grandpa, Orange Chauncey, one of the first settlers of Sag, came here from England, wedded an Irishwoman, and cleared the farm. When he died, the farm should have gone to Uncle Denny, but he wanted nothing to do with farming, as he had a good job on the railroad. Uncle Jimmy died young in a farm accident, so Pa took over the farm, married Mam, and had me and Sally. When Pa died, Mam had no use for farm life, and Sally and Mick wound up running it, as Mick was a born farmer. Sooner or later we'll have to straighten it all out.

As I finished setting the table, I heard someone whistling a tune in the lane, and knew Packey was home. Fancy whistling was one of Packey's talents. I went out on the porch and watched him push his bicycle into the barn and then stride to the house without stopping his tune. I smiled as I waited, marveling again at his energy and cheerful nature, even at the end of a long hard day and after pedaling home.

Packey's broad smile brightened the room, and he threw his arms around me and lifted me from the ground, as he did every day. He never got to thinking hugging me that way would hurt the babe at all, and indeed it did not, and I *loved* his arms around me, I did, and never would I think of asking him to stop.

I hugged him back with all my strength, stood on my toes to rub my forehead against his cheek, bristly this late in the day. I ran my hands through his thick dark hair, smiled into his sparkling blue eyes, and then buried my head in his muscular chest. Oh, how I *love* my Packey, and I giggled in delight, sure all this greeting business would be waking Sally from her nap, and not caring the least little bit.

"How's Mavourneen, my Darlin'?" an' my baby Darlin'?" Packey patted my bulging tummy as he said this. The babe made a great kick and Packey laughed in delight. "'Tis like a fine strong boy this wee one is acting, takin' after his Dah already, he is."

"None of that, Packey," I said with a giggle in return. "This feisty wee lass can kick with the best, like her mam, you'll see."

"How are you both, an' what did you do all this fine day?" he inquired, boisterous as was his way.

"Well, an' I spent the day with Mam, so how do you think that may have gone?" I replied, laughing. I didn't feel so grumpy now, nor so put upon.

"Ah, that's right," Packey nodded. "'Tis Monday an' I forgot all that. Well, 'tis over now, is it not? An' you're none the worse for wear, I see."

"No worse than usual, I must confess. But when I got back Sally was exhausted an' cranky, so I volunteered to make supper an' sent her for a rest. An' how did your day go? Are the men still grumblin' an' did they give you trouble at the quarry today?"

"Ah now, Darlin', doan be worryin' your head on that. You have enough to fret about with the farm an' the babe an' your Mam an' all. Let me be doin' the worryin' about the job. 'Tis nothin' I can't handle, you know."

In the past few weeks I had seen a troubled look on Packey's face when he didn't know I was watching. He denied anything worrisome going on, and I hoped that was the truth, but I feared otherwise. I changed the subject, as I knew he wouldn't want to be talking about work troubles.

"I saw Maggie today. Mam sent me to the general store in Lemont, an' I met Maggie on the 'lectric car. She'll be at the picnic on the Fourth. I'm so looking forward to the picnic, Packey. 'Twill be the last real fun before the babe comes. I miss bein' around people these days, especially smart people who are usin' *new* things an' movin' up in the world. Someday, when the babe is older, we will do that too, Packey. I know we won't always be on this farm, an' we'll go places."

"That's grand ideas, Darlin', an' surely we *will* have a grand life. But for now, we'll have a fine time at the picnic, won't we? Is it your stew I'm smellin' now?"

"Yes, 'tis," I said.

"I knew 'twas yours. I can tell by the grand oudor comin' from the stove, without me tastin' it yet, a treat such as no other lucky husband has in these parts. Let me just go an' wash up a bit, an' change these dirty clothes of mine with the rock dust an' all, an' I'll be back soon to do your meal justice, I will."

It was quiet in the kitchen after Packey left. I knew he would take his sweet time, and Sally would not come down until I called, takin' full advantage of a rare chance to rest. Mick might be in town a while yet, and the stew was simmering and needed no attention. I guessed I would have the better part of an hour alone in the kitchen.

I had an hour for myself.

I smiled and went to the secret place where I kept my journal that not even Packey knew.

Chapter 20

I always forgot how much work picnics are for women. Sally and I worked like the devil all morning to get ready, and it made me wonder why I was looking forward to the picnic at all. By the time we fried up chicken, made potato salad, chipped ice for keeping, and every blessed thing was done up and packed up, I was ready to go back to bed, not to start a full day of socializing. Heaven be thanked at least we did the baking yesterday and got that out of the way. Uncle Denny promised to make ice cream. I wondered if he'd make chocolate—my mouth was watering thinking about chocolate ice cream.

I did recover a wee bit while riding over in the wagon. The men unloaded and Mick took the horses to graze in the shade. Since he was likely to run across distractions on his way back, I sat on a chair near our table to relax before friends and relatives came. I wondered again why Mick was so grumpy these days. He didn't talk the whole drive over. I s'pose he was worried about the farm.

It was a perfect day, not so hot as the Fourth of July usually was, and a gentle breeze helped make it comfortable, even in the bright sun. Mam was so excited about getting out for a day of gabbing she didn't go on at Sally and me for a change. She had to inspect the food for sure, but looked satisfied well enough, even said she liked Sally's fried chicken, which took Sally by surprise.

Mam caught sight of an old neighbor right off and went to chat, and Sally went to talk to friends too. Packey settled me on a blanket to lean my back against a tree before going off to find out about the games. I knew what he'd want to know: about the base ball game, and surely if someone was organizing a boxing match. The ring wouldn't be at the picnic grounds, as such matches weren't legal. The men would want Packey to fight. I wasn't fond of that, but Packey's the best prizefighter around, and there'd be no escaping it for sure.

With everyone gone for a while, I rested in the shade and watched the goings on, and planned to find Maggie, wander around and chat with friends later. It was lovely in this grove, all shady with great old trees and overlooking the valley, the river, and the canals, the old canal and the new one. I closed my eyes and listened to people chatter as they went by. This was a grand place to hear the latest gossip, and I expected to have my fill of it before the day was done.

Some men walked by complaining about wolves killing their sheep. Wolves were common here before the farmers settled, but that was a while ago, and the wolves were supposed to be chased off. Now it seems they came back, probably attracted by sheep, and the farmers were trying to clear them out again.

"Are they goin' to offer a bounty for wolves this year?" one man asked. "I hear the beasts howlin' at night agin', so seems we have work to do."

"I hear they're postin' a five-dollar bounty like they done last year," another man said.

"I spotted a female near my herd last week," a third voice said. "Her teats were heavy swollen, so she must have a den nearby. I thought they stayed in their den when feedin' their young."

One man answered in a confident voice, as if he thought himself an expert. "Most likely someone shot her old man. The mate brings food for the mama and her pups before they leave the den, but if he's gone she has to hunt."

"We better be on the lookout for that den, or there will be a whole new batch of wolves to contend with come fall," one of them said, as they wandered out of earshot.

I opened my eyes and looked to see if I knew the men, but I didn't. Wolves haven't got any of *our* livestock, but I've heard them howling at night. I set back against the tree again.

Two women came by, struggling with baskets and huge jars of lemonade, and didn't notice me looking at them.

"Fourth of July picnics used to be so much more fun before they moved the river, don't you think? Remember when we used to go out on the island, an' swim an' fish? An' the children played in the sand? Now it's all swampy an' buggy, an' of course the islands are gone. This place is okay, but it's not like the good old days."

I grew up doing the things they talked about too. After the river was moved to a new channel to make way for the canal, the valley wasn't the same. Still, I wondered why people kept talking about the good old days, when so many new and exciting things were happening in *these* times.

Her companion shifted the items she was carrying before stating her opinion, which was more like my point of view.

"The railway may finish buildin' that new park soon, an' maybe next Fourth picnic we can take the train to it. Imagine—the train will stop right in the park! They're makin' a lagoon, an' an amusement park. We can rent boats an' row around, swim or fish, an' there'll be a big fancy pavilion where bands will come to an' play dance music. Wonder if our husbands have any romance left in 'em?" Both women laughed, and their voices faded as they walked away.

Uncle Denny arrived, carrying fixings for ice cream. "Hey Meg!" he greeted me cheerfully. "Let me get this stuff started, and I'll come set with ya a while. How ya doin'?"

"I'm just fine," I replied, watching as he unpacked the churn and supplies. He loaded the churn with salt and surrounded it with layers of newspapers to keep the cream and ice cold.

"What flavor are you makin'?" I asked.

"Chocolate," he replied.

" 'Tis neither here nor there, but I'm glad 'tis chocolate," I said. "Chocolate's my favorite!"

He sat down next to me, wiping sweat from his face with a handkerchief, despite the breeze. "I have a grand story to tell, if you haven't heard about McWeeney's will."

"I haven't, an' who would McWeeney be then?" I asked him. Uncle Denny heard a lot of things working on the railroad, and he was famous for telling outlandish tales.

"McWeeney was a big shot at the police department down in Chicago," he started, "but I s'pose you don't remember he used to live in Lemont, until he made so much money managing the drainage ditch he got too big for the likes of this little town."

"Ah, yes, that McWeeney," I said. "I wondered what happened to him an' all."

"Well, McWeeney was said to have made a great pile of money, not always legal-like, but shrewd he was, so he niver was caught, an' you know how officials are these days, here an' in Chicago. Be that as it may, he died an' left a fortune, over five hundred thousand dollars it is said. With no wife or children, it was all to go to his nephew Lyman, an' he made a will that said so. There were other bequests to relatives, to the Methodist Church, an' a great sum for a fancy tombstone."

"Well, 'tis sad McWeeney's gone, but surely the Reverend Tully an' the relatives were glad for the money," I said.

"An' they would have been," he went on, "only it appears there may have been some funny business. It seems a new will was signed just before he died, an' *that* will didn't mention the nephew, or the church, or the other bequests. The second will said the estate amounted to *two* hundred thousand dollars, an' the rest of the money was not accounted for. Large sums were left to people who were not mentioned at all in the first will, an' the homestead was left to McWeeney's housekeeper instead of the nephew, along with a great sum to her as well."

I shifted to make myself more comfortable, and Uncle Denny got up and fetched a towel, which he folded up to cushion my back.

"Rumors were flyin' all over as the circumstances became known. One day I went to Chicago on railroad business, an' on the train I sat beside John Taylor, who had a forty-year lease from McWeeney for his store here in Lemont. I asked Taylor if he knew McWeeney had died, an' he said he was there when it happened."

"No!" I said. "What did he have to say about the will then?"

"Taylor told me he was a *witness* to the new will durin' his final visit to McWeeney. I asked him if McWeeney was able to write at the time, an' he answered, ' 'bout as well as a dead man,' he sez."

"How could that be?" I asked Uncle Denny, as I was truly astonished.

"It appears another man took up McWeeney's hand an' made the writin' on the will."

I threw up my arms in protest. "How could Taylor ever sign such a thing?"

"I asked him that as well," Uncle Denny said, reaching over to pull a few blades of grass through his fingers. "He said the witness' statement only said he saw the will signed by McWeeney's hand. That of itself was a true an' honest statement, an' so he signed the paper."

I was flabbergasted. "Surely the new will didn't stand up in court!" I exclaimed. "Was it contested? What did Walker say in court?"

Uncle Denny shook his head. "I don't know that part, but sure an' it was not *my* place to criticize the man. But since he told *me* the truth, I think he probably would do so on the stand as well."

Uncle Denny left me then, and I leaned against the tree trunk and closed my eyes, waiting for everyone to get back. We would have food, then games, and we would pack up the wagon before the evening's dancing. The band would come at seven. I hoped the men would not be too far in their cups and spoil the fun, but in this town that was never certain.

People still strolled by, and my eyes drifted shut again, but I heard more bits of their talk, filling me in on what the townsfolk were thinking.

Many people didn't believe the newspapers that said the economy was recovering from what they now called a depression, but we just called it hard times. Businesses, including the department store and the soda company, failed this summer. A horse market opened—which was supposed to help—but most people were against it, as it brought rough people to town who tried to sell old and sick horses, and there was the fear of diseases infecting Lemont livestock.

Others talked about politics and Smokey Row, with its unsavory characters and criminals and all. Some sided with Reverend Tully, who was trying to rid the town of saloons and bordellos. Others felt these establishments brought money to town. One man claimed the mayor and police chief were making personal profits off Smokey Row. Still others were of the opinion, now the drainage ditch was finished, it would only be a matter of time before the workers moved out of town and the undesirable business dropped off on its own.

~~~

It seems I drifted off to sleep for a wee bit, and woke up thinking I heard

Packey. I opened my eyes to look around, but no one was near, so I closed them again. A few minutes later I heard Packey's voice, telling someone not to disturb me. Seems I sensed somehow that Packey would be back, and woke up before he came. That is something I often do, and I can't explain it, just some silly gift of mine.

"Oh, no," I said, and struggled to sit up. "Please, I came here to have a good time an' be with people, not to sleep, an' I'm refreshed now." Packey helped me to my feet and I walked to the table and chairs he and Mick had lugged here.

Packey had brought Jacob Luther with him. The man was the new supervisor at the quarry, who had come from Pennsylvania, where his previous experience was with running mines. That wasn't quite the same as running quarries. To make matters worse, the man had no experience handling a crew of immigrant Irishmen, such as those who worked the quarries, and didn't have a clue how to break up their squabbles. The laborers took advantage to press for wage increases and shorter hours, and Packey, as foreman, was caught between labor and management.

I offered Mr. Luther a glass of iced tea, and he smiled but refused. I supposed that beer would probably be more to his liking, but we didn't bring beer.

"How do you like our town, Mr. Luther?" I asked him.

"It seems a fine place," he said. "I'm still getting used to it, but I must admit there's a fair difference between the way things are done here and how they're done in the East. I wish all the men were like your husband, Mrs. Hennessey. I wonder how long it will be before I manage to get these everlasting disputes settled."

"You are referrin' to our Irish laborers, I assume," I answered him. "The gentlemen who break their backs for ten hours a day an' get $1.50 for their efforts." I smiled at him, to let him know my words didn't mean I was taking a side in the matter.

Packey picked up a twig off the ground and began to peel bark off it as he exchanged a glance with Luther and laughed. "Jacob," he said. "Didn't I iver tell ya what an outspoken woman me wife is? An' stubborn to boot. She may be tiny, but just one look at that fine head of red hair should let you know 'tis an Irish spitfire I took for me wife."

"Yes, I should have known then," Luther said, chuckling. Then he turned back to me. "I have no control over wages. The owners told me they'd like to pay more, but they're struggling too, and digging into their own pockets as it is, trying to keep the quarries running in these bad times."

"The men would say that's all fine and good, but it doesn't put food in their children's bellies. The workers don't see the owners' children goin' hungry, only their own. Their wages are less now than they were ten years ago," I said.

"And the owners would say there always seems to be sufficient pay to put whiskey in the workers' bellies."

"Ah—that would be the single workers, not the family men," I pointed out.

The same disagreements have gone on for years, and Mr. Luther seemed uncomfortable as he removed his hat and rubbed his head. I thought he seemed a nice enough man, but out of his element. I feared the situation at the quarries was more than he could handle.

"Have you lived in Lemont long yourself, Mrs. Hennessey?" he asked, changing the subject.

"All my life, Mr. Luther, born an' raised right here," I told him. "Grandpa Chauncey was one of the first settlers, an' Grandpa Dolan came from Ireland to build the railroad. Packey an' I are still livin' on Grandpa Chauncey's farm. It's one of the few farms around that wasn't bought with land scrip."

"What's land scrip?" Mr. Luther inquired, furrowing his brow.

"The contractors that built the old canal in the forties ran out of money to pay the workers, so they gave them certificates to purchase cheap land along the canal. I surely hope the quarry owners aren't thinkin' about doin' any such thing, as we have as much land as we can handle now," I told him with a laugh.

He turned toward my husband. "I didn't know you were a farmer too. Is there no end to your talents?"

"My talents *end* with farmin'," Packey joked. "I can barely tell a sheep from a pig. 'Tis not us who farm the land. Meg was workin' in Chicago when we met, an' when her Pa died, Meg's sister an' her husband took over runnin' the farm. Meg an' I are only livin' there an' helpin' out 'til the babe comes. We'll be lookin' for our own place."

"I'm glad to hear you're no good at farming, as I was feeling pretty inadequate thinking you had so many skills. Were you an early settler too?"

"Not me, no. I come here from Ireland back in '90, to dig the drainage ditch. When we finished the Lemont section a couple of years ago, I knew Meg by then, so of course I wanted to stay." Packey had by now taken all the bark off the twig, and threw it back to the ground and brushed off his hands. He smiled at me and took my hand in his big one.

"How did you meet Meg, if she was in Chicago?" Mr. Luther asked.

"Ah, Meg, you see, she come to this same picnic ev'ry year, and 'tis where we met, we did. An' we wouldn't be missing the July Fourth picnic now, would we, it bein' like an anniversary of sorts."

I squeezed Packey's hand and he looked at me fondly. "Packey found work in the quarries then, when the diggin' on the canal wound down, an' I moved back to the Sag to marry him."

Packey and Mr. Luther continued to chat for a while about matters at the quarry, and it was clear both wanted to do the right thing for the workers as well as the owners, but they were at a loss as to how to do it. They feared a strike. During the last quarry strike men were killed and the militia was called. It was not a matter to take lightly, and an inexperienced man in charge made the situation even more risky.

I liked Mr. Luther though, and I felt sorry he had such problems.

Finally Mr. Luther made his excuses saying he had to visit other workers. "Now don't you disappoint me," he told Packey as he was leaving. "I expect to eat all week off the bet I placed on you to win."

"I'll do me best," Packey assured him, looking at me from the corner of his eye. He knew I wouldn't be happy about the boxing, but I didn't say anything. Packey was the town champion, and the men who followed prizefighting wouldn't let him out of the match. I knew Packey was a boxer before I married him, but I couldn't make myself like it.

'Tis not like me to be a worrier, but I had a sudden feeling of foreboding. Maybe that's something else that comes with pregnancy. All the troubles I listened to today, like wolves, and the depression, and Smokey Row and corrupt officials. Like struggles to make ends meet and quarrels at the quarries. I wondered what kind of world my babe would be born into, and if I would be able to keep her from harm. How would we survive all that, and her Pa a boxer besides? Our life is hard, but we've had no personal tragedy. Pray God it will not strike us too.

It was too much to think about. This day was for fun, and I pushed concerns out of my mind.

Sally and Mick returned. Mam came back and sat down to watch us set out food. We wouldn't expect her to help, but at least she didn't spoil things harping at us. She jabbered on with gossip she heard around the grove.

Uncle Denny returned with a neighbor's young sons. He promised them as much ice cream as they wanted if they did the churning. They were excited and fought over who would be first to turn the handle. I wondered how long it would be before they tired of the task.

"I saw you talkin' with Packey an' that Luther fella," Uncle Denny said, as I uncovered the chicken and set out plates and napkins. "Did you get to talk with your women friends?"

"I never did leave, an' Maggie hasn't come by yet. Later, when the games start, I'll look for her. She must be busy with family too. With all that's goin' on, we could wind up too busy for people we most want to see."

"Next year that little one you're carryin' will be winnin' all the games, you just watch," Uncle Denny bragged.

"Next summer the little one won't be a year old yet. A bit young for games, don't you agree?" I said, picturing a one-year-old in a three-legged race and laughing at the idea.

"Not if he's anythin' like his mother. He'll be out there tellin' everyone he's the one to beat. Not too soon for my great-nephew," he insisted.

I felt an urge to hug him, and I did. I did not disappoint him by saying I was sure the baby was a girl, not the great-nephew he hoped for.

The grove was full of activity. Surely there were hundreds of people, children running and squealing, women chattering in loud shrill voices, men laughing and shouting over each other. It was going to be a *grand* day.

Chapter 21

On the Sunday following the picnic, Mick dragged Grandpa Chauncey's old surrey out of the barn and drove us to Saint James for Mass. Mick has been so busy, I was surprised he took time, but was grateful for it, as I was getting heavier by the day, and never would have been able to walk so far. It made up a bit for his grumpy mood. I didn't want to miss Mass. Few women have trouble these days, but I'd rather play it safe and be right with God before I go into labor.

Walking up the hill was a struggle, but I leaned on Packey, and he went slow and patient with me. We went through the cemetery and past the ushers tolling the church bells and into the church.

Saint James is small but 'tis lovely. The men of the parish built it, and it was the first church in these parts, that replaced the old log cabin. The men who had property donated property, and those who had supplies donated supplies, and those with nothin' donated their labor. Only recently we put on the finishing touches, the lovely stained windows and the steeple. Light now streamed through the Eye of God window above the altar. The window was well named, a thing of great beauty and mystery like God.

Our priest is Father Fitzpatrick, a big strong man like my Packey, although from the looks of his great girth he hasn't been pushing back from his supper table soon enough. He came to Saint James ten years ago with grand ideas and started remodeling the church and building the rectory and parish hall right away. Some think he isn't right for our wee parish because he's forever planning something new and you can't never hold him back. In my opinion he has grand ideas but makes us work too much.

But I must admit he has done many good things. We didn't have the summer bazaar before he started it, and that surely is a grand event, when the entire parish gets together on Sundays for six whole weeks to display and sell our goods and all. People come from Lemont and all over, even from Chicago. 'Tis great fun and we make extra money, some for ourselves and some for the parish, and extra money is surely welcome these hard days.

Father Fitzpatrick didn't come from another Irish parish in Chicago or from any big city, like most of our priests. No, he was a chaplain in the Army, and he served in the War Between the States, and helped men on the battlefield. 'Tis said he was a hero and received a medal for all he did. He knows little about farm families, but he knows hardship and he knows kindness and comfort. Perhaps he's not so bad after all.

I do think he gives a grand homily, though some say he's opinionated. I don't mind if he's opinionated as I generally agree with his opinions. Today during the homily he asked the men to come tonight to discuss how the church is to be maintained. All that building we did will be put to waste if we don't take proper care of it, he said. He pointed out a stain on the ceiling where a leak in the roof was fixed. It looks shameful, it does. There's not enough money for repairs, and the rest of the property is showing neglect too. The men need to provide labor, and will make a list of the work each man can do, how to get materials, and many other details. Father asked for a show of hands, who will come tonight, and Packey raised his hand, along with about a dozen other men.

I wasn't all that keen about Packey going to the meeting. Although I was proud of his generosity, I hoped he wouldn't be away long, as my time to have this babe is near. I was being a tad selfish for his attention. I wished Father wouldn't ask so much of the men, but I tried not to be irritated.

When we left the church, one of the men who raised his hand for the meeting tipped his hat to me and motioned to Packey to step aside to chat. They didn't talk long, but Packey looked surprised at what the man said, and then he frowned, waved his hand at the man like he wanted him to go away, and strode to catch up with me, and he was wearing his angry face.

"Who is that man, an' what did he want with you?" I asked, taking Packey's arm and watching his face.

"Just a man I know from town," he answered. He seemed distracted, but the red color in his face was fading, and he gave me a great smile. I wasn't fooled, as I sensed he was trying to throw me off.

"It seems he made you angry," I observed.

"Oh, no, 'tis just a matter we'll talk about tonight, as we don't see eye to eye. 'Tis not important—don't worry your wee head," he assured me. He reached his arm around and gave me a hug. I was getting hard to reach around.

~~~

Everyone was quiet on the ride home after Mass. Mick and Packey both stared at the road, each considering his own thoughts, I s'pose. To make things worse, Sally said she wasn't feeling well. So I couldn't have any conversation at all, with no one willing to talk.

When we got to the farm, Sally went right to her room. I heard her throwing up in the chamber pot, and I went to her door to ask if she wanted help. She begged me not to come in; in case she started a fever she didn't want me or the babe to catch sick. There is always fear of the cholera, the typhoid, the small pox, or the influenza, and so it was best to be cautious.

So once again it was left to me to make the supper, although I wanted nothing more than to lay down on the porch swing in the shade, as I was mighty wore out these hot days and found the easiest tasks tiring.

Packey washed up the supper things, which was unusual, and I wondered if he felt guilty about leaving me to go to the church this evening.

Before I set down, I lumbered upstairs to Sally's door and called to her through it. She said she felt feverish now, and she was coughing and her bowels were loose. The rest of us weren't sick, so perhaps it was something bad she ate, but I feared something worse. I thought it wouldn't be the typhoid though, which starts slow, not sudden. Sally wanted to sleep, so I went downstairs.

I went out on the porch, where it was cooler. Mick was in the barn checking on the cow, which was ready to drop her calf. Seems I wasn't the only one about to give birth on this farm. Packey sat with me and sipped a cool glass of water. A breeze started and the sun moved down the sky. It was lovely on the porch.

Packey held my hand, and it felt good, it did, us sitting there alone together, but something was bothering me. I picked this time to talk to Packey about it.

"Packey, 'tis grand that you won the prizefight at the picnic, but will you still be fightin' after the babe is born?" I asked, gazing off down our lane instead of at Packey.

I sensed that he turned to me, but still I did not look at him, worried what I would see.

"Oh Darlin', I know ye're not fond of the fightin'," he admitted, "but 'tis something I grew up with, in the Auld Country, an' I'm a verra good boxer. 'Tis also an important thing for the men for me to win. They have so little to feel good about these days, an' they depend on me to be their champion, ya know."

"They keep puttin' you up against men who are harder to knock down, an' you come home with your lovely face all cut an' battered. I can hardly bear to see it." I turned to him now so he could see the earnest look on my face.

Packey squeezed my hand. "That's what fightin' is all about, Darlin', to face a fierce opponent," he said. "Surely 'twould not be excitin' otherwise. My face heals just fine, ya know it does. The men put up their hard-earned money expectin' me to knock the opponent down, an' it would not be fair to deprive them of their fun, or their *money*, as they have so little of both. I always win, Darlin'. The men would be fair disappointed if I didn't fight."

I knew Packey was proud of his fighting, and I wanted him to feel good about himself, but was torn between that and the danger of the sport. Not wanting him to see my confusion, I looked away again. "So what if the coppers come then? What you're doin' isn't legal, you know."

"Oh, the coppers don't bother with us. 'Tis all taken care of. The men must have some fun an' all." He gave a great laugh, as was his way.

I pulled my gaze back to him and accused, "Someday you will fight someone you cannot beat. Or maybe a man will cheat or get a lucky punch."

He laughed heartily again, and I was sure he was thinking I could not comprehend this fighting business, and he was right. I did *not* know, as I would never let myself watch him fight.

"Now who would it be could take me out that way?" he teased.

"Maybe that Gentleman Jim Corbett who was here last fall," I suggested.

Packey leaned back in his chair and smiled, and I knew he was remembering the evening the famous Gentleman Jim Corbett came to Sag for the big match. Every barge on the canal came loaded with men from Bridgeport and other places along the way, and crowded around the ring to see the famous boxer. After the fight the townsmen insisted Jim meet their local favorite, Packey, and the two of them spent hours in one of the saloons, talking about their experiences.

"Ah, Gentleman Jim...." Packey reminisced, his gaze drifting unfocused toward our lane. "That *would* be a fight, it would. I would be honored to try my fists against such as Gentleman Jim. But fine enough it was to watch the match an' to toss down a beer or two with him after the fight. An' I must tell you, Darlin', Gentleman was an apt name for the likes of the great man."

"Yes, Packey, you did tell me, don't you remember?" Truly, I had heard him tell about that night many times, and not only me but anyone who would listen.

"Well now, all you say about *needin'* to fight may be true, but 'tis also true you *enjoy* it," I accused.

"Darlin', it's in me blood," he explained, looking at me with a shrug.

I let out a long slow breath in resignation. "So I guess there is no hope of stoppin' you. *When* do you think you may quit the fightin' then?"

I could see Packey struggling to make the right decision. It seemed to take a long time, but at last he looked in my eyes, and he must have seen my concern and fear there, for he said gently, "Darlin', you an' the babe are more dear to me than any fight. If it means so much to you, then I will fight no more after the babe comes."

I pulled myself up clumsily and managed to balance my great weight on his knee and wrap my arms around him. I nuzzled my face against his neck and murmured, "I love you so much Packey. I wish I didn't feel so about your fightin', but I fear it will come to no good."

He rubbed my back and promised, "There are three fights already scheduled, an' the bettin' has started. I'll tell the men they will need to find a new champion after that."

Nice as it was on Packey's knee, my big body would not let me stay there in comfort for long, so I squeezed back into my chair. We sat a spell, thinking and watching the wildlife gather for their evening browse. The killdeer were running through the fields with their strident cries, picking around for food and protecting their nests in the ground. We tried to follow the swallows darting through the air catching insects, but they flew so fast we caught only their motion.

"I don't see rabbits," I said. "Shouldn't rabbits be out now?"

"Perhaps it's wolves that are catchin' the rabbits, like they were sayin' at the picnic," he said. "I haven't seen one, but did you hear the howlin' last night?"

"I did hear it, an' 'tis a mournful sound, but beautiful an' mysterious at the same time," I said.

Packey pointed to a deer emerging to graze at the edge of our field, and we watched her for a while.

"I wish you would just sit with me tonight and enjoy the lovely evenin'," I implored, although I knew he would never go back on his word to Father Fitzgerald. "This evening will be no fun at all. I will be alone, with you gone, an' Sally sick, an' the Good Lord knows what's the matter with Mick of late, he's so grumpy an' makin' himself scarce every chance."

"I wish I could stay, Darlin'," he said, "but I canna disappoint Father. He doesn't think the men work so well if I'm not there. Every man will try to be his own boss, an' they will fight among themselves. Father says I have the gift of gab and of directin' work without lettin' on that it's orders the men are gettin', so each man thinks it's his own idea to be doin' such a thing."

"I'm sure you do just that. You will make the men happy by fightin' an' then you won't disappoint Father either. I wish that priest wouldn't ask so much, an' would leave the men alone for a while instead of dragging them away from what little time they have with their families. I'm truly upset with him, I declare. Well, I guess *my* day is comin' soon," I said. I could feel my face growing red and blinked quickly to hide the moisture gathering in my eyes. I had won my way about the boxing, but I was still peeved with Father, and feeling a wee bit hurt.

"Now Darlin'...," Packey began.

But I didn't let him finish. Just as sudden I realized I was thinking only of myself. "That was just malarkey, Packey, an' I'm sorry for it. I didn't mean to sound so spiteful."

Packey looked like he didn't know whether to believe me or not, so I went on.

"But that man will be there," I said, and this time I watched his eyes, as I sensed he didn't want to tell me something.

"What man would that be?" He avoided my gaze, and I'm sure he knew what man I meant.

"The man who chatted with you after Mass. The one who made you angry."

"Oh, don't think I was angry at all. He just sees things a different way, an' I canna agree with his way. We will work it out tonight, niver fear your pretty head." He shifted his weight restlessly, and scratched at his leg.

"I didn't like him," I said, and I tossed my head and lifted my chin. "I don't know why, but I didn't like him. Is he new in town? I haven't seen him before."

"No. He's been here some months, but seems he just now got around to joinin' Saint James."

"Then I wonder why he volunteered right off. Don't you think that's strange?"

Packey turned to me at last. "Oh, surely he's interested in makin' the right impression on the priest an' the other men. Don't you think that may be so?"

"Maybe it 'tis. But how do you know him then? An' why did he talk to you in private?"

He turned his gaze toward the farmyard again, and folded his arms across his chest. "I met him in town. He works at one of the quarries down by Lemont, and 'tis rumored he fires the men up with labor complaints."

"Ah—I see then. You would have no patience for that rabble-rousin'."

"You're right. I have no use for the likes of that," he agreed, nodding.

"Is that what he talked to you about then, about wages or some such thing at the quarry? Was he lookin' to include you in his nasty business then?" I pressed.

"No, 'twas another matter entirely," Packey said, avoiding my eyes again.

"And what was that other matter then?" I wouldn't give up.

Packey looked uneasy, and stood up. "Come now, Darlin'. None of that," he said. He pulled me from my chair and drew me to him, smiling warmly at me as he brushed a stray strand of hair from my cheek. "Darlin', I really have to be leavin' now, 'tis getting close to meetin' time. I promise I will tell you all about it when I get home, an' 'twill be all resolved then, I know. 'Tis no great matter in any case."

Packey hugged me for a long moment, and I nestled my face into the warm space on his neck. He rubbed his cheek against my hair and then sought my lips for a long gentle kiss. He stroked my cheek once fondly, then placed his cap on his head and headed out for the church, whistling in his merry way as he walked jauntily between the trees that lined our lane. I watched him fade into the gathering dusk, the sound of his whistle growing softer until I could no longer hear it.

As I stood at the porch rail and watched him stride off down the road and out of sight, I had a feeling of uneasiness. But I trusted my Packey, and I know no man better able to care for himself. Sure and if he rode his bicycle it would get him there faster, but it would be dangerous to ride home after nightfall, and hard to ride carrying a lantern. I shook off my misgivings and turned my mind to other matters.

Mick had not come back from the barn, so I figured the cow still needed tending, as all the other chores were likely done by now. Or perhaps he found some other task after all. There was always some task that needed doing on a farm. It was no big thing, as he wasn't happy company lately anyway.

I maneuvered myself back into my chair and sat alone, watching the sun go down, thinking about my talk with Packey and wondering about the new man, who he was and what he was up to. Then I thought about my Darlin' baby girl again, and it was not long before I found myself wanting to nod off. I went into the house and took out my journal, to make a note in it before going to our room. Soon I would be a busy mam, and there would be little time for journals and such.

Chapter 22

I don't know what woke me up. Maybe it was Sally moving around in her bedroom. It was dark and too quiet in the house, not even the usual snoring noises. I heard rumbling in the distance, probably thunder from lightning I saw going on for the past few nights, far off but no rain ever fell.

I reached over to Packey, but he wasn't there. I got up and lit a match to check the clock and it was two in the morning. How could that be—two A.M., and Packey wasn't home yet? Perhaps he *was* home but didn't come to bed yet. I listened carefully, but I didn't hear any sounds at all, so I went to look for him.

Lighting the lamp, I looked around the room. None of the clothes Packey had been wearing were there. I pulled my robe as far as it would go around my bulging belly and stepped into my slippers, then made my way downstairs, carrying the lamp. He wasn't downstairs either.

I went out on the porch, and no one was there, but light came from the barn. Relieved, I lumbered out there to greet Packey, despite the late hour. I half expected he would meet me on the way, but he didn't.

As I entered the barn, I heard distressed animal sounds, which I realized were coming from the cow. A voice called out, "Who's there?"

It was Mick. "It's me—Meg," I said. "Why would you ever be out here this late? Is the cow in trouble?" I shuffled across the dirt floor toward the stall.

"Yes, Meg—she's in big trouble," Mick said, his tone upset, "an' I don't know as I can save her *or* the calf. The calf is comin' wrong way, an' I don't seem to be able to turn it or help her move it down at all. Bossie's been bawlin' these last few hours an' she's gettin' weak. I don't know how we can stand to lose one more thing on this farm."

Mick sounded like he was near to tears. I made my way to the door of the stall and looked in to see what was going on.

Sure and I spent much of my life on the farm, but I was like Mam in that I wanted little to do with takin' care of the barn animals. I would feed them or water them if there was no one else to do it, or set them out in the pasture, or put them in the barn. But milking or hitching or doctoring or breeding—those were all things I knew nothing about and didn't *want* to know about. There was plenty to do in the fields and in the house to be of help, but I drew the line when it came to the animals.

Yet when I looked into the stall it didn't take much to see the cow was in a bad way. She was lying on the ground and thrashing her legs and her head, and rolling her eyes, and bawling in the most pitiful way, and it was clear she was in agony. There was blood and somethin' more on the barn floor near her tail, and I looked away quickly as the sight of it made me queasy. Mick was sitting on the milking stool and looked almost as miserable as the poor cow, disheveled, sweating, and eyeing the wretched animal anxiously. He wiped sweat from his face with his sleeve and looked up at me.

"Why are you out here, Meg? Why aren't you in bed an' sleepin'?"

"I came down to find Packey," I told Mick. "He isn't in the house, an' I saw the light in the barn, an' so I came down. Did you send him for help?"

Mick threw me a surprised look. "I haven't seen him since supper. I've been in the barn that whole time. Wasn't he goin' to the church meetin'?"

"Yes, an' I saw him leave for the church, but that was long ago, before dark. I went to bed early, an' now there's no sign of him." I tried to stay composed, but my heart was racing with worry and I felt blood draining from my face. Where was Packey?

Mick stated the obvious. "He should have been back long ago. Somethin' must have happened."

"God, Mick!" I cried, unable to hold back a sob. "What *could* happen? I hope there was no trouble at the church. Maybe he fell walkin' home, an' broke his ankle or some such thing? He could be waitin' for us to help him! Or maybe that wolf the farmers were talkin' about...."

Bossie let out a long loud bellow and heaved her body as if to get up, and then fell back to the ground and thrashed her head continuously. I couldn't help but have a moment of fear that I would have such difficulty when it came my own turn to give birth, but I forced it out of my mind for the more urgent fear for Packey.

Mick went to Bossie, placed a hand on her neck and then on her hindquarters to calm her, and when he stood up at first he had his back to me. When he turned around I could see the whites of his eyes and a muscle in his jaw was jumping.

"The last thing I need right now is you cryin', Meg. I have more to worry about than you an' Packey." He dropped his face into his hands and swayed to and fro, making a growling sound. When he looked up again he was more composed, but his face still looked irritated. "I don't know anyone who can take better care of himself than Packey, but he'd be home now unless somethin' happened. Someone has to go find him," he said. "'Tis best if we don't wait for mornin', as he may need help. No—someone has to go *now*." He glanced around, seeming undecided despite the determined words.

I stood there taking deep breaths as I waited for him to go on, hoping his next words would be that he would go right out to find Packey.

"I can't go, Meg," he said, shaking his head. "The cow an' the calf will die if I don't stay for the birthin', an' we can't lose them. We've only been able to afford the one cow. With everything else, it would be the last straw an' the end of the farm, an' no way to provide for us all. There's no one else—I have to stay here. Why does this have to happen now of all times?" He stamped his foot on the ground and banged his fist on his thigh and his gaze roamed the barn as if he could find some answer there.

I heard myself say, "I'll go." I found it hard to believe Mick thought the cow more important than Packey, but my anger at him made me face the fact that if anything was to be done I would need to do it myself. It would be simple, I was sure. I pictured how it would go in my head— I'd drive the wagon down the road toward the church and somewhere along the way Packey would be there holding his poor ankle or some such thing. I'd get him in the wagon and bring him home. It would be fine and not hard to do at all.

It would not be hard to do, that is, if the someone doing it was not about to have a babe and could drive a wagon. That someone was not *me*,

but I would manage. " 'Tis not far, an' I will go slow an' careful, watchin'
with the lantern, an' Packey will drive us home after I find him. It will
only take a short time."

Mick had a guilty look, but was not of a mind to back down. "Maybe Sally can go. Or maybe you can wake Donohue an' he will go out to
look." The Donohues were our closest neighbors.

I wished that was an answer, but I knew it wasn't. " 'Tis likely not a big
thing, Mick—Packey could be close by, maybe just out of sight down the
road. Donohue's place is as far as the church an' in the opposite direction.
It makes no sense to wake him an' cause a great alarm unless we know
'tis not a simple matter of sendin' the wagon for Packey. Sally is too sick.
No, I must go, Mick. I can do it." I took a deep breath and straightened
my back for confidence. Truth be told, Mick's attitude, besides making
me angry, also made me stubborn and determined.

Mick was still shaking his head. "All right," he said. "I'll start hitchin'
the mare. But first go an' wake up Sally, an' ask if she's able to go, or if
she'll ride along at least."

I went to ask Sally.

When I knocked on Sally's door, she didn't answer for a long moment.
Finally she called out to me weakly. "Don't come in Meg. Please—stay
outside the door."

Through the door I told her about Packey and Bossie's troubles, and
that Mick wanted to know if she was able to drive the wagon or sit with
me. I could hear her weeping through the door, and I figured she was
not only ill but distraught. She managed to tell me that if she tried to get
up she got dizzy and threw up. She said she was so sick and weak now
she couldn't even move from the mess she was making in her bed. I knew
she wanted to help, but it was clear she was not able to.

I told Sally I'd ask Mick to find a few minutes to clean her up, and I'd
be fine on my own. I went to my room and dressed.

I watched Mick finish hitching the mare to the wagon and securing
the fastenings. He helped me into the wagon seat, put the reins in my
hands, and hung a lantern within reach. He told me he had put his shotgun in the wagon just in case, but certainly I would not need that. As if
I knew how to use a shotgun, but how hard could it be?

"Keep her at a slow walk, now," he instructed. I surely wouldn't do anything else, but nonetheless I found his words reassuring. "There's no need to hurry, as you aren't going far. The mare will know what to do, an' she'll just move slow an' easy followin' the road with no real help from you. Lift the lantern high now an' then where you want to check the road for Packey."

I promised him I would do that, and made him promise to run upstairs and clean Sally up. I flapped the reins and the horse and wagon moved slowly down our lane to the road.

I drove the wagon down the dry dirt road, kicking up a cloud of dust. Now and then a wheel bounced through a hole or over a mound. I listened carefully, as surely if Packey needed help he would call out to any wagon passing by, but he did not call. I heard only rustling of the cornstalks as the night breeze passed through them, an occasional night bird, the clopping of the horse and creaking of the wagon.

I made my way through Sag, skirted the edge of town, and took the turn toward the church. I was more than half way to Saint James, but knew I wouldn't get much further without emptying my bladder. It was a maddening inconvenience of pregnancy; I had no control over the matter, and cursed myself for not remembering in my anxiety to take care of that before I left the farm. Dreading the struggle to get out and then back in the wagon, I was nevertheless forced to look immediately for a place to stop, somewhere I could keep the horse from walking off.

This part of the road ran along the railroad and electric line tracks. A thin moon passed in and out of clouds, providing only scarce and intermittent light. I had been on this road only in daylight, and tonight things near the road that I would surely recognize in better light were dark and mysterious, the trees spooky. Frightened in the gloomy surroundings, anxious about Packey, and now the added urgency of a bladder feeling about to burst, I nonetheless knew there was no avoiding the need to stop. I made out in the dim light a small bridge ahead and remembered that on the far side was a pile of railroad ties. This would be a protected place to stop, where no one at Sag would see my lantern, and I could tie the horse to one of the electric line poles that ran along the tracks.

I stopped the mare and climbed down successfully, holding carefully to the wagon seat and box while maneuvering myself to the ground, and tied the mare. I reached for the lantern to be sure I didn't trip in a hole or some other hazard as what probably happened to Packey, and I made my way to the great pile of wood tossed any old way near the road, and looked around to be sure there was no danger. Confident I was not being watched, I set down the lantern, pulled up my skirts, pulled down my drawers, squatted, and with blessed relief let my bladder empty.

As I stood up and readjusted my clothing, I heard a rustling sound and another noise like a low whimper. I reached for the lantern and held it high. The lantern revealed a pair of eyes at the far end of the wood pile, and as I watched a wolf moved slowly into the light and stopped to glare at me. I never thought to bring the shotgun down with me, as a shotgun was not something I thought of at *any* time. I wished I had done so, but then I sensed, for some reason I could not explain, that this wolf was no threat to me.

She—it was a she, as I could see her swollen and drooping teats— did not approach, but only watched me. She was a poor animal, thin and hungry-looking with a matted coat, and her eyes looked sorrowful and beseeching. Knowing that wolves are pack animals, I pulled my eyes away from her to see if there were other wolves about. What I saw was near a half dozen wolf pups, which I thought to be about a month old, all lying crushed and bloody on the ground.

It was dim-witted, I'm sure—perhaps intuition told me this wolf wouldn't attack me. She was grieving for her slaughtered pups, and her watchful gaze seemed to say she knew I was about to become a mother too. She whined, and a look of sympathy passed between us—two frightened mothers, the wolf from starvation and tragedy, and me worried to distraction about my Packey and my pregnant condition. I had no fear of her when I turned and lit my way back to the road, stopping to drag a block of wood to help me get up into the wagon. Once seated, I lifted the lantern high again, and she was no longer where I had left her, but gone.

I hoped the mare would not be skittish at the wolf and that turned out to be the case, as she gave no sign of having sensed the creature nearby. I was struck by immense sadness as the mare plodded, continuing toward the church. I guessed at what happened. A she-wolf had made a den for her pups in an isolated area, where shelter—a wood pile—was already in place and water convenient nearby. Her mate would have brought food to her and the pups, but I was willing to wager hunters killed him, either in fear for their livestock or for the bounty. She was forced to find food, and while away from her den, hunters located it and destroyed the pups. Perhaps it was the same men I heard talking at the picnic, and this was the very den they were looking for. They probably left the dead pups there to be sure the female would return and they could collect another bounty.

The sorry experience increased my anxiety for Packey, and I began to fear it was something worse than a turned ankle that kept him from returning home.

There was no sign of Packey along the road. Either he never left the church or never arrived there. It was a great mystery.

When I got to the parish hall, I turned the wagon into the church-yard and tied the mare there. A slender moon came out from behind the clouds. It afforded a poor view of the surroundings, but I could make out the path I knew led away from the yard uphill to the rectory, then veered through the cemetery and up to the church. I heard breezes moving through the forest surrounding the property and the rumble of distant thunder again. I couldn't see anyone about.

I went to the parish hall first, where meetings were held. The building was dark and the door locked. I called out, asking if anyone was there, and walked in my slow way around the building, holding the lantern in front to avoid tripping, and I didn't find anyone.

It hadn't been easy to navigate the hill up to the church this morning, and it was no easier now. I saw no one, and I despaired of finding Packey, but I had nowhere left to look. I had come this far, so I would make a fair search of the church property and even the cemetery in the event he wasn't at the church.

I stopped at the rectory first and tried the door. It was locked. Surely the door wouldn't be locked if Packey was still inside. I walked around the rectory, holding up the light to look on all sides and even behind the shrubbery, although it made no sense for him to be in the shrubbery, and of course he was *not* there. If I found nothing in the church or cemetery, I would go back to the rectory and wake Father Fitzpatrick to see if Packey had come to the meeting.

I didn't want to disturb Father for no good reason, but part of me said it would serve him right to disturb his sleep, as it was due to him we were being put to such bother and worry. But I'm not a spiteful person, so first I'd look about, and be quiet about it.

The cemetery gate was locked, but it was a flimsy affair between the stone columns, and with a bit of finagling I got through it and into the cemetery yard. As I walked up the path, I held the lantern high and looked on both sides.

As I approached the church, I called out softly. "Packey, 'tis Meg. Are you here?" I wasn't surprised when there was no answer.

I reached the church doors and tried them. They were locked too, so there wouldn't be anyone inside. I circled around to the back of the church.

"Packey," I whispered a bit louder now. "Are you here, Packey? It's Meg!"

There was no reply.

I moved carefully behind the church. The building now blocked the rectory as well as any moonlight, and the only light here was from my lantern. I could see something on the ground about fifty feet ahead, and with my heart in my throat I made my way toward it. I lifted my lantern as I crept closer, and when the light fell on the ground it revealed Packey lying there, and my breath and my heart stood still in stunned horror!

I caught my breath, gasped, and cried out in desperation. "Packey! What has happened, Packey?"

I bent down to the ground and now I could see blood on the ground around his dear head. I dropped down to turn him, and when I did so there was such a large crushed place above his left ear! I implored him, "Packey! It's Meg! Wake up Packey!"

In a panic I shook him, and I called to him, but he didn't or couldn't answer. I put my hand to his mouth but couldn't feel a breath. I put my ear to his chest, but instead of a breath I heard what sounded like a hoof striking a stone and a soft nicker. I started to get up, to turn and see what made the sounds, but before I could do so there was another noise close behind me. I felt tremendous pain on the right side of my head, a bright flash and a roar like thunder.

Is it the lightnin'? I wondered, and then I felt nothing at all.

~ ~ ~

I have no idea how long it was before I woke, if waking is what I did.

There was such tremendous pain—pain in my head and pain in my back and my belly. My whole body was gripped in a tremendous cramp, and at first there was only the agony.

Then the pain faded for a brief moment, and I struggled for consciousness, trying to remember where I was. It was night and I was on the ground in an open place. I made an effort to turn my head to look around, but movement made the pain unbearable. I had a glimpse of tombstones, so I must be in a cemetery. Then I remembered that my dear Packey was dead. That was all I recalled before the cramp returned. Consumed by pain, sorrow, and panic, I blessedly lost consciousness.

When I woke again, the torment was unbearable and now it felt as if the area between my legs was ripping apart. I could feel wetness, and something bulky there between my legs, and a feeling like a knife cutting me apart. I groaned uncontrollably. I realized I was dying, and then I knew this pain was my Darlin', my wee lass, trying to get out to save herself.

I tried to get up, to help my body in its spasms to assist my Darlin's escape, but I found I couldn't move the left side of my body at all, only the right, and I was so weak! I thought Father Fitzpatrick would appear at any moment to save us, but he did not come. The pain in my head! Oh God…I canna stand that pain! I stopped my efforts, and with my head now turned to the right I saw eyes glowing in the moonlight.

"Father Fitzpatrick! Help me!" I whispered weakly. "Oh, please, help my Darlin'!"

The eyes belonged not to Father but to the she-wolf, the same one I saw earlier. She moved slowly toward me, watching intently. When I saw she did nothing else, I tried with my right arm to reach between my legs, and with a tremendous effort I managed to do that. My hand found something warm and slick there, and a pulsing cord-like thing. I pulled on the cord, which I knew was attached to my Darlin', to help her, and I pulled her tiny body to my belly. My Darlin' wasn't moving, but she was warm, and so I had hope for her.

Throughout my struggles I tried to scream, to call for help, but my voice did not seem to work as it should, and no help came.

I was able to pull my Darlin' onto my belly, but no further. With the weak use of only one arm, there wasn't much I could do. She didn't seem to be breathing, and I didn't know why, as the cord was still pulsing below her. I found her mouth and put my finger inside to see if anything was blocking her throat, but I couldn't find anything. I slapped at her, and I pushed on her wee chest, but I could *not* make her cry or breathe, and after a time I could feel my Darlin' was growing cold, and so was I.

As my strength faded, so did my panic. What was left of me was emptiness and despair. But then came a moment of clarity, and of resolve.

I cannot, and will not, believe that my Darlin' is dead. Somehow she will survive this night, and she will be found in the morning, even if I'm no longer here to know it. My Darlin' will be expecting me, her Máime, to care for and protect her all her life, and I vow that I will do that. Even if I should not survive, I'll never rest, but I will stay with her, and no harm will ever come to her. I will be fierce in protecting my Darlin'. This I vow!

Exhausted and in terrible agony, sleep was overcoming me.

The she-wolf sat patiently watching this whole time, unmoving. With a final effort, I looked into the animal eyes. "She is cold," I whispered to her. "My Darlin' is cold."

The wolf padded over. She nuzzled and then laid her head next to my poor Darlin', and she rested her long body next to me, nestling alongside us, giving us her warmth, and I thought my Darlin' was not so cold. I turned my face into the wolf's soft fur for whatever comfort I could find there and allowed myself to sleep.

You run like a spirit on a moon-lit night
And you travel the woodlands without a fright
Shifting through leaves like the midnight air
Nobody can see you but you are there
Like a guardian angel you follow the silent trail
Protecting your pack and helping the frail

…So if you hear shifting of the leaves, don't run and hide
It's just your guardian walking by your side

—Rick Cantalupo, "The Guardian," 2005

Cora

2012

Chapter 23

Father McGrath had lost consciousness. Cora and Cisco watched anxiously, relieved to turn his care over to Jean's experienced hands. In rapid succession, police and paramedics arrived, questioned Jean, stabilized the priest, and loaded him into an ambulance.

Cisco put an arm around Cora and pulled her to him after the ambulance left. "Are you okay, Hon?" he asked, holding her and rubbing his cheek against her hair as they stood in the driveway. Cora nodded her assent, despite her tears and shaking hands and legs. Her gaze kept going back to the blood on the ground beside Father's car, darkening near the still-open car door.

A police officer, a large man with a crew cut and oval wire-rimmed glasses, walked around the priest's car, closed the door, examined the ground and made some notes in the notebook he carried. He approached Cora and Cisco. "I'm Officer Jeff Rogers," he said, addressing Cisco. "Did you see what happened?"

"Yes—we both did." Cisco described the attack and told him the animal ran away after Cora pulled it off the priest.

Officer Rogers eyed them for a moment, looking first at Cisco, then at Cora. "What kind of animal? A big dog? Can you describe it?"

"Uh...about a hundred pounds, grey, pointed ears, thick fur, wild and mean-looking."

"Your wife's pretty brave to grab it like that," the officer noted, looking at Cisco and rubbing his chin.

"I tried to stop her, but she pulled away...I went for something to hit it with."

"His golf club," Cora said, blinking.

"Have you seen this dog around here?" Rogers pressed.

"Uh...," Cisco glanced at Cora. "No."

Rogers raised his eyebrows. "Why did you hesitate?"

Cisco squeezed Cora's arm, nodding to show he would support what she said.

Cora hesitated, then went on in a rush. "Officer, this will sound crazy, but we think the animal might be...uh...a wolf."

"A wolf," Rogers repeated, eying Cora over the rims of his glasses.

Cora felt her face turn red, and set her jaw defiantly. "I'm probably wrong. I think I've seen one around before—a number of times." She crossed her arms and looked at Cisco for encouragement.

"If you thought it was a wolf, why'd you pull it off?" Rogers asked.

She shifted her eyes away and then met his gaze. "We had to stop it. It seemed like the only way."

Rogers put his pen in his pocket and scratched his head. "Okay," he said. "Looks like the animal's gone, but we'll canvass the neighborhood and issue a lookout for it. Here's my card, and I'll get back to you if we have more questions." He handed a card to Cora, and leveled a look at her.

"It must've been a dog," he said, and moved toward his car.

~~~

Cisco called Saint Brennan's rectory to notify them of Father McGrath's injuries. Cora was frantic he would say something in the house to further inflame Angel, but fortunately he didn't.

It was growing dark by the time they drove to Mother of Good Counsel Hospital. Cora, badly shaken, appreciated Cisco's company after the terrible events—a day that seemed never-ending, relentless, beginning with Angel's startling message and ending with crisis.

Cora typically showed unusual strength under stress. Cisco knew this, but nonetheless expressed concern. "Are you sure you feel up to going to the hospital?"

She didn't answer, but propped her elbow on the car's window frame, trying to decide how far from the house they had to be before Angel could no longer overhear them. "Give me a minute to calm down and gather my thoughts," was all she said.

Finally she told him her fears. "Cisco, back at the house, I was afraid you'd say the wrong thing, but thank God you didn't. I think—no, I *know*...Angel hears us there, but I don't think she does when we're somewhere else. And I think she gets mad if she hears us plotting against her. That's why Father was attacked—because he wanted us to do something she didn't like. I don't want to make matters worse, or make her mad at you too. We have to be *very* careful!"

Cisco said nothing, kept his eyes on the road and let her finish.

A few hours ago he pooh-poohed her belief in Angel, but Cora thought he would surely see things differently now. She eyed him hopefully, but he remained silent, apparently considering what she had said.

After a moment she asked, "Well? Are you going to tell me what you're thinking?"

"I'm working on it. I admit there *is* more going on than what I thought—I'm trying to get it to make sense."

Cora ran her hands through her hair, folded her arms across her chest and looked out the side window, disappointed he didn't immediately accept her reasoning. Well, at least he was open to discussing the matter. "What are some things you *can* agree about?"

"Are you sure you want to talk about this now?"

She drew in a breath and turned toward him. "We have to. It could be dangerous if we don't sort things out before we go home."

Cisco took his eyes from the road to watch her. "Okay," he said finally. "Well, *possibly* I'm ready to believe there's a wolf. I don't think that animal today was a dog either. Maybe it *is* a wolf."

"I noticed that you yelled, 'Get away from that wolf'. You didn't yell 'Get away from that dog'. Your first reaction in the heat of the moment was to cry 'wolf'."

He smiled, watching the road again, although Cora didn't notice the humor. "True. But I don't know if I'm ready to believe the wolf has anything to do with your Angel. What connection could they have?"

"I haven't figured that out yet." Cora was in better control of her emotions now that she was *dealing* with the day's disasters instead of *reacting* to them. She watched the road, thinking. "But all this crazy stuff happening at the same time...it has to be related! Are you ready to believe there *is* an Angel at least—now that I told you she replied and about the diary—I think you were right when you said it could be hers. And Father's opinion?" She turned to watch Cisco's face.

Cisco hesitated. "I see why you believe it, but it's hard for me to buy it. An entity from another world?—things like that just don't happen. And it's not *my* direct experience; it's secondhand to *your* experience. Can't there be any other reason for this?"

"Will you at least watch what you say in the house, if I'm right...?"

"Sure," he conceded. This would not be difficult, as he was normally close-mouthed about personal matters.

"And will you help me dig into this business and resolve it? Even if you still think there has to be another explanation?"

"Of course I will, Hon. You know I will."

She was reassured. She turned her eyes away and fiddled with a strap of the purse in her lap.

"Well, let's pretend I'm right again and try to get a handle on what just happened," she said, taking an analytical approach. "The way I see it, Father advised us to try to stop Angel. We want to do that, but assume Angel would be upset if we interfere. *She* thinks she's doing good..."

"Protecting you," Cisco interjected.

Cora nodded, eyes still on her purse. "Yes, protecting me. She thinks she's protecting me, like she's done for years, but for some reason now she wants to step it up...so the last thing she wants is for anyone to *stop* her. That's why we have to be careful."

She looked up at Cisco. "She's protecting me, but not you. I'm afraid she might do something to you if she thinks you're in her way."

He raised an eyebrow and tilted his head in her direction. "If she's so dangerous, I can't believe you're not at risk too."

"Believe it. She's never hurt me and she won't."

"Is that why you ran in to pull the wolf off Father, why you knew it wouldn't turn on you?"

"I didn't think about it—it was just reaction, intuition, but yes. I never thought I was in danger."

"If she's been protecting you all these years, and punishing people who crossed you like you propose, then how come she only hears us in our house? Seems she's other places, not just our house, don't you think?"

"Well, we talked about those people at home, and in fact I got even more angry at them telling you about it. I can't explain that part yet, but there's a *lot* I can't explain."

"This is supposition, but let's go on. Father was trying to stop her, so she got mad. And then what? She sent a wolf to attack him?" Cisco glanced at her skeptically.

Cora's face hardened, insistent. "Yes—exactly. She sent a wolf to attack him. The same wolf that attacked Valerie, the same one we saw in the woods."

"How could she do that?" Cisco asked, turning the car off the dark road into the well-lit parking lot in front of the hospital.

"I don't know. We have to figure that out. Frannie and I have been working on...."

"Frannie. Oh, yes, you and Frannie have been digging into this, haven't you? And have you two come to any conclusions?"

Cora clenched her jaw in a moment of anger. Just as quickly she turned away and blinked furiously to hide tears of disappointment, and said in a meek voice, "We have some ideas, and some information, some research. And we're looking into more things."

"Do you want me to drop you at the emergency room while I park?" he asked, slowing the car, not noticing her reaction.

"No, I'll walk with you."

Cisco found a parking spot, pulled in and turned off the motor. Cora stayed in her seat and reached for his hand. With his free hand he stroked her cheek gently. "Are you okay, Hon? Are you sure you want to go in?"

"No," she admitted, as she dropped his hand and squared her shoulders. "But I have to find out how Father is, and let him know we're here. I'll talk to his doctor...maybe we can answer some questions for him. Then we can go home."

~~~

"Only immediate family is allowed in the emergency room," the woman at the information desk said.

"He's a priest," Cora argued. "He has no immediate family."

The woman was unmoved. "He'll need to send word out that he wants to see you."

Cisco chipped in, "He was unconscious. That's not going to happen."

Finally Cora was able to get through to the woman to let a nurse make the decision, and they were directed back to an ER treatment room. Father was still unconscious. Large dressings covered his throat, both arms, hands, and his right cheek. His ankle was wrapped and elevated on pillows. He was pale and agitated, tossing his head and moaning, but seemed to be breathing normally with the hissing oxygen cannula in place. Monitors and an IV were connected, making the expected beeping sounds.

They introduced themselves to the nurse attending Father and explained their relationship to him. "The paramedics told us a garbled secondhand story about a priest being attacked by a wild dog," she said. Cora admitted that was pretty much what *had* happened.

They waited in uncomfortable chairs, keeping their coats on in the chilly room, as nurses and aides performed their tasks and moved in and out. Finally a doctor arrived and asked them to step into the hall.

After they answered the doctor's questions, he told them, "As you see, he's stable and the lacerations to his face, arms and hands have been taken care of, but he'll need repair of the neck and ankle as soon as the surgical team arrives."

Cora and Cisco nodded, and asked about the extent of the injuries and what surgery was needed.

"I'm not supposed to discuss the case under privacy rules, of course. But as you were there you already know what happened." He looked seriously from Cora to Cisco.

"We'd appreciate whatever you can tell us," Cora said. "Not only is he our friend, but it happened at our house. I'm sure he'd want us to know."

The doctor took in a long breath, let it out again. "Well, the ankle, of course, will need repair. The Achilles tendon was completely severed. The severity of the injury is unusual and he could be left with a limp."

"And his neck?" asked Cora, white-faced.

He scratched his head. "That's not so easy. He had many layers around his neck, and that probably saved his life, but the damage is severe." He paused, then went on. "Fortunately there doesn't seem to be serious penetration of the larger vessels, but there are a lot of structures in the neck. Best case, a simple vascular repair, or over-sewing of severed vessels, is all he'll need. However, if injuries are extensive, he could need a vascular surgeon, a head and neck surgeon, or a neurosurgeon."

Now it was Cisco who turned pale.

One of the nurses interrupted to say the pastor of Saint Brennan's was on his way.

The doctor turned back to Cora and Cisco. "It will all depend on what the surgeon finds. The trachea may need repair, and there could be damage to the voice box. He's breathing well on his own, and that's a good sign. It's unlikely there's penetration of those structures, but there could be some crushing or bruising to contend with."

"But he will live?" Cora implored, through the fist she held to her mouth.

"Yes, he will live, unless there are complications we can't foresee."

"But he may limp, and...." Cora hesitated. "What about brain damage? Was there loss of blood to the brain?"

"We don't think so. The neurological assessment doesn't substantiate brain injury, but the work-up isn't complete yet."

"But he's not conscious," Cisco said.

"He's sedated, and had significant trauma and shock." The doctor edged toward the door, and Cora assumed he felt he'd spent enough time with them.

"Just one last question," she said. "If the voice box is damaged, will he be able to talk?"

"The voice should return, but he may sound different, even bizarre, but he'll be able to be understood. In all likelihood therapy will improve that."

Soon after the doctor left, Father McGrath opened his eyes and put his hand to the bandage around his neck. He looked at Cora and tried to speak. Wincing at the effort, he lifted his eyebrows and both hands in a questioning way. Cora understood he wanted to know what was going on. She took his hand and explained gently what the doctor said.

Chapter 24

Cora couldn't sleep. Her mind kept replaying the events of the day. She tried reading, and she tried listening to talk radio, strategies that usually made her sleepy, but her thoughts wouldn't shut off. She couldn't get comfortable. Her neck hurt, and she had leg cramps, despite the bar of soap she kept at the foot of the bed. She admitted there was no reason soap should help, but she had had no leg cramps for three years, since she put the soap there. Finally she dropped into a restless sleep about five in the morning and woke two hours later. Her neck was stiff, and one eye hurt from digging it into her pillow while she slept. Her vision was fuzzy from dry eyes.

No...yesterday had certainly *not* been a good day!

Still in her sleep shirt, she dragged herself to the kitchen. "I feel like I've been beat up," she announced. "Every muscle in my body aches and my head is foggy. Is coffee ready?"

Cisco, an early riser, poured a cup for her. "Stress will do that," he said.

Cora sighed dramatically, staggered to the table and sat staring at her cup, her chin resting in her hand, deep in thought.

"How are you doing this morning?" Cisco asked automatically, returning to the paper.

"Other than feeling beaten up and too brain-dead to think, you mean? Other than that, how am I doing?" she replied sarcastically.

Cisco raised his eyebrows and gave her a meaningful look over his glasses.

"Not rested, that's for sure," she said. "I'd like to take things easy today.

Do we have to keep that appointment with the accountant? Can't we go another day when I can think straight?"

"Not a good idea. She may not have another appointment before the end of the year, and tax planning needs to get done. You know how busy she is."

"I guess you're right," Cora conceded, with another deep sigh.

The phone rang, and Cora got up to answer it. She listened to her daughter-in-law Marty chat about the grandsons and Thanksgiving plans. "You sure you don't want to join us at my sister's?" Marty asked.

"No—that's okay. Thanks, but I've been tired lately, and a quiet day at home looks pretty good. I'm not in the mood for a crowd." Marty was from a large family so Thanksgiving would be boisterous, but Cora was speaking for Angel's benefit. Nor did she want Marty to know what was going on, at least not at this juncture.

After ending the call, Cora dialed Father Parrilli, the pastor of Saint Brennan's, for an update on Father McGrath's condition. Thankfully, the surgery had gone well. The parish would arrange for someone to pick up Father McGrath's car.

Cisco rattled off a list of errands to the bank, the hardware store, and other places, and left a short time later. The errands weren't real. To appear normal to Angel, they devised a plan on the way home from the hospital last night. Cora should be alone to confront Angel, they reasoned, as she had never contacted Cora when Cisco was nearby. They were meeting Frannie later that day, not their accountant.

To continue the ruse, Cora went about her morning routines. She straightened the kitchen, went upstairs, washed up, brushed her teeth, put music on, hung clothes. The phone rang again as she headed to her office.

This time the caller was Officer Rogers. They hadn't been able to find the animal that attacked Father McGrath, and he asked if Cora had any ideas. They needed to test it for rabies, talk to the owner, capture and cage the animal. Cora had nothing to suggest. She was dismayed to imagine Father enduring rabies shots along with everything else.

"You knew plenty about the animal yesterday—I thought you might have some ideas. Why did Father McGrath visit you anyway?"

Cora didn't want to tell Rogers they had been talking about a ghost.

He didn't seem to think her story was reliable as it was.

A door slammed loudly somewhere downstairs. The sound was unmistakable.

That's odd. No windows should be open.

"Oh, we've been friends for years. He just drops in. By the way, how did my neighbors describe the animal? Did anyone else think it was a wolf?"

"No—they said it was a large dog or coyote. Most got there after the animal was gone and didn't see it."

Cora went downstairs after the call. All the outside doors were closed and locked, exactly as they were before she went upstairs. All interior doors were wide open.

What slammed? Okay, I should be used to this by now. Angel wants my attention.

She reheated a cup of coffee and carried it to her office. She felt a sudden urgency, a sense of time wasted on phone calls and interruptions. How would she force Angel to stop her little hints and communicate with her? She raised her chin in determination.

I have to know more about her and why she's doing...whatever it is she's doing.

She opened a blank Word document on her laptop, inviting communication with Angel. She sat in front of the screen gathering her thoughts. She jotted notes on paper to help stay focused during the anticipated battle—words carefully chosen as safe for Angel to see.

—Did Angel cause the wolf attack on Father McGrath?
—If so, why, and how, did she do that?
—Doesn't she realize Father McGrath is my friend and hurting my friend hurts me?
—What does she want me to do?
—Does she recognize the diary, and why does she want me to read it?

That was what she wanted to know. She decided to jump right in, take things as they came, and react to whatever Angel said....

If she answers—a big if.

Feeling silly, she addressed her computer, saying in an angry voice, "I am *very* upset. Did you have anything to do with the attack on my friend yesterday?"

She waited. Nothing happened.

"I know you can hear me," she insisted. "I'm not giving up until you answer."

She waited again, staring at the screen. No words appeared.

"I don't understand why you would attack him. How can I do whatever it is you want me to do if you won't *tell* me what you want? You're making me guess—and I'm stumped."

Previous communications from Angel appeared when Cora was out of the room. She would try that. She went into the bathroom, washed her hands and face, and returned to her chair. The document was still blank.

Cora snapped—she'd had enough of Angel's games. "Damn you!" she exclaimed. "What kind of chicken-shit spirit hides when confronted? Why won't you talk to me? Are you *afraid*, Angel?"

Suddenly a cold wind blasted into the room, throwing Cora forward in her seat and blowing papers off her desk. The office door slammed with such force the walls shook. Holding her desk for support as the wind whipped her hair and papers around the room, trembling, Cora watched wide-eyed and open-mouthed as a five-drawer file cabinet, forty inches wide, shook and clattered violently, then slowly tilted forward and crashed to the floor.

My God, that thing must weigh 500 pounds!

The wind stopped abruptly, papers drifted to the floor, and the room was completely silent. Cora's scalp tingled with horror and she clutched her upper arms, digging her fingers into them, as she watched the cabinet inch itself upright again, lifted by an invisible force back into place, the drawers closing one by one with a clang, seemingly of their own volition, leaving the contents of the upper shelf and cabinet-top fanned out across the floor. An earthy smell, like a damp forest, permeated the room.

White-faced, shaking, with a racing heart, Cora sat in her chair, gripped the chair's arms until her nails bent, mustering courage to face Angel head on. She forced herself to think clearly. She couldn't match the spirit's physical strength, but intellectually she might have a chance.

I called her and she's here—be careful what you ask for! I have to get control!

She couldn't show fear. She took a few deep breaths to stop shaking and resorted to her customary standby for stressful situations, sarcasm.

She hasn't hurt me—so far.

She pushed herself up and stomped to the office door, threw it open, and banged it against the wall to demonstrate her anger. Then she plopped into her chair and glared at the laptop, arms folded across her chest. "Well, I guess I got your attention," she said. "I don't suppose you'd consider picking that stuff up."

The room was silent.

Frustrated, Cora leaned forward, her face inches from the computer screen, and burst out, "He's a *priest*, for God's sake! How can you attack a *priest?* He was trying to *help* me!"

At last, words slowly—letter…pause…letter…pause—started to appear on the screen. No box enclosed the words, just letters in a large bold font, starting in the center of the page, the line lengthening toward both margins as each letter appeared.

Don't trust Father Fitzpatrick, Darlin'. It's all his fault.

"Okay. An opinion. One that doesn't *apply* in this case, but it's a start," Cora wisecracked. "It's Father McGrath, not Fitzpatrick. So you did have something to do with his attack?"

There was no response. Perhaps Angel didn't answer direct questions, but responded when provoked. "I'll take that for a yes. Do you turn yourself into a wolf, shape-shift or something?"

No response. Cora chewed on her lower lip, considering what to say next. "Another yes. So why did you attack Father? He's a good man trying to help me. You call me Darlin'—I assume that means you care about me. If you care for me, why would you attack my friends?"

New words appeared, replacing the ones on the screen:

She is my only friend! We protect Darlin' from that man.

Cora was confused. The response didn't make sense. "She? We?" Cora asked, her brow furrowed. "Who is *she?* Who is your friend? What does your friend have to do with what happened yesterday, or *anything?*"

This was not easy. Angel responded, but only with cryptic phrases and clues. She was controlling the communication, saying what she wanted to say and disregarding Cora's questions.

So—this is a game to her. A game of wits—Cora against Cyber-Angel.

Cora concentrated. Angel's first response came when she provoked her, and then to correct her. Could she use that to get answers to her questions?

I just accused her of changing into a wolf to attack Father. Maybe that's wrong.

"Are you saying you *didn't* attack Father? That a friend did? Is your friend a spirit too?" Cora shook her head slowly.

I'm already dealing with a spirit and a wolf—how many entities are there?

Her mind raced. No response meant Angel agreed with what Cora said—or didn't care. Was she on the right track? Who was Angel's friend? Her eyes opened wide as the answer came to her.

"The wolf! The wolf is not *you*. The wolf is your only *friend!*" This time there was an answer.

Wolf is She.

Wolf is she. No—wolf is She! That's it!

"She! That's the wolf's name! And *She* is your only friend! That's right, isn't it?" Cora was excited. She was getting somewhere.

No reply. Cora smiled. She was getting the hang of this. "I'll go with that, Angel. So *She* is your friend, and you somehow got *She* to attack Father. Right? Why attack my friends, Father and Valerie, and who knows who else?"

No response. Cora readjusted her position and gripped the chair arms firmly again with both hands. "You told me you were fixing things. I think you mean you're protecting me—that I'm your Darlin'. People did nasty things to me and I thought you were paying them back for hurting me. Well, I don't like that, but at least it makes a *little* sense. This attack on Father, though—that's different. He was helping me, not hurting me. You didn't do this because of me. You did it because you were angry…because you felt threatened for *yourself*, not for me. You're not protecting me. You're just in a *snit!*"

Cora threw the word out, realizing "snit" was ridiculously inadequate to refer to the attack, but the word popped into her head and she used it, feeling it was a word that would challenge Angel, who appeared to have no sense of proportion when it came to offense and vengeance.

No answer. "I'm right, aren't I?" No response.

"Angel, I don't *want* you to punish people I know, let alone my friends! What *you're* doing hurts me more than *they* ever could." Her anger turned to despair as she pictured Father's panic-stricken face, and her eyes began to shine with tears.

"What do you want me to *do*, Angel?" she whispered with a choked voice.

She felt a loss of connection, hopelessness, and leaned back into her chair and rubbed her eyes. Had Angel left, or was she just not answering?

"Why do you want me to read the diary? Why did you pick a place to read? What am I *looking* for?" she tried, guessing that reading the diary might answer some questions but create others.

Cora asked question after question, made assumption after assumption, but Angel was done. Too pumped up to sit, she paced the room, picking things up and placing them in different spots aimlessly. Cora had survived a direct contact with Angel and was beginning to understand her. She had seemed to be Cora's protector, but now acted more like a child that didn't get her way. She grinned—Angel was vulnerable. She could use that. Cora could do this.

But on the other hand—why did she say Father Fitzpatrick—who was that? Was it Father McGrath's comments or something else that made her distrust priests? The irrational and confused communications and behavior, and the damage to Cora's office, demonstrated increasing power and mounting danger. It confirmed her instinct to be careful, to avoid implicating Cisco or anyone else.

What do I do now?

Cora turned off her laptop, leaving the mess Angel made on the floor for Cisco to see. She took the diary to a comfortable reading chair in the guest room and opened it to the page Angel had indicated.

Chapter 25

Cora could hardly wait to tell Cisco and Frannie about her contact with Angel and what she read in the diary. The Lemont Area Historical Society was open for only limited hours, so the building was usually vacant by mid-afternoon and was a good place for private conversation. To save time rehashing events, Cisco and Frannie had already met to bring each other up to date. Cora had not seen Cisco since he left the house early in the day, so neither of them knew about her latest encounter with Angel. Now Cora unlocked the entry door and led them to the choir loft, where they took seats around the library table, and sipped from takeout cups of coffee.

"Did you bring your pad and pen?" Frannie joked.

"Sure did," Cora said, fishing for them in her bulky purse. "Brought my *favorite* pen. Makes me feel confident, working with a good pen."

In spite of her brave words, Cora looked around nervously to be sure they were alone. "I know this is *my* problem, and I appreciate your help." She looked into one set of eyes and then the other. "I think we agree now there's good evidence Angel is real, and after this morning I don't think there's any doubt." Cisco started to open his mouth, but Cora held out a hand to stop him.

"Let me finish. She's also violent and unpredictable. I don't think she'd hurt me, but she *is* a danger to people around me. That includes you." Her gaze rested on Cisco. "We have to prevent that."

"I still don't know how you can feel so sure *you* aren't in danger," Cisco objected.

Cora didn't answer him. Admittedly the information she got from Angel that morning was scanty and left a lot to interpretation, but now she had confronted Angel, knew her better, and felt less impotent.

Frannie reached into her purse, pulled out some notes and waited for someone to begin.

"It was quite a morning." Cora rolled her eyes, then took a deep breath. "Let's see if we need to fill in any gaps before I tell you about it."

Cisco and Frannie looked at Cora expectantly, knowing she would have something in mind. They were well aware of her management skills, one of which was running meetings. Cora's mother often said she was *born* in charge, and was so headstrong it was easiest to just give up and let her take over. She liked to be in control, and management as a career choice had suited her.

"Cisco, Frannie told you what she found out about wolves and spirits?"

"Yeessss." Cisco's doubt was reflected in his shifting eyes and clenched jaw.

"Did you tell Frannie what happened yesterday?"

"That poor man—how awful!" Frannie's eyes blazed, shaking her head, lips tight with anger.

"Cora thinks something Father said made Angel angry enough to make a wolf attack him," Cisco said.

"Uh huh." Frannie paused a moment. "Well, that's no crazier than anything else we been considering. How do you figure this mother business relates to that?"

Cisco frowned and shifted his eyes between the two women. With the rapid succession of events and limited discussions in their home, Cora hadn't told Cisco that theory yet. "Father suggested Angel might think she's my mother, since she used the word Máime, which is Gaelic for Mommy—or maybe I was reacting to grief over Mom's death."

Cisco examined Cora's face for a clue. "Well…" he said, "he's a psychologist, so I guess he *would* ask you about grief. But he thinks she's real, a ghost or something, doesn't he?"

"Either way, maternal feelings could be involved—mine, or Angel's— or both." Cora's voice shook, and she looked down at the table.

"I should have realized how much your mother's death was bothering you," Cisco said, reaching out and taking her hand.

"I've been hiding it, Hon—pretty well, I guess." She gave him a little tight-lipped smile. "Trying to man up…it's not your fault." She squeezed his hand. "Angel couldn't be my mother's spirit, of course, she was around long before Mom died. After she died, I kept feeling Mom wanted to know what I was doing or that she left things for me to find. Sometimes I thought I heard her call me."

"Doesn't that happen to a lot of grieving people?" he suggested.

"I suppose…you could be right." She pulled her hand away but gave him a warm look before saying, "We'd better get busy."

She began shuffling through papers on the table, straightened her back, looked at Frannie, and said, "I think a lot of what we talked about yesterday is barking up the wrong tree. Father's attack and this morning's events have put a whole new light on things."

She paused and looked at Cisco. "After you left, I heard from Angel."

"Really? Our plan worked?" Cisco sounded surprised.

"Yes. Not at first, but then I said something that made her mad, and she threw that big file cabinet on the floor…"

"What?" Cisco exclaimed. He probably thought she was exaggerating.

"…and picked it up again…"

"What?" Frannie said, her mouth dropping open.

"…she pretty much admitted to masterminding the attack on Father. 'Don't trust Father Fitzpatrick, Darlin'. It's all his fault,' is exactly what she said."

"On your computer again?" asked Cisco.

"Yeah, and some other things, too…not very clear, but I think I can fill in the blanks with guesses."

"Who's Father Fitzpatrick?" asked Frannie.

Cora went on to describe in detail Angel's tantrum and how she had provoked Angel's responses. "Father Fitzpatrick was from old Saint James, I read that in the diary, and I guess Angel has a dislike of priests for some reason. She seems to be confusing him with Father McGrath."

"Right, spirits get confused, remember," Frannie said.

Cora leaned back in her chair and watched while her husband and friend considered the developments.

"The cabinet…" Cisco began.

"Dramatic, wasn't it? I'll let you pick up the mess." She gave a little chuckle.

"How can you joke about this?" Cisco asked.

Cora blinked rapidly and averted her eyes. "It's how I cope. You should know that."

A muscle in his jaw jumped and he started to open his mouth, then thought better of it and closed it again. Instead he asked a question. "She didn't actually say she caused the attack?"

"She alluded to it. I don't think she wanted to explain, so she wouldn't answer," Cora said. "I accused her of attacking Father because she was in a snit when she heard him say he wanted to stop her. I think I was right. The wolf isn't her, made manifest or some such thing, but a friend—her only friend, she said. Angel even told me the wolf's name, which is She—that's gonna get confusing, but it is what it is."

"What were her exact words?" asked Frannie.

"The first response I told you, and the second was: 'She is my only friend. We protect Darlin' from that man.' The third was: 'Wolf is She', with a capital 'S' for She. That reply came after I suggested that she—Angel—didn't attack Father herself, but that She—the wolf, Angel's friend—attacked under Angel's direction. See what I mean about the confusing name?" Cora gave a half smile.

"After the attack, I saw the wolf look at the window. You mean Angel was telling it what to do?" Cisco asked.

"That's what I think."

In the end Cisco and Frannie agreed with Cora's reasoning. Cora felt a sense of relief that Cisco finally accepted the idea of Angel's reality, was ready to explore the implications and discuss plans to take action.

"Cora, you write somethin' down on your little pad now, stuff we know," Frannie cut in. "Here's what to write. You say, 'Angel gets this she-wolf to attack Father, because he's getting in the way.' She's in a snit, so she calls her friend—this *she*-wolf—that's where the name came from, I figure."

"That's about what seems to have happened," Cora said, nodding.

"This Angel confuses me, though. One minute she wants to be your mother, next she's like some kid having a hissy fit because things don't go her way. And what does she want with you? Why you, not someone else?" asked Frannie, narrowing her eyes, unable to make a connection between Cora and the spirit.

"I don't know that yet—but I think I know who she *is*," Cora said, leaning back in her chair, arms folded and eyeing them smugly.

"It *was* her diary, wasn't it?" Cisco said, grinning.

"I think so, yes. You said that sarcastically, but I think you were right."

"You read it?" asked Frannie.

"Yes, right after she stopped communicating with me. Not the whole thing, but enough to convince me." This was going to take a while to explain, so Cora settled herself more comfortably, took a sip of coffee, cleared her throat, crossed her arms and rested them on the table, watching their expressions as she told them what she read.

"I'm convinced Angel is the spirit of the woman who wrote the diary—a young Irish woman who lived over a hundred years ago, who was murdered at Saint James. When I brought the diary into the house, Angel recognized it. I even think I know where the wolf came from."

In the silence Cora looked from face to face. Cisco frowned and furrowed his brow, not yet convinced. Frannie raised her eyebrows, grinned, and rubbed her hands together, excited.

"That's got to be it! A ghost don't rest sometimes because of a violent death—I read that. Here's what I think—this has got to be a *murder* mystery!" Frannie said.

"Right. The woman who wrote it, Meg, or Mavourneen, grew up in Sag Bridge, where Bridey lived. And, as Bridey told me when she gave me the diary, the woman who wrote it was killed in the summer of 1898, along with her husband and unborn baby. How many murdered women are there that could be my ghost?"

Cisco was listening intently, but he didn't say anything.

"Meg began keeping the diary when she was in her teens. There are almost ten years of entries here—I didn't have time to read it all, so I skimmed it until I got to where she wanted me to start," Cora said.

"Did it say who killed her?" asked Frannie.

Cora grinned. "She could hardly write about it after she was dead, could she? Clues, you mean, or something she knew that pointed to who killed her?"

Frannie nodded, and now Cisco did too.

"Nothing obvious. We'll have to spend some time analyzing it in detail. Here's the short version. Meg would have been in her early twenties, and she was married, happily, to Packey, a foreman in one of the quarries.

She left Sag Bridge to work in Chicago, but returned to marry Packey. That reminded me of you, Frannie, coming home to a former life."

"I'll have to think about that—it didn't turn *me* into no ghost," Frannie said.

"She was pregnant, near term, with her first child. She and Packey lived
on the family farm with Meg's sister and brother-in-law, but her mother lived at a boarding house in town. Meg described her mother as an
irritating woman who made their lives difficult, and she was determined
to be a better mother than her own Máime, which is what she called her
mother."

"Máime! That does it. This has to be your ghost!" said Frannie.

"Yes, and the diary was filled with descriptions of inventions, gadgets,
and toys—clearly that interested her, and could explain why she's using
my computer to communicate," Cora theorized.

"But none of those people would have killed her," said Cisco, waving
his hands as he talked.

"No, not likely. She seemed to care for all of them, even her irritating mother."

"What do you think Angel wanted you to see?" he asked.

"I'm not sure. The first revealing information I read, after the page she
said I should start, was about a picnic on the Fourth of July and extensive gossip Meg heard that day, including trouble at the quarries where
Packey worked. And the last entry was about a man she didn't know who
approached Packey after Mass, and that her sister was very sick. She had
an argument with Packey about a number of things, why he wouldn't tell
her what the man at the church wanted, why he let the priest—Father
Fitzpatrick, like in Angel's note—drag him into so much work at the
church, why he had to keep boxing, which she didn't like. She was upset
with her brother-in-law, Mick, who was being distant and crabby. Her
final words were about patching things up with Packey before he left
her alone that evening to meet with the priest, how eager she was for
the birth of her baby girl, who she called Darlin', and she was very tired."

"Darlin'," Frannie said, nodding. "That's important too. How did she
know her baby was a girl?"

"She said she believed it was a girl, she couldn't *know* in those days, of
course. There was no more after that, but we know, of course, that Packey,

Meg, and her baby girl were found dead in the cemetery, by Father Fitz-patrick, at least, that's the story. And no one knew who killed them."

"Other than the killer or killers," Cisco put in.

"If you still aren't convinced for any reason," Cora went on, "the big-gest clue that this is Angel's diary is the strong reaction she had to it. It was like, as soon as I brought it into the house—where did that come from? Where did you get it? She must have recognized it, and it's ex-tremely important to her. Once I got the idea Angel was Meg's spirit, things started falling into place, although I didn't like the connection. I found myself liking Meg, and it was hard to think of her as violent."

Cisco had a thoughtful look on his face. "You said you liked *Angel* too, before you started connecting the violent stuff."

"So Angel is a spirit…she was alive once, and isn't anymore. The next question is, what kind of link does she have to Cora? Why is Cora her earthly contact?" Frannie said.

"Good question," Cora said.

They looked at each other, and Cisco and Frannie waited for Cora's opinion.

"What?" asked Cora, and then exhaled, rested her elbows on the table again, rubbed her eyes, and took a moment to think. "From what Frannie found out about spirits, they focus on either a person or a place. I have no idea why she'd pick me. I didn't live here when she started visiting me, and she's followed me for years, wherever I moved. She doesn't stay put."

"Maybe ghosts can tell the future, and she knew you'd move to Lem-ont someday," Frannie suggested.

"She only hears us in the house, you think," Cisco put in. "And she's been more active since we moved to Lemont. That must mean some-thing."

"Yeah," Cora said, shrugging and holding the palms of both hands out.

"It's a question…write that down," Frannie dictated. Cora jotted a note on her pad.

"So we'll assume Meg is Angel. We don't have any better ideas, let's go with that one," Frannie said. "What places would be important to her?"

"The place she lived," Cora guessed.

"No…," said Cisco thoughtfully. "…the place she *died*." They ex-changed looks of agreement as the thought sunk in.

"He's right," said Frannie. She paused, then ordered, "Write that down."

Cora ripped two pages from her notepad. On the top of one she wrote: *Known or Theorized.* On the second she wrote: *To Find Out or Do.*

She placed both pages on the table for Cisco and Frannie to see.

"Ah!" Cisco teased, tapping a finger on one of the pages. "Cora's famous lists!"

"You ever notice," Frannie said, poking Cisco with an elbow, "the look she gets on her face when she crosses something off one of her lists? It's almost like sex."

"I noticed. I should be so lucky," Cisco replied.

"Let's do this," Cora said, ignoring their banter. "We can't prove Meg is Angel, but we strongly suspect it. So let's write down what we know, or think we know, that *might* prove it. Questions go on the list of things to find out. It could help us sort out what to do next, don't you think?"

They spent some time brainstorming and making notes. Frannie consulted her research now and then. Cora wrote items down as they sorted facts and suppositions from unknowns.

"Angel is a spirit—probably a young Irish woman who lived here a hundred years ago," Cora began.

"Spirits stay spirits because something keeps them from being at rest. Let's say that's the murders. Angel can't accept being killed, her husband and baby too," Frannie added, nodding.

"Angel says a wolf is her friend—a wolf named She, and She carries out Angel's orders," Cora added.

"There's some connection between Cora and Angel we don't know. There must be a reason she protects Cora," Cisco said. "And she wants Cora to do something—something important to Angel. What is that?"

"This Angel's been around years, follows Cora from place to place, but all of a sudden gets mean and starts coming around just about every day. What made her kick into high gear out of the blue?" Frannie asked.

"Why *did* Angel latch onto Cora? Why not someone else?" Cisco asked, rephrasing his thought.

"Clues—calling herself *Máime* and me *Darlin'*—suggest she thinks she's my mother. Why? Could that be a motive?" Cora theorized.

"You're both Irish," Frannie noted.

"She seems to have limitations—she doesn't seem to react to things unless they happen in our house, but vengeful acts happen other places," Cora said. "So far. What she did this morning shows she's getting stronger, or was holding back before, so I wonder if she'll start to follow us other places—if there's anywhere we can talk safely."

"Meg, her husband and baby, were murdered, but we don't know who did it," Cisco said. "What about that man Packey talked to the day they died?"

"Meg's sister was sick. Does that mean anything?" Cora asked.

"What went on at that church? Angel doesn't like priests. Did the killings have something to do with the priest?" Cisco asked.

"What about the brother-in-law. Any idea what kind of guy he was?" Frannie said.

"I have to read the whole journal. Maybe there are more clues," Cora said, shaking her head slowly.

"What about the quarries? You said men were making trouble and Packey was foreman," Cisco said.

"My money's on that stranger. Everyone else seems like nice guys, that's what I think," said Frannie.

"Everyone we know about—there's bound to be other people," Cisco pointed out.

"I can pull out news stories about the murders at the historical society. A story like that must have had a lot of coverage," Cora noted.

"Okay, I think we've beaten this to death," Cora said, scanning both lists and marking notes by some items. "Let's prioritize and figure out what to do."

"Yeah, but wait," Frannie said. "I remember another question. Where did that diary *come* from? How did Bridey get it? Put that down too."

"Oh, I forgot," Cora said, tapping her forehead. "After I read the diary I wondered that too, and I called Bridey. How could I forget to tell you? It's interesting.

"A friend of Bridey's father worked for public works in Lemont. This was many years later—about the 1950s, Bridey thinks. They were boarding up all the old tunnels because they were dangerous..."

"Tunnels? What's this about tunnels now?" Frannie interrupted.

"Lemont has a spiderweb of connecting tunnels running under the old part of town. It was a very busy canal port at one time, and it was easier to unload barges and carry materials to businesses at canal level than to hoist stuff up to the streets and down again. Digging tunnels was no big deal after digging canals and quarries."

"So this friend of her father...?" Cisco circled one hand impatiently.

"Yes—well. Years later the tunnels started collapsing, so they boarded them up. In the process they found stuff that was stored in them and forgotten. Bridey had no idea how the diary got left in the tunnel. Maybe somebody who bought Meg's farm found it, handed it over to the village or the police, and it got into some inactive file. Her father's friend found the diary. Meg's family was gone, and the friend remembered Bridey's father telling Meg's story, and thought he would like the diary since he knew Packey, so he gave it to him. Bridey got it when her father died."

"Seems the historical society would've been a better choice," Cisco said.

"True, only it hadn't been started yet," Cora pointed out.

"Wait now. You said we'd know where the wolf came from. Where *did* this wolf come from anyhow and why is *She* Angel's friend? How'd you figure that?" Frannie complained.

"I could be wrong, but going back to the story Bridey told me, when the pastor of Saint James, Father Fitzpatrick again, found Meg and the baby dead, a wolf was lying with them, and started to attack him. He had to shoot and kill it. I think that's Angel's wolf, and it's a spirit too—a wolf spirit, like the one in that Algernon Blackwood story you told me about," Cora proposed.

Frannie pressed her lips together, wagged her head, and held out her hands. "Could be. So you think maybe Angel sent her, because wolves live in forests and travel around, this She wolf can do things and go places Angel can't?"

"I guess I missed part of Bridey's story," Cisco said, and then shrugged his shoulders and raised his eyebrows. "Hard to believe we're serious here, but if you buy into any of it...."

"Let's get back to the list, then, and figure out what to do. What jumps out at you?" Cora asked.

"The *To do* list is a whole lot longer than the *What we know* list," Cisco said, shaking his head and gesturing with his hands.

Frannie laughed, but Cora was dealing with a sudden thought and hadn't noticed Cisco's remark.

"I'm going to do something we didn't put on the list." She paused dramatically. "I'm going to Saint James tomorrow."

Frannie and Cisco looked at each other and waited for her to explain.

"I've been there before, but I didn't know any of this then. Things appear different when you put them in perspective, and I want to see for myself where this happened. Maybe it'll give me a clue." Noting the others starting to open their mouths, Cora held up a hand. "I want to go alone."

Chapter 26

After Frannie left, Cisco said, "I don't want you going out there alone. I should go with you."

"Please, Hon, let me do this my way. I just want to put myself where Meg was, to try to understand her better. I have to be alone to do that. We've been out there a dozen times—what could happen?"

She didn't mention the sixth sense that compelled her to go unaccompanied, as she could think of no way to explain that.

~~~

The next morning Cora picked up Meg's diary and went through all of it this time, hoping to know and understand Meg as well as she could before going to Saint James.

The entries were well written and entertaining. She wondered if, had she lived, Meg would have achieved her ambition to be a writer, as noted by the uncle who gave her the book. In fact, the diary itself was publishworthy, in Cora's opinion, presenting a delightful picture of a young woman at a particular time and place. Perhaps when this was all over Cora would look into what it took to publish it.

Cora tried to take notes that might help to solve the mystery of Meg's death, but had no idea what details could be important, and soon became lost in Meg's life and set the note pad aside. Cora began to view Meg as a friend—a close friend.

She was amused to read of trivial day-to-day events like buying new clothes, gossip among school friends, and spats with her sister. It seemed she and her sister were very different people who battled frequently, but besides frequent outbursts of anger, she wrote of occasionally standing up for her against their mam or anyone who treated Sally poorly.

Meg gave very vivid descriptions of her thoughts about the Columbian Exposition, and what it was like to be a single woman living and working in Chicago. She had worked at Marshall Field's Department Store as a clerk, and told a story about how Marshall Field had sold his interests in a store in Sag Bridge to open his store in Chicago. The Sag store had apparently been doing quite well, and the partner laughed at Field's decision, calling him a fool. Cora had heard this story before, but had never been able to find any facts to back it up.

She talked about meeting Packey when returning to Sag for a Fourth of July picnic, and how he immediately swept her off her feet with his commanding presence and infectious good humor. She admitted to arriving at the picnic with her nose in the air, in a stylish dress and hat unlike what local women were wearing, feeling better than "this old town". Packey told Meg what attracted him from across the grove was not her stylish clothes, but how she moved with energy and confidence, which reminded him of the red-headed "spitfires" he had known in Ireland. Throughout the diary Meg wrote about how much everyone loved and admired Packey, and how fortunate she felt to be his wife, missing her life in Chicago, but never regretting her decision to marry Packey and move back to Sag.

She talked about life on the farm before her father died, and how decisions were made about where her mother would live and who would run the farm after his death.

As she read, she recalled Bridey's stories. Bridey's father was a young boy when Meg died, and Cora envisioned him at the farms and in the town of Sag, fishing and visiting the quarries where Packey worked. Bridey said Packey had sometimes given her father fossils.

She then scanned historical documents online about Saint James and found the location on MapQuest, zooming in for a virtual tour of the cemetery.

In addition to its historic status and unique setting in the middle of a forest, the church was popular with psychics and ghost-hunters. Many reports of sightings and supernatural events had occurred over the years and attracted thrill-seekers.

Resurrection Mary, in nearby Willow Springs, was the most famous ghost, but Saint James had its share of followers due to its isolated forest location and evidence it was built over an Indian burial ground. Cora had described her own experience there in her talk on *Fright Night* a few weeks ago.

Was it only a few weeks? So much has happened since then!

One ghostly legend told of a young housekeeper at Saint James who fell in love with the pastor's assistant. Planning to elope, the lovers arranged for a wagon to pick them up in the middle of the night. When it arrived, the horses spooked and the wagon overturned, killing the woman. Afterwards, reliable witnesses saw a young woman and wagon at Saint James on multiple occasions, the woman calling "Come on!" before both she and the wagon disappeared. Cora noted the date of the first sighting was 1897, near the date of Meg's tragedy, and she wondered if the legend developed from Meg's murder.

A further, and surprising, discovery was that Meg's farm was near where Cora now lived. She pulled old maps out of her Sag Bridge folder and determined that the land her home was built on was probably in Sag, not Lemont as she thought. She would look up land records at the historical society and see who originally owned it.

~~~

It was midafternoon when Cora finished her research and pulled onto Archer Road, the same road Meg would have traveled in 1898. Cora now imagined the scene as it looked in Meg's day: a dirt road, ditches on both sides, wide enough for wagons to pass. Horses, wagons, bicycles, and feet were the means of transportation then.

Along Archer Road today were homes, banks, gas stations, mini-malls, golf courses—these weren't along Archer in 1898, of course. There were a few old frame two-story homes, one with a front porch, and occasionally a dirt road led off the highway. Cora realized these were probably updated farm houses and lanes that dated back to the 1890s. She drove this road frequently but hadn't noticed them before.

She stopped for a red light, which she now knew was at a corner that once was the heart of Sag Bridge. She imagined a few small shops on a dirt road with tracks down the middle and electric poles on one side, a hotel on a corner, riders gossiping on the porch waiting for their train. Beyond were poorer dwellings and shanties. Today there was no sign of the town. There was a subdivision, a field, a street that led up a hill, and Archer widened to four lanes here and became an elevated road with a series of bridges that traversed four waterways ahead. On one side was an abandoned quarry, now filled with water, a popular fishing area and part of the county's forest preserves.

Cora drove over a wide working canal that passed by warehouses, docks, and trucking and stone yards. When Meg lived here, this canal wasn't yet excavated. The area then was flat farmland with only a small ditch where the canal was now.

Cora stopped for another red light at the end of the first bridge and looked around as she waited. She knew from her research that she was on the edge of a hill overlooking two valleys that came together at this point. Today's driver wouldn't realize this was a hill or a vantage point, as the elevated road gave the impression the land was level. Meg, on the other hand, would have had to make her way from the valley floor and climb steeply.

Archer split off here to become a two-lane road, and after a short distance through a densely forested area Cora came to the entrance to Saint James. She pulled off the road to picture the land Meg would have come through, with a log tavern directly across from the church lane. Cora had read the foundation of the tavern could still be found there. Meg would have seen farms, not woods, and beyond them a railroad, with two other canals and then the river a half mile away.

Cora drove through iron entry gates at Saint James. A single car was parked near the rectory. She picked a spot close to the parish hall and turned off her motor, unsure what to do next. Looking around, she realized much of the property was unchanged from 1898, as most building was completed before Meg's death. She knew from her research that the rectory in Meg's day was a frame building with a front porch, the parish hall a low wooden structure. Both were replaced by stone buildings of similar size at their original locations. The iron entry gates had been added, and the lot and lane were now paved.

Cora got out of her car and wandered around the grounds. Meg wrote in her diary that Packey went to a church meeting just before she made her last journal entry and went to bed. Either someone woke her up and asked her to go to the church, or Packey didn't come home so Meg went to look for him, Cora surmised. It must have been important, because in Meg's condition she wouldn't go out alone in the middle of the night otherwise. Sally was sick, but Cora wondered why Mick, the brother-in-law, didn't go.

Whatever the reason, Cora knew from Bridey's story that Meg went and was killed, and she guessed it was because she interrupted Packey's killer. Unless Meg was the target of the killer instead of Packey. Bridey hadn't mentioned rape. Cora assumed Packey was killed before Meg, but maybe not.

What would Meg have done when she got here? It was likely she drove a wagon and carried a lantern. The meeting Packey went to was probably held at the parish hall, so perhaps Meg went there first, and if no one was there, she would have looked further. It must have been late, since no one witnessed the killings and the bodies weren't found until the morning. It was logical to think the rectory was dark and the priest asleep. Would Meg want to search the grounds before she woke him up?

Cora wished she had looked up the news articles about the killings before coming here, but time had run out. She would do it later.

The day was sunny, the temperature moderate, there was no wind, and Cora was comfortable in her leather jacket. It was a nice day to amble around the peaceful premises, she thought, as she crunched through fallen leaves. She imagined she was Meg, searching for Packey, and followed the path she thought Meg would have taken. Cora circled the parish hall but found no reason to linger there. As she started uphill through the parking lot, she was jolted back to the present when a woman left the rectory, looked at her, smiled and waved before she got into her car and drove away. She probably thought Cora was there to visit a grave or the rectory.

Cora skipped the rectory, as she figured Meg did, climbed the hill, entered the cemetery, and followed the path to the church. The church doors were locked. She went behind the church, where the bodies were found, and a short way into the graveyard.

She stood looking at the gravestones and trying to imagine how the place would look in the middle of the night. Based on Bridey's descrip-

tion, she was near where the bodies were found. She could not see other buildings, as the church blocked the rectory, and the parish hall was
below the crest of the hill. With her back to the church, she was facing east. Assuming again that this happened late at night or early in the
morning, the moon, if there was a moon, was descending in the west, and
that side of the church would be dark. Cora saw a small stone building,
which she knew from her research was there to hold remains during winter months, until the ground thawed and burials could take place. To her
right the hill dropped sharply to an area of dense brush. Cora thought it
probably was the same in 1898. She figured both places provided ample
cover for a killer to hide, even on horseback.

Lost in thought, Cora wandered among the gravestones, randomly
noticing names and dates. Most names were Irish, but not all. Some small
graves were simply marked, INFANT, testifying to high infant and child-
birth mortality and harsh living conditions of the time. She noticed that
the gravestones all faced east and remembered they were placed so that
on Judgment Day the deceased could sit up and face the rising sun.

She came to a simple stone that marked the graves of John and Mary
Chauncey. That would be Meg's mother and father, she knew from the
diary, and the dates made sense. Meg's mother, Máime, apparently lived
to a ripe old age, surviving many years after Meg's death. Cora wondered
who took care of Máime after Meg died and how Máime's husband felt
about spending eternity buried next to such a witchy woman.

*Meg's probably buried here too. I wonder where her grave is...it's not here
with her mother....*

A sudden gust of cold wind blew a scattering of dry leaves across the
ground, and Cora caught a scent of something foul. She shivered and
looked around nervously but saw nothing unusual. The sun emerged
from behind a cloud and all seemed warm and peaceful again. Her attention was drawn to the northwest corner, and she headed that way, as if
pulled, no *guided*, in that direction. She was reminded of an occasion
years ago when a similar compulsion led her to follow an abandoned
road, where she experienced an amazing display of butterflies and discovered a different sort of cemetery, where nuclear waste was buried. That
was only a short distance through the forest from her present location.

She noticed a tombstone carving: ILL MOUNTED VOLUNTEER OF THE

BLACK HAWK WAR, and she remembered reading that a section of the cemetery was set aside for people who died violently. Most stones were simple flat markers, weathered and difficult to read. Despite the warm day, a shiver went up her spine at the thought of finding Meg's grave. As she searched the stones on the ground, she caught motion with her peripheral vision, looked that way and saw a woman moving slowly in her direction.

Strange. I thought I was alone. I didn't see any cars pull up.

She checked the parking area, which she could see clearly from where she stood, and indeed her car was the only one in the lot. A woman was coming from the far side of the cemetery, adjacent to a wooded area separated from the cemetery by a fence. This was puzzling—why would she be coming from the forest, and how did she get through the fence? Was she in the cemetery all along, or was there another path? Cora had already walked through that area and not seen anyone, or a path or opening in the fence. Cora stared with a rising sense of comprehension.

As the woman walked, her body stayed in the same plane, with little up and down or side to side motion, as if she were gliding. She wore no coat or jacket, unusual in November. A dark, full-length skirt, was softly tailored and flared below the knee, and her white blouse fit loosely, the standup collar trimmed with lace, as was the upper bodice. The long sleeves were puffed at the top, tight across the arms, with lace at the wrists. She held her skirt a few inches off the ground, and Cora got glimpses of neat black boots. She was young, perhaps in her twenties, a small woman with striking auburn hair parted in the middle, braided and wound into a tidy bun at the nape of her neck. She was pretty in an understated way, and she carried herself erect.

Cora froze in place, unable to take her eyes away. She knew who the woman was, and illogically her initial reaction was one of pleasure, as if spotting a dear friend she hadn't seen for years.

The feeling quickly changed as her mind processed that she was seeing someone who had been dead for over a hundred years. Her scalp, fingers and toes tingled, and she was lightheaded, but oddly calm despite the surreal aura. She put both hands to her mouth, trying to think rationally. Should she leave—run off? Or was this an opportunity? Was she led here today, and did Angel orchestrate the encounter? If that was so, Angel, materialized as Meg, could inhabit the cemetery as well as Cora's home.

A spirit, in the flesh…no, not in the flesh! Is this happening? What does she want? What should I do?

The apparition moved past Cora without speaking, her face emotionless. She looked through Cora rather than at her, unfocused, as if confused or dazed. She went about twenty feet past, then stopped at a particular grave. She lowered herself to the ground, rested her cheek against the gravestone, closed her eyes and moaned softly.

Cora didn't know what to do. Should she approach the clearly grief-stricken woman? Maybe the apparition didn't know Cora was there; perhaps she should sneak off and leave her undisturbed. As she stood there undecided, the age of the graves touched her, the bodies in them dead so many years. She realized Meg—who else could she be seeing?—had been grieving all this time. Cora felt she knew her now, and didn't feel she could just walk away.

Angel had never hurt her before, why should she now? Cora approached her. "Are you okay?" she asked softly. "Can I do anything to help?"

The woman, Angel/Meg, turned her face, met Cora's gaze, but said nothing.

Cora took a gamble, and lowered herself to the ground. "Do you mind if I sit here with you?"

Meg didn't reply, but laid her head down again and closed her eyes. The gravestone was one of a group of three, and Cora turned to read the names. The closest one said, PACKEY HENNESSEY, AGE 33 – BORN AUGUST 7, 1865, LAID TO REST JULY 11, 1898. The middle one read, MAVOURNEEN HENNESSEY, AGE 23 – BORN JANUARY 15, 1875, LAID TO REST JULY 11, 1898. The third, the grave the woman was resting on, said, INFANT GIRL HENNESSEY, BORN AND DIED JULY 11, 1898.

Cora's eyes filled with hot tears. Was it because she was finally face to face with Angel? Was she moved by Meg's tragic story, made real by the manifestation of her spirit?

She put both hands on the ground, leaned back, and asked in a soft voice that broke with emotion, "You're Meg, aren't you?"

The woman turned her head, eyes full of pain. She rolled to a sitting position but made no sound, merely gazed at Cora, as if inviting conversation.

"I'm glad to meet you at last," Cora began. They regarded each other. "I read your diary, and I'm very sorry about what happened to you." She moved closer, and reached out to the woman, wanting to offer the comfort of a gentle touch.

The woman's eyes flew wide and she pulled away violently in terror, commanding in a guttural voice, "No!"

Cora withdrew her hand and moved back. The woman relaxed, and said more calmly, the voice now high-pitched, "Touch...afraid...."

Cora considered the words. Why was everything so cryptic with Angel, even face to face? "You're afraid for me to touch you? Something bad could happen if I touch you? Bad to you, or bad to me?"

Meg gave a single nod, paused, opened her mouth as if to reply, but before any sound came out she began to fade, became transparent. She closed her mouth and lifted her arms, as if struggling or gathering something, and her substance slowly returned. In a calm, soft but clear voice, normal-sounding woman's voice, she implored, "What happened...to us?"

"You don't know!" Cora remarked in surprise. "That's it, isn't it?"

Meg, Angel, dropped her eyes, and then looked back up. Cora realized she was indicating the guess was correct.

"When I brought your diary home, you recognized it. You wanted me to know who you were, and you wanted me to tell you who killed you and why, that's what you wanted, wasn't it?"

Meg repeated the sign. In view of the earlier fading, Cora speculated that speech reduced her strength.

"You wanted me to tell you about the murder, and Father McGrath was getting in the way, so you had that wolf go after him."

Meg's eyes blazed with emotion, and she started to fade again. Cora watched as she struggled to fight it off, gathered strength, regained substance.

"I'm so sorry Meg, but I don't know what happened," Cora said softly. "No one ever found out who killed you or why. I wish I could tell you, but I don't know."

Suddenly Meg seemed charged with energy, and became radiant. She shot to her feet, a powerful and fearsome being that stood glaring at Cora. "You...find out!" she commanded in the deep, guttural voice that echoed with emotion, then just as suddenly started to wilt before Cora's eyes. "Do it for Máime, Darlin'," she pleaded softly, the voice high-pitched again, like an LP record played on high speed, thin, exhausted. "Time... to know...you and me...hurry...before..." Meg seemed to collapse. She stood small and weak with Cora at her feet, then turned and moved away, indicating the visit was over.

"Wait!" Cora begged, jumping up to face Meg, unanswered questions tumbling out in a disordered rush. "Why do you want me to hurry? What's so urgent? I don't know how to find out, but I'll try. Why *me*, why did you pick me? Why do you call me Darlin'? Why did you wait so long to reveal yourself? What changed? I don't *know* enough to help you!"

Meg turned to Cora, but she was losing substance once more, and this time she didn't stop. As she faded she said in a weakening voice, so soft Cora couldn't be sure she wasn't imagining it, "Over forty years to find you, Darlin'. Can't leave now...."

Chapter 27

Cora pedaled an old balloon-tired bicycle, a little girl in a scout uniform behind her, arms clinging around Cora's waist. Cora panted for breath and her legs burned. She stopped at a church and watched the girl run off.

She pedaled frantically, then stopped and locked the bike to a rack. Next she was banging on a door. A woman answered, accusing. "You're late."

"Only five minutes…sorry." Cora smiled, trying to break through the woman's bad attitude. Another woman came into the room and showed Cora what to do—take tall stacks of documents, scan them, and save them to a DVD. There were so many documents! Cora had to hurry—she had to be somewhere else. The women glared at her, angry.

Back on the bicycle with the little girl, Cora rushed. She was late again—who would watch the girl? She was distraught. A creek ran under the street. She sent the girl to play there. She looked around and Cora's mother appeared, standing on a bridge and watching the girl. Her mother was young and healthy.

Cora was in an empty store. She called…two women came from the back. Cora said she had to leave right away, she had to take care of a little girl, but she could come back later. The women were angry—they had to leave and Cora had to take over. Cora's mother came into the store. She was aged and frail. She had to eat or she would be ill. Cora sent her across the street for food. Cora watched as her elderly mother dodged cars across six lanes of traffic, terrified she would fall or be struck. Her mother stumbled, regained her balance and disappeared into a restaurant. The little girl was alone.

Cora was frantic. She had to take over the store…the little girl needed her, *unaccompanied by a dangerous creek…her mother couldn't fend for herself. She could do only one thing. Which would it be? She screamed in frustration, "When is it my turn?"*

Distraught, unable to make a decision, Cora woke up.

~ ~ ~

Cora couldn't get back to sleep, thinking about the dream. Beside her, Cisco snored softly. His snoring usually disturbed her, but tonight she found the sound a comforting reassurance of his presence. After the stressful meeting with Meg at Saint James the previous day, Cora tried to put it out of her mind. She discussed the experience extensively with Cisco, then retired early. Surprisingly, she was able to sleep, until the urgency of the dream woke her.

She glanced at the clock. Two in the morning. She needed rest badly, but she tossed and turned, finally gave up and let her restless mind go where it would, taking advantage of an opportunity to think things through.

The symbolization in the dream seemed clear to her. The little girl represented her family, children and grandchildren. Rushing to commitments on the bicycle revealed the emotions Cora struggled with, trying to balance personal and family life with other responsibilities. She wanted to give back after she retired and did a lot of charity work, but she took on too much. How could she do it all—be a good mother, daughter, wife, when so many other things, although worthy, tugged at her and monopolized her days? Where was time for herself, to relax, to read? Life was full of stress, and she was unable to enjoy anything she did—there was simply no time as she raced from one thing to another.

Leaving the girl with her elderly mother at the stream in her dream indicated poor decision-making. Another set of obligations was added when her mother moved in with Cora—at first she was a little help but soon became yet another responsibility. When was it Cora's turn?

A lump in her throat, Cora closed her eyes tightly and buried her face in her pillow, feeling sorry for herself, worn by life's many burdens. She had tried to make her mother's last years happy. It was an impossible task, as she couldn't make the ordeals of old age go away. She was kind and patient, but she admitted she felt resentful. She herself was aging, and she wondered if there would ever be time for things that were important to *her*, rather than to others.

Now Cora's mother was gone, Cora's children raised. Just when life started to fall into place, someone else came along with claims on her—Angel. Cora was becoming convinced that Father McGrath had identified an important fact—Angel was trying to fill a spot in Cora's life where her mother and family resided. She wondered if she had enough strength to deal with the demands and contradictions of Angel.

She opened her eyes, turned onto her back, pulled the covers under her chin, and gazed at the ceiling, thinking about Angel—perhaps she should be calling her Meg now. What did Meg think about her own family and responsibilities, and how did Meg become entwined in Cora's life? What was Angel thinking now? Was she thinking as Meg would have, or were her thoughts altered by her altered state? Signs of her confusion were clear: Angel could be likeable, heartrending, demanding, or violent. What was really going on?

After reading Meg's diary, Cora thought she had some insight. Meg didn't get along well with her "Máime," who was a difficult woman. Cora's mother had been irritable at times, but never mean or demanding. Their personalities were widely different, so they weren't exceptionally close, but they cared for and respected each other. Her mother accused her of being bossy, and Cora would reply that's how she was raised, and they would laugh. She wondered if Angel was jealous of the relationship between Cora and her mother, as Meg didn't have a similar rapport with Máime. Yet Meg was the one who visited Máime and supervised her care—Meg probably had some feelings for her mother.

Meg was excited about expecting a child and described in detail how she would be a better mother than her own. Meg would have stayed home and devoted every moment to her child. Cora felt a stab of guilt, as her own career severely limited family time, but she rationalized that in Meg's day mothers stayed home and didn't help support the family.

Had Meg known she was dying, or did she die instantly? Was the baby girl born before or after Meg died? What would she have thought if she had any conscious moments before death? Certainly pain, but she would have felt grief, for Packey, for herself, and for the baby. But perhaps she never knew her baby died with her. Perhaps she thought she had to remain a spirit to take care of her baby. Cora had no idea what motivated a spirit, but if Meg knew she was dying, she would have been desperate to know how her orphaned baby would be cared for.

Was this why she attached herself to Cora and took on the role of protector? Did she believe Cora was her child? If so, Cora asked again, why did Angel think Cora, rather than someone else, was her child, and why the recent violence?

During the encounter at the cemetery, Meg was sad and struggling, yet displayed moments of anger and violence. Something was up, something so important it forced Angel to materialize, which seemed tremendously hard for her. It was as if she had two distinct personalities, one outgoing, sensitive and nurturing—the good guy. The other, the bad guy, was angry, vengeful, confused and vicious. It didn't make sense. Was her behavior based on Cora's needs, or motivated by a personal agenda Cora had yet to discover? Was she motivated by love, or jealousy, or revenge?

Why did Father McGrath upset her so profoundly? She had used a different name, Father Fitzpatrick. Perhaps that priest did something bad to Meg. Surely if he abused her Meg would have mentioned that in her diary. Was anything going on at Saint James that led to the murders? Cora was drawn there before she knew about Angel, even before her own marriage—why?

Why was she in a hurry now, when all Cora's life she was content to remain unknown? Why did she want Cora to be involved now? What caused the recent urgency and desperation?

What did Angel think of Cisco? How about the rest of Cora's family, and her friends? Were they in danger? Did Angel see them as a threat? Why? What would make her leave them alone?

How am I going to defeat her?

Do I really want her to go away—I've spent a lifetime with her.

She wants me to hurry, find out who killed her. Will that stop the violence?

It was not in Cora's nature to take no for an answer; she would find a way. She finally drifted into an uneasy sleep.

She woke to the smell of fresh coffee and the sounds of Cisco rattling around in the kitchen. Groggy from another night of restless sleep, she rolled over and got out of bed to face the day.

~ ~ ~

"Ania, I'd like to find newspaper articles from 1898. How should I go about that?" Cora asked.

"Oh, we don't have much from back then. There are a few really old papers on this bottom shelf...." Ania pointed out a shelf of binders and flat boxes. Cora examined the materials and lifted the lid of a box. Inside were yellowed and crumbling papers, pieces of which drifted to the floor as she handled them.

"We have some newspapers on microfilm, but I'm not sure any go back that far. You could try the *Tribune* archives, or some of the big libraries in Chicago, the Harold Washington, the Newberry, or the Chicago Historical Society. Or the Lincoln Library in Springfield has a large newspaper archive. That's where we send people." As she talked, Ania was entering recent deaths onto note cards for genealogy records.

"I'm looking for a local story—wouldn't local papers have better coverage?"

"Let me think...the *Lemont Observer* and the *Lemont Optimist* were the local papers in 1898, but they both went out of business years ago. Once a paper goes out of business there's no one left to maintain an archive, and that's long before the historical society started, so just the odd old issue turns up, if somebody donated one. A really big story might have been in the *Joliet News* or the *Joliet Daily Republican*...but they're not around anymore either," Ania rambled on, then looked up. "What's the story? Maybe I know something about it."

"You probably do—it's about the murders at Saint James, the young Irish family that was killed out there."

"Oh, Lord, yes, that's a very well-known story. I'm surprised you haven't run across it before. They never found the killer, you know." Ania leaned back in her chair, a sure sign the ladies were about to fill Cora in.

"I heard about it when I was a child," Emily said. "Our parents used to scare us with the story to keep us from going out there. Because of the ghosts, kids wanted to go to the old cemetery at night, but some boys got wild and destroyed things, so they had to stop them."

"Emily and I can tell you the story, and there are written anecdotes too, over with the family history and anecdote files. It would take some digging..." Ania began.

"I'll look at those, but I have good anecdotal information already,"

Cora interrupted, not wanting Ania and Emily to know about the diary. She was interested in what they had to say but in a hurry to assemble research materials before they left. "I'd like to see what was in the papers. I'm looking for details that could have been missed or interpreted differently now."

Ania's eyes widened and her jaw dropped. "You're looking for clues? You're trying to find the killer? After all this time?"

Cora laughed at her expression. "Well, why not? It would cause a commotion, wouldn't it? Maybe even generate more interest in the historical society."

"You're serious," Ania said.

"Yes, I'm serious." Cora's wide eyes sparkled with humor as she nodded.

Ania and Emily looked at Cora, waiting for her to explain, but Cora didn't want them to know her personal involvement.

"Good luck with that," Emily said finally. "It will probably turn out to be a waste of your time, but you young folks have plenty of time to waste, I guess."

Cora and Ania exchanged a look and laughed, wondering when was the last time they were called young folks.

"Let's get started," Cora prompted. "I hope I can find what I need here—not have to go downtown or anywhere. But I need another favor—before you leave, could you show me how to find microfilm from 1898 and how to work the viewer?"

"Let's do it now," said Ania. She got up from the table and showed Cora how the microfilm strips were filed and how to thread them into the viewer. It was laborious. "Now remember to push the base of this bulb with one hand while you advance the film with this little wheel here," she said, demonstrating. "Otherwise the light will go out. And you can't see the whole page at once, you'll need to keep moving the text around with these little dials." It appeared the viewer had seen better days. Cora resigned herself to hours of reading, and hoped the bulb wouldn't burn out before she finished.

After the others left, Cora found they did have microfilm from 1898, and she pulled out filmstrips from three months before the murders through three months after. Cisco and Frannie would arrive in an hour, and she hoped to locate articles about the murders by then. Fortunately she knew the date—that would make the search easier.

She was resigned to tedious examination of documents from a variety of sources, much as she had tediously gone over Meg's diary. At least Meg's diary had been entertaining, but today's research would be less so. However, she was hopeful that comparing what she found here to what she knew directly from Meg would be revealing. A mental image of Meg at the cemetery popped into her head, standing over her and pleading in that surreal high-pitched voice, "Do it for Máime, Darlin'... hurry...." Cora lined up the filmstrips next to the viewer and forced the image from her mind—she didn't have time for distractions.

Before wrestling with the viewer, she examined the old newspapers, an easier task. There were four shelves of them, most after 1920. There were none prior to 1890, and none after early 1901 until 1920. Three binders and a newspaper wrapped in clear plastic were from the 1890s, and a flat box also contained papers from that period. She lugged the materials to her desk.

She turned the papers over one at a time, listing the name of the paper and issue date. As she made the list, the names and dates seemed familiar. Checking labels on the microfilm strips she had pulled out, she realized the issues were the same as the filmstrips. The microfilm was probably made from these papers. Thank God, she wouldn't have to struggle with that idiot viewer. She re-filed the microfilm strips. A waste of time, but she was ahead all in all.

Returning to the papers, she wondered why this ten-year period had been preserved and guessed that either the period or the murders had historic value. That could explain why the story of the murders was so well known, as it was the only time period for which they had documents. She was anxious to read them but knew it would keep her from finishing before Cisco and Frannie arrived, so she continued to list the pertinent issues.

She picked up the oldest issue, the *Lemont Observer* from March, 1898, a weekly paper. She discovered there were many newspaper publishers during those years, four from Lemont, one from nearby Lockport, and two from Joliet, a major city in the 1800s that printed both daily and weekly editions. She would also be interested in the *Chicago Tribune*, but after she dealt with the local news.

As she thumbed through each issue, she wrote down dates, major events, and names of important people. The notes would identify people and happenings shortly before and after Meg's death and could point to a motive or a killer, providing it was someone from town and not a vagrant. Packey could have walked into a hot issue, so knowing the town's conflicts should prove helpful. Gathering information over a range of time, Cora hoped, would prompt a connection to jump out at her— some fact overlooked in 1898, by a police force more concerned with goings-on at Smokey Row than solving the murder of some Irish immigrants from the Sag. In fact, based on the colorful history of early town corruption, someone from the police force or a town official could even be the killer.

Having organized the materials, she jumped ahead to early July to look for stories about the murders. And there, July 15, front page, was the headline—"Mystery at Saint James". She read the article, and one that came out a week later. Cora already knew most of it. The articles confirmed that Packey, Meg, and a newborn baby, with the umbilical cord still attached, were found dead in the cemetery in the morning by Father Fitzpatrick. He discovered a horse and wagon in the churchyard, and wondered where the owner was. He thought it might belong to someone at the meeting the previous evening, but was puzzled why it was left behind. Once again an image of Meg jumped into her mind: Meg gliding past her, and then lying on the graves. She pushed it away.

The reporter noted that Packey had sustained many crushing blows to the head, whereas Meg seemed to have died from a single blow. No reason was given for the death of the baby. Cora didn't think it would have been exposure, as it was mid-summer, but wondered if the umbilical cord had anything to do with the baby's death. She also wondered why the brother-in-law didn't go instead of Meg, and why he didn't come to investigate when Meg didn't return home either. Perhaps because he had no transportation? That seemed a poor reason. Maybe his wife got worse? Nothing was said in the papers about them.

Cora smiled wryly after reading one interview. "Mary Chauncey, mother of the deceased woman, was understandably distressed. 'Why did my daughter go out in the middle of the night? My no-good sons-in-law were probably drunk for all I know. Who will care for me now?'" the reporter had written. How like what she knew of Máime!

She heard a knock on the door and ran down to open it for Cisco and Frannie. Instead of revealing answers, the articles had brought up more questions.

Chapter 28

Exhausted by recent events and lack of sleep, Cora wished she could call it a day and go home to nap. She, Cisco and Frannie sat around the table in the historical society loft, finishing fast-food sandwiches while Cora told Frannie about the meeting with Meg.

"Great—Angel's not enough to stress about, now we got to find a killer too. Well, no point wasting any more time trying to figure out is Angel in your head—we got us a bon-a-fide ghost." Frannie put the last bite of sandwich in her mouth, and followed it with a slug of bottled water. "But tell me again, why all the hush-hush? Shouldn't Angel be happy knowing we're digging into her murder? Isn't that what she wants?"

"I keep thinking about Father McGrath. We don't know who or what sets her off." Frannie blinked and nodded. Cora went on, "I think I'm the only person she trusts—she could even be suspicious of Cisco."

"What'd she look like?" Frannie asked, as she put food wrappers and napkins in a bag and crumpled it.

Cora looked out into the sanctuary as she pictured Meg, watching her walk from the woods. "She was pretty. Neat. Dressed in clothes from the period. I thought she looked dazed, not quite present, you know? But with flashes of awareness."

"She's not telling you enough. These short answers and messages on your computer, it's not enough. She needs to explain better. She needs a blog," Frannie said.

Her comment broke the tension and got them laughing.

"Whole thing don't make much sense," Frannie went on. "This Angel or Meg, whoever, she's one confused ghost, you ask me. Course she don't make sense because spirits *don't* always make sense, that's a regular thing with spirits. Who knows ghost rules—I sure don't. Every one of those supernatural websites says different things—too much room for interpretation."

"Yeah, well, we have to try," Cora said. "Too bad I couldn't give Father McGrath's books to you, Frannie. I'm afraid Angel might go nuts if she sees me touch them."

"I looked at them," Cisco said hesitantly, avoiding Cora's eyes.

"You did?" Cora exclaimed, lifting her eyebrows and turning to him. Of all people, Cisco was the last person she'd expect to investigate spirits. But he had a sharp instinct for honing in on practical information, and considering his reluctance, she was interested in his take on the books.

"I have to admit I found some interesting stuff—along with a lot of garbage—sorry." He picked up the remains of their lunch and got up to put it in a waste basket, stopping by Frannie's chair and addressing her. "Have you been able to understand *how* Angel can communicate, what her so-called powers are, and where she '*is*' so to speak? Don't we need to know that if we're trying to manage her?"

He had the women's attention. "Think about it." He waved an arm in the air. "She's gone from messing with little things, like paper clips, to flinging around file cabinets, she materializes as an apparition, then backs off. We think she's bound to our house, but Cora saw her at the cemetery." He sat back down, continuing to wave his hands for emphasis as he talked. "There's no consistency—shouldn't we try to explain that?" He held both hands, palms upward.

Frannie rubbed both hands on the table and wiggled in her chair, anxious to give an opinion. "What I think, we should decide if Angel has attached herself to a person, namely Cora, or a place."

"She must be attached to Cora, because she followed her from house to house and to her workplace. I saw that myself," Cisco reasoned, giving Cora a glance to see if she noticed his admission.

"But she doesn't seem to know what we do here, yet she *does* know what happens in your house." Frannie put her elbows on the table and pointed a finger in the air. "We know that because she only reacts to things she could find out at your house, but not to things we talk about other places. Like she didn't react to the diary until Cora brought it into the house.

Now we know she's at Saint James too. We would expect that, since she died there—violently, which is important to spirits."

"To make it more confusing, the books say spirits can be in more than one place at the same time," Cisco added.

That stopped them short. Cora put her chin in her hand and stared across the room, Frannie scratched her head, and Cisco drummed his fingers on the table.

"What about when she took revenge on people for Cora? They weren't at the house or the cemetery," Cisco said.

"No, but maybe she didn't go herself. Maybe she sent that old wolf out," Frannie speculated. "Maybe wolf powers are different from Angel powers. Wolves go all over, live outside—could be that wolf goes places Angel can't."

Cora said nothing, making aimless scribbles on a sheet of paper in front of her.

"What I read...spirits need energy from some source to do anything. They feed on someone's energy, or send it back to affect their feelings, emotions...even actions. They can even do it remotely, entering their minds...." He gestured, expressing with his hands energy in and out, pointing at his head.

Excited, Frannie interrupted, "Wait! I got an idea—Angel could punish people if she sent negative energy to make them harm themselves or do things that led to disaster. It didn't have to involve the wolf. Angel wouldn't even have to be there to make it happen. That's what I think." She leaned back in her chair with a smug smile.

"The theory is—" Cisco said, nodding, "a spirit has to attract energy to act or materialize, but there's probably not enough to do it *fully*. The energy source is affected too, so lights blink and mechanical things malfunction when a spirit is around."

"Like computers," Frannie added. "She has energy in your house, and can see and hear there, and do things poltergeists do. That's why she played with your batteries and threw the clock on the floor, for the energy. She uses mechanical and electrical things there, but outside she's limited—she needs more energy from somewhere, or sends She-wolf."

"Or her energy relates to mine...." Cora said, gazing into space. "Which may explain how I know stuff about Angel, with no reason I *should* know."

Cisco searched Cora's face. "You have more figured out, don't you?"

She met his gaze. "A lot of it, I think," she said softly, hands motionless on the table.

Cisco picked up a pen and tapped it on the table, and Frannie leaned back with her arms crossed, waiting for Cora to explain.

"I think Angel *is* attached to me. That's how we began, and she followed me from home to home, and to work. She thinks I'm her daughter, and always has, but I don't know why."

She put her hand out to stop an interruption she saw coming from Cisco. "She's *also* attached to *places*, not a single place. Our house, which is why she got stronger when we moved to Lemont—she wasn't this strong in our other homes. And she's attached to Saint James, the strongest energy source...which is why she can manifest there, especially if I'm there too."

"So it's not either–or, it's both," said Cisco, nodding. He began flipping restlessly through a stack of papers on the table without looking at them.

"Yes. So she followed me each time we moved, but not until she built up enough energy—it could have taken years. She followed me to work, but once there at first she only had enough energy to do little things, like closing drawers. She affected my life by sending out positive energy, to give me what I thought was a charmed life, to make accomplishments come easy. But it all took time." She stopped talking and took a sip of the soft drink in front of her.

Cisco said, "I bet she didn't have enough energy at the cemetery to materialize and communicate at the same time...that's why she faded in and out. And maybe why her communications are so cryptic too."

Cora took a deep breath and let it out slowly. "I think Angel and I share energy—pass it back and forth. We depend on each other—sometimes she supports me, other times I get it from her." She blinked a few times, gazing toward a stained glass window at the end of the room.

"She's doing what a mother would do, trying to give her daughter a good life. Like when Mom needed me to take care of her, and didn't want anyone but me to do it, now Angel needs *me*, and she's terrified and in a hurry. What I don't know is what *changed*—what brought this all to a head." She looked over at Frannie. "Didn't you say once that spirits don't have a sense of time? I don't understand this urgency part."

"Listen to me a minute," said Frannie. "I bet this is because she's got too much energy now. You, and the locations, a lot of time building up energy, a lot of emotion and drama, they all come together. They make her real strong." She shook a finger at Cora. "But you got to remember ghosts are confused. All this here sudden strength combined with confusion and terror you're talking about, that's your Angel, and it's made her unstable and vicious too."

"Terror," said Cisco, clearly intrigued by the word. "What's she terrified of?"

Cora chewed on a thumbnail thoughtfully. "I have an idea. The last thing she said to me in the cemetery was 'Over forty years to find you, Darlin'. Can't leave now.' Maybe it relates to that."

Cisco's face turned pale and for once his hands were still. "What are you saying, Hon? Who's leaving—you or her? Do you think she knows something's about to happen?"

"I think she's realized I'm getting old." Cora's voice broke and Cisco covered her hand with his. She wiped tears away and explained. "Angel watched me take care of my mother until Mom died. I don't know who she thought my mother was, maybe an adoptive parent, but she had to know I loved Mom, and hurt along with me. It could have made her realize I'm going to die someday, and she'll be left between worlds, a spirit with no more Darlin'. What will she do then?"

"What did she do during the forty years it took to find you? Go back to doing that?" Cisco suggested.

"She won't want to look for another baby—she thinks she's found hers—me. She doesn't want to accept her baby died, nor will she want to accept it when I die."

Cora met their eyes. "Her motivation, her attachment to earthly life, it falls apart without me. She's scared."

They sat thinking. "If we tell her what she wants to know, it could help her move on, put her at peace," Cora reasoned.

Cisco shook his head. "How do we do that?"

"By solving her murder. She asked me to find out who killed her, remember?" Cora closed her eyes, put her forehead in her hands, and added, "If I can get her to accept the circumstances of her death and that of her husband and baby, and convince her I'm only a substitute, maybe she'll leave the spirit world."

"You think she wants you to find out about the murders now because you're the only one who would care enough to want to do that, before you get too old?" asked Frannie. "Not that I think you're getting old or anything, but who knows what Angel thinks," she added quickly.

"You'd think she'd have a little sympathy for her Darlin' if she thinks I'm getting so old, and not *add* to my troubles," Cora said with a smirk.

"Well, what do you think?" Cisco asked, looking at them for indications of their opinion.

"I think it's all guesswork, that's what I think!" said Frannie. "What've we got except guesswork, though? Who's got experience with this kind of thing? But it's educated guesswork, considering how hard we've all been working."

Cisco shrugged. "We can try, I suppose. We don't have any other ideas. We should do *something*." He threw his hands into the air. "Okay, where do we start? Cora? Ideas? You know her best."

"We need a strict safety plan."

"A safety plan. Right," said Frannie. She looked at Cora and blinked. "What safety plan?"

"I still don't believe you're not in danger too," Cisco said.

"But I'm sure. I've met her, remember?" She squared her shoulders and held his eyes. "What I mean is, we can't expect Angel to be logical, and she doesn't trust anyone but me. She won't necessarily believe what I tell her either, like a child with a hand in the cookie jar, but she won't *hurt* me."

Cora paused a moment to gather her thoughts. "She's not only illogical, she's paranoid. We can't let her get suspicious—so we have to let her know some things, but not stuff that would make her mad."

"Assuming she'll follow you if she has enough energy, she'll follow us *here* sooner or later. We should think about how we're going to handle that," Cisco said.

"Makes sense. If she's getting stronger, and has a sense of urgency, that could happen soon," Frannie said.

"We'll change it up," Cisco agreed, nodding.

"So let's see if we can figure out who murdered Meg. Here's some stuff to look at...." Cora described the materials she had assembled, showed them the old newspapers, and explained how she listed people and events Packey may have been involved with, hoping to come across clues to who killed him or why.

She read the news articles about the murders aloud. One had an interview with Father Fitzpatrick, in which he described finding the bodies and a wolf lying with them. At first the wolf watched as if guarding the bodies, but then it attacked and he shot and killed it.

"That's the priest Angel confused with Father McGrath. It seems she didn't trust him for some reason." Cora made a note as she said this.

There were no pictures of Meg or Packey, but there was a photo of Father Fitzpatrick and another of the location the bodies were found. The pictures were of poor quality. Cora made two copies of the articles, one to take home, and one for Frannie. The copies would provide ready reference and show Angel Cora was working on a solution. They agreed the articles contained no useful clues.

"I'll finish with the papers—maybe something will click. If not, at least that part will be done," Cora said, and let out a long slow breath. "I'm too tired to do anything else today—I wouldn't be productive...I really don't want to lug all this home...." She swept her hand over the table, pointing out the documents covering it. "I'll have to come back tomorrow and finish."

"Why're you spending so much time with these old papers again?" Frannie asked, frowning. "Why're you so convinced you'll find a motive or a killer in there? Maybe this whole thing's some personal reason nobody ever knew about."

"Two reasons," Cora said, holding up two fingers. "Meg's diary said everyone loved Packey. So why would someone kill him, unless he got in the middle of something important? That could have been in the paper."

"Assuming the killer was after Packey—maybe he was looking for Meg," Cisco suggested.

"I thought of that," Cora admitted, considering. "But don't we still need a motive?"

"Great—motive for some guy a hundred years ago, on top of a motive for Angel acting up. I guess you're making sense, though," Frannie admitted. "What's that second reason now?"

Cora worked her mouth and averted her gaze as she shrugged. "I can't think of anywhere else to look," she admitted.

Frannie and Cisco exchanged a glance. "Works for me," Frannie said, and shrugged too.

"Got to start somewhere," Cisco agreed, nodding and gesturing.

"We probably shouldn't waste any more time reading about spirits, now that Cisco helped with that part," said Frannie. Her eyes sparkled and she was rapidly tapping her foot, clearly excited. "I love solving this old cold case. How about if I track down what they wrote in the *Chicago Tribune?* That rich Chicago paper—with all their people—could be they have information the local papers don't—experts, interviews, better pictures. I can see what's online and check the library databases. I can find where the archives are and go there. Paper like that must have archives somewhere."

"That's a great idea, Frannie," Cora said.

"What can I do?" asked Cisco.

Cora laughed. "I need you to take care of everything else, so I can spend all my time on this. Isn't that enough?"

"No, it's not enough. I want to do something," he persisted.

Cora thought about it. "You got along with that policeman, Officer Rogers, better than I did. Why don't you tell him you're helping me look into this story for the historical society? Ask him how they'd investigate now, versus what they might have done in 1898. Ask him what he would do if he was trying to solve these murders."

"I love it!" said Frannie. "The three of us should've been detectives for real." She wiggled in her chair and drummed her heels on the floor.

"Uh...maybe there are four detectives," Cora said, looking at the ceiling.

"What do you mean?" Cisco asked.

"Angel," Cora said haltingly, not looking at them directly, as the thoughts occurred to her. "Why do I feel so positive about my ideas that deal with her? Sixth sense? Coincidence? Where are the thoughts coming from? Are they mine or hers? If we're sharing energy, maybe she's in my head, too?"

They started gathering belongings, preparing to leave, silent as they considered Cora's suggestion.

"Wait a minute though, before we go. I got another question," said Frannie, setting her purse back on the table. "You got anything up here that can tell who owned your house way back when? You say Angel's attached to your house some kind of way. Maybe we can clear that up. Why don't you look into that tomorrow too?"

"Actually, yes—we can do it now—it's not hard." Cora started moving around the loft as she rambled on. "That's a good idea, Frannie—I meant to do it, but there's so much going on...it's not the house of course, as we know it was built in 1995—but who owned the land and lived on it back in the 1890s? Let's see...."

Cora moved to an old wooden cabinet with wide flat drawers about two inches tall, and opened them one after another. "Okay now, yes—here's the one I want...." She pulled out a map and spread it on the library table. "This is the Sag area in 1900. We need to find where our house is from landmarks, note the section, etc. It would help if we had our survey, but we'll figure it out...Archer should be on this map—yes, here's the intersection. Now measure out where our house is...here's the section number...where's our house in reference to the borders of that section...." Cora looked up. "Isn't it interesting? These sections were laid out by surveyors before settlers came to the area." Cisco and Frannie exchanged a glance and rolled their eyes. Cora's enthusiasm for historic details escaped them.

"Okay, here we are—where our house is," She pointed to a spot and jotted down some numbers. "Now, we look it up." She walked to a shelf, searched, withdrew a book. "Here's the census data from 1890—it will show names, addresses, and family members. Here, you start looking in this," she said, handing the book to Cisco. She walked across the room and took down another book. "This one has property records for the period. We should find listings in both of these."

The room was quiet as Cisco and Cora turned pages carefully in the fragile books. Frannie leaned over one shoulder, then another. Cora and Cisco both found what they were looking for at the same moment, and their eyes met.

"John and Mary Chauncey," said Cora.

"Living with two daughters, Mavourneen and Sally," said Cisco.

~~~

When Cora got home, she wanted to rest before dinner, and not think about Angel, Meg, or old murders. She went to wash her hands, grimy after handling the old documents. At the sink, she heard the unmistakable chime that announced Windows was opening. Strange—she had shut the computer down before she left the house that morning, and Cisco hadn't come in yet, out picking up debris that had blown into the yard. She walked into the room, and saw the logon screen displayed. As she watched, although she touched nothing, the password box filled, and the desktop screen appeared. The cursor moved to the task bar and launched Word. A new document opened to reveal a message in large bold font:

What was Packey doing with those books, Darlin'?

Chapter 29

Angel's message was another indication of her confusion—she must mean *Cisco* was reading the books, not *Packey*. Cora exploded. "Don't you *dare* question my husband!" she ranted, enraged and terrified.

"He's trying to help me solve your murder." Cora paced the room, waving her arms.

"He's *not* a threat to you, and he's the *most* important thing to me. I'm sure you want that to be *you*, but that's never going to happen!" She grabbed the diary from her desk and hurled it to the floor. The fragile binding separated, fanning pages across the room.

"I swear, Angel, I won't help you—I'll stop trying to find out who killed you if you do anything to Cisco!"

Hearing Cora's yelling, Cisco rushed into the office. Seeing the fury on her face and the diary pages scattered on the floor, he read the message on her computer screen and his face turned white. "Maybe we should leave the house," he said in a whisper.

"What good will that do?" Cora shouted. "She'll just find out where we are and follow us sooner or later. We have to get this over with."

"Cora, be careful," Cisco cautioned, pointing a finger in the air to indicate Angel was listening.

Cora waved him off. "We have to find the killer, so Angel will leave us alone."

She directed her next comments to the unseen Angel. "I don't know how you expect *me* to solve your murder. I'm no detective—just a retired woman who wants to live peacefully and do things I waited my whole life to do. Why can't you let me do that? I don't want to fight you—I just want to be left alone!"

Cora threatened and pleaded, using every line of reasoning she could think of, every argument that might resonate with Angel. She grabbed Cisco and hugged him to demonstrate she wouldn't tolerate anything Angel did to him. Cisco said nothing. This was between Cora and Angel—he was a bystander, watching participants doing battle.

The scene was insane. Cora raved like a lunatic as Cisco looked on, with no third person, no object of her outburst, in the room—like the old movie, *The Invisible Man*. Throughout the tirade Angel remained silent. No message, no objects or furniture moved to indicate her presence, but Cora knew she was listening—what she didn't know was if she convinced her.

~ ~ ~

The next morning, Cora couldn't decide if she was furious, frightened, or determined—if she wanted to collapse and give in to hysterics, get back into bed and pull the sheets over her head, or march out of the house to finish her research. There was no outside help she could turn to, now that Father McGrath was out of the picture—only Cisco and Frannie, and now Angel was threatening *them* too. She couldn't seem to get ahead. Every time she built up a little confidence, thought she had a plan to resolve matters, Angel threw her a curve.

Cora asked Cisco to leave the house with her. She made a great show of reassembling the diary, wrapped it carefully and took it with her. She mentioned going to the historical society, and her intent of studying the diary and old newspapers. If Angel followed, so be it, but she hoped Angel hadn't gathered enough energy for that yet. Cisco would try to track down Officer Rogers and meet her later. Frannie wouldn't join them today.

Maureen, the part-time LAHS secretary, was in her small main floor office when Cora arrived at the historical society. "I'll be upstairs most of the day," Cora said. "There's some things I'd like to finish."

Upstairs, Cora sat at the large table and spread out the materials she had gathered: newspapers, note pad, pen, and the diary. She opened the diary and began to list facts about the last few months of Meg's life.

She began on January 1, 1898, noting events, people, and entry dates in chronological order.

She listed the immediate family: Meg Hennessey (AKA Mavourneen, AKA Angel); Packey Hennessey, husband; Máime (née Dolan, AKA Mary Chauncey), mother; Sally Keating (née Chauncey), sister; Mick Keating, Sally's husband. She skimmed for names of extended family and friends, and sketched a brief family tree.

She then turned to other names, acquaintances and people around town who could have played a part in Meg's or Packey's lives: McCarthy, mayor of Lemont, and the Police Chief, Sweeney; Mr. Luther, quarry supervisor; Father Fitzpatrick, pastor of Saint James; Reverend Tully, pastor of the Methodist Church; an un-named stranger.

Cora contemplated each person. She eliminated family and friends as suspects, only because she didn't want to think a family member could be so brutal. She could always add them back later if she had to.

What did she know about the remaining people? According to the diary, the mayor and police chief had questionable reputations. Packey's boss was described as a nice guy, but inexperienced and incapable of handling the workers. Did Packey get in the middle of some dispute at the quarry? His boss, and maybe quarry owners, should be suspects.

What went on at that meeting at Saint James? Was there an argument? Were men angry with the priest for asking too much of them, and was it hushed up afterwards? Why was Angel upset with the priest, and why did she say he couldn't be trusted? Reverend Tully was trying to clean up Smokey Row—that was a potentially violent situation. Did Packey get involved, maybe because of his boxing?

Who was the stranger? He seemed an obvious suspect. Meg said he was getting the quarry workers riled up, another reason to suspect a quarry dispute.

Cora preferred not to think the killer was after Meg, unless a reason to do so turned up.

She closed the diary and headed a new page in her notebook, *Info from Old Newspapers*. She opened the oldest paper and looked for names on the diary list or anything else that seemed to relate to Packey's or Meg's lives.

The paper was only an eight-page weekly, but it was poorly organized and going through it was tedious. A column labeled *Happenings* listed pages of random topics: social events; visitors; fires; crimes; elections; trips; board meetings; personal opinions; ads; and medical advice. There was also serialized fiction. She had six months of issues to examine.

After three long hours, Cora found information to confirm what Meg had recorded in her diary and filled in a few details. Businesses and farms were failing in the poor economy, and local bankruptcies were reported. Illegal activities were taking place at a new horse market, which brought undesirable elements to town. The earlier issues carried a crazy story about a swindle attempt and court battle against the estate of a man named McWeeney—an odd name, Cora thought. Reverend Tully had brought the suit, so Cora made note of it.

Mayor McCarthy and Police Supervisor Sweeney were acquitted of charges of corruption brought against them by Reverend Tully; the American bantamweight prizefighting title bout was fought and won in Sag; quarry workers struck the previous year over low wages and preferential treatment, and the striking workers were fired. Father Fitzpatrick defended his need to keep Saint James buildings maintained, answering complaints from parishioners.

"Too much information!" Cora exclaimed aloud, faced with an abundance of vague motives.

Maureen's head appeared at the top of the stairway. She carried a stack of papers and needed to use the copier. "Is something wrong?"

Cora laughed. "No, no, nothing. I just got a bit too thorough, and made too much work for myself."

Maureen sighed. "I wish I could pare *my* work down." She started running copies, grumbling about the quality of the images and the complexity of the new copier. "Used to be you'd just put the paper down, press a button, and the copy came out. Now you have to pick the size, the orientation, set the darkness level, number of copies, sort options, and then when you're all done it gives you an error code anyway. Crazy newfangled piece of junk!"

Cora laughed with her, grateful for a break, but impatient as she had no time to waste. It seemed Maureen had urgent work too. She finished quickly and went back downstairs.

Cora spent the rest of the morning carefully considering each person and event she had listed. She selected four suspects as most likely, and guessed at motives. Then it was time to meet Cisco. She put the news-papers away, gathered her notes, the diary, and her coat, and went down-stairs, setting her personal belongings on a bench before stopping to use the restroom.

In addition to the entry and sanctuary on the main floor and the library in the loft, the historical society maintained a small museum in the base-ment, divided into a number of exhibits, recreating a schoolroom, a doc-tor's office, a general store, and more. The basement also had a kitchen, storage rooms, and the only restroom in the old building. Windowless, it had stone walls and a concrete floor, probably poured over a dirt floor years after its construction. It was creepy, and the restroom was inside a storeroom at the far end of the basement, the only light operated by a switch behind a wall, necessitating entry into a dark room and feeling around a corner for the switch. Cora couldn't enter the deserted area without expecting something to jump out at her.

She entered the restroom, and while washing her hands an idea burst into her mind. "The tunnels—what else was in them?" The words were so clear she thought they were spoken. She jumped and looked around the tiny room, then giggled sheepishly. Bridey had told her Meg's diary was found when the town boarded up its collapsing tunnels, but Cora gave that no further thought until now. Where did the sudden words come from? She mentioned yesterday Angel could be guiding her thoughts, but was reluctant to believe that. Was this Angel's idea? Had Angel fol-lowed her here, or was she planting ideas in her mind remotely? She shook her head and dismissed the thought.

Yet as she left the restroom she wondered if the Old Stone Church *had* been connected to the tunnel system and felt compelled to search for places a tunnel could have been located, boarded up along a wall. She knew what to look for, as she had seen a boarded passage in another old building. Like her other intuitions, she couldn't shake the feeling this was important.

The furnace was in the same storeroom as the restroom. It was likely the church was once heated by coal, because of the radiators throughout the building. There should be a coal storage bin and a window or other opening where coal was delivered via a chute—or a tunnel. It should be close to the furnace to shovel coal easily. Cora examined the outer wall near the furnace, but there was no space there for a bin. The wall wasn't patched, so no window was ever there, and no alley or street access for a delivery truck or wagon. No, there was never a coal chute there, but was there once a tunnel? The canal was in that direction, so it was a logical location, but she rejected the idea due to the intact wall.

Turning around, she saw an old interior door made of painted boards. She hadn't noticed it before, but she opened it now, to reveal a small storage area with a dirt floor and stone outer walls. A pull chain dangled in front of her, and she pulled it. Light flooded the room, and Cora jumped back involuntarily. An eerie man with red, black-rimmed eyes stared at her. Her racing heart slowed when she recognized Bill Mum, the spooky manikin that stood at the church entrance on *Fright Night*, and she laughed at herself. One wall faced the alley with a boarded window that allowed a bit of light to pass through the cracks. This had been the coal bin. She examined the walls, moved a few items, but found no boarded area or changes in the stone walls to suggest underground access. She turned off the light, closed the door, left the storage area, and went into the museum.

She carefully explored the outer walls of each exhibit, entering to look behind large items. She found only stone walls, no indications of boarded areas or wall repairs. She checked the kitchen, looked behind shelves and in cabinets. Nothing. She was ready to admit there had never been a tunnel in this building.

Why am I so sure there's something here?

My instincts have been right before…and there should be, that's why. This church is right on top of the tunnel system. It's more strange that I'm not finding a tunnel than if I did!

Turning to leave, disappointed, at the bottom of the stairs she realized she had overlooked a small space that separated the general store from the staircase and housed an old printing press and a manikin dressed as a printer's assistant. No bigger than six feet by six feet, it was lit only by whatever overhead basement lighting penetrated the area.

Cora went upstairs to Maureen's office. "Do you have a flashlight? I dropped an earring, and it rolled near the printing press," she fibbed. She wasn't wearing earrings, but Maureen didn't notice. She was on the phone, but pulled out a desk drawer and pointed to a flashlight. Maureen motioned she would come down to help when she finished the call. Cora shook her head, indicating it wasn't necessary, not wanting Maureen to know what she was doing.

Cora flashed the light behind the press, revealing a drape over its back wall.

There's no drape over any other wall down here.

The back of her neck tingled with excitement. She pulled the cloth aside. Fixed to the wall behind it was a large and rather ugly painting in poor condition. The frame was nailed to unpainted boards that were attached directly to the stone. It was about six feet tall and four feet wide. Cora grinned.

I knew it! This is the size a tunnel opening would be! Pay dirt—pun intended!

She looked around the edges of the frame. Did she feel a slight change in temperature from the surrounding walls, or was that her imagination? She tapped on the painting. Was that a hollow sound, or was that just what she *wanted* to hear? There would be at least a small gap between the canvas and whatever was behind it. A tunnel here would lead under and across the street, to another old church built a few years after this one. Could the painting cover the opening to an underground passage between the churches?

She went back to Maureen's office to return the flashlight, carefully controlling her excitement, and sat to ask some questions. "Do you know how they heated this building, back when it was built?" she asked.

Maureen leaned back in her chair, seeming to welcome a break. "Oh, I don't know about when it was *first* built, but for a long time it had a coal furnace," Maureen explained. "I don't know if you noticed that old storeroom near the restroom? That was where the coal came in and was stored—" She would have gone on, but Cora cut in.

"That's interesting. I just peeked in there and that's what I guessed. I know they stored coal in the old tunnels. Did the bin in the basement connect to them?"

"Oh, I go down there all the time and never saw anything like that. They just delivered the coal down a chute from the alley, I think. I never heard of any tunnels in this building. I go in there a lot— there's so little space to store stuff here and we have so much stuff...."

"You'd think there'd be a tunnel, though. The church was built during the canal days, and there were passages all over town. Wouldn't you think this building would have one?" Cora raised her eyebrows, inviting Maureen's opinion.

"Well, that was before my time, of course. I never saw anything like that, and I've been here almost twenty years—I think I would've seen a tunnel if there's one down there." She gave a high-pitched giggle. "I don't know a lot about them, as they were caving in so the village boarded them up long ago and all. You might ask the board members, someone might know something. Or maybe Public Works, the Building Department, they might have some maps or other information—"

Cora interrupted again. "Do you know anything about a big painting behind the curtain in the printer's display?"

"There's a painting back there? I never noticed that! I'm sure the cleaning girl knows but she never mentioned it to me. She's been here for five years and surely she's wiped it down, she's very good, even with all the items down there...."

"Do you know what the basement looked like before the displays went in? Was it all bare walls? Was there a big old ugly painting lying around?"

"Oh my—I'm sure I wouldn't know that. The museum was already down there when I started—I've just been adding to the exhibits. I never noticed anything behind that old dusty curtain, didn't want to touch it if I could help it, it might crumble like other old stuff does if you're not careful. You have to be real careful handling stuff, you know. No one ever told me about any old painting either...."

Now the idea was in Cora's head, whether it was her idea or Angel's, she had to see if there was a tunnel and what was in it. Why would Angel want her to look there? She didn't know, but she *did* know it wasn't a good idea to cross Angel.

Chapter 30

Cisco sat in a comfortable chair reading a golf magazine when Cora arrived at the public library. She knew his relaxed posture didn't reflect his level of dedication to their problems. She had her coping mechanisms, and Cisco had his. He had much more patience than she did, though, and would wait without complaint for long periods—especially if a golf magazine was handy. They moved to a comfortable seating area near a window to talk privately.

"I got a lot done, but first, did you reach Officer Rogers?" Cora asked.

"I reached him, but I don't know how much help he's going to be. The idea of looking into such an old murder case intrigued him, though."

"Will he help? Did he tell you what an investigator might do?"

"To some extent."

"Well—what's he going to do?" Cora tilted her head and raised her eyebrows.

Cisco explained, gesturing elaborately, "Well, he's a beat cop, not a detective, but he knows a little. He thought they'd pull out old files, read over the notes, interviews, see if any evidence is still around. After so much time, new technology could be used on old evidence. Maybe something was overlooked or couldn't be tested in 1898." He took off his glasses, wiped them on his shirt, rubbed his eyes, and then put the glasses back on as he talked. "For example, maybe something had fingerprints but no database to compare them to, so it wouldn't have meant anything. Not that they'd have fingerprints that old either, but you get the idea. Then they'd look at the suspects and see what those people did years later. Were they involved in other crimes, or did something happen later that tied them to the killings?"

Cora eyes widened, excited. "Would he give us a list of people they suspected?"

"Hold on—" Cisco held up a hand, "it's not that easy. If files still exist, which is a big if, and if any evidence is still around, which is even more doubtful, it'd take time."

Cora's face fell. "How much time?"

"Depends on how busy and how interested he is. Turns out the guy's a local history nut, though, and he said around then the Lemont police had a reputation for bribery and graft. You ever think how that could impact this case?"

Cora nodded. "You're right. They might have investigated carelessly or kept poor records. One of them might even have been the killer, or knew the killer and covered it up."

"I thought I'd get further with him trying to capture his interest, otherwise why would he want to help? There's no one left to put behind bars."

She reached out to grab Cisco's arm, giving it a little enthusiastic shake. "We have other things to do now anyway," she said, reaching into her purse for her notebook.

Cisco glanced at the page she opened. "Lists," he said, frowning but with twinkling eyes, "what else?"

"Of course, lists—that's what I'm good at." She laughed. "But look, they start long—," she held up a page and dragged her finger down the columns, "and they finish short, or at least short-er."

She dragged him to a sofa, sat down next to him, and pointed at a page. "I honed it down to most likely people and events. Look, let's review it together...."

Cora went over her criteria for selecting and narrowing her lists, sketched her thought process, and then gave Cisco some time to think it over. As he did so, she went to the front desk and picked up some reports for an upcoming board meeting. As she sat back down and put the thick envelope in her purse, she said, "I hope we have this all settled soon, or I may not be able to attend this board meeting."

"You just got re-elected, so hopefully we can get this done," he said without looking up, then pointed at a section of a beginning list. "You crossed out people that didn't pose a threat to Packey, assuming the murderer targeted him. You think Meg was killed because she surprised him," Cisco observed.

She nodded. "I left the mayor—something shady going on there—and Packey's boss, because he was new in town and we don't know much about him. I left Father Fitzpatrick and Reverend Tully, because they were involved in other disagreements, and Angel mentioned Fitzpatrick."

Cisco jabbed a finger at one of the names. "Why do you think no one in her family could have killed them? What about the brother-in-law? Does it make sense that Meg, ready to have her baby, would go out in the middle of the night? Why did she go looking for Packey instead of him? Why didn't he look for her when she didn't come back, instead of leaving the horse and wagon in the churchyard all night?"

"You're right," Cora said, and added Mick's name back. "That leaves the stranger Meg mentioned. Is he the most likely suspect only because we don't know anything about him? I couldn't find anything in the papers to suggest who he was." She repositioned herself into a corner of the sofa and met Cisco's gaze. "That leaves five—no six—possibilities with Mick. Unless the killer isn't on the list."

"What about motive?" Cisco asked.

"It had to be something Packey was mixed up in—something so important someone had to kill him."

She leaned forward, turned over a page, and pointed to her list of issues. "Here. Packey couldn't have affected the depression, bankruptcies, changes on the sanitary canal, the McWeeney business, or the horse market, so I crossed those out."

"The McWeeney business?"

"We'll talk about that later. Trust me, it's not a motive. So, four possible motives left." She moved her finger down the list as she read them off. "One, Smokey Row, Reverend Tully, the saloons and illegal fighting are related. Two, police or official corruption. Three, problems at the quarries. Four, Father Fitzpatrick and the work projects at Saint James." She leaned back again and tried to read his face for his thoughts.

He ran his hand over the top of his head. "Nothing stands out—except the stranger. If he was important, wouldn't he have been mentioned? The town wasn't that big."

"Let's pick something and check it further. If we can eliminate anything we're getting closer." Cora reached over and shook Cisco's arm with both of her hands and a big grin.

"What?" Cisco said, examining her face. "You're enjoying this too much. What happened?"

She laughed. "It *is* fun, and now I've actually met Angel, I see her as a person, and that changes things."

"Be careful Cora. You know that could be dangerous thinking." He frowned and shook his head slowly from side to side.

"I will." She dismissed his warning, still grinning and eyes sparkling with humor. "I saved the best for last. You had to know everything first, so you'd know *why* we need to do this."

"Do what?" asked Cisco, eyebrows up, hands held out, curious.

"Break into a tunnel," Cora confided, lowering her voice.

Chapter 31

"Think about it," Cora said, after she told Cisco what she found and explained why she thought the painting could be covering one of the old tunnels—a tunnel that could contain missing records, and maybe even clues to the killings.

"All this time since the killings nothing came to light. Somebody must have known something, even if it was only the killer. Would he go to his grave with that? Wouldn't he have said or written something—that's human nature. So why didn't it turn up? Because he did it years later after people stopped looking for the killer, then he forgot it, misplaced it, or hid it and it was never found. Why couldn't it be in a tunnel? Other stuff's been found there, including the diary, I'd like to remind you." She changed her seat again as she spoke, to a chair facing him, subconsciously positioning herself to give her an advantage in presenting her argument, and peered intently at him for signs he agreed with her.

Cisco raised an eyebrow. He didn't seem convinced. "You figured this out, huh? Why are you so sure an old picture attached to a wall is hiding a tunnel? What if it's just wall back there?" He raised an arm and flicked his wrist at a wall in emphasis.

"I don't know *how* I know, I just know," she said evasively. "So if it turns out it *is* just wall, there's no harm done, right? We've just lost some time, we put everything back, and no one will know." She gave him a pleading look.

Cisco said nothing, just looked off into space and drummed his fingers on the arm of the sofa.

"Hon, I have a sixth sense about it." Her words came out in a rush. "I think there's a tunnel public works missed, and something important is in it. I know it doesn't make a lot of sense, but my intuitions have been right lately." She raised her chin.

"I suppose you think that's Angel's doing? Planting thoughts in your head to help us find the killer?" He shook his head, but couldn't hide a small smile. "If she knew something, wouldn't she just tell you to go there?"

"I don't think she knows either. If there *is* any information, it has to be either hidden or lost. She knows her diary was lost in a tunnel, because we talked about it, and would remember the tunnels from her day. Whether the idea was Angel's or mine, the historical society seemed a good place to look."

"Okay, okay, I give. You won't talk about anything else until I do. Besides, you can't take down the painting and whatever holds it to the wall by yourself, or move that printing press—my God, how heavy is that thing?" He flashed her a grin. "Besides, it could be fun. When should we do it?"

"Right away." Cora grinned back. "We shouldn't go at night—if anyone sees us going in at night they could call the police. I'm authorized to be there, but it could be awkward."

"Are there tools there?" Cisco asked, ever practical.

"I don't know. We'd better go home and get our own. But we don't want to be seen carrying a whole bunch of stuff in the building," she said, avoiding Cisco's eyes, not wanting him to realize she was nervous. "What do we need?"

"Flashlights. Two—two good ones." He thought it over. "We may have to run to the hardware store. A claw hammer. Maybe a crowbar. Long nails to put the painting back."

"And if we find a tunnel?"

"A shovel maybe, if we need to uncover or move something, or run into crap."

"We'd better bring a long tape measure, a notepad and pencil. And don't forget the camera," Cora added.

"I don't know why you need that, but whatever. We're not going past any obstructions, right? If it looks crumbly or dangerous, we stop?" He watched her face.

"Uh, yeah...," Cora dithered. "I mean, what if we can see something just ahead? We can decide while we're in there, right?"

Cisco shook his head. "I should be used to this by now—you're gonna do what you're gonna do. Be sure to take the cell phone, at least, in case the whole thing comes down on us and one of us is still alive to use it," he stipulated. "And a baseball bat, in case we find rats in there!"

~ ~ ~

Cisco and Cora went home to change clothes and pick up supplies. When the garage door opened it revealed Cisco's golf bag, empty of clubs, in the middle of the garage floor. Open-mouthed, their attention fixed on a club protruding *through* the garage wall into the family room on the other side. It was bent and twisted at angles that held it firmly in place. Eerily, the wall itself was undamaged—the handle of the club stuck through the wall as if it was growing there.

"I'm afraid to go inside to see the rest of the house," Cora said, her voice weak and shaky. Her legs were shaky too.

"Have to face it sooner or later," Cisco murmured. He put an arm around her. "Ready?"

The mess, an understatement, was mostly confined to the family room. A mass of twisted golf clubs were scattered on the floor, curled around the light fixture, buried in Cisco's favorite chair. One was seen through a window, twined through the deck railing. Pictures previously hung on the wall were now in a neat stack at the opposite end of the room. The wall was also unscathed, the head end of the golf club through the garage wall similarly bent and twisted on this side.

Cisco stared, transfixed, while Cora looked around. "It all seems to be in this room."

"Only my clubs are damaged, nothing else," Cisco said woodenly.

"Why did she leave the bag in the garage and wreck the clubs in here?" Cora said, bewildered.

"She didn't. She made them come *through* the wall. She left the bag in the garage and one club in the wall to be sure we knew. Even took the pictures off the wall and piled them." Clearly Cisco had no further doubts about Angel or her abilities. "She wants to be sure we know her powers are greater than ours—the extent she'll go to if we don't obey her. That's what this is about."

"What set her off?"

"She knows I read Father's books, how poltergeists and spirits can penetrate walls. It has to do with absence of time, parallel worlds, energy transference, living in two planes...I don't know." He scratched the back of his neck. "I don't know *how* it happens, but this warning is for me, because she saw me reading about supernatural powers and behavior."

"How do we fight this? Should we call Officer Rogers?" Cora asked.

"To do what? To arrest Angel—put her behind bars? You think anyone is going to take us seriously? We're on our own here."

"Sshh—" Cora said. "She's hearing us."

"I don't give a damn!" Cisco exclaimed. "She *expects* us to react—that's what she wanted, and it worked. But she's one fucked-up spirit if she thinks I'm not gonna be pissed off about it! Let her hear me, I don't care!"

~~~

"I'll be damned!" Cisco exclaimed. "It *is* a tunnel!"

With considerable effort, Cisco and Cora had moved the fragile manikin and heavy printing press away from the wall. They tied the drapery to one side, and Cisco pried the painting off the wall. The picture was mounted on wood surrounded by a sturdy frame. The frame was nailed to a wooden border edging a dark, dank opening.

"You'd think they'd have done a better job of boarding this up," Cora remarked, sliding behind the press and peeking into the darkness. "I bet I know what happened. I bet someone from the church, before the historical society got the building, saw rats or mice coming from the tunnel, and this ugly picture was laying around, so they just nailed it up to keep them out. When the historical society took over, they just left everything in place—no idea a tunnel was back there."

"Why didn't public works board it up?" Cisco countered.

"Maybe they just missed it. I asked at the building department for maps of the tunnels once. No one knew what I was talking about."

"Think the rats and mice are still in there?" Cisco rolled his eyes.

"God, I hope not! Let's use a lot of light and make a lot of noise...I got an idea—hang on!"

Cora ran upstairs while Cisco peered into the opening, using a flashlight, hesitant to step inside.

Cora returned with a small gooseneck lamp and a reel of extension cord, and Cisco plugged it into a fluorescent fixture in the museum ceiling, smiling. "This will be better than flashlights."

"I hope we don't have to go far, just across the street, but we'll see. Are you ready?"

"You want me to go first?" Cisco asked.

"No, I'll go. In case I need you to pull me out!" Cora chuckled but was half serious. She turned on the lamp and held it near her waist, sending a beam of light ahead into the gloom.

Cora expected earth and wooden supports boring through a narrow passageway, but the excavation immediately widened to seven or eight feet, and beyond the doorway it was about six feet high. Most of the walls were rock, with few support beams. What she saw made sense. A tunnel had to be tall enough for dockworkers to walk, wide enough for a cart to pass even with supplies stacked along the walls, and the town was built over massive deposits of limestone, hence the quarry industry.

Looking for crumbling walls, holes in the floor, piles of debris, or creatures, Cora moved the lamp in all directions. The floor appeared solid, but the tunnel narrowed ahead, which could mean a cave-in, something stored, or only light distortion. "What do you see?" whispered Cisco.

"A lot of rock, a lot of dark," Cora replied in a soft voice. "Why are we whispering?"

"I don't know," Cisco replied a bit louder. "The situation just seems to call for it."

Cora giggled and had a hard time stopping. "I don't see anything moving or caving in. Let's go."

She reached back to take his hand, tested the floor, and held the lamp higher. "You got the flashlights, in case this goes out?"

"One in each pocket," Cisco patted his thighs. "Ugh! It stinks in here, damp and musty."

"I don't hear squeaking though. Wouldn't we hear squeaking or scurrying or something if there were rats in here?"

"I s'pose...how should I know?"

Cora stepped into the tunnel and moved forward tentatively, sliding one foot forward and gradually shifting her weight onto it before taking another step. Cisco followed, keeping a tight grip on her hand to steady her or pull her back if need be, but the tunnel appeared solid and empty.

"Does it get narrow up ahead, or is that my imagination?" Cisco asked, looking past the light.

"I thought that too. We'll have to get closer to tell—the light doesn't go that far."

"How far do you think we've come?"

Cora spun around, turning the lamp to look behind. Cisco jumped and gasped. "Hey! Don't do that without warning me!"

"Sorry...Hon, I don't think we've come fifteen feet yet. Seems we've been in here a long time, doesn't it?" She had another attack of giggles.

Cisco wasn't laughing. "Let's do what we have to do and get the hell out of here. I never thought I was claustrophobic, but this place puts me to the test."

"Okay." Cora walked a bit faster. An occasional support beam made her hesitate, but she went on. They neared the narrowed area which now appeared to be a bend in the passage.

"Where do you think we are, Hon? Any idea?" Cisco asked.

"Under the street? Midway? The street would be about forty feet from the entrance. If this doesn't turn again it'll connect to Saint Paul's Parsonage in another forty feet or so. Does that sound right?"

"Yeah. How much farther you want to go?" he asked.

"Let's see what's past the curve." She moved forward.

At the curve, the tunnel widened on one side to reveal a recess cut into the wall creating a small storage area about six feet in diameter. It was filled with boxes. "I didn't expect alcoves down here!" Cora said, trying to push the light into the chamber. "I'm out of cord. We'll have to switch to flashlights."

"Or we can just stop right here."

"I want to see if this only goes to Saint Paul's or if it branches. We're more than halfway—it seems safe enough."

"And if it does branch off?"

"I don't know...we'll have to see. Okay, okay— we'll save that for next time," she conceded, sensing he was irritated.

He switched on both flashlights, handing one to her. "Next time," he grumbled under his breath.

"What?" Cora asked. She moved the flashlight to check his face. He turned away but not before she caught his grin.

"I'll lead this time," Cisco said, ignoring her question and continuing down the tunnel. "We came this far, might as well check it all out."

There was nothing more to see. The tunnel went straight until it hit a dead end at a door. They couldn't budge it. They returned to the storage area, and Cisco held the lamp and lit around the boxes with his flashlight while Cora examined them more closely. "What do you think this stuff is?" Cisco asked. He tried to lift one. It was heavy.

There were seven wooden crates, all the same size, approximately fifteen inches by thirty inches and fifteen inches tall. They were sturdy, as if made for permanent storage of items of some importance. The lids were nailed closed.

"They're the right size to store records. This could be what we're looking for!" Cora said excitedly. "We've got to open one!"

"I don't suppose you'd agree to just *tell* someone what we found, would you?"

"What's the fun in that? It's *our* discovery. It might not be important anyway."

Cora saw his eyes sparkling with excitement in the dim light. "I want to know too. Let me go back and get the hammer then," he said.

"Wait—I'll go with you. I need to measure."

He turned to her. "Measure? Measure what?"

"Measure how far it is from the historical society wall to this recess and from Saint Paul's doorway to where the boxes are." Cisco lifted the lamp to see her face better, the eyes sparkling with humor, the smug smile.

"What for? It's the only storage area in here! It's not hard to find, is it?"

"For ownership, that's why. If the boxes are as old as we think, the original owners are all dead. Whoever's property they're on owns them— Saint Paul's or the historical society. But if they're under the street, that's public land, so *we* can claim them. That's why!" Cora explained. "I don't want to have to hand them over until we know if what we're looking for is in there."

"And you know this because...?" Cisco asked.

"Because I called a special collections librarian to find that out, before I met you at the library, Hon," Cora said, proud of her forethought. "Better bring the camera too, so we can get pictures to document where they are before we move them."

"You're bragging, aren't you?"

Cora just grinned.

When measurements were taken, the boxes were forty feet from the historical society doorway, and an equal distance from Saint Paul's Parsonage entrance. The boxes were under the middle of the street.

"Why do you suppose they didn't take the boxes out of here when they sealed off the tunnel?" Cisco asked.

"When they boarded Saint Paul's entrance, they probably couldn't see this pocket because of the bend. I bet they didn't go in, and assumed it ended or would be explored from the other side, the historical society side. Which never happened."

When Cisco opened the boxes, they did contain old documents. The two they opened in place dated from 1890–1900 and 1900–1910. Some were church documents. Others appeared to be Village of Lemont documents.

With difficulty, they lugged the heavy boxes to the library loft to examine the next morning.

"As it turns out, it's a good thing we don't have plans for Thanksgiving. We'll have the long weekend alone here to go through the boxes. I wonder if Frannie can help," Cora said.

"You'd better have an excuse in case someone drops in."

"I'll say a neighbor found some boxes in the attic of her old farmhouse and asked me to look through them for anything of historical significance."

If Frannie joined them, they would finish more quickly. That could expose Frannie to danger if Angel found out, but there had been no sign of Angel in the building and there were a lot of documents so it might be worth the risk. They would let Frannie decide. They would *not* reveal their discovery to Angel—yet.

Chapter 32

Early on Thanksgiving Day, Cora, Cisco, and Frannie faced one another around the historical society's library table. In front of each was a box of documents, and four boxes were piled on the floor, which made it difficult to maneuver around the crowded loft.

Frannie, with no plans for the holiday, had been eager to join them. "Sure thing," she replied. "You're not about to leave me out. Frannie the Ghostbuster be there with bells on!"

After Cora told Frannie what they found in the tunnel and why they were in a hurry to examine the boxes, Frannie was excited. "I missed all the fun!" she grumbled. "Why didn't you ask me to go down there?"

About the destruction of Cisco's golf clubs, however, Frannie for the first time showed apprehension and looked around nervously. "Girl, you about to see a black face turn all white! You think Angel would take out after me, if she finds out I'm helping you?"

"Yes, Frannie," Cora said, searching her friend's eyes. "We talked about this from the beginning—the danger, the need for secrecy. You were the one who said Angel was escalating, remember? We've been talking about her doing one awful thing after another—this can't be a surprise."

Cora looked away and her voice shook as she said, "I'm not worried about myself. I'm scared to death something awful will happen to one of you if I don't do everything right." She lifted her head to reveal eyes glistening with unshed tears. "Angel couldn't have picked a worse thing to do than threaten Cisco." Cisco placed a reassuring hand on her arm. Cora forced a tight-lipped smile.

Frannie leaned back in her chair and stared at the tabletop with her lips pressed firmly together. "I guess this spooky stuff's coming too close now. You know you never really believe danger is gonna touch you personally—not me! Well, I guess this is just a moment of truth, what you said about Cisco's clubs. This is real, isn't it? This game Angel's playing, she's got all the powers and we got nothing good to fight back with, only our heads."

"That's about it," Cora nodded. "Would you rather bow out, Frannie? Much as we appreciate your help, Cisco and I can handle it."

"Yeah, well, maybe it's too late for that. What if Angel knows I'm involved already and doesn't like it? What's my protection then? Seems to me, my only chance to get through this business is to stick near you and help solve these murders real quick."

"True, but…I hope that's not the only reason. I mean, I can't tell you how much it's meant to have you believe me and help me." Cora rubbed her forehead. "But if you want to give up…."

Frannie let out her loud laugh. "Give up? Who's talking about giving up? Cut the crap, girl! You just *try* to keep me away! You think I'm gonna sit back and watch while you have all the fun? No way! I had a moment of second-thought is all, and now third-thought's come and gone, and I'm raring to go. We find this guy, and tell Angel the truth, and she'll stop pestering us, and it's quicker with *all* of us working at it."

They exchanged glances and grinned.

"One more thing. It's great how you found these old boxes, but maybe we're getting carried away by that. How do you know there's anything important to *us* in these here papers? Why are we gonna take all this time looking through this old stuff?" She waved both hands at the boxes surrounding them.

"Actually, I *don't* know," Cora admitted with a lopsided grin. "Just like I didn't know an old tunnel was downstairs, or these boxes were in it. Like I didn't know I'd meet Angel at the cemetery." She poked a forefinger on the table as she made each point, then looked up with her jaw set. "I can't give you any more reason than gut instinct. It's been working up to now."

"Don't ask, Frannie," Cisco commented wryly, rolling his eyes. "Cora's always right, aren't you Cora?" he asked, giving her a significant look.

"Well, pretty much," Cora replied sheepishly. "I try not to say *anything* until I'm sure it's right. Why would anyone want to say something *wrong*? That makes no sense!"

"Most people do though. They're not all perfect," Cisco said.

Cora lifted her chin and grinned good-naturedly. "They're not me!"

"Whatever," Frannie said. "We make a good team, don't we? Cora got through this research stuff in no time, and got us all organized. I did the online part and don't forget the propping up part, and Cisco's out there hoofing it, making calls, reading stuff and providing muscle."

"Okay then, fearless leader," Cisco said, straightening his back and drumming both hands on the table. "What have you got in mind? What do you want us to do?"

"I bet it involves lists in some kind of way," Frannie said, throwing Cisco a smirk and nodding.

Cora laughed. "You're right. You know me too well." She went to the copier, made copies of a page she had been writing on, and handed one to each of them out.

"It's more an inventory than a list," she began.

"Not much difference, is there?" Frannie said under her breath to Cisco.

"There is in *my* mind," said Cora. "A list is things to *do*. An inventory is things we *have*. Sort of. Anyway, let's identify each document in these boxes. We don't have to read the whole thing, just enough to note in these three columns."

She held up a page and pointed at a column. "One: date. If there's no date, estimate. Month and year is enough." She picked up a document and showed it to them. "This seems to be a bill of sale for lumber. It's dated May 29, 1899—an exact date, so I'll use it." She filled in the date on the page in front of her.

She held up two fingers. "Two: names. Put down every name you think is important—people, organizations, towns. Anything else that jumps out at you, keeping in mind what we're looking for. Let your sixth sense talk to you. If you don't think you have a sixth sense, pretend. Think of it like picking words for a Google search." She held up her page again. "This is a purchase by Jim Fischer from Joseph Tedent." She wrote down the names.

"Now, the last column, the *description* column, note briefly the purpose of the document. It could be a bill of sale for lumber, an agreement to sell a farm, or a letter to relatives in Pittsburg. If it's not obvious, then let's talk about it and decide. This one is a simple bill of sale. Got it?"

"Got it," said Cisco.

"Got it," said Frannie, looking up with a frown. "We have seven boxes, right? We expect to get through more than a couple of inches? There's *thousands* of documents in these here boxes!"

Cora shifted her eyes away and promised, "It'll go fast once we get a sense of what to look for and develop a rhythm. That's what happened when I went through the newspapers. We'll recognize important things and move on. Our sorting will also help the historical society when they try to find permanent homes for the documents."

Frannie rolled her eyes with a lopsided grin. "Good to know—I'll try to keep that in mind." She reached into her box and moved a stack of files to the table in front of her. "I sure hope there's plenty of paper in that copier—we're gonna need a shitload of it!"

"One last thing," Cora said, "let's review what we're looking for. That would be: village officials; Packey's boss—Jacob Luther; Father Fitzpatrick; Reverend Tully; Mick Keating—the brother-in-law; and someone new in town that could be our mysterious stranger. The time frame is 1898. Look for events and activities about Smokey Row and Sag Bridge, political or police corruption, quarry 'quarrels', and dissent at Saint James. We want names involved in those issues and any other things Packey could have been involved with, especially if controversial or violent. If you think you've found something, let's talk about it right away."

Cora pulled out her cell phone and checked the time. "Let's stop after an hour, compare notes, and decide if we should change how we're doing this. But first figure out what we have." Cora had fallen naturally back into her lifelong habit of giving orders. There was no time for niceties— they'd just have to deal with it. Cora, the administrator, was in high gear.

~~~

An hour later, after tediously recording numerous bills of sale, payrolls, permits, tax records, registers, minutes, and other documents, they agreed on a simpler approach. They sorted each box by source, type of document, and date. They put ledgers, tax documents, and bills back in the boxes for another time. They set aside correspondence, minutes, clippings, court or legal documents, church registers, and papers with lengthy text for closer immediate attention. This reduced the materials by about eighty percent.

They tackled the remaining boxes in the same manner, and by early afternoon they had a good idea of the contents of all the boxes.

Three boxes contained Village of Lemont records, one from 1890 through 1899, another from 1900 through 1909, and the last from 1910 through 1919. Two boxes contained records from the First Methodist Church, dating from 1890 through 1900 and from 1901 through 1910. The last two boxes were from Saint Paul Lutheran Church, containing records from the same years as First Methodist.

Along with financial documents, the church records included registers of members, weddings, deaths, and baptisms. "Saint Paul's will be glad we've found these," Cora said. "They had a fire in the 1920s and thought all their records were destroyed. They must have forgotten they stored some in the tunnel."

"Too bad the stranger was a Catholic instead of a Methodist. We could have just looked at men who registered in 1898 for him," Cisco said. Cora jotted a note to check if Saint James had such records.

They took a break and Cisco went for sandwiches. "I hope he gets a bottle of wine too," Frannie quipped. "A bottle of wine would make this afternoon go a whole bunch better."

"It would put me to sleep!" Cora laughed.

After they ate, Cisco took the Village records, Frannie took Saint Paul's, and Cora the Methodist Church. "It's fitting, since I spend so much time in this building," she explained.

The monotonous work dragged on. Cisco had *not* brought wine, but they still had trouble staying awake. Most of the materials were exceedingly dull, and only the process of recording summaries on the inventory sheets kept them marginally alert. With no exciting finds, their enthusiasm dropped, conversation lagged, and the only sounds were the rustling of pages and an abundance of loud sighs. The light began to fade, and Cora was about to suggest they call it a day when she picked up a file that brought her up short.

Buried between the pages of the birth, death, wedding and baptism registers for the year 1907 was a folder an inch thick. Written on the front was *Personal, Reverend Tully, 1907.*

"Whoa! Look at this," Cora said, holding it up. "The great abolisher of evil himself—he was still here in 1907, I guess. That's long after our murders, but I wonder what's in here."

"Haven't we done enough for today? said Cisco.

Cora ignored the suggestion. The dreamy, tingly sensation that accompanied her premonitions surged through her. "Let me just take a look."

She paged quickly through the file. A few letters seemed to be from family or personal friends—she would read those later. A few bills for personal items, an expired bank passbook—zero balance—news clippings, funeral cards...and a large sealed envelope. Cora's scalp prickled with excitement. In a neat script, characteristic of the fancy handwriting of the day, she read, "Daniel J. Cavanaugh, January 1, 1907. Do not open until after my death."

The blood drained from Cora's face and her heart beat faster as she held the envelope up for Cisco and Frannie to see. "Look," she said, whispering. "Should I open it?"

"He's got to be dead by now," Cisco observed. "Even if he was ten years old when he wrote whatever is in there, he'd be a hundred and fifteen today. I think we can assume we're not violating his wishes."

"Yeah, girl!" said Frannie, taking a deep breath and stretching her arms over her head. "Open it! I'm ready after all this mind-numbing drivel. I hope there's something good in there. You like this stuff, huh? Baffles me why. I don't know how you stand it week after week. I wouldn't last a day."

The envelope had long since failed to hold its seal. Cora easily slipped out the contents, many hand-written unfolded pages. The paper, although showing signs of age, was not crumbly, the ink only slightly faded. Quickly scanning the opening paragraphs as Cisco and Frannie watched, Cora looked up, eyes bright with excitement. "It's a confession!" she said. "A long one...." She flipped through multiple pages.

"This'll take the better part of an hour to read, especially with this old flowery handwriting." She looked around the dim room. "It's getting dark. We might not finish, and we shouldn't show any light in here. What do you want to do? Find somewhere else to go or wait until tomorrow?"

"Fuck the lights. Risk it," said Cisco. "If this is what we're looking for, let's find out here and now."

Chapter 33

To be *read after my death:*

Daniel J. Cavanaugh—A Confession

This letter is the product of a year's contemplation, but it is fitting to begin the New Year by sealing it away for my lifetime. I write now with deep regret for sad events of a number of years ago, and a desire to clear my mind of a certain matter, a matter known to no one but me. It was Reverend Tully's suggestion to set down on paper these troubling events, my part in them, and the reasons for my actions, in the hope that in the telling I will achieve some measure of peace and surcease from tormenting thoughts.

I leave this letter in the hands of a man who has become a friend, although we began as fierce opponents. That is Reverend Tully of the First Methodist Church. Yes, the same Reverend Tully who is credited with ridding our town of drunkenness, brawls, and crime in the streets. When I first came to Lemont I was among the men profiting from such sinful occupations, as I too gave in to temptations and greed. My poor sainted Máthair, God rest her soul, would grieve that such temptations led me away from her strict Catholic teaching. I have since returned to the better path, and I wish to be known not for past errors, but for more recent endeavors, and to be remembered as the honorable man I have become.

Reverend Tully is unaware of what happened at Saint James and the contents of this letter and I will not tell him. He is an astute man, however, and he knows something is burdening me, and for that reason he suggested I take this course, to write my story and seal it away, in the hopes it will help me gain peace and relief from disturbing dreams. I know it will be safe with him, and he can be trusted to deal with it per my wishes.

You know me as the owner of Cavanaugh Brewery, a fine local business that not only makes grand beverages for local consumption, but distributes them widely to stores and establishments, as men from many states enjoy my brews. Perhaps you are also a patron of Cavanaugh's Saloon and Cavanaugh's Liquor and Cigar Emporium here in Lemont, other fine businesses in which I take pride.

It was Billy Lynch that started the brewery some years before I arrived in Lemont, and at first he met with great success. As the company grew, he discovered he was a fine production man, but a poor businessman. When the company started to decline and arrived at the brink of bankruptcy, I bought into it and built it up again. Eventually I bought my partner out. At first he did not want to sell at the price I offered, but I pointed out certain things and eventually he saw the practicality of the deal. He has moved on now, I do not know where, as I do not hear from him. We did not part great friends.

In the event you are among those who disapprove of alcoholic beverages, then surely you know me as a Village Trustee. You have elected me for a second term to that trusted position, which I hope to hold for many terms to come. Many of my fine ideas have been implemented and have resulted in notable improvements in the village.

Some would say the mayor, police chief, and I personally benefit from our good works, but even if that were true it cannot be denied that the taxes brought in by our encouragement of certain businesses, though they may not be embraced by all, have nonetheless profited the village with such assets as our fine schools. The mayor, police chief and I work well together, as we have been doing for many years, even before my investment in the brewery or election to local office.

I find I am at last in exactly the situation I sought when I came to America in 1897 from County Wexford in Ireland. Arriving in New York City, I left the East a year later for Illinois, like many others, for better opportunities for those of Irish descent. I came to Lemont early in 1898 with grand ambitions, and they have come to fruition as I envisioned. But I started with nothing, and, as I hinted in the opening words of this letter, my journey to becoming a respectable, and reasonably wealthy, businessman was one of difficulty, and actions that led to my prosperous situation are now troubling. I wish at this time to express remorse regarding the outcome, and to make an explanation of those circumstances.

Upon my arrival in New York, I soon discovered Irish immigrants the likes of me were not welcome. The city was filled with an abundance of unemployed Irish men, and my own countrymen viewed me as competition for the few remaining jobs open to them. I was unskilled in any work, friendless and near to starving. But there was work near Chicago, it was said, for Irish men to help dig a canal, a grand idea to change the flow of the Chicago River, a sanitary canal they called it, to provide clean water and a better transport from the Great Lakes to the Mississippi River. So I went to Chicago.

Once again my timing was poor, for when I arrived I found that the canal was almost done, and the battle for jobs on the small portion that remained was fierce. But in Lemont jobs were available in the quarries, and so I worked there at first. I had an idea, you see, to save enough money to settle here and start a business.

Alas, I soon found the quarries no better than my other poor attempts. Conditions there were very sad. The work was back-breaking and men worked long hours for very little pay. Many of them spent what little they made in the saloons and brothels, but I wanted no part of that, as I had a grander plan. I was better than those men, I knew, smart and shrewd, and confident in my abilities, and did not want to limit myself to a life of digging and loose living. I determined to make my stake here, and not move on again. I had enough of moving on. But a large amount of money would be needed to start a business. Where would I get it?

Shortly after I came to Lemont, I made the acquaintance of a feisty lass named Kitty Hurley. Kitty moved to Chicago from Lemont at the request of an old man she kept house for, James McWeeney. We met when she came to visit her family here, a shanty Irish family I am sad to say, but Kitty was fun and accommodating, and I often took the train to Chicago to be with her. When she told me McWeeney's situation, that he was near to dying and with no wife or child, we cooked up a scheme to have him deed his money to Kitty. Of course, I would need to marry her to gain control of the funds, which gave me second thoughts. But although I was not in love with Kitty, it was a fair price to pay to stake my ambition, and I was willing, as she was a pleasant enough lass and all.

So we prepared a will that left most of the old man's assets to Kitty, and we waited for his demise, which was not very long. When he died, we called a witness to the bedside, and put a pen in McWeeney's dead hand, and moved it to make his signature on the new will. "Did you see this document signed with McWeeney's hand?" we asked the witness, and he said that he did, and signed his name below McWeeney's, as it was the truth, although without the details.

Well, it was a good attempt and all, but we did not get away with it. That was my first encounter with Reverend Tully, as it was he who brought Kitty to court. His church was to benefit from the original will, and he contested the new one in court, and won. He never did know I was behind the deception, but blamed Kitty.

I thought it best not to associate with Kitty after she lost the inheritance, and her reputation in the bargain. Being around her would hurt my own status and I could not afford to have that happen. She did not agree at first, but I found ways to persuade her, and she decided to move on. The less said about that the better, as our relationship did not end well.

Then I thought perhaps I could put a bit of money aside if the men from the quarry paid a fee to me to fight their battles with the owners, to organize them and get better wages and shorter hours as they deserved, and to be sure the Irish workers got the best opportunities. I made some noise and gave it a good try, but it was a failed attempt, and in the end the men cursed me because they gave me their money and nothing came of it, and the owners relieved me of my job. After that no other quarry would hire me.

At that time, Lemont was in poor shape, recovering from the depression. To make matters worse, workers moved away after the canal was finished, and businesses failed. Jobs were scarce, and none at all for a new immigrant such as me. I came to this country and this town in search of success, and I had nothing to show for my efforts.

I was desperate. I had little saved and no prospects. I tended bar at some of the local saloons on the odd day, but there was no future in that. One thing I enjoyed was the prizefights that took place down at the Sag on weekends. The matches were not legal, but the men fought nonetheless. We Irish dearly love to fight. I was not much of a boxer myself, as I could not bear getting hit, but I attended matches as a spectator.

One night, coming off a shift as bartender, I had a few dollars in my pocket, and thought I would wager them on Packey Hennessey, our local favorite. It was hard to find someone to bet against him, but eventually I did, and even at the odds I had to give I wound up increasing my few dollars. That small win inspired a new plan.

I knew something about wagering from back in Ireland, but surely the rules were a bit different here in the States. How hard could it be to find out? I asked around, and followed not only local matches, but others I heard tell of, and I studied how it was done. I started with small bets, and it turned out I had a real talent for figuring out how best to work a wager to my advantage, and it was not much different from wagering in Ireland.

I thought it important to keep a low profile. I did not want to be well known, as that would make my methods predictable, not a profitable thing in the gambling business. I attended local fights, but made my wagers other places. If I did bet at the Sag, it was only with men from Bridgeport or other men from out of town.

Occasionally I bet on Hennessey, as I could count on the outcome of his matches. Hennessey always won, without fail. I took bets at short odds against him from new men who did not know the local fighters, and with men who badly wanted some other favorite of theirs to win.

One day it occurred to me that a great deal of money could be made if Hennessey lost. I could not shake that idea, and so I worked it all out. If I betted for Hennessey to lose, and gave long odds, and approached the local men who did not know me, they would think I was a fool and be glad to take my money. If I used everything I had, I could make a killing on only the one fight, and I could take that money and buy a business. I would have it all, everything I had ever wanted. I would only need to do it once and I would be done.

If Hennessey lost.

Would it be so bad if Hennessey lost, just once? Would it not really add to the excitement of the sport, if Hennessey did not always win, if he was fallible? Would it not be better for the game in the long run? Surely Hennessey would understand this, when I talked to him. Because of course I would need to talk to him, to convince him to agree.

I needed a way to approach Hennessey, who did not know me. I had heard talk about the man, including the great help he was at his church, Saint James, where many of the Irish families went. I started to attend Mass there, and one Sunday I called Hennessey aside after Mass for a little talk.

As it happened, I was mistaken about Hennessey knowing me, because he remembered me from my days at the quarry, and did not realize I was no longer employed there. Since he was a foreman, he had a poor impression of me, and said we would have nothing to talk about. It was not an auspicious beginning, but I reasoned that it was a poor time for such a talk, with his family and his pregnant wife standing nearby.

An alternate plan came to me, as I recalled Hennessey raised his hand to come to a meeting that same night at the church. If I went to the meeting and pretended to help, and we talked after the meeting instead, and after the beer or two Father would likely provide the men, why surely Hennessey would be agreeable to losing just one fight.

I had already inquired of some men to see if they were interested in taking my wager, and one of them found me in O'Shea's Saloon that afternoon, where I was having a few pints and planning what to say to Hennessey later in the evening. The man took up my offer, and said he had arranged for a group of friends to put up the entire amount for the next fight, almost a week away. It could have been the challenge, or it could have been confidence in my plan, or it could have been the beer. Whatever the reason, I accepted the wager then and there. I did not have enough to cover it if I lost, but it was no real risk at all, as surely Hennessey would agree and the result of the fight was a sure thing that would go my way.

At the church meeting, Hennessey sat on the other side of the room, and I suspected he was avoiding me. I tried to convince the men in the room, and Father Fitzpatrick, that I was a grand fellow, a good and religious man, and very anxious to help the church in any way, and so I volunteered every time it was asked. I was trying to make an impression on Hennessey, and it did seem to have that effect, as he looked me in the eye with some surprise. It was a good thing, as it turned out the priest did not provide beer for the men after all.

After the meeting ended, I offered Hennessey a ride home, as my horse would carry two a reasonable distance. I asked him if first he would explain to me one of the projects Father wanted done, so we walked from the hall through the cemetery and up to the church. No one was there, as the other men left as soon as the meeting ended. I asked Hennessey if he would agree to lose the fight next Friday night.

Unhappily, he would not listen to reason. No argument I made about it being for the good of the sport and ultimately helpful to the men carried any weight with the obstinate man. He would not see my point at all. He could not betray his men, he said, or his own ethics, he said, or his pride, he said. He was not a man to take a fall, his reputation would be diminished, he would never feel right about himself again, and on and on he went. I pleaded. It was only the one time, I said. I would lose everything, I told him, and when the men found out I could not make good on the wager they would come after me, and would beat me, and maybe even kill me, and he said that was not his fault, it was mine.

He turned to walk away, and I was desperate, and I ran after him and pushed him, and he hit his head against a gravestone as he fell, and it opened a great bleeding gash above his ear.

He got up and made a sound I could only call a roar, and he reached for me. I was panic-stricken. I had not meant harm, but he was coming for me and I could never fend off Hennessey, the champion boxer, I could never do it. Somehow a rock was in my hand, and I swung it, and it hit right where the great bleeding gash was, and he went down. I lost control and violently fell on him, and I hit him again, and again, and again, and I lost count of the number of times I hit him with the rock, as I was consumed with panic. It was not me, but overwhelming passion that caused the deed. And the man was dead.

I stood and looked down at him and did not know what to do. After a while I took him by his feet and dragged him a short distance into the graveyard. He would not be seen there easily if someone came to the church. I ran to my horse, and I rode out of the churchyard and onto the road, and spurred my horse to go as fast as he could away from Saint James.

When my terror diminished, I let the horse slow, and tried to think clearly. No one knew I met with Hennessey, and there was no reason to associate me with his death. But it would be better if they did not find him right away, so I should go back, and hide his body. But where to hide it? It seemed to me that Hennessey was in the right place already, in a cemetery, and a Catholic cemetery, where he would want to be buried. So to bury him there, that was the right thing to do, the right thing for Hennessey, and the right thing for me. I would get a shovel, and I would drag him to a far corner where no one would notice the disturbed ground, and I would bury him there.

I rode home and I got a shovel. An Irish man always has a shovel handy, I could not help thinking. Even at the worst of times, the solution for an Irish man is his shovel. It took some time to muster my courage to go back.

It was very late when I returned, after 3:00 A.M., and I would need to work fast to get Hennessey buried and get away from the church before light. I tied my horse out of sight in some trees down the hill, where he was nearby but could not be seen. I took the shovel, and looked for a distant spot where the soil was easy to dig. I found such a spot near the road in a far corner, and returned to get Hennessey.

The horrors of the night would not end, because when I got close to where I left the body I heard a cry and saw that Hennessey's wife, heavy with child, was leaning over his body and calling to him, and then she dropped down to hold him, crying out his name again. I was behind her, and the horse nickered, and the wife pushed herself up to turn around and look. I could not let her discover me, and I did not think of anything else, but I had the shovel in my hand, and I swung it, and it hit her head, and she went down.

And did not move.

Oh my Lord! I had only wanted to stop her and make my escape. It was but an accident the shovel landed hard. It was never my intent, but I had killed again!

As I stood looking down at what I had done, I heard the plaintive howl of a wolf, which sounded very near. I did not know that wolves inhabited these forests, but the cry was easily recognized. I shivered and an intense fear overcame me.

I could bear no more, and could not find it in me to complete my task. It would soon be dawn, and no time remained. No time now to bury not one, but two. I fled. Grabbing my shovel, I ran to my horse, untied him, and rode home at a gallop. The cries of the wolf followed me, or was it only fear and my imagination? The thought of wolves chasing me down and tearing into me fed my panic.

Through no effort on my part, fortune went my way after the events of that evening. The bodies were found in the morning, but the deaths were never associated with me. The priest, and the men who attended his meeting—the last men to see Hennessey alive— were questioned, but we had no helpful information. The only person who may have known I had talked to Hennessey was the wife, and she was dead.

The prizefight bets were called off, of course, because the fights could not take place, so I kept my money. I was no worse off. I stopped betting on boxing. I had no more appetite for it. Nor could I face returning to Saint James.

Bad luck continued to plague Hennessey's family, what was left of it. Hennessey's sister-in-law left her husband, moved in with her máthair, and sold the family farm. Her husband, surely a weak man, picked up odd jobs on the railroad after the farm was sold. The town turned against him, blaming him for letting Hennessey's wife go out to search that night, and for waiting until morning to check on her when she did not return. He took to the drink, a damaged man. His body was found in the rail yard some years later, and it was assumed he stumbled onto the tracks while inebriated. Hennessey married into a no-account family, all right.

My own luck, on the other hand, changed to good, and my intelligence, shrewd judgment, and willingness to do what was required to achieve my goals fit nicely with things happening in Lemont. I discovered that the mayor and the police chief were involved in profit-making schemes, and I offered my services. They took me up on it, tentatively at first, but after the opportunity to fully evaluate me, I became their partner. I quickly accumulated the nest egg that allowed me to buy into and then take over the brewery.

My reputation as a shrewd businessman increased, and I found I enjoyed the role of kindly business owner and responsible elected official. I switched my allegiance to the Methodist Church, and became a benefactor. I enjoyed the company of Reverend Tully, and we became fast friends. He introduced me to fine literature, and I became not only an honest citizen, but a moral and literate one. The only blight on my contentment was that events from my past began to trouble me, and I lay awake many nights, and had troubled dreams.

Now that the entire story is written, it is easy to see, regrettable as was the outcome of that evening's events, it is not so much a matter of finding fault, rather that all involved had fallen victim to circumstance. This written exercise has succeeded in its purpose to set me at ease in that regard.

Despite my present Methodist faith, I find myself falling back upon my Catholic upbringing as a young boy in Ireland, and so I end here in an appropriate way, with my act of contrition, a final step before I seal this envelope for my lifetime.

O my God, I am heartily sorry for having offended Thee.
I detest my sins and every other evil
Because they displease Thee, my God,
Who, in Thy infinite wisdom, art so deserving of all my love.
I firmly resolve, with the help of Thy grace,
Never more to offend Thee, and to amend my life.
Amen.

With sorrow, and trusting in Your understanding, I am,

Daniel J. Cavanaugh
This first day of January, in the year of our Lord, Nineteen Hundred and Seven

Chapter 34

Cora, Cisco and Frannie sat in silence, thinking, looking around the room, anywhere but at each other. Each of them reacted differently to Cavanaugh's letter, which Cora had just finished reading aloud.

Cisco's face was relaxed, his eyes wide and clear. Cora supposed he was relieved, thinking the letter solved the mystery and led to the end of their problems.

Frannie gazed, unfocused, across the room. Legs crossed, she jiggled one foot up and down. Cora thought Frannie's mind was ticking away, trying to understand Cavanaugh and wondering what their next step should be.

Cora's own thoughts refused to follow a single path, and she struggled with her emotions, but couldn't understand why. Why wasn't she simply relieved, like Cisco? Shouldn't she be elated that they found what they were looking for? Instead, she had an empty feeling in her gut, and a sense of trepidation, of more unpleasantness to face. She sat with her arms crossed, head bowed and eyes closed.

Was she confused by the tragedy, her sympathy for Meg and Angel? Although Meg and Angel were the same, her mind separated the living woman from the spirit. For the first time she considered how she would feel if Angel left for good—after all, she was part of Cora's life as long as she could remember. Was she afraid to tell Angel what they found out? Or all of it.

"So that's it then," Cisco said.

"A fit of passion, that's what this whole business is about. What a sanctimonious, hypocritical jackass!" Frannie ranted, as she uncrossed her legs, stomped her foot on the floor, and banged a fist on the table. "That Cavanaugh didn't feel any more sorry when he wrote that letter than when he killed those poor people for no good reason. You catch how he justified everything, like what he did was accidents, not *his* fault? *He* never did a damn thing, just putting words down way later like everybody should feel sorry for him getting caught up in bad stuff."

"Yeah, we caught that," Cisco said, leaning forward with his arms on the table. "But I don't think he was a murderer by nature—just a selfish man carried away by greed. He didn't see anything wrong with stealing from his partner, or ditching Kitty after what he did to her. And he never felt sorry for his victims, just himself. Called the poor family slobs."

"Amoral, don't they call it? Where was this guy's head? He rationalizes away his guilt, just circumstance, then he makes an Act of Contrition? For what, I say? To cover all the bases? Here's what I wonder—I wonder how many killers want to make a confession before they die, and how many want to die with their secret. I say he wanted to take credit for what he did, not look for forgiveness. He was bragging, not complaining."

"This guy wouldn't write a confession for anything but a selfish reason—he was too preoccupied with himself," Cisco stated.

"Wonder how that letter got lost in the first place," Frannie said, leaning back and crossing her arms.

"I bet the Reverend Tully moved and it just got mislaid. Tully didn't stay here all his life, isn't that right Cora?" Cisco turned to Cora, who was sitting quietly, hands tucked under her armpits, eyes still closed, deep in thought and trying to shut out their voices.

She opened her eyes and shook her head slowly. "I can't talk about this now. I have to go to sleep and face it in the morning."

Cisco tipped his head toward Frannie. "She calls it incubating. She believes if she doesn't think about something for a while, her subconscious will come up with answers. It doesn't work all the time, but often it *does* work. Maybe she'll have an idea in the morning—or maybe not."

"You guys go on home if you're not afraid Angel will get you," said Frannie. "I don't know where I'm going yet, but not home. I'm not about to be going anywhere she might figure out I could be!"

Cisco looked at Cora. "She's got a point. Maybe we shouldn't go home either. Want to check into a hotel for the night?"

Cora thought it over. "That's probably smart. It might be overkill, but better safe than sorry."

"What makes no sense to me is why we're still calling this spirit *Angel?*" Frannie complained, as she stood up and gathered her belongings. "She's not acting like any kind of angel I know, more like we're dealing with the *Devil!* Puts me in mind of something I read about making liquor. Some alcohol evaporates when it's aging, so the barrel's not full when it's done. They call this missing part the Angel's share. Maybe *our* Angel spirit is partaking of her share of some alcohol spirit. That could be why she's so confused all the time!"

"Thanks to you, Frannie, we're ending the day with a laugh," Cora said, glad for the break in tension. "But in answer to your question, I've been calling her Angel for so long, I don't think of her by any other name."

"Let's get out of here," Cisco said, taking charge. "There's a Holiday Inn a few miles away. We'll get a couple of rooms tonight and figure out what to do in the morning."

~~~

In the hotel dining room the next morning, Cora, Cisco and Frannie ate mechanically. None of them had rested well, and they found it impossible to drag themselves out of bed any earlier than 9 o'clock. The restaurant was almost deserted, as most hotel guests had left for the opening day of Christmas shopping.

Distracted and jumpy, Cora didn't join the conversation. Her subconscious had not magically created an action plan during the night. She poked at her pancakes. "I shouldn't have ordered these—I don't feel like anything sweet," she said, and sipped her black coffee moodily.

Cisco and Frannie tried random talk, but the conversation was strained. Finishing his oatmeal, fruit and dry toast, Cisco broached what was on all their minds.

"Okay, so what are we going to do next? Now we know about the murders, what are we going to do with that? What are your thoughts, Cora?"

Cora set her coffee cup down and looked at him. "I don't know. I can't think about anything besides this, but...I still can't make *sense* of my thoughts. It would be dangerous to rush into it and do the *wrong* thing, don't you think?" She wrung her hands together.

"What do you think Angel will do when you tell her? You *are* gonna tell her, right?" Frannie asked, setting down her fork.

"If I can't straighten out my own thoughts, how can I predict Angel's?"

"You think she's crawling around in your head messing it up? She's more of a Guiding Angel than a Guardian Angel, seems to me. She's both the problem and part of the solution."

Cora smiled grimly. "I don't think she's in there right now, but who knows? I can't sort out what thoughts are my own anymore." She paused. "It's hard for me to think about Meg, that sweet person whose diary I read, then compare her to Angel, a spirit obsessed with me and convinced she's my mother, and now she's a danger I have to put an end to. Sometimes I'm afraid, then I'm sympathetic, then doubtful, or guilty...and I'm not sure how I'll feel if I make her leave."

Frannie exchanged a puzzled glance with Cisco. "You're as confused as Angel—you can't be thinking she shouldn't leave! She has to be told. Maybe this thing will just play out by its own self. What experience do we have to help us do this, anyhow?"

Cora exhaled loudly. "You could say I have a *lifetime* of experience. Problem is, everything I thought I knew has changed. I can't just dash off and wing it. A lot's at stake, and I have to know I gave it my best shot, even if it turns out to be wrong. I need to talk to someone," she said, draining her cup.

"You are talking to someone—two someones," Frannie said.

Cora ignored her comment. "Why don't you guys stay here—it seems to be as safe as anywhere. I'm going to see Father McGrath. I don't know how long I'll be—as long as it takes. I'll come back here when I can think more clearly."

Cora wasted no time. She got up, gave Cisco a hug and a kiss on the cheek, smiled at Frannie, and strode away, leaving them staring after her, and then at each other.

~~~

Cisco and Frannie, too close to the action, would have a tough time with Cora's reluctance and indecision, but Father McGrath would understand.

It was six days since his injuries, and Cora was pleased to find him sitting in a chair beside his hospital bed, alert and picking at a tray of food. The dressings around his neck were less massive, his ankle was in a brace, and bandages covered his arms, hands, and face. A pad of paper and pen were on the over-bed table in front of him, along with a food tray. She concluded he could eat, but was discouraged from using his voice.

He smiled when he saw her, and reached for the note pad, wrote, then handed it to Cora. *Glad to see you! I'm told you saved my life!*

"I guess it's debatable if I saved it or jeopardized it," Cora said with embarrassment. "Do you remember the attack?"

He wrote another note. *Some, not all. They may come get me for therapy. Our visit may be cut short.*

The food tray contained an assortment of soft foods and liquids. Father took a fork-full of scrambled eggs, chewed briefly, then swallowed with some difficulty. He took a sip of coffee and then pushed the tray aside.

"Therapy for your voice or your leg?" Cora asked.

Either one. Seems I need both. He passed the note to her.

She inquired about his progress, and was delighted to learn he would recover, except his voice could sound different and he might walk with a limp. He took it in stride, referring to God's Will. *I have an opportunity to be a fine example of triumph over adversity, and I expect to make the most of it.* He grinned as he turned the page toward Cora.

"I'm glad to see you doing so well. Any idea when you can go home?"

As soon as I convince them I can get around on this leg, can eat and eliminate what I eat. It should be soon.

Cora explained that a lot had happened, and she would sit it out during his therapy sessions if need be to tell him about it. Father wrote: *That sounds serious.*

"It seems I'm always talking and waiting for a written answer these days, first from Angel, and now you." She smiled at him fondly.

Father's face went through a series of expressions, odd sounds, a grimace of pain, and ended with a smile and twinkling eyes. *Don't make me laugh!* he wrote.

"Well, Father," Cora said, turning serious, "let me bring you up to date. I'll do most of the talking to spare you the paper." Not knowing how long they would have, she wanted to move things along quickly.

She told him she thought it was a wolf that attacked him; at first surprised, he nodded noncommittally as she gave her reasons, and described the communication from Angel alluding to her part in the attack. She reminded him of the diary, and explained how they decided Angel was the spirit of the woman who had written it. She told him Meg's story as disclosed in the diary. Father's keen, intelligent eyes gleamed with interest, and when she asked if he was with her so far, he waved his hand for her to continue.

"Next," she went on, avoiding his eyes as she expected him to be skeptical, "I went to Saint James Cemetery, and Meg, or Angel, showed herself to me." She wrinkled her forehead as she watched for his response, wondering what he was thinking, but he only waved her on again.

She described the encounter in detail, along with her conclusions that Angel/Meg thought she was Cora's mother, Angel didn't know who killed her, and wanted Cora to find out what happened and who did it. Father tapped his temple with a forefinger. "Good thinking?" Cora asked, and he responded with a smile and a nod. He patted Cora's hand in reassurance.

Cora told him about their search for information, and explained how it led to the discovery of old documents in a long-lost tunnel at the historical society. She described how Angel threatened Cisco by destroying his golf clubs.

"I was afraid she would take out after Cisco or Frannie, like she did after you. We had to act fast and secretly. Yesterday we found this in the old documents," she said, handing Cavanaugh's letter to Father. She wanted him to see something concrete, to add credence to her deductions.

He reached for the pages and read, glancing up at Cora now and then. After he read a few pages, a therapist arrived, pushing a wheelchair into the room. "Time for PT," she announced brightly.

He reached for the pad and pen, and wrote. *Something important has come up. Would it be difficult to schedule my therapy for this afternoon instead?* The therapist frowned, clearly not welcoming a schedule change. However, after making a call, she found an open appointment, and agreed to come later.

When he finished reading, Cora opened her mouth to comment, but Father held up a finger for silence, and closed his eyes in thought. When he opened them, he reached for his note pad. *You're going to see her at the cemetery again, aren't you? Today?*

"As soon as possible," Cora agreed, nodding firmly. "As soon as I figure out what to do and say."

He scratched on the pad and handed it to her. *I'm not sure I'm the right person to advise you. Look what happened the last time I gave my opinion.* A sound came from him that Cora realized was a chuckle, but it was unlike any human sound she had heard. She tried to hide her astonishment.

He took the pad back and wrote at length. *I'm afraid I have to say you're on your own here. As a priest, I can't advise you to go confront a spirit. As your friend, I don't think I can do anything constructive to coach you. She trusts you, and your instincts seem to have been right up to now—better than my advice. Why do you doubt yourself?*

"I can get through telling her about the killer. I can do that. But I don't know how she'll react. I'm guessing, trying to figure out what motivates her. Will telling her what she wants to know stop her violence? Will it do any good at all?"

Father reached for the pad again, and wrote another lengthy response. Cora was hopeful he was laying out a plan for her, but when she read the note, it contained only more questions. *You think I'm a better guesser about what motivates a spirit? You want me to assure you that answering her questions will do the trick? That resolving the murders for her will allow her to rest, accept her death and those of her family, give up her attachments to the material world, and move into the afterlife?*

Cora read his words and nodded. "Something like that. It could have the opposite effect, make her angry and she'll lash out even more violently."

Do you think that's likely? He held out a hand in question.

"No, I don't think she'll do that."

What do you think she will do?

The muscles around Cora's mouth begin to quiver, her eyes grew hot with tears, and in a small choked voice she said, "I think she'll go away. Go away forever." She brushed the tears away hastily.

Father took the pad back, wrote. *Up to now you've done what you could to stop her violent acts and make her go away. And in a more kindly way, you tried to help her achieve peace. Now you don't know if you want her to go after all. Is that what's bothering you?*

"I've been concentrating on making her go away without a thought of what it will be like when she's gone." She sniffled.

Father held his hands out in question.

"She's been with me all my life, protecting me like a second mother. Shouldn't I miss that? She's like two people, the motherly adult Angel, and the angry child that strikes out when she doesn't get her way. I feel like a traitor."

He wrote: *And you met Meg, and you have empathy for her. Life doesn't always give us clear choices.*

"I can't help feeling like she's a part of me, and I am sending her away! I let my real mother go away!" Cora blurted, shifted her eyes and put a hand up to her mouth.

What do you think is keeping Angel here in the material world?

"I think she doesn't understand why they died, and she thinks I'm her daughter and she needs to protect me."

Then what would allow her to go to the spirit world?

"If she knows why they died and doesn't need to protect me anymore."

Father wrote: *If you hold on to Angel now, what's her purpose?*

Cora's eyes blinked as she considered his question. If she couldn't convince Angel she wasn't her daughter, she could try to convince her she didn't need her anymore. But what would Angel's purpose be then, and ultimately once Cora herself died? If her ability to accept the death of her daughter made her miserable now, how much more so if Cora took all purpose away from her? Wouldn't she be better off if she ended it now instead of putting her through that?

"She won't have one. She'll be worse once I tell her, won't she?"

He took the pad back and wrote. *You watched your mother die, and felt you should have been able to find a way to keep her.*

The gentle reminder made Cora realize she was doing the same thing, selfishly trying to hold on to her spirit mother when it would be kinder to let her go.

"It's the right thing for *her*, to let her go, isn't it?" asked Cora. The question could barely be heard.

For her, and for you.

"*Where* will she go, Father?"

You know that, Cora. The place she should have gone a hundred years ago. She'll be happier there than she is here.

Cora asked weakly. "Can I tell her without weeping like a damn fool the way I am now?"

Let her see your sorrow Cora…it will validate her. But she needs to know you'll be safe if she leaves.

She used a forefinger to rub out the wetness gathering under her eyes again.

Chapter 35

The temperature was near forty degrees but a blustery wind and cold mist made it seem frigid. Cora walked through the cemetery, her winter coat pulled tightly around her, her discomfort intensified by anxiety and fear.

Wouldn't you know it—the weather turns wicked just in time to add misery to such an important...what do I call this? Meeting's not a good word. Confrontation? Revelation?

Despite her efforts that morning, she had no real plan—she would just tell Angel about Cavanaugh and wing it, the very thing she had said she didn't want to do. Cora's talk with Father McGrath gave her a better understanding of her own conflicted emotions, but how she would go about revealing the killer to Angel would have to be spontaneous.

She paused, turned and glanced at Cisco sitting in his car, staying in the parking lot as he had promised. She could barely see his head through the windshield, and couldn't see his face, but was grateful he had insisted on coming, despite her objections. She rested her hands in her pockets; gloves didn't keep her warm enough, and covered hands took away her sense of control. Today of all days she needed to feel in control. Her mission was vitally important, a battle of sorts, and she wasn't going to go about it gloved or distracted by the weather.

Cora faced into the wind and trudged her way to the graves of Meg, Packey, and Darlin'. As Cora hoped, and felt sure she would be, Meg was waiting, seated on Darlin's grave.

Angel/Meg was dressed as before, neatly, for summer, not winter, as she would have been dressed when she was killed. She wasn't watching

Cora, but looking at the woods that separated the graveyard and the road. She didn't turn at Cora's approach.

Maybe she's as nervous as I am.

"Hello, Meg," Cora greeted her. "Do you think we could move closer to the church, where there's a bench? I'd rather not sit on the cold ground. I'm not young anymore, as I'm sure you're aware."

After a moment, Meg turned to face Cora. The spirit seemed stronger today and wasn't exhibiting energy fluctuations.

Meg fixed her unblinking eyes on Cora, and then said in a hollow, flat voice, "Ground's no colder than anywhere—'tis all cold." Her voice was high and rapid, reminding Cora again of an old vinyl record played on a faster speed.

Cora sighed. "I guess you're right—from your perspective." She seated herself on the ground facing Meg, careful to place layers of coat beneath her. She shivered as the blustery wind found its way past her scarf and down her collar. Her knit hat kept her head warm, but the mist was cold and damp on her cheeks.

"You seem stronger," she observed, her voice flat as she struggled to keep from revealing her emotions.

"There's energy in the woods," Meg replied.

A sudden memory flashed into Cora's mind. "The nuclear waste—the butterflies. Is that what you mean?"

Meg met Cora's eyes but said nothing.

"I wanted to be with you when I told you," Cora said, and waited.

She watched Meg wrestle with her emotions as she realized Cora was about to disclose the reasons for her death and that of her family. Her eyes grew intense, seeming to glow with their own light source. She stood, floated, twirled in a circle, then noticed something, stopped abruptly, her gaze fixed on the parking lot, and in a low, raspy voice close to a roar she demanded, "Why is Cisco here? What are you plotting? Are you afraid of me, your Máime?" She began to float toward Cisco.

Cora jumped up. "Wait," she entreated. "He's no threat to you! If you want to know, wait! Hear me out first!"

The spirit slowed, stopped, and turned toward Cora, but came no closer.

Cora's words tumbled out in a rush as she tried to keep Angel away from Cisco. "He won't come here. I made him promise. He'll stay where he is. He's only watching me. He loves me, Meg, like you do. He wants to protect me, same as you do. He's no threat to me—no threat to you either. You're wrong to suspect him. Please, come and sit down. I can tell you what you want to know. I know it all now, and I want to tell you." Cora gathered her coat around her and made a great show of sitting again, to convince Angel—and herself—she was in control.

Cora could see Meg's energy fluctuate as she struggled with her fury, in, out, in, out, in, out, in; then she dropped slowly, her feet touched the ground again, and she glided back to the grave, resumed her seat near it, and waited silently.

"I brought a letter that tells it all, and I'll read it to you. But I want something from you. If I tell you what you want to know, if you know everything, will you promise to never harm anyone I know? Not to take vengeance? Ever again? Will you promise that?"

"How can I?" Meg insisted, in a soft, almost normal voice.

"I can take care of myself, and I have others who protect me. If I convince you of that, will you promise?" Could she change the spirit's convictions? She had to try.

Meg stared at Cora, then dropped and raised her eyes. The last time she and Meg talked, that sign had meant agreement.

"Okay then," Cora said. She fumbled in her pocket, drew out Cavanaugh's letter, squirmed in the brown, damp grass. Meg checked to be sure Cisco hadn't moved, and then turned her unfocused gaze to the grounds behind the church as Cora began to read.

~ ~ ~

From his car, Cisco watched Cora walk across the cemetery to an area devoid of standing headstones. He supposed the grave markers there were recessed in the ground. A fence separated the graveyard from an area of sparse trees and brush, and beyond it a two-lane road could be made out through bare tree limbs, an infrequent car passing by. Someone sat on the ground where Cora was headed, but he couldn't tell if it was a man or woman. Cora didn't seem to see the person yet. Who would sit on the ground in such weather? Was that Angel?

After all they had been through, and all the evidence pointing to the existence of a spiritual entity, despite all they had learned, the possibility of actually laying his eyes on a spirit was surprisingly unsettling.

This can't be real! It can't be happening!

As Cora approached the figure, Cisco found it harder and harder to remain in the car. He stifled an urge to run after Cora, to drag her away, run off with her. Only his promise to Cora, and the fear that his actions would make matters worse, kept him still.

His heart pounding, he bit his lower lip and watched. Cora was talking to the person now, and sat down on the ground too. It seemed peaceful. Then suddenly the person jumped up and seemed to shimmer in front of him, with glowing pulsations, and floated off the ground, twirling like a top, then stopped suddenly and moved rapidly in his direction!

Cora jumped up too, waved her arms frantically, and he heard her call out, although he couldn't make out the words. The spirit—he had no doubt of this now—halted, and turned back toward Cora.

Cisco reached for the door handle, alarmed, ready to rush to Cora's aid, although he had no idea how to protect her from a spirit known to be violent and possessing unearthly powers. At least they would be together when Angel took vengeance. But the spirit seemed calmer, so he paused, and it lowered itself to the ground, glided toward Cora, and both sat on the ground again. Cora reached into her coat and unfolded the letter, as she told him she would do if all was well, and he took a deep breath and leaned against the car seat, but did not relax his vigil.

~~~

Cora finished reading Cavanaugh's letter aloud, rested in it her lap, and looked up at Meg for her reaction. Meg's energy levels were pulsing again, but gently, like breaths, and she kept her gaze behind the church. Cora wondered if Meg was reliving—living?—the events of that fateful night. Meg showed no sign of anger or violence.

Cora glanced toward Cisco; he was still in the car watching them. She addressed Meg.

"Do you want to see it? The letter? Will it help you to touch the letter, to know it's real, to see it's authentic, not something I made up? It's not, you know—not a fake. I found it in a box of old documents, in one of those canal tunnels. I came here first, to tell you, so I haven't researched

Cavanaugh yet, but I know it will prove out—I'm sure of it." She held the letter out, but the spirit didn't move to take it.

After a long time, Meg probed Cora's eyes with the laser-like light of her own. She spoke at last. "So 'twas over nothing after all...nothing important...just a greedy man. All that pain and torment...." She trailed off.

Cora folded the letter and put it back in her pocket. They sat in silence for a time, and then Cora asked, "What will you do now?"

There was no answer.

"I did this for you, and for me," Cora said. "I solved your mystery because I thought it would give you peace, but also because I want to enjoy my remaining years without the stress you're causing me."

Meg/Angel still did not speak.

"Why did you want to know about your murder? Was that keeping you from peace, not knowing? Or is it taking care of me? Are you staying here because of me?"

Meg's gaze traveled from place to place, anywhere except toward Cora.

Cora had many questions, and this could be the only time to get answers. "Was it you who made bad things happen to people who hurt me, all through my life?"

Meg paused, and then dropped her eyes to the ground, the gesture Cora took as agreement. "They hurt themselves. I gave them ideas."

Cora was thoughtful. "I see. You facilitated their self-destruction."

" 'Twas satisfying."

"What about the little things, drawers closing, moving stuff, things like that?"

Meg made a sad little smile. "I thought...you would feel me—'twas fun."

"You wanted me to know you? And you wanted to have some fun? In your diary you seemed to love to have fun."

Meg just smiled gently.

"Was that you I saw here when I was in college, the story I told on *Fright Night?*"

"You came, on your own. 'Twas a surprise."

"An opportunity you couldn't pass up, as I was right here? How much of my life did you manipulate? Did you orchestrate our move to Lemont too?"

"You were older. I wanted you near."

"The first time we met here, you got into my head then, didn't you? It wasn't my idea to check out Saint James, it was yours, because you wanted us to meet, and you can only materialize here."

Meg turned her head and gazed toward her grave. They sat quietly, Cora's last question unanswered.

"Why me, Meg?" Cora asked. "You could have picked anyone for your daughter. Why did you pick me? I'm not your daughter. I wasn't born until more than forty years after your daughter died. You can love me and pretend, but I'm not your daughter. The letter I read to you, from your killer, and articles I saw in the paper—they all said your baby died."

"You *are* daughter. Earth Máthair returned you." The spirit's eyes glowed as she said this.

"I don't understand," Cora said, knitting her brows in confusion. "I really am your daughter, and someone called Earth Máthair brought me to you? That doesn't make sense. I'd be over a hundred years old if that were true. Can you explain?"

The glow in Meg's eyes faded and she only looked at her sadly and refused to say more. Cora could get no further with that question.

She returned to the promise she wanted from Meg. "Are you going to stop hurting my friends? If you love me, then listen to me and please stop doing that."

Meg's reply was so soft, Cora couldn't understand it.

"I'm sorry, I didn't hear you," she said.

"Naïvvveee," said Meg, more clearly, singing the word.

"I don't understand," Cora said, knitting her eyebrows and narrowing her eyes, puzzled by the comment.

Meg stared, and then stood up to face Cora, who was still sitting in the same place. "You explain murders. Then…simple…I go away," she said, her eyes hurt and pleading.

Cora didn't know how to answer, and her eyes filled with tears. "Angel, I don't know *what* I want. What you've been doing…you're hurting people, and I don't want people hurt because of me. You say you want to protect me, but you've got the wrong people, the reasons are trivial. Your judgment is no good—you have to stop!" Distressed, Cora didn't notice she was calling the spirit Angel again instead of addressing her as Meg.

"I need reeessst. Soooo tiiiiiired." The words were drawn out; her voice was a moan, as if made by a tree creaking in the wind, and she threw her head from side to side.

Cora choked up and had no reply.

Angel looked around, distraught. "Protect…you…Darlin'!" she insisted.

Cora felt tears running down her cheeks, or was it the mist? She left them there, remembering Father McGrath's advice that Angel needed to see her sorrow. "Angel, I can take care of myself. Don't you know that? Haven't I proved my strength throughout my life, especially in the last few weeks? And my husband, my family, my friends, they're all with me when I need them. Cisco will keep me safe, see, he's there in the car watching me right now, and he'll always do that." Once again Cora was grateful for Cisco's foresight, as his presence testified to her words.

Angel didn't look at Cisco as Cora asked, only rolled her head around and emitted an eerie cry full of anguish and despair that echoed throughout the cemetery and the forest. Cora looked toward the car and saw Cisco jump out, hesitating by the door.

Cora stood up and faced the spirit. "Angel," she choked. "I'm getting old. Your powers can't keep me from dying. I hope to live another twenty years, maybe more, but what will you do then? Who will you have to live for, if not me? What will happen when you see me die too? You can't stop that. Why should you keep struggling when you're ready to go *now*? I'll be okay without you, on my own, but not alone, with my husband and friends. It's okay…you can rest now."

Angel calmed, and gazed at Cora sadly. The light in her eyes no longer blazed, and they looked human, like a mother fondly watching her sleeping child.

"Miss me?" she asked.

"Oh, my God, Máime, can't you see how much I'm going to miss you?" Sobbing now, tears flowing freely, Cora continued to let them fall. Trying to control her voice, she continued, "I never knew who you were, but you were there, I felt you. My life wouldn't have been the same without you. If you need my love, you have it."

Angel looked deep into Cora's tearful face. "You…called me…Máime…

Darlin'!" she said, moving closer to Cora and opening her arms to her.

"No!" Cora cried in fear. "You can't touch me! You warned me before! You didn't know what would happen. It's dangerous!"

But Angel glided to Cora and wrapped her arms around her at last. Cora felt the warmth of a mother's embrace for a heartbeat, and then it was over.

~ ~ ~

Cisco, watching from the car, didn't see threatening behavior, but he heard an eerie cry, and he leaped from the car again and stood beside it, ready to sprint to Cora at any sign of danger. Cora didn't indicate she needed help. She was still sitting on the ground, wiping her eyes, and he thought she could be crying. Angel stood looking down at her.

Then Cora stood up too, facing Angel, and the two kept up an intense conversation. He saw Angel move toward Cora with open arms, and Cora cried out and backed away. Angel reached out and embraced Cora, and as he watched, the two figures appeared to merge.

A rumbling sound, like thunder, seemed to come from underground. The ground heaved up and down rhythmically, as if breathing. The asphalt surface of the parking lot cracked and split, throwing him to the ground. When the ground stopped rising and falling, he struggled to his feet. A single figure lay unmoving in the cemetery. Was it Cora, or Angel? He couldn't tell.

Cisco raced toward the figure, his heart in his throat.

You now are sorrowful;
Grieve not: I will again behold you,
And then your heart shall be joyful,
And your joy shall no one take from you.

　　　—John 16:22

Look upon me:
I suffered for a little time:
Toil and labor were mine;
And I have found, at last, comfort

　　　　—Ecclesiasticus (Sirach) 51:35

I will give you comfort,
As one whom his own mother comforts.

　　　—Isaiah 66:13

　　　Johannes Brahms, *A German Requiem,*
　　　fifth movement (texts selected
　　　by Brahms from the German Bible)

Epilogue

Cora paused in the bedroom doorway, her eyes surveying the room. This was the room her mother had occupied. Although it was now a guest room, Cora had made no changes to it since her mother's death, and she still referred to it as "Mom's room". When her mother first moved in with Cora and Cisco, they furnished the room with her old traditional mahogany bedroom set so it would feel familiar to her, the furniture her mother bought when she was married in the 1940s. Her mother had picked paint, window coverings, and bedding and put favored pictures on the dresser and walls of her new home.

Today, with Christmas only two days away, Cora had sent Cisco out for last-minute errands and purchases. She stayed home to get rooms ready for her family's expected arrival the next day. There wasn't a lot to do—tidying, dusting, changing bed linens and such—and Cora approached the task in a languid mood. She moved around the room, touching things at random, and then sat—only for a moment, she told herself—in a comfortable chair beside a window that looked onto their quiet residential street.

Christmas was a sad time for Cora, especially setting up the Christmas tree. Her mother had always put the finishing touches on the tree, hanging the "special" ornaments, and the memory was so embedded in Cora's mind that she found decorating the tree an emotion-laden experience.

She looked around the bedroom, her eyes lingering on her parent's wedding picture, another picture of them from the 1980s, and a picture of her mother with her only sister, Cora's favorite Aunt Pauline. She blinked, got up to open the blinds, and then sat, gazed out the window, and let her mind wander.

Since the final encounter with Angel, Cora had not allowed herself to dwell on the dramatic events or indulge in her feelings about them, characteristically avoiding upsetting matters until she was better able to accept them—until it didn't hurt as much. Perhaps today was a good time to let go the restraints. As she looked out the window now, she replayed parts of that day a month ago.

Right after Angel left, Cisco found Cora sobbing uncontrollably when he reached her side in the cemetery. He mistook her emotion for relief, saying over and over, "It's okay—I'm here," as he held her. He buried his face in her hair and kissed the top of her head, and in the process knocked her hat to the ground, but she left it there. Cora clutched him tightly even after her sobbing stopped, and then broke the embrace and took his hand.

"Let me show you where she is," she said, pulling him a few steps to Meg's grave. Headstones in a nearby section had been toppled, from the earthly upheaval that occurred when Angel left. They stood hand in hand looking at Meg's grave, Cisco with an arm around her, Cora leaning, her head resting against his shoulder. Tears ran silently down her cheeks, and she caught her breath now and then with a soft sob.

When Cisco opened his mouth to say something, Cora reached over and put a finger gently over his lips. "Not now," she had whispered, loving him for his concern, his strength, and his willingness to be there with her. "I can't talk about it now. I'll explain it to you another time, when it's less painful—we'll talk about it then...."

They *had* talked about the events later—but not about Cora's emotions.

Initially she hadn't been able to tell Frannie the full story either. "We're safe now though, right?" Frannie had asked, and Cora had reassured her. Frannie was especially interested in how Angel had remotely manipulated the minds of Cora and others.

"She won't be doing that no more, right?" Frannie had asked.

Cora didn't tell her that Angel never promised to leave them alone, saying only, "She's gone, Frannie. Her departure was quite dramatic."

She had let Cisco describe that experience. "First these rumbling sounds came out of the ground and then the whole place started rising and falling," he said, waving his arms to demonstrate. "It sounded like air whooshing in and out, like loud sighing. It must have been an earthquake, but it seemed more like swelling than shaking. It threw me right off my feet."

"Maybe Angel leaving triggered some kind of phenomenon," Frannie had guessed. "Or maybe she did it herself, a departing gesture or getting rid of her remaining energy. Wow! That's one powerful Angel we got! Who else we know as powerful as all that!"

Only the three of them, and Father McGrath, knew the whole story, of Angel's existence and the probable cause of the "earthquake", and they were amused when they read the guesses the newspaper printed. Parts of the story would remain their secret. Who else would believe it? "I can't remember when I had so much fun," was what Frannie said, now that she believed the danger was over.

Now Cora went downstairs to make a cup of tea and returned to her mother's room and her mother's chair, propped her feet on the end of the bed, leaned back and closed her eyes with a smile on her face, holding the cup with both hands in her lap to warm them. After the mild autumn, December had turned brutally cold, and a few corners of the house did not seem to get warm enough.

Her smile was brought on by the remembrance of subsequent developments. When she disclosed the findings of the tunnel, the old records, Cavanaugh's letter and the story behind the old murders, it generated much excitement at the historical society. To keep the existence of Angel secret, when questioned about the discoveries she said it was accidental, she continued to explore out of curiosity, and one thing led to another. Local papers covered the story, and generated increased interest in the historical society. Some large donations arrived, visitors wanted to see the tunnel or take a tour, and a few new badly-needed volunteers signed up, one with vital experience in museum management.

As for the documents they found, Cora didn't need them any longer and turned them over to the historical society to manage, donating a copy of Cavanaugh's letter but keeping the original.

She owed Bridey a visit, to thank her and return the diary. Even though she had made multiple copies of it, she put off giving it back, hating to part with something that felt so personal to her, wanting to hold in her hands the same book that belonged to Meg. Cora had a vague idea of looking into publishing it, or at least preparing an anecdotal document. Bridey was delighted by the idea, and her part in events.

"You deserve to keep it, Cora," Bridey had said. "I don't have anyone to pass it on to, and you'll do more than just put it back on a cabinet shelf. You should have it."

Especially interesting to Cora, Cisco, and Frannie had been what the ladies in the archives discovered about Cavanaugh. After they read Cavanaugh's letter, they were unanimously indignant and determined to learn the end of his story. No one wanted to know that he lived happily ever after, and he didn't. A clipping found in the archive of Lemont businesses described the failure of Cavanaugh Brewery, and another exposed him for diverting funds and other shady stuff, using his position as a village trustee. The mayor and police chief, no altar boys themselves, denounced him, but before he could be arrested, he disappeared.

That seemed to be the end of the trail, until Ania did a search on other names in Cavanaugh's letter, and found an obituary for Kitty Hurley, the woman who left town in disgrace after the fraudulent McWeeney will. The obit was detailed due to the unusual and interesting circumstances, and revealed that Kitty died in a Kansas jail where she was incarcerated for killing Daniel Cavanaugh. It seemed they met up again after he left town and either she killed him because he caused all her troubles or over something else.

"She would have been in her seventies when she died. What goes around comes around," Cisco had said when she went home and told him about it. "Well, he got what he deserved, but I'm sorry for her." All in all a satisfactory conclusion, Cora thought. Except she still didn't know why Angel had chosen her. She supposed she never would.

She opened her eyes now and looked out at the snow on the ground. All was quiet and peaceful, but that would change when their family arrived the next day. Her tea was cold, so she set the cup down. She got up to finally empty her mother's dresser so guests could use it. Boxes were piled on top of the bed, carried from the basement for that purpose, and she opened the bottom drawer of the dresser.

Papers that related to her mother's final illness, burial, and financial records took up half of the drawer. There was no reason to save most of them, but she would have to go through them page by page to separate out those she had to keep. She took them out of the drawer and stacked them in a box labeled *Sort*. Next were a number of jewelry boxes of varied sizes. She had taken out the pieces she wanted and given others away as mementos, so she put these in another box to go to charity for resale. A flag, from her father's burial, a Knights of Columbus sword, a box with harmonicas, an ocarina, and a Jew's harp—these all had belonged to her father and went into a box to save. There was also an old picture album, sealed carefully in plastic with the intent—perhaps mistaken—that the plastic would help preserve it.

Cora checked the clock on the nightstand. There was plenty of time. The last time she looked at the album could be close to ten years ago. It was too much trouble to unwrap and then locate materials to rewrap it when she finished. She was nostalgic today—why not go all the way and look at it?

The album had not belonged to Cora's mother but to her mother's *grandmother* and dated back to the 1880s and 1890s, coincidentally when Meg was alive. Cora remembered sitting on the sofa with Grandma on the first floor of her two-flat in Chicago, turning page after page while Grandma told Cora stories, long forgotten, about each person in her own mother's album. The pictures were studio portraits, no candid pictures at all, and a few tintypes. None of the faces smiled, and the clothing was dark. It must have been the custom at that time to be serious and formal.

No one recorded the identities of the portraits, and they were lost when Cora's grandmother died. Cora's mom, never interested in anything old, was of little help. The last time she and Cora looked at it together there were only three pictures she recognized. One was a picture of a baby in a long dark plaid dress that Cora's mom said was a baby picture of Grandma. Another was a stern-looking woman, half-turned from the camera in a dark dress with a bustle, her hand on a pedestal. This, her mom said, was Grandma's mother, Cora's great-grandmother, and the woman who had owned the album. The last was of a child of three or four wearing a dress, who Cora's mom said was a boy, and that it was common for young boys to wear dresses in those days.

Cora carefully unwrapped the album now. It was twelve inches by nine inches and three inches thick, covered with dark green velvet that was worn through in places, with a large brass bell and a small mirror on the front cover. The binding was broken and the pages loose. It hooked onto a brass stand with a shelf to hold the album and a small memento drawer below the shelf. The drawer had lost its pull, and Cora used a letter opener to get into it. It contained only an envelope with some religious cards and relics Grandma must have sent for, of no significance to Cora.

Cora returned to her chair by the window, set the album in her lap, and began to carefully turn the pages. Each page had marbleized shiny brown paper on both sides, mounted on stiff cardboard-like board, each leaf almost a quarter-inch thick with slots into which pictures of various sizes could be slipped. The paper was beginning to delaminate from its board, and some of the board was likewise separating, deteriorating like the rest of the album. Cora handled each page carefully, looking for tintypes and the only three pictures she knew but casually glancing at others.

A few pages in, she came to one that was completely in pieces. She thought this probably happened because an envelope had been forced behind one of the pictures, creating a bulge that separated the paper from its backing. Cora had never seen an envelope in this album, and doubted her mother had known of it either. It must have been there, forgotten all this time, until it was revealed when the page separated.

Intrigued, she set the album carefully on the bed and examined the envelope. It was addressed in a fancy script to Josie Dubicki, Cora's grandmother. The sender was Cora's great-aunt Stella, Grandma's sister, from an address in Lemont. Cora didn't know she had lived in Lemont.

The envelope was unsealed, and Cora opened it. Inside were a crumbling yellowed newspaper clipping and a letter in somewhat better condition. Cora read the letter first.

My Dear Josie:

I know Agnes did not want anyone to know how Cora was born, but I thought since you are her mother, you would want to have this article from our paper. You can do whatever you like with it, show it to Agnes or not, or just throw it away. But I thought you should see it.

I won't ever say a word about it to honor Agnes' wishes like you said, although I must say I'm having a hard time understanding why she doesn't want anyone to know. What could be wrong that a baby came a little early? It's not so early as to suggest any hanky-panky before marriage and get anyone talking. If they were going to talk about anything at all it would be about how Agnes wound up married to Jack when he was engaged to Pauline and everyone expecting him to marry her instead of all of a sudden marrying Agnes. I never did know how that came about, but I guess these things just don't always go the way we expect. They're both such fine girls, and I know Agnes wouldn't have set out to make that happen, she loves her sister too much for that. But I do wonder how hard it has been for Pauline to go on with no man in her life now.

Anyway, Agnes has always been such a quiet and private person, so maybe that's all and I'm looking too hard for reasons, or something to explain how the accident happened. Well, it all turned out fine, and everyone is healthy, so I promise from now on I'll never bring this up again.

I hope you can find someone to bring you out this way soon Josie. I miss my big sister!

Love, Stella

The color drained from Cora's face and her heart pounded. She stared at the letter unseeing, then at the wall. How Cora was born? The accident? Agnes doesn't want anyone to know? Her father was engaged to her Aunt Pauline?

Cora remembered something else, something she dismissed long ago. Other old albums, the ones that were assembled by her mom. Many of the pictures taken before Cora's birth were of family picnics and parties, and many showed her father hugging, carrying, or posing with her Aunt Pauline. More, in fact, than pictures of her mother and father together. Cora had thought that was odd, and asked her mother about it, but her mother just laughed and changed the subject. She hadn't seemed like she was hiding anything, at least Cora hadn't thought so.

She carefully unfolded the newspaper clipping.

Lemont Observer, August 29, 1942
Surprise Birth at Saint James at Sag Bridge
When she reluctantly agreed to accompany her family and friends to a picnic and swimming outing at our Lemont quarries last Sunday, August 23, a young wife never thought she would return home carrying a baby girl.

Although she was in advanced pregnancy, her baby was not due for a month, or so she thought. She had followed her doctor's orders, but failed to realize that even the best doctors have been known to miscalculate due dates.

A resident of Chicago, the young woman was standing at the edge of a quarry with her sister, watching family and friends swim, when she fell into the water. When she was pulled out, she soon went into labor, perhaps brought on by the accident. Her husband quickly put her in the car, intending to rush her to Evangelical Hospital in Chicago, where her delivery was scheduled.

As they drew near Saint James Church, the husband realized the birth was imminent, and he had no recourse but to pull into the church parking lot for delivery. Her sister, best friend and friend's husband had followed in their car, and the sister ran to fetch the priest, who was enjoying an early dinner when interrupted by pounding on the rectory door.

Happily, we can report the birth was without incident. The priest's housekeeper immediately called an ambulance, but the baby girl had been born by the time it arrived. Father McNally of Saint James baptized the little girl on the spot. Ambulance attendants provided further assistance, then transported the mother and child to Evangelical Hospital at the mother's and father's requests.

The mother was reluctant to discuss the experience with me, and asked that her name not be mentioned. She did not understand how she got in the water, and said her sister was looking the other way and did not see it happen either. "I didn't want to go to the quarries because of what happened before, but I let the family talk me into it. The only other time I was here, someone stole my new shoes and my mother wouldn't talk to me for days. Times were tough, and shoes were expensive. I warned everyone I had a bad feeling about going back to the quarries, and I was right. But we are both fine, and no harm done in the end."

Saint James at Sag Bridge is reputed to be built over an ancient Indian burial ground, and is associated with stories of ghostly appearances, as well as the documentation of a triple murder over forty years ago. It is a curious circumstance that Saint James comes to our attention once more due to a pleasant event this time, the birth of a darling baby girl, named Cora. Mother and child are in excellent health, a happy ending to our tale.

Cora sat staring through the window. It was starting to snow again, and there would be a white Christmas. Her mind registered that but ran on, jumping from one thought to another, memories mixing with new revelations, as she realized, white-faced and shaky, what the article meant.

She looked over at her mother's dresser, at the photo of her mother and her Aunt Pauline, cheek to cheek, smiling happily. Cora had taken that picture herself, maybe ten years ago, before her aunt's final illness and death.

She had been close to her aunt, riding to her house on her bicycle when young to spend time with her during school breaks, sharing stories her mother didn't want to talk about. Her mother was secretive about things that embarrassed her, typical for second-generation immigrants who didn't want to call attention to themselves. She'd say, "What do you want to talk about that for?" Her aunt was the one who wrote down the family history, two more generations back, named everyone in the family tree, gave their birthplaces and birthdates, and entrusted it to Cora, knowing no one else would be interested enough to keep it. That's how Cora knew it was Grandma's sister who had written the letter and sent the clipping to her.

A letter and clipping her mother probably never knew about, as Grandma apparently honored her wishes, keeping the information but hiding it where her mother, uninterested in the old photo album, would not find it. And she hadn't. Grandma, who was close to her own sister, Stella, as Agnes and Pauline had been. And Meg was close to her sister too. It went on and on, too many levels to process. Cora would put it on paper someday, pull out the history Aunt Pauline had sent, draw lines to connect and understand the generations of relationships between the women in her family.

Cora's eyes moved to the photo of her mother and father hanging on the wall. Her father had idolized her mother, treating her like a queen. In fact, he even jokingly called her "Her Honor," Cora recalled. It now seemed her observation, denied by her mom, that there had once been a romantic relationship between her father and her aunt, was correct. Aunt Pauline had a strong silly streak and was a lot of fun to be with. Cora's mom had been quiet, careful, not likely to make people laugh, but she loved to laugh at the antics of others. Her father was a joker too, and would have been drawn to Pauline, but it made sense that Cora's mother became more attractive to him because of her quiet but delighted appreciation of his antics. Who doesn't like to be appreciated? Or see a pretty woman's face light up at something you've done?

Was there a further mystery about how her mom fell in the quarry? The article seemed to imply her mom and Aunt Pauline knew how it happened but didn't want to say. Did they quarrel, push each other? Was it over old resentments? Is that why they didn't want anyone to know? Cora could never find that out, but if it did happen that way she was sure they patched things up, because she knew their affection was genuine. As long as she could remember they had always talked fondly of each other, her mom referring to her "Big Sis" and her Aunt Pauline to her "Little Sis", always with smiles on their faces.

Cora's birth certificate gave her place of birth as Evangelical Hospital. That was seventy years ago. How particular were hospitals about recording place of birth back then? The ambulance brought her to the hospital, and whoever filled out the information there could have taken a pick of place of birth as hospital, ambulance, or parking lot. The clerk was probably used to writing in the hospital name.

Cora smiled now, thinking about what Frannie would say when she told her. She'd probably have some goofy comment like questioning whether or not she was legitimate, and she would have to scold her for casting aspersions on her mother—or mothers.

How did her birth remain a secret all these years? Well, it had. The family kept it quiet, they lost contact with friends that knew what happened—somehow they pulled it off. Knowing how private a person Agnes was, Cora could easily imagine her mother behaving in this way.

Just as she could imagine Angel, a formless, hidden Angel, hovering over the cemetery searching for her baby girl, and watching Agnes bringing her Darlin' to her at last.

~~~

Cora's eyes flew open. Lying in bed, she searched the room. Although it was the middle of the night, there was adequate light, due to a full moon shining through a skylight in the adjacent bathroom, brightness reflected from the snow covering the ground. Something awakened her, but what? Then she heard it clearly, the howling of a wolf, distinct despite the closed windows.

If the sound woke the neighbors, they might talk about in the next day, chalking it up to a dog or a coyote. Cora, however, knew this was no dog howl, nor the call of a coyote, but something personal, meant for her.

She entertained for a moment a temptation to wake Cisco to listen with her, but decided to savor the cry as a private communication. She rolled toward Cisco and nestled against him, nuzzling her face into his back. *All is well,* she thought. *All is really well.*

Cora drifted back to sleep, smiling and lost in the recital, feeling safe, feeling content, feeling loved.

Afterword
History versus Fiction

The Mystery at Sag Bridge is a work of fiction: the characters are ficti-tious, and so is the story. That said, residents of Lemont, a suburb some twenty-five miles southwest of Chicago, Illinois, will easily recognize their town—and perhaps some of its history.

Lemont is perched on a bluff overlooking the Des Plaines River Valley, and, when I moved to the village in 1998, I quickly became enthralled by its unique geographic features and fascinating history. This led to many hours of exploration and, ultimately, an affiliation with the Lem-ont Area Historical Society. I vowed that, should I ever achieve my ambi-tion to write mystery novels, Lemont would be featured prominently in those books.

The historical background and geography of Lemont are described with as much accuracy as possible in the story. However, in that much of what passes for "history" is oral tradition and sometimes question-able, I wanted freedom to take the story where it needed to go in those instances that fact and story did not agree. Any errors or misrepresen-tations are solely mine.

So what is true? What is fiction? Cora and all characters and events from the 2012 time period are fictional. The geography of the area is accurate. The exact location of the fictional Meg's farm and Cora's home were intentionally left vague. The conversion of the land from forest to farmland beginning in the 1830s is accurate, and much of the area, pur-chased by the Forest Preserve District of Cook County after the 1893 Columbian Exposition, was turned back to forests. The lakes that cur-rently enrich the area's forest preserves are man-made. Much of the work was done by the Civilian Conservation Corp during the Great Depression. The building of the Sanitary Canal (AKA drainage ditch) was completed in 1900, and the Cal-Sag Channel in 1922. These waterways did indeed replace much of the real town of Sag Bridge, the remainder of which is now incorporated into Lemont. Thus in Meg's day, the I & M Canal, opened in 1848, had been present before she was born, the Sag Bridge portion of the Sanitary Canal would have been completed, and the Cal-Sag Channel had yet to be thought of. And yes, the Des Plaines River was moved to allow the Sanitary Canal to occupy the original river bed.

What was the "bridge" in Sag Bridge, and what is "Sag"? The answers are speculative, just as the history is murky. The term Sag probably derived from a Potawatomi Indian word, *Saginaw*, which may have meant "swamp". The Sag Valley was a low-lying swampy area, and it is presumed that a bridge may have provided transport across it. The name could also refer to the geographic coming together of two valleys, the Des Plaines and the Sag. When one considers that recorded history of the area relates that the first white settlers to the area arrived in 1833 and that the oldest grave at Saint James Cemetery is that of Michael Dillon, buried in 1816, further fuel is added to any doubt about the accuracy of the history.

Saint James at Sag Bridge is a real Catholic Church still in operation, and its history is essentially as presented in the story. It is located on a peak of land between the Des Plaines and Sag Valleys, once Mount Forest Island in prehistoric Lake Chicago. Father Fitzpatrick, Meg and her family and friends, and the events surrounding the murders depicted in the novel are all fictional. The Old Stone Church also still exists. Built in 1861, it was originally a Methodist Church, and currently operates as the Lemont Area Historical Society. Reverend Tully is a fictional character loosely based on the real Reverend Clancy of the Lemont Methodist Church, who battled against the evils of Smokey Row. Smokey Row, begun in the 1860s, became notorious after the 1893 Columbian Exhibition in Chicago. It is said to have had over one hundred taverns and brothels. Crime of all sorts, including murder, was plentiful on the sin strip, which really did exist as described, as did the questionable activities of Village and police officials during the period.

The stories about Marshall Field and McWeeney and his will are part of Lemont lore, and I will not venture an opinion regarding their truth.

In any case, the name in Lemont's anecdote about the will was not Mc-Weeney. There were a number of real McWeeney brothers during the same time period: John was a Chicago police superintendent, and James was a Chicago policemen for a year and then went on to coach football at Notre Dame. I thought the odd incident needed an odd name and used it. Orange Chauncey was real, an early settler of Lemont in the 1830s, and his name was used for a fictional character in the book, again to lend some color.

There is no tunnel at the Old Stone Church, but tunnels in other parts of Lemont are real. The quarries and the disputes that took place there are historic, including the Lemont Massacre of 1885, at which time the militia was called to put down a worker strike, which resulted in a number of deaths. After the quarries closed, they filled with water and became popular swimming destinations, although swimming is no longer allowed.

Argonne Laboratory, where some of the Manhattan Project took place, was originally located in the woods on the south side of the Des Plaines Valley, where the burial site's monument described in the book is still located. Dellwood Park was constructed in nearby Lockport to provide a destination stop and increase profits for the railroads. Among its features were a picnic area, a lagoon for pleasure rowing, and a dance pavilion. The park still exists, but of the lagoon and pavilion only photos remain.

Due to the large Irish community in both Lemont and Sag Bridge in the 1890s, prizefighting, although illegal, was hugely popular. There is, however, no record that Gentleman Jim Corbett ever fought there. Corbett won the heavyweight championship in 1892 and lost it in 1897, so he could have been in the area around the time of the fictional character of Packey. Whether he would have staged an exhibition in Sag is doubtful—but not impossible. The American bantamweight crown was won in Lemont by "One-Eyed" Jimmy Barry in 1894.

Extensive research was done for this novel, of which *Lemont and Its People*, by Sonia Aamot Kallick, was invaluable. Sonia's book is available through the Lemont Area Historical Society. I urge interested parties to visit the historical society web site at www.lemonthistorical.org or the author's website at www.patcamalliere books.com for additional historical information.

Acknowledgements

I am indebted to all of the people who provided vital assistance and encouragement, without which I would not have had the fortitude to complete *The Mystery at Sag Bridge*. The following writing support groups provided honest critiques, taught me to recognize good, along with ineffective, writing, and gently suggested improvements: The Lemont Library Writers' Club, the Downers Grove Writers' Workshop, and the Chicago Chapter of Sisters in Crime. Your insights and experience have been invaluable.

The following friends and relatives agreed to read early drafts and give feedback: Clare Dempsey, Dorothy Bogan, Gail Ahrens, Patsy Hackel, Judy Langowski, Marilyn Panush, Carolyn Jamieson, Susan Donohue, Chris Camalliere, Mike Morrison, Ellie Fletcher and Christine Myles. The obligation to develop the promised chapters on a regular basis kept me on deadline, and without their comments and encouragement this book would never have been completed.

Amika Press believed in this book and gave me the tools to bring it to life. I am indebted to Jay Amberg for his faith, guidance, and encouragement; to John Manos—I couldn't have found a better editor—who pointed out what was keeping my work from being the best it could be, who was patiently faithful about my ability to fix problem areas, and who maintained an upbeat attitude and sense of humor throughout; and to Sarah Koz, an indispensable go-to person, who provided the book's excellent design features and bolstered the spirit of a first-time writer.

My thanks to those who helped with fact-checking: Robert Dempsey,

M.D. and Dolly Quispe, M.D. for medical questions, Chief Kevin Shaughnessy and Kelly Morrison, for police, EMT, and animal control procedures, and Daryl Morrison for historical archive questions. Thanks to John Dempsey for his insightful opinions, and to Ruth Hull Chatlien and Jim Stahulak for advice on book promotion. Thanks to Rick Cantalupo for permission to include his poem, "The Guardian", and to Richard Hoyt Lee for his excellent photography.

Many women played roles in my life and inspired the book's underlying theme that relationships women share, family members across generations as well as friends, develop and strengthen our lives. This is especially true of Mom, who remains a superb and constant example of the vital and often misunderstood role mothers play in the lives of their daughters.

And lastly, thanks to the man who was there at the start, at the end, and at every moment in between, my ever-so-patient husband, Chris. With his unfailing belief in me as a writer, he was always my reliable sounding board (despite the times I so vehemently disagreed with his opinions!). He withstood my grumpy spells and allowed me to vent, and he also took care of many household details to allow me time to write. I could never have done it without you, Hon.

Book Discussion Questions

1 Why does Angel wait so long to reveal her existence to Cora? Why does she communicate by computer?

2 Angel is sometimes vicious and sometimes sympathetic. In your opinion, does she evoke fear or compassion?

3 What are the similarities in the relationships Cora and Meg have with their mothers? The differences?

4 What do you think Angel would have thought of Cora's birth mother? Who might Angel think Cora's birth mother was?

5 Cora has outstanding organizational skills, yet she struggles with clutter in her personal life. She outwardly appears strong and capable, yet she employs many coping mechanisms, such as avoidance, procrastination, and reliance on routines. Do such apparent inconsistencies in her character make her more human or annoying to you? How do they affect her ability to deal with Angel?

6 Does Cora find any enjoyment in her battle to rid her life of Angel? In what ways?

7 Compare and contrast the motivations and personalities of Meg and Cora. What role does intuition play for both characters?

8 Why didn't Meg want Packey to go to the meeting at Saint James? Why was she angry with Father Fitzpatrick? How did that affect Angel's feelings about Father McGrath?

9 Discuss the relationship between Cora and Cisco. How do their disagreements and different interests and habits affect their ability to deal with Angel?

10 Discuss Frannie's place in the story. How much help does she really provide? How does the relationship between Cisco and Frannie change during the story?

11 Cavanaugh explains himself as a victim of circumstance. Is there anything sympathetic about him?

12 Discuss Father McGrath's place in the story. Should he have had a more reality-based opinion about Cora's situation?

13 Cora, Cisco and Frannie plunge themselves into tedious research on a number of occasions. Do the details of their search enhance the story?

14 At their first face to face meeting, Angel says, "Over forty years to find you, Darlin'. Can't leave now...." Do you think she is referring to Cora leaving, or herself?

15 When Cora is in a position to send Angel out of the material world, she becomes reluctant to do so. Discuss why she would feel this way. How would you feel?

16 What was keeping Angel from leaving the material world? If her task on earth was to protect her daughter, then why did she want Cora to find out who killed her and her family? What finally allowed her to enter the spirit world?

17 *The Mystery at Sag Bridge* suggests a single mystery. Do you think the author is referring to the murders, the reason Angel believes Cora is her daughter, the ties among the characters, or something else?

18 In chapter 12 the author makes a thematic statement regarding the generational bonds between women, past and future. How would you describe the relationships between the women characters in the story?

19 How do you think Agnes fell in the quarry?

20 What do you infer from the ending scene when Cora woke up to hear a wolf howling?

An avid reader of mysteries and historical fiction, Pat Camalliere recently utilized her skills—developed writing historical papers and programs, newsletters, and website content—to create her debut novel, *The Mystery at Sag Bridge*. She lives with her husband in Lemont, Illinois, a suburb of Chicago. Visit her website at www.patcamallierebooks.com.